Praise for May McGoldrick's Breathtaking Novels

"Love triumphs in this richly romantic tale."
—Nora Roberts

"Wonderful! Just the right blend of historical detail,
romance, and intrigue."
—Jill Marie Landis

"May McGoldrick brings history alive, painting passion
and intrigue across a broad, colorful canvas."
—Patricia Gaffney

"No one captures the magic and romance of the
British Isles like May McGoldrick."
—Miranda Jarrett

"Fast-paced, emotionally charged . . . rich in
historical detail, sizzling with sensuality."
—*Romantic Times*

"Impressive. . . . A splendid Scottish tale,
filled with humor and suspense."
—Arnette Lamb

"Brilliant. . . . A fast-paced, action-packed historical
romance brimming with insight into the
sixteenth-century Scottish-English conflict."
—*Affaire de Coeur*

The Promise

May McGoldrick

A SIGNET BOOK

SIGNET
Published by New American Library, a division of
Penguin Putnam Inc., 375 Hudson Street,
New York, New York 10014, U.S.A.
Penguin Books Ltd, 27 Wrights Lane,
London W8 5TZ, England
Penguin Books Australia Ltd, Ringwood,
Victoria, Australia
Penguin Books Canada Ltd, 10 Alcorn Avenue,
Toronto, Ontario, Canada M4V 3B2
Penguin Books (N.Z.) Ltd, 182–190 Wairau Road,
Auckland 10, New Zealand

Penguin Books Ltd, Registered Offices:
Harmondsworth, Middlesex, England

First published by Signet, an imprint of New American Library, a division of
Penguin Putnam Inc.

First Printing, September 2001
10   9   8   7   6   5   4   3   2

Ⓟ REGISTERED TRADEMARK—MARCA REGISTRADA

Printed in the United States of America

PUBLISHER'S NOTE
This is a work of fiction. Names, characters, places, and incidents either are the product
of the author's imagination or are used fictitiously, and any resemblance to actual
persons, living or dead, business establishments, events, or locales is entirely
coincidental.

To our mothers

Chapter 1

London, England
July 1760

The nervous hand, fluttering across the worktable, knocked over the inkwell, spreading the liquid on the surface and staining the young woman's skirt as she leaned quickly to right the well.

"Have mercy, Lord," Rebecca whispered under her breath as she quickly blotted the ink on the table with used scraps of paper. The sudden appearance of the serving girl at the door only added to her growing anguish. "Ah, Lizzy. You are . . . you are back."

"Sir Charles wants you now, miss . . . and he ain't one for waiting." The serving girl's quick eyes surveyed the room, taking note of the damage. "You'd best be on your way before the master really gets angry, if you don't mind me saying. You don't want him coming after you himself. Here, let me see to this mess."

Rebecca found herself being pushed aside as Lizzy took charge of cleaning up the spilled ink. She stared for a moment at the rag the serving girl had stuffed into her hand.

"Is . . . is Lady Hartington back?"

A knowing smirk crept onto Lizzy's young face as she scrubbed the surface of the table. "The mistress just left for the opera an hour ago. She won't be back for hours, I shouldn't think."

Rebecca was having no success at all wiping the stain off the palm of her hand. "I . . . I think . . . I should go and check on the children. I believe . . . little Sara wasn't feeling very well during our reading lesson."

"Maggie's in with them, miss. And that's her job, anyways."

Lizzy straightened from wiping the table and met Rebecca's gaze. "Look, there is no putting it off. You'd best go off and have done with it. He'll have his way sooner or later."

Have done with it! She felt the words reverberate in her mind. *Have done with it!*

But she had only been ordered to go down to Sir Charles in his library. Alone. While his wife was gone for the evening. While his children slept only a floor above in their bedrooms.

The shiver that wracked Rebecca's body was violent. She shoved her trembling hands into the folds of her skirt and started for the door.

"I . . . I have to see to this dress first."

"He won't care. He won't give a damn what you're wearing." Lizzy's words rang sharply with experience.

With tears burning her eyes, Rebecca fled the room.

But there was to be no escape as she came face-to-face with the butler in the corridor leading to the main portion of the house. Desperately, Rebecca tried to fight back her emotions as she stared at the buttons of the man's dark waistcoat.

"Sir Charles is waiting, miss."

She could not lift her gaze to meet the old man's eyes. She knew what Lizzy had said was true. She had sensed it herself. For the fortnight since Sir Charles Hartington had come back from the Continent, she'd felt his eyes upon her constantly. Several times he'd come to the room where she tutored his children, leaning over her, pressing against her. His attentions were unmistakable.

What made her think they would stop?

With the continual presence of his wife and the other servants in the house, though, Rebecca had fooled herself, hoping that she would be safe. Safe, at least, until her plea to Mrs. Stockdale was answered. In her letter she had begged her old schoolmistress to begin searching out a new position for her. But even with the new mail coach going directly to Oxford, Mrs. Stockdale may not have received the letter yet.

"You should be going to him now."

The young woman willed herself to look up at the butler. "I cannot. I think . . . I will just remain in my room until Lady Hartington returns."

The man's perpetual frown only deepened. "Sir Charles will not be pleased. He is master of this house. If you know what is best, you will do as he bids."

"I was engaged by Lady Hartington to tutor his children. The children are all abed—my work is finished for the day."

"If you do not go down to the library, Sir Charles will surely come up for you. He is not one to be disobeyed . . . and in the years I have served this family, I must tell you I have several times witnessed his temper. . . ." He didn't have to finish the words. The warning was clear.

The taste of bile was burning in her throat. Rebecca placed a hand against the wall to steady herself. It took a moment for her to find her voice, and to gather her strength. When she spoke, her voice sounded far clearer, far more self-assured, than she'd expected. Far more than she felt.

"I will not go down to him, Robert. I believe . . . I will go to my room and pack my things. I am leaving Sir Charles's service tonight . . . now, in fact."

There was a momentary look of disbelief on the butler's face. Then, for the briefest of instants, the old man's eyes glinted with something akin to respect before he bowed and allowed her to pass. But the rewarding feeling she gained from Robert's approval lasted only as long as her next thought.

Leaving . . . tonight . . . but to where?

Rebecca's mind, as she hurried on, was in total chaos. Where was she to go? It would take her only a moment to pack. As a tutor she had little need for an extensive wardrobe, and she had brought very little from Oxford. But the uncertainty of where she was to go, in the middle of the night, with no carriage or company or any means of protection . . . the confusion was nearly paralyzing.

But one thing was clear. Staying in this house even a moment longer than necessary was *not* a choice.

For as long as Rebecca Neville could remember, she had lived at Mrs. Stockdale's Academy for Girls, next to the vicarage of St. George's in Oxford. Until a month ago, when she had left the school at the age of eighteen, she had never spent a night anywhere else. Until she had come to the London mansion of Sir Charles Hartington, she had never known any other home than the room she had occupied on the school's second floor.

As far as she knew, she had no family. Rebecca had only an anonymous benefactor about whom she knew nothing whatsoever. All Mrs. Stockdale would ever say—all she was allowed to say— was that funds for Rebecca's education and upkeep came twice a year from a law firm in London. Growing up, she'd always envisioned London to be filled with kind and generous benefactors.

Rebecca took her cloak off the peg on the wall. Despite the warmth of the summer night, she wrapped it tightly around her. Opening up her small purse, she quickly counted the money. Three pounds, five shillings, and some copper. Hardly a nest egg, Mrs. Stockdale had said when Rebecca left to take her new position. Nonetheless, her coach fare of four pounds and eight shillings to London had been paid by her employer, Lady Hartington, and with a salary of ten pounds a year plus room and board, Rebecca had been sure she would need nothing more. What Mrs. Stockdale had failed to warn Rebecca about, though, was the danger presented by men like Sir Charles Hartington.

The small window was open to the darkness outside. A breeze, still exceedingly warm, wafted through her chamber. She did not feel it, though. Rebecca was chilled, inside and out.

Tucking her purse inside her traveling bag, she glanced at the small but tidy room that had offered so much hope, so much promise, not a month earlier.

Most of the girls Rebecca's age who had attended Mrs. Stockdale's school in Oxford had returned to their well-to-do families some time during the summer of the past year. As she had watched their carriages roll away, she had been struck once again with the hard fact that she was the only student with no place to go. She had no future awaiting her beyond the front door of the academy. To Mrs. Stockdale's credit, the old schoolmistress had never even hinted that she should seek a position, but the young woman had been coming to the realization for a long while that she must take her future in her own hands. She could not live forever on the generosity of her longtime benefactor.

The sound of steps coming down the corridor launched Rebecca into action. She picked up her traveling bag without another moment's delay and headed straight for the door. Outside, the corridor was empty except for two of the upstairs maidservants, who stared at her with surprise as they rushed past. She could hear their whispering as they moved down the hall.

Though her heart was racing, Rebecca's feet were leaden as she descended the paneled staircase. A tavern on Butchers Row. A clothing shop on Monmouth Street. The household of Sir Roger de Coverley on St. James Square, where she'd heard they were forever in need of servants. All these possibilities of employment presented themselves at this moment of desperation, affirming her decision.

She'd find a position. Perhaps not as a tutor, but as a servant. She'd do anything. All she had to do was to find a place for the night. In the morning she could seek employment in any of the places she'd remembered. There had to be so many more. She'd certainly be fine, if she could only last until morning.

"I did not believe Robert when he told me of your insolent intentions."

She was only a few paces from the stairs leading to the ground floor. She could see the front door.

"Stop where you are."

Her steps faltered at the command. Cold panic washed down her back as Sir Charles approached from behind. She gripped her bag tightly and tried to hide her terror as she half turned to him.

"I meant no insolence, sir. I only informed him that I am leaving your house."

"With night already upon us? With gangs of young brigands roaming the streets? Why, you'd only find yourself rolled in a barrel down some hill. Or perhaps they'd do something far, far worse." Rebecca repressed a shudder as he drew near, but his voice was low and his insinuation unmistakable. The smell of brandy and cigars hung in the air. "What kind of a gentleman do you take me for, Miss Neville? Do you think I could possibly allow such a delectable creature as yourself to leave here unprotected?"

"I ask for no protection, sir." She tried to step away, but the man's sudden grip on her arm halted her escape. "Sir Charles, please let me go."

"Not before we get to the bottom of this precipitous decision of yours, Miss Neville."

She found herself being pulled toward the baronet's library. With a cry, Rebecca planted her feet and jerked her arm free as she turned sharply to him. "No, sir! I want you to release me this second."

The man's pale blue eyes sharpened in an instant. Color edged into the angular planes of his face, betraying his rising temper. Rebecca took a step back and clutched her traveling bag tightly before her.

"What do you have in that bag?"

His question stunned her, and she looked down uncomprehendingly at the bag. "My . . . my belongings."

"Not very likely, I'd say." He had Rebecca's elbow in a death grip before she could utter a word and forcibly dragged her toward the library. A serving maid appeared down the long hallway, and he called out to her, "You! Get Robert and the others. I want this house searched for what's missing. The silver and the plate. My wife's jewels. Yes, be sure to check my wife's jewels!"

Rebecca found herself thrown roughly into Sir Charles's library, and heard the door slam shut as she whirled around. They were both holding on to her bag, and she released it, backing away from him. With a look of satisfaction, he turned the key in the lock. Rebecca backed away to the farthest wall until her shoulders were against the shelves of leather-bound books. She could see the look on his face, and it horrified her. Her eyes looked for some avenue of escape. There was none.

"Sir Charles, there is nothing of yours or your wife's in that bag."

"My dear Miss Neville. You are not only young and tender, but a dolt, as well."

"If you think so poorly of me, sir, then why not let me go?"

He laughed as he tossed her traveling bag aside and shrugged out of his coat. "Letting you go, my dear, is not even a remote possibility. You see, young chits like you need to learn a lesson in life. You are just so very fortunate that I will be the one to educate you."

Nearly frozen with panic, she forced herself to move, edging behind the exquisite mahogany desk. Tears burned in her eyes as she saw him reach for the buttons of his waistcoat. "Why me? You . . . you can have anyone you want! You have a wife! Please, please . . . not me!"

He flashed her a brilliant smile and crossed the room slowly, like a cat on the hunt. "You, my dear, are the one that I *must* have. You see, you come from—how shall I put it?—from a very fine line."

She pushed a chair in his path and backed away as he circled the desk. "You are mistaken! I am no one. Nothing special! Please, Sir Charles! There can be no satisfaction in ruining a nobody like me."

"A nobody?" he repeated, unfastening the buttons of his tight breeches. "A nobody you might be with regard to title and fortune, that is true. But as far as your lineage . . ." He shook his head. "Nay, my dear. You are far from a nobody."

Rebecca was shuddering violently as the front of his breeches fell open, exposing his aroused sex. His face was a mask as he continued toward her.

"Do not proceed, Sir Charles. I *beg* you! You are mistaken about . . . about whomever it is you think I am."

He stood still for a moment, eyeing her across the desk.

"Mistaken?" He shook his head. "Your secret is out, Miss Neville. But to tell the truth, I had no difficulty at all finding out who you really are. Imagine, the daughter of the notorious actress Jenny Greene under my own roof! A fine mother she was, I'll grant you, though, to shield her offspring from the effects of her reputation for so long. And so near to London, too."

Rebecca could hardly comprehend his words. Confusion had set her brain spinning, and she could only think of escape. She backed away from the desk a few steps until she found her back against the marble mantel of the fireplace.

"But the first moment I laid eyes on you, I sensed it. The same stormy blue eyes. The same golden-red hair . . . the color of sunset." His eyes swept over her body. "I knew it."

Her hands searched the space behind her. He was so much bigger than she was. A great deal stronger. He was in the center of the room now. There was no escape.

"As a lad I used to sit in the upper gallery at the theater in Haymarket, lusting after your mother. I would watch the fops who paid an additional charge to visit the celebrated Jenny after the performances. I would pine for her, wishing it was I enjoying her charms."

He came closer, his protruding manhood belying the almost casual manner he now affected. She held her breath, looking to the side as he reached out and pulled the ribbon of her straw cap. Dropping it on the floor, he took a tendril of her hair beneath his fingers, rubbing it back and forth as she felt his eyes fix on her face.

"Full lips that cried out for *me* to kiss." His gaze shifted downward, his voice a husky whisper, "Breasts made to be suckled by *my* mouth."

Rebecca cried out as his hands reached beneath her cloak, encircling her waist and pulling her roughly against his chest. She stared up at him. She could feel his manhood pressing insistently against her.

"I finally enjoyed your mother, you know. I took her this past week after her play at the Covent Garden Theatre. A little gin and she was chattering like a magpie. Getting her to talk about you was easy. I had to have her . . . for old time's sake. But also, so that I could compare the mother with the daughter."

She turned her face away as he tried to crush his mouth down on hers. She pushed roughly at his chest and tried to turn in his arms. He laughed.

"She was willing. Easy. Hardly as exciting as you are now. Of course, she is not the woman she once was." He was squeezing her breasts, hurting her, and all she could do was to restrain her sobs . . . and pray. "I knew you would be better. Much better."

She felt the tie of her cloak pull free from around her neck. She glanced wildly at him. He had the look of an animal on his face as he took hold of the modest neckline of her dress.

"How much?" Her voice was barely a croak. She forced out the words. "You paid my mother. How much will you pay me?"

His eyes sobered for an instant as they came up and met hers. His lips curled nastily. "A harlot . . . like the mother."

"How much?" she snapped with a firmness that was pure fraud. "I shall remain in your household. I shall keep my position, and . . . and you can use me as you wish."

His teeth flashed, but he released the neckline of her dress. "What's your price?"

She pushed back, taking a half step to the side. He let her, one hand still gripping her arm. "Your wife hired me for ten pounds a year. Make it twenty."

His pale blue eyes studied her suspiciously for a moment. "And you will do whatever I command you to do?"

She swallowed once. "Whatever."

"Are you a virgin?"

She stared at his shirt and nodded. "I am."

Silence ruled the chamber while she waited, and then relief swept through her as he took a step away, releasing her arm. "This could prove quite . . . diverting."

He stepped back, eyeing her, his hands on his hips. She fixed her gaze on his face.

"Very well. I'll pay you the difference. And my wife shall not know anything of our arrangement."

She nodded.

"Then I command you to take your clothes off . . . very slowly. And when you are finished, I wish for you to lie on the desk."

Rebecca stared at the dark mahogany desk. Her gaze moved away, lighting for an instant on Sir Charles's sex, blotchy and swollen and horribly potent. She turned quickly toward the hearth.

"As you wish," she said, bending to pick up her straw hat.

It was there, just as she'd hoped it would be. It was her only chance.

There was no hesitation in her actions now. Her hand darted to the poker, her icy fingers closing on the brass handle. Then, in one swift movement, she whirled around and smashed the iron rod with a sickening crunch into the head of Sir Charles Hartington as he leaned, quite exposed, against his desk.

Chapter 2

She had killed the man.

Dropping the poker, Rebecca covered her mouth to stifle her own scream of horror. The crimson liquid pumped from Sir Charles's scalp and soaked into the rug in a rapidly widening arc. He lay sprawled facedown on the floor, his head away from her. In her haste to reach the door, she tripped over an outstretched foot and landed heavily on her hands and knees beside him. Immediately leaping to her feet, she gasped at the sight of her attacker's warm blood covering her hands. She stared from her hands to his inert body.

She had certainly killed the man.

"No!" she sobbed, running her palms again and again over her skirts. "No!"

Her fingers were trembling violently as they tried to unlock the door. Glancing fearfully over her shoulder, all she could see of him was the head of powdered, golden hair now streaked with the dark shades of his own mortality.

The key turned, and Rebecca stumbled into the hallway. She only managed a few wobbly steps toward the staircase, though, before crouching down and retching violently on the brilliantly flowered carpet.

"Miss Neville . . . Rebecca."

She lifted bleary eyes and saw the butler coming down the stairs. The serving maid Lizzy was directly behind him.

"Oh, my God! What have you done?"

She had no chance to answer Robert as another serving maid began to screech at the library door.

"Blood!"

And still louder.

"Murder!"

Rebecca covered her ears and shook her head as she staggered to her feet. The shouts and the chaos surrounded her, but she couldn't answer. There was no sound in her throat but broken gasps for air.

And then she ran.

She felt hands reaching for her. Shouts behind her. She didn't stop, though, flying down the steps to the front door and opening it before they could reach her.

On the street she saw flashes of faces in the yellow arcs of lamps. Voices and shouts. On she ran as fast as her feet could carry her. She was not even a block away, though, when cries of murder rang out. The sounds of running footsteps. More shouts.

At the crossing street, Rebecca turned the corner and then stumbled off the high curb and into the thoroughfare. Regaining her balance she tried to dash across as the darkness of the park on the far side caught her eye. But the rush of a carriage coming straight at her froze her in her tracks. She could not move, could not breathe. Stunned, she watched the hooves of the horses pounding toward her.

So this was to be her end. There would be no hanging. She would be trampled escaping the murder.

"Get out of the way! *Out of the way, you fool!*"

Rebecca saw the coachman struggle with the horses, but she couldn't move. The carriage veered to the left. The horses reared as they plunged past, and she felt a hand pull her away as the wheels of the carriage thundered by.

The next moment, she found herself sitting on the street. Faces were staring down at her with evident concern and surprise, but not one of them looked at her accusingly.

With senses suddenly acute, she looked up as the carriage stopped a short distance away. The driver was shouting at his team of horses and trying to start the carriage again. From the tiny window, a young woman's ashen face peered out.

When their gazes connected, Rebecca knew. In that face she saw a desperation that matched her own. She dragged herself to her feet and ran toward the carriage, stretching out a hand.

"Help me!" she called. "Please, take me!"

From the corner of her eye, she saw a mass of people rounding the corner.

"Murderer! Hold that woman!"

The carriage was already rolling when she saw the door swing open. She could barely hear the weak commands from inside, but saw the driver look back at her.

With renewed strength, Rebecca dashed for the open door and climbed inside as the driver cracked his whip. The carriage jerked forward and in an instant was racing through the streets of the city, leaving the shouting throng far behind.

The pale woman in the carriage drew the curtains, and darkness enveloped the two riders. It took a long moment before Rebecca managed to catch her breath. As her eyes adjusted to the dark, she heard the driver shouting at the team of horses as he slowed to turn a corner.

The woman who sat across from her stared searchingly at Rebecca. On her lap, beneath a well-made cloak, she held a small bundle.

"I am innocent." Rebecca heard herself blurting out. "My name is Rebecca Neville. I . . . I lived at Mrs. Stockdale's Academy in Oxford up until a month ago."

Her rescuer continued to study her in silence. The woman was young . . . not much older than Rebecca. Her clothes bespoke obvious wealth. But there was fear in her drawn, pale face—a look of desperation that Rebecca could see now even more clearly.

"I . . . I was hired to be a tutor . . . by Lady Hartington . . . for their three children . . . and then her husband arrived . . ." She lost the words as a knot rose in her throat. She dashed tears off her face with the back of her stained sleeve. "He tried to . . . he attacked me . . . the wife was away . . . I swung the poker at him. I killed him . . . and now they are after me. But he tried to . . . to . . . I . . ."

She couldn't continue. Burying her face in her hands, Rebecca leaned forward and lost herself in her own misery as the carriage jerked roughly from side to side. A moment later, a delicate handkerchief was tucked into her hands. She took it gratefully and wiped her eyes.

"I am sorry. I shouldn't have involved you with . . ."

"Do you have family?" The woman's voice was kind, but weak, as if she were in severe pain.

"I don't . . . although I was told tonight that I might have a relation." She shook her head hopelessly. "I have no one to go to. For all of my life I've been told I was an orphan."

"No matter what he did, they will hang you."

Rebecca stared down at her hands in her lap. The stains from Sir Charles's blood, mixed with the ink she'd spilled earlier, created grotesque markings on her dress. The white handkerchief against it was a shocking contrast, even in the darkness of the coach.

"I would not have acted any differently, even knowing the consequences."

She stabbed again at her tears. There was a noise from the woman's lap. A small mewling cry. Rebecca's eyes rounded as she watched her rescuer push aside the cloak and reveal an infant tightly swaddled in blankets.

"He is awake." There was tenderness in the young woman's face as she looked down on the baby in her arms.

"So small!" Rebecca found herself whispering as she leaned over to look at the child.

"He was born only this morning."

Her eyes lifted to the pale face. "Are you . . . the mother?"

The woman smiled faintly. "I am Elizabeth Wakefield. And yes, I am the mother."

The carriage lurched and Rebecca laid a hand on Elizabeth's knee as the woman winced with pain.

"You are not well. It is too soon for you to be leaving your bed after delivering a child."

"I . . . I am well enough . . . to look after my son." She ran a finger over the infant's furrowed brow. "I am calling him James."

There were other questions racing through Rebecca's mind, questions more important than the child's name. Where was her husband, for example, and why was it that Elizabeth was traveling alone at this time of night with her infant son? But the sadness that enveloped the woman, the love that shone in her eyes as she looked down on the baby, restrained Rebecca from asking anything more.

Instead, she sat back, thoughts about her own situation crowding her brain. Thoughts about how insignificant her entire life had been. Thoughts about how quickly it was going to end when they tried her and hanged her for Sir Charles Hartington's murder. Her hand drifted unconsciously to her throat as she wondered for a moment how painful it was to hang.

Her eyes focused again on the mother and child across from her, and she wondered if there had ever been a moment such as this in her own life. She wondered if her own mother had ever held her with such tenderness and . . .

She shook her head and looked away as emotions tightened like a fist in her throat. Too late for such thoughts, she scolded herself. Even if Jenny Greene were indeed her mother, it was far too late for such thoughts.

From the time she'd been a little girl, Rebecca had been raised with Mrs. Stockdale's constant reminders on the value of virtue that must accompany the improvement of a girl's mind. Indeed, she had grown into womanhood schooled on the difference between right and wrong and, more importantly, on the fragile nature of a woman's chastity. Much more so than with the other students, it seemed, the schoolmistress had been keen on constantly reminding young Rebecca about the necessity of hiding her "unusual" looks, of binding and taming her willful and flame-colored tresses. No, nothing should ever be allowed to steer her—even momentarily— off the narrow path of decency and respectability.

It all made sense now. Mrs. Stockdale's persistence had simply been the result of her suspicions about the "bad" stock Rebecca had probably issued from. Indeed, she wondered with a pang of bitterness, though, what her former schoolmistress might think of her actions tonight.

The carriage rumbled to a sudden stop. Rebecca's heart leaped into her throat. She clutched her skirts in her hands and stared at the closed door of the coach. She could smell the rank odor of fish and rotted wood, and guessed they were close to the Thames. "I suppose . . . this is the end."

"There is a boat waiting for me here."

Elizabeth's words drew Rebecca's gaze.

"I am taking a boat from here to Dartmouth where James and I will be boarding a ship headed for America."

All Rebecca could do was hold her breath.

"I am . . . I am not well. And we are traveling alone."

A tear rolled down Rebecca's check as she stared into her guardian angel's face.

"I want you to come with us."

Chapter 3

Philadelphia, in the Province of Pennsylvania
April 1770

"We cannot teach a deaf boy in our school, Mrs. Ford. We simply cannot do it."

Rebecca forced herself to remain seated on the wooden bench and stared irritably at the headmaster of the Friend's School. "Jamey is not deaf, Mr. Morgan. Hard of hearing, that is true, if you are standing by his bad ear. But not deaf."

The middle-aged man adjusted the spectacles on his nose and stared down at the papers on his desk. "I have had both of my teachers spend time with thy son—separately and together. They each say that thy son hears not a word. The lad cannot even speak, for all they can tell."

"He is only nine. He was . . . quite nervous the day I brought him here."

The headmaster shook his head. "Mr. Hopkinson tells me he saw the lad running on the wharf with some other boys last week, and he didn't respond to his greeting in any way."

"How many nine-year-old boys do you know who would speak to an adult while they are in the middle of mischief-making?"

"So, thy son is a mischief-maker, as well?"

Rebecca let out a frustrated breath and unrolled the papers she was holding on her lap. "I was speaking of boys at play. Jamey is *not* a mischief-maker, Mr. Morgan. He is a very bright and vigorous lad who shows great promise in learning. Just look at these papers, sir." She placed the sheets on the man's desk. "These are samples of his handwriting. He can read, too. And I have already been tutoring him in mathematics, and he does quite as well as many of your own students."

The headmaster took the papers and leafed quickly through them.

"Now, you tell me, sir. How could I be teaching him these things if he were deaf?"

"Mrs. Ford . . ." He paused, carefully rolling the papers up and holding them out to her. "Thou art a talented teacher. Many of our students have benefited greatly by being tutored by thee over the past few years. A number of parents cannot praise you highly enough for thy way with their young ones. But about thy son . . ."

Rebecca took the rolled bundle from the man's hand.

". . . with regard to Jamey, thou art better off continuing as thou have begun. Perhaps 'tis the bond that exists between a mother and son that allows thee to overcome the lad's handicap. 'Tis thou . . . and only thou . . . that he appears to respond to."

"But there is only so much more that I can teach him. There is only so far in life that he can go if all of his education comes from me."

"Based on what thou showed me here, thy son has already surpassed what most . . . laborers . . . or tradesmen might need as far as schooling in life. He has already done quite well by thee."

"No, Mr. Morgan! I will not allow my son to think that becoming a laborer or a tradesman is the best he can do with his life." Rebecca fought to restrain her growing fury. "Despite one deaf ear, regardless of a misshapen hand, I will raise my son to be whatever he wishes to be. If he decides to be a doctor, then he shall be. If he wishes to become a lawyer or a clergyman, then I will see to it that nothing shall stop him. I will make sure that Jamey has every opportunity that exists for a boy growing up in Pennsylvania."

"Thy intentions are quite admirable, Mrs. Ford."

She glared fiercely at the headmaster and leaned forward on the bench. "Admiration is not what I came here for, Mr. Morgan. I came for understanding, openness, equality . . . things that you and the Society of Friends say you stand for. I came here seeking the opportunity of an education for my son."

The headmaster's face turned a reddish hue, and he stared down at his hands. "I am sorry, Mrs. Ford. But we *have* given thy request quite some time and attention. But with only two teachers and myself, we are already handling over a hundred pupils. There is simply no way we can handle someone with thy son's difficulties at this school."

Rebecca stared for a long moment at the headmaster's balding head, at the thin spectacles that had slipped farther down on the man's nose. She stood abruptly.

"Good day to you, sir."

The afternoon sun was lying like liquid gold on the spire of Christ Church when Rebecca stepped out onto High Street, though she was hardly in the frame of mind to notice it. With one hand wrapped tightly around Jamey's papers, and the other clutching the ribbons of her purse, she pushed through the bustle of activity that showed no signs of easing despite the lengthening shadows of the afternoon.

"Good day to you, Mrs. Ford."

She turned her head and nodded blindly while making her way along the brick sidewalk. There were other schools. Perhaps the school in Germantown. But how to get Jamey there, day in and day out?

"Fine afternoon, Mrs. Ford."

"That it is, Mrs. Bradford." Rebecca forced a polite smile at the heavyset woman. Hiding her frustration with the headmaster, she lengthened her strides.

They would move. If that was the only way she could get Jamey into a school, then so be it. She was willing to do whatever it took. New York. Boston. Wherever. And as far as jobs that she had here . . . there had to be other positions in other cities.

Rebecca ignored the cries of vendors hawking everything from meat pies to apples to Dr. Franklin's *Gazette*. As she turned the corner into Strawberry Alley, the curses of a carter driving his slow-moving team of oxen into the activity of High Street hardly even registered as she pushed along the crowded dirt street.

She had made a start—a life for herself and Jamey in Philadelphia over the past ten years. People knew her, respected her. She was never short of work, whether it be tutoring or sewing or helping in the bakery whenever Mrs. Parker needed to tend to her ailing husband.

She passed under painted signs extending from rows of neat brick dwellings, signs noting drapiers and glaziers and cobblers and butchers working hard at their trades inside. Yes, there was work here, but if she had to go . . . well, she would find work in another city . . . in another colony. Anywhere, so long as she could find a school willing to overlook Jamey's differences and treat him like any other boy.

Rebecca carefully stepped across the alley—avoiding puddles and muck and traffic—to the red brick building that housed Mrs. Parker's bakery. There, above the ever-expanding Butler family, she and Jamey rented two snug rooms beneath the sloping roof.

She nodded to Annie Howe as the thin, squint-eyed worker from the Death of the Fox Inn stepped out of the bakery with an armload of bread.

"Oh, Mrs. Ford. There was a gentleman inquiring after you at the inn this afternoon."

She stopped on the landing. "Thank you, Annie. This gentleman . . . was he looking for a tutor for a young one?"

"He didn't say anything about that, ma'am. But I shouldn't think so. He arrived in the city two days ago, intending to stay at least for a few days at the inn. Demanded a room to himself, if you can imagine."

"Well, thank you, Annie." Rebecca opened the front door.

"He is a lawyer, you know . . . from England."

A tight knot gripped Rebecca's middle and she froze with her foot on the doorstep. Slowly, she turned to the woman. "Who . . . who was it *exactly* that he . . . asked for?"

Annie shifted the bundles of bread in her arms. "For you. He asked for you. The mother of the boy with the crippled hand. To be perfectly honest, my first thought was that your Jamey must have been up to no good again down on the wharf. If I were you, I'd box the lad's ears once a day whether he needed it or not. I've been meaning to speak to you about it. I've seen him down there myself,

Mrs. Ford. Don't think I mean to give a dog a bad name and hang him. I mean, he's just a lad, to be sure, but you don't know the way he runs wild down there, scaring the fancy lassies coming off the ships with that claw of his, and then running off with those hellions who live beneath you." The woman squinted up meaningfully at the Butlers' windows.

The tension in Rebecca's belly eased a bit, but not much. "Thank you for telling me all of this, Annie. I'll have a long talk with him."

"A good strong willow reed across his backside is what he needs, if you ask me, Mrs. Ford. If your husband was alive—"

"Very well, I'll see to it. Thank you." Rebecca didn't wait to hear any more, and with a quick wave she closed the door and started up the narrow steps to the upper floors.

There was not much of what Annie had said that she didn't already know. Jamey had become a little wild this spring, but with so much going on, with Rebecca working at so many jobs, there were only so many hours in the day that she could be tutoring him, or watching him, or scolding him. Not that she had the heart to do much scolding. After all, he needed to stretch his wings a bit.

But this was another reason why she had to find him a school. He needed a place where he could find some direction for his energy. He needed a way to mold the growing defiance in his character into a positive quality.

As expected, Molly Butler's door was open as Rebecca passed, and the neighbor—her belly big with child—waved her into the all-purpose front room. A small fire was crackling in the fireplace on the far wall, and Molly turned her back to stir a pot of stew hanging from an iron rod over the hearth. Satisfied, the rosy-cheeked woman eyed Rebecca as she sat heavily on the large settle beside the fire. Twin girls, barely toddlers, were napping side by side in a little bed in the corner.

"You don't have to tell me. Your face shows it."

Rebecca dropped the scroll of paper and her bag on the table before walking to one of the two front windows. "That's not the last school. There are others."

"You know I love him like my own, but not for your Jamey, I shouldn't think."

She didn't feel like arguing, and let the comment pass.

"I can tell, you are already thinking."

Rebecca turned and smiled. "You know me, Molly. I'm always thinking."

As she sat beside her friend, the pregnant woman cut a slice off the loaf of bread that sat on a small table next to the settle. Without asking, she set the table in front of Rebecca and pushed the small pot of apple butter next to the bread. "You didn't have any lunch, darling, and seeing how pale you look, I'd wager you didn't eat anything this morning, either."

"Jamey is not back yet?"

"Don't fret about him. I sent my Tommy along with George and Jamey. With the older brother along, there is only so much trouble those two urchins dare to get into."

Thomas, the oldest of the Butler's four children, was twelve and quite grown up for his age. He was already riding along occasionally when Mr. Butler would carry passengers Mondays and Thursdays from Strawberry Alley to the Trenton ferry for the first leg of the journey to New York. George, on the other hand, was exactly Jamey's age and just as unruly.

"Rebecca, I still think you should consider Mr. Butler's advice and let Jamey start earning his keep by working in a smith's shop or—"

"I can't." Rebecca shook her head, staring at the slice of bread before her. "I am writing to the headmaster at Germantown. There is a good chance they'll take him at the school there."

"Mr. Butler tells me they have over two hundred pupils there already, and even if they were more understanding of your Jamey's situation . . ."

"I have to keep trying, Molly."

Molly shook her head. "You, of all people, a woman who gets nervous when your son spends half a day out of your sight. How are you going to cope with him boarding with strangers in Germantown? Worse than that, Rebecca, how are you going to afford it?"

Rebecca took a bite of the bread. She could not bring herself to reveal to Molly her plans of moving. The two women had been friends from the time Rebecca and Jamey had arrived in Philadelphia. In this very house, the two families had lived for nearly ten years. In this very room, Rebecca had learned so much about child-rearing from her friend.

But there was more to their friendship than that. Much more. Many a night Rebecca and Jamey had joined the Butler family at their table for supper. How many Christmases had they shared together? From the beginning, there had always been a gift for the two of them, as if they were kin. And when Jamey was burning with fever as a child, Molly had sat with her at his bedside. And in the same way, when Molly was ready to deliver the twins, Rebecca and Jamey had taken in Tommy and George for a fortnight.

With John Butler away as much as he was, running the "coachee" to New York, the two women had formed a friendship that only deepened with the passage of years. There was no denying it, outside of Jamey, the Butlers were the only family that Rebecca had known in all of her life.

But right now, as tired as she was, as dispirited as she felt, talking about a move that would change everything was not Rebecca's idea of an inviting discussion.

"Forget about eating. Seeing how pale you look, you should go upstairs and lie down before your afternoon lessons. I'll send some of this stew up when it's ready."

Rebecca shook her head. "I'm fine . . . really I am."

She came quickly to her feet at the sound of Tommy and George shouting up from the street. Crossing to the window, she spotted the two boys looking up at her.

"Is Jamey back yet?" the older boy called as she raised the sash.

Rebecca leaned out the window. "I thought he was with you two."

"He was," George said. "But this fancy-dressed gentleman stopped us on the corner of Front and High Street. Said he wanted to have a *private* word with Jamey."

Molly's voice shrieked over Rebecca's shoulder, waking the two girls. "You're not telling us you left him alone with a stranger, are you?"

"Nay, Mama," Tommy hurriedly responded. "But we couldn't hear what the macaroni says, either, as they stood a few paces from us. Then, a couple of sweeps come a-shoving and a-barging along the bricks. Well, by the time the bloody soot-suckers cleared off, all we see is Jamey pushing the man away and running. I ain't never seen him run so . . . except maybe the time we snuck up the bell tower of Christ Church and got almost caught coming down—"

"You did what?"

Rebecca pulled abruptly back from the window, giving room to Molly to question the boys about this latest misdeed. There was something very wrong. What was it that Annie had said about the lawyer who had asked about her? But he really had been asking questions about Jamey.

She had to find her son.

Without another word, Rebecca rushed to the door and started down the stairs. She hadn't descended even two steps, though, before spotting his folded form on the bottom stair.

"Jamey!" she cried, crouching next to him. She took his face in her hands and brought it up until she could look into his face in the dim light of the stairway. "What's wrong, Jamey?"

There were tears in his eyes. He wiped away at them with the back of one sleeve. Before Rebecca could ask again, though, he threw his arms around her and buried his face in her lap.

"Don't let him take me away, Mama. Please don't let him take me away."

"I would *never* do that." She lifted his head until he was looking into her face. "Do you hear me? I promise you I will never let anyone take you away!"

She crushed him against her chest, rocking him in her arms as the tears flowed down his cheeks.

Molly appeared at the top of the stairs. "Praise God, he's back. I'll skin those two rogues of mine. . . . What's wrong?"

Rebecca shook her head at her friend. "He's fine, Molly. Just tell the boys he's here."

Clutching his hand, she led him up the stairs to their rooms. Molly followed them up, carrying the pot of apple butter and the bread.

Jamey just shook his head at Molly's offer of food and escaped into Rebecca's tiny bedchamber.

"Something's wrong," Rebecca muttered to Molly before going after her son.

In the other room, she found Jamey curled up on her bed and clutching tightly to her old shawl.

"Do you want to tell me what is wrong?"

He didn't respond. She crouched down next to the bed and took his chin, turning his face until his large blue eyes met her gaze.

"What happened, Jamey? Who was the man that stopped you on the street?"

Fresh tears glistened in the boy's eyes.

"What did he want?" She gentled her tone. "What did he say?"

She caressed his sandy blond hair, pushing it away from his brow. She used a kerchief from her sleeve and wiped his tears.

"He already knew my name, Mama. But . . . he called me . . . James."

"What else, love?"

"He grabbed my arm and stared at my hand."

"Hush!" she cooed as more tears rolled down his cheeks. This wasn't the first time that the child had faced people looking at him as an oddity. True, she had made every one of those incidents a battle—a battle against ignorance—but she didn't remember Jamey ever reacting as strongly to it as he was now.

"I love you, Mama. I promise to do my best." There were hiccups mixed with the words. "I promise I will never pretend not to hear. If you take me back to the Friend's School, I give you my word this time I'll behave. I'll answer their questions and everything. Just don't send me away."

"I love you, too. And you are not going anywhere without me. But I need to know," she said more firmly, "what that man said to you, Jamey."

But before he could answer, Molly appeared at the door. Rebecca looked up in surprise.

"There is someone here to see you."

"Take their name, Molly. Send them away."

Her friend shook her head and motioned for Rebecca to come into the other room.

A fear as potent and as crippling as the one she'd felt in that library in London so many years ago pierced her body. She ran a hand over Jamey's forehead before forcing herself to her feet. Her movements were slow, almost painful, as she closed the door behind her.

Molly motioned toward the door leading to the stairs.

Rebecca took a deep breath and opened it, her fingers tightly wrapped around the latch.

"Mrs. Ford?"

She nodded at the fashionably dressed gentleman on the landing.

"I am Sir Oliver Birch, ma'am, of the Middle Temple in London. I am here on behalf of the Earl of Stanmore."

"What can I do for you, Mr. Birch?"

"I am here to collect and accompany James Samuel Wakefield, the future Earl of Stanmore, back to England."

Rebecca stared at him for only an instant before slamming the door as hard as she could.

Chapter 4

London

The white silk slid upward over the muscled back of her lover. As he pulled the shirt over his broad shoulders, however, Louisa's lips curved into a practiced pout. She stretched like a cat between the rumpled sheets of the giant bed and watched him dress.

Carnally fulfilled she was, but the familiar sight of Stanmore leaving her bed and her house immediately after their lovemaking never failed to diminish her pleasure. Even now, the acrid, metallic taste of disappointment was in her mouth, but she forced herself to look casual, soft, alluring.

She was not above asking him to stay. She was not even above pleading with him. But she refused to yield to such a fatal inclination. She was far too clever for that. Louisa Nisdale had no wish to join Stanmore's long list of castoff paramours. She had invested the entire three years of her ridiculous marriage and the first two years of her widowhood keenly studying—albeit from a safe distance— the man and his restlessness. Samuel Wakefield, the Earl of Stanmore, was openly disdainful of the women who swooned at his feet. He was impossibly arrogant toward the men of his station, especially those who tried to engage him in activities he saw as frivolous. Drinking, gaming, and whoring were beneath him, it seemed. It certainly seemed to matter not to him that the rest of his class found the diversions entertaining.

No, the Earl of Stanmore took his politics seriously. A hero of the French wars in America, he was now an outspoken member of the House of Lords. He was regal in bearing and fiercely proud of his lineage, with ancestors who had served their kings back to the time of William the Conqueror.

More important than any of that, though, Lord Stanmore was incredibly generous with his friends. And this was a virtue that Louisa highly esteemed in him—particularly in light of her highly developed taste for gambling and spending.

It was like a lovely play, she thought. And credit her own astuteness as a player, for here she was at the end of nearly a month's run of pleasure and passion . . . and no hint of a finale in sight.

Cheered by her own thoughts, Louisa pushed the covers away and rolled to the edge of the bed. From here she had a full view of Stanmore's handsome face in the mirror as he tied his cravat by candlelight. She savored the heat spreading through her at the sight of his eyes darkening as they traveled the length of her naked back and buttocks. She rolled onto one elbow, giving him a full view of her breasts.

"About Lady Mornington's invitation for Friday night . . ." She gathered her long mane of blond hair in one hand and rolled back onto the pillows. His eyes followed her movements in the mirror. She tilted her head up and casually kicked what remained of the sheets off her legs. "Could you arrange to come for me here at six thirty? I much prefer to arrive there *with* you and—"

"I've already declined Lady Mornington's invitation."

"But she is such a good friend of mine. She shall be greatly disappointed if we do not go."

He moved away from the mirror and reached for his waistcoat. "I only spoke of my own plans regarding this engagement. You are, of course, free to do as you wish."

"I cannot understand what you have against her. This is the fifth invitation from that good lady that you have declined in the past month."

"If it were the fiftieth, I would still decline. I have no interest in gaming establishments nor in gambling."

"But that's not all that she offers her guests. Why, she is a respected—"

"I have no interest in attending."

Louisa heard the change in his tone. It was a subtle shift, nearly imperceptible, but she'd heard it before and recognized it. Stanmore did not raise his voice, but the note of danger was unmistakable.

"Ah, well . . ." she said, sliding gracefully off the bed and walking slowly toward him as he pulled on his jacket.

She knew that a little time was called for. Time for his flash of temper to subside. Time for his eyes to focus on her body once again and appreciate the display of her charms. But the earl seemed distracted, if not disinterested, and this alarmed her more than she wanted to admit.

Louisa Nisdale, however, had a gambling soul, so she picked up her dressing gown of the sheerest silk and draped it loosely around her.

"In fact, Stanmore, I have a much better idea." Running a finger along the taut skin of his neck, she drew his gaze to her face. She moved into his arms and rubbed her body seductively against him. He towered over her. The dressing gown fell open, and a thrill raced through her at the feel of her soft skin against the superfine cloth, at the sight of her own creamy flesh pressed against the black fabric, at the heat of his buckskin-clad thighs pressed against hers. "You and I . . . Saturday evening . . . strolling through the pleasure gardens at Ranelagh. As we pass by the arches with all the parties sitting at tea, you can whisper in my ear all the wicked things you'd like to do to me. And I, in turn, can whisper all the—"

"No, I think not." Gently but firmly, he pushed her away and turned toward the door.

She reached out quickly and took hold of his sleeve. "We don't need to go anywhere," she said, working hard to keep the note of panic out of her voice. "Perhaps here . . . we can—"

"I'm leaving town for Hertfordshire for a few days. Perhaps I'll see you sometime next week, Louisa."

She stared at him for a moment. *Take me with you,* she nearly cried out as he leaned down to place a kiss on her forehead. But she knew better and bit back the words, instead sliding her arms around him and lifting her lips to be kissed.

Again, he disengaged himself from her and started for the door. She felt the color flood into her cheeks.

"I understand. You are restless because you are impatient with the waiting. It has been several months now, has it not?"

He came to an abrupt stop at the door and looked back at her. His eyes were black, but she could see that distinctive light gleaming deep in their depths. She felt the danger heat the air around her. She had overstepped her position, but now she knew she had to hold her ground.

"*What* exactly has been several months, Louisa?"

His voice was even lower, now, than it had been before, and she pulled the sheer gown around her.

"I . . . I've heard things." She could not maintain eye contact, so instead she picked up the silk belt to the gown and made an elaborate show of knotting it at her waist. "I just wanted you to know . . . well, that I understand . . . and that I am here if you need me."

She gave him a smile that she hoped was convincing.

"What is it *exactly* that you have heard?"

She ran her hands up and down her arms to ward off the chill she felt. There was no escaping this. He was waiting for an answer.

"I hear rumors of things all the time. I simply heard that you had sent someone to the colonies . . . well, to retrieve your son. Everyone is talking about it. You know how people talk. Everyone knows how hard it must be on you after ten years and . . . of course, if Elizabeth decides to return, also . . . well . . ."

The words withered on Louisa's tongue as a hardness she had never seen crept into Stanmore's dark eyes. His face had taken on a look of carved granite. Cold and formidable. She took an unconscious step back.

"I only . . . I was only concerned about you."

"Concerned?" The shake of his head was barely discernible. His tone was cool, even, and tightly controlled. "We have taken pleasure in each other's company, Louisa, but do not presume that there is anything more between us. Make no mistake about our connection." He turned sharply and pulled open the door. "In the future, madam, you will *not* concern yourself with my affairs. Not now. Not ever."

Louisa Nisdale watched him go and then sank against the edge of the bed. She stared at the door for a long moment and then stood up. She had erred in that skirmish, but she was hardly defeated.

No, she thought. She'd been formulating her strategy for too many years to throw it all away now. Conquering Lord Stanmore might require doing battle, but it was a campaign that she had no intention of abandoning.

Not now. Not ever.

Philadelphia

Rage and fear, like two iron-clawed creatures, tore at Rebecca's insides as she turned her back on the door and looked wildly into the face of a surprised Molly. There was another knock at the door.

"Send him away, Molly! Get him to leave us alone. Tell him . . ." Hot tears suddenly scorched her cheeks, and she felt the knot rise in her throat at the sight of Jamey's frightened face peering out from behind the bedroom door. "Tell him he has the wrong boy."

The knocking was louder now, more persistent.

"Tell me what this is all about, darling. . . ."

Rebecca shook her head at her friend's question and moved toward the young boy in the doorway.

"Please, Molly," she pleaded. "Just send him away."

"Aye, very well, lass. I'll do what I can."

Jamey's arms wrapped around her waist like small bands of steel. Rebecca quickly drew him inside the bedroom and closed the door.

"'Twas the same man, Mama," Jamey hiccuped, holding her still tighter. "He was the same one who stopped me. The one asking the questions. He's going to take me away. He told me so himself. But you won't let him, Mama, will you?"

"I shan't, sweetheart. No one is taking you away."

"Please tell me you won't let him take me."

She pulled him to the middle of the room and loosened his grip as she knelt down and looked into his face. "I shan't, Jamey. No one is taking you from me. You and I are a family."

Fresh tears spilled from his blue eyes, but just as she was ready to pull him into her embrace, his fingers tightened on her shoulders, and he looked into her eyes with that same piercing intensity that always cut straight to her soul, "You promise! You *promise* to keep me safe . . . keep me with you!"

She could feel her heart being clawed open, but she swallowed her anguish and nodded. "I promise, my love."

He melted against her, guided by the trust that she had so wrongfully instilled in him. No, she thought fiercely, *not* wrongfully. It is *not* wrong for a child to trust his mother, and Jamey was her son as sure as there was a God in heaven. He was her son because Elizabeth herself had placed him in her arms and made her promise to love him as her own. He was her son because she had nurtured and cared for and loved him from the time his life was still measured in hours.

And he had been hers from the day she had stood by the railing of that ship and watched the gray-green waters of the Atlantic receive his mother's corpse.

Her hand shook as she caressed his hair, stroked his back, and soothed him as she had done for nearly ten full years. He was her son, and she had never loved anyone and anything more than she loved him now.

But she felt herself strangling with the thought that she might lose him.

Rebecca stayed with him, comforting him with hushed words of affection until Jamey ran out of tears. As she sat on the bed with his head on her shoulder, she felt him gradually relax. His eyes drifted shut, as he once again clung to the old shawl. Rebecca held him, grief lodged in her throat, burning and raw.

Molly looked in on them several times, once whispering that she was sending the afternoon pupils away. Another time, she quietly offered dinner, but Rebecca just shook her head.

Rebecca was relieved when the fading light of evening came on. She was also thankful that the boy had not sought any answers beyond what she was willing to give.

Some time later, while Jamey still slept, Rebecca carefully tucked him under the bedclothes and then stood watching him.

Night had descended upon the town outside her window, and with it feelings of darkness descended upon her spirit. Feelings of desperation about their situation. Feelings of fear.

She knew Molly was waiting. She had heard her coming heavily up the wooden stairs again.

"You look like the dead, darling. Twice buried and dug up again," her friend said as Rebecca emerged from the bedchamber.

She hurt too much to smile. Rebecca pressed her fingers to the puffy slits that had once been her eyes. The light of the candles threw shadows across the room, and Rebecca shivered and moved to the window, shutting it against the cold demons no doubt hovering outside.

She rested her head against the pane of glass and tried to fight the renewed feeling of misery swelling in her chest.

"I've brought some dinner up for you and Jamey. I sent Tommy down to Mrs. Parker's for something, as well. Nothing like a fresh sweet roll to—"

"Oh, Molly!" Rebecca croaked, turning away from the window to find her friend already standing at her side. "What am I to do?"

Despite the bulk of her large belly, Molly gathered her in her arms and consoled her as she wept. It was some time before Rebecca pulled back and let herself be led to the bench, where the two of them sat down.

There was so much that needed to be said. Ten years of lying to this woman who had accepted the two of them as her own. Rebecca didn't know where to start, though, even though she knew that her friend's possible disapproval of her was really only the least of her troubles.

"I know Jamey is not yours, darling."

Molly's quiet statement drew Rebecca's gaze to the woman's face.

"I guessed the truth the moment you arrived in Mr. Butler's coachee from New York that summer so long ago. Why, seeing you holding that wee one in your arms like a piece of fine china rather than your own flesh and bone . . . you were more worried about the right way of caring for the babe than for yourself. And what with all the unfamiliar things that were facing you in this strange city. I knew right then that you'd not birthed Jamey yourself."

"But you . . . you didn't say anything. You let me go on and lie to you all."

"Who am I to interfere with a woman caring for a poor child?" Molly smiled and pushed a strand of hair out of Rebecca's face. "Seeing the wee thing that Jamey was then, and hearing his screams—by the saints, they were loud enough to wake the dead— seeing how blind you were to his misshapen hand, and how you've loved him so much." She shook her head. "You've been as good as his mother, to be sure. If not better."

Rebecca gripped Molly's one hand tightly with both of her own.

Molly patted the backs of her hands. "You were . . . you are the hardest-working woman I've ever known, Rebecca Ford—or whatever your real name is. You were and are the most caring friend a woman could have." She reached up and wiped away Rebecca's tears. "'Twas a blessing for me and my family that you came here . . . and I nearly had to bust a head with my rolling pin once or twice to keep you from harm's way. Though I hadn't meant to ever tell you."

"Your rolling pin?"

"Aye, my Mr. Butler—the sweet thing—nearly took it full on his thick skull, let me tell you. But 'twas his own doing. He has a matchmaker's soul, you know."

"Mr. Butler?" Rebecca managed a smile.

"Aye, darling, and over the years, he always thought it a shame to see a young lassie such as yourself working so hard to take care of yourselves. The way he saw it, you were a widow, so there should be no trouble finding you a good husband. But I put him in his place. I was thinking . . . you could tell all the stories you want about your dead husband, but when it came to men, I felt certain that you were . . . well, an innocent. And how were you going to explain *that* away in your marriage bed, with a lad you're passing off as your own son?"

Rebecca blushed crimson at the thought of the husband and wife discussing her in such a manner. "Molly, you know I've never spent a minute looking to find a husband . . . and I never will."

"I told Mr. Butler so in nearly the same words. But besides, even if you were looking, I've not seen a man about here worthy of you. Why, I don't know a man who could match your learning or your wit . . . or your quality, and you know that don't sit well with most of them."

Rebecca let go of Molly's hand and rose to her feet. "My troubles now are much more serious than finding a husband." She glanced anxiously at the closed door to the bedroom. "That man . . . the lawyer . . . what did he say?"

"Actually, I was ready to toss him—stick, hat, and all—right out into the alley. But he was a gentleman about it all from the moment I opened the door on him. Why, I've never heard an Englishman apologize for anything, and this fellow couldn't have been more civil in his manner if I'd been the queen herself. Anyway, I believe he is sincerely sorry for the way he approached you." Molly frowned. "But all that aside, darling, he means what he said."

Rebecca turned pleading eyes on her friend. "Tell me what he intends to do."

The other woman paused, her kindly face strained. "He means to take Jamey back. He says that he wants to go about this as quietly and in a manner, he says, that would be 'mutually agreeable to all concerned.' He's a lawyer, all right. He is staying at the Death of the Fox, and he wants you to send for him when you are feeling better and ready to talk."

Rebecca felt more tears burn her eyes, and she looked away.

"Is this really the truth? About Jamey being an earl's son and all that?"

"I don't know. I only met the mother," Rebecca murmured, walking to the closed window. "Elizabeth Wakefield was her name. She died on the ship coming from England. She was a young and beautiful thing."

"What was she doing on that ship? Where was the husband?"

Rebecca shook her head and continued to look out. "She never told me any of that. I had a feeling, though, that she was running away from him. Jamey was only a day old when the two of us boarded the ship. Elizabeth was clearly very weak, but she forbade me to go after anyone until we were far out to sea. And then, suddenly, she just drifted away. There was a doctor onboard, on his way to New York, and I brought him in. But there was nothing he could do. Elizabeth gave me Jamey, and then she just died."

In the pane of glass before her, Rebecca could see that gray dawn. The rolling whitecaps on a dark sea. The wailing child in her arms. The canvas shroud draped over the mother's corpse on a plank.

Rebecca remembered so clearly her own misery that morning. A bitter taste of salt was in her mouth as she watched the two sailors solemnly drop the body over the side. With the trailing terrors of her past and the uncertainty of her future, she had entertained a momentary thought of giving in to her woes and casting herself into that dark watery waste.

But then, the infant had stopped wailing for a moment, his dark blue eyes staring up at her. Helpless, sad, and so incredibly alone in this world. Before that morning, no one had ever needed Rebecca Neville. No one had ever depended upon her for his existence. Until now.

"When we raise our children, we give each of them a piece of our heart." Molly's gentle voice came from directly behind her. "But as they grow older and move away from us, they keep the piece that we gave them. It hurts, darling, and it don't matter how old they are or how strong they become, it still hurts to let them go."

Rebecca stared at her own reflection in the glass. Tears glistened and continued to slip down her pale face. Her lips trembled, and she brought a hand up to quiet a sob.

"You've been wanting the best for your Jamey for as long as I've known you. This fight you've been taking on lately . . . of finding a school for him, of wanting him to do better than apprenticing to a tradesman or becoming a common laborer earning his living by the sweat of his brow. Can't you see, darling? The good Lord is giving you an answer! He is trying to help you now."

Rebecca shook her head, but she couldn't turn around and face her friend.

"That lawyer says that your Jamey is an earl's son. Not a merchant, nor a tradesman, nor a clergyman, even . . . but a peer of the realm. With all the love you have in your heart for the boy, how could you sit back and deny him that kind of future?"

Rebecca pressed her fingers to her eyes. Suddenly, her head was pounding painfully.

Molly put a hand on her shoulder and persisted. "Having lived with all the hardship he's had to endure—with his claw hand and his deaf ear—are you willing to refuse him this blessing, lass?"

She was selfish. She wanted him all to herself. She wanted him by her where she could care for him forever. But Molly's words were battering at her defenses, cutting her heart to pieces.

"I cannot!" she cried finally, wrenching the words out. She turned away from the window. "I cannot deny him what is rightfully his. But . . . but I also cannot simply trust this man with Jamey, either. His wife—Jamey's mother—was running away from something . . . or someone. What if this . . . this earl is evil? What if his intentions regarding his son's future are not as noble as we are being led to believe?"

"If that's true, then this Lord Stanmore has spent a pretty penny just to hurt a wee lad." Molly cocked her head to the side. "That makes no sense, darling."

"But you don't know these people . . . their kind." Rebecca shook her head fiercely. "I could never entrust Jamey's life to a man I do not know. Rank has nothing to do with honor, Molly. I know that the most privileged can also be the most vicious." She started pacing the room. "This father—the Earl of Stanmore—he doesn't even know there is anything wrong with his son. What happens if Jamey arrives there and the earl doesn't like what he sees? Think of Jamey's hurt at being sent away by me and then being rejected by a father he does not even know. I cannot let him be treated so—"

"Then go with him," Molly cut in. "Go with Jamey to England, darling. Make certain for yourself that he's settled well."

"I . . ." The breath was suddenly knocked out of Rebecca's chest. She could feel the noose snap tight around her neck.

"The lawyer," Molly continued, "he seems like a reasonable man. I'm certain if you explained your concerns to him, he'd arrange to pay your passage. And I've a good feeling Mr. Butler might have a few shillings tucked away."

Rebecca sank onto the bench. Fear hammered away in her brain. In her mind's eye, she could see herself running out of the London house of Sir Charles Hartington. In the image, she could see the blood, feel it thick and warm on her hands. Unconsciously, she wiped her palms on her dress.

"'Tis clear as day, darling. This is the only way you'll be contented." Molly sat down heavily beside her on the bench. "There is nothing here that you cannot leave behind for half a year . . . or a year even. Your rooms and your belongings, Mr. Butler and I will look after while you are gone, if you like."

Rebecca planted her elbows on her knees and covered her face with hands of ice. Jamey's face was now all she could see.

Keep me, Mama. Promise you'll keep me.

"This is the answer to a prayer, Rebecca. You'll just have to take Jamey back to his father yourself."

Chapter 5

London

The men lounging in the training room of the Marlebone Street club quickly cleared a space as the flashing swords of the two opponents threatened to slice both friend and foe alike. As word of the contest spread, onlookers immediately pushed to the railing of the gallery above, though the eagerness in their faces stemmed more from the prospect of a wager than from the desire for self-preservation. Within minutes, the factions had formed, bets had been laid, and the cheers began to break out as one group's champion or the other took an advantage. Bets of a thousand pounds and more were not uncommon, for the two battlers each had impressive years of military training behind them.

"Five ships, Nathaniel!" the taller of the men said through clenched teeth as their sabers locked.

The noise of the crowd above covered the words exchanged by the combatants below.

"One was all that I promised," Nathaniel replied, spinning away, and parrying the slashing blade of his opponent.

"What difference to you? The work will be the same."

Sparks flew as the swords clashed.

"One could be construed as an accident." Nathaniel stepped up his attack, managing to drive the other back across the room. "Five would be seen as open warfare."

The advantage was only temporary, as the taller man deftly side-stepped a fierce blow, staggered Nathaniel with a fist to the face, and then pressed forward amid cheers from the gallery.

"It would only be open warfare if we put their entire fleet . . . damnable as it is . . . to the torch. But now that you mention it . . ."

Sir Nathaniel Yorke, the Surveyor of the Navy, continued to back away under the ongoing onslaught of his opponent's saber. "I'm surprised, you blackguard, that you haven't tried that yet."

"It is a bloody business, Nathaniel." The tall nobleman backed up and swung his sword, forcing his opponent's thrust to slide away from his body. "It is barbarous to ruin human lives for a few pieces of gold."

"Everyone knows how you feel."

"Well, there are more than a few in Parliament who are already supporting the cause. It won't be long until the law sides with justice."

Nathaniel drove forward, but the other fighter deflected his blows and suddenly the two were again face-to-face, the crossed swords locked between them.

"And how," he asked breathlessly, "would Parliament feel about the confiscation of five new ships?"

"However Parliament feels, I will continue to cut away at the assets of these slave-trading dogs until no dockyard in England will accept such a commission, no matter what price they're willing to pay."

With a quick move, Nathaniel pushed his opponent's sword downward and held it there, saying in a low voice, "Aren't you afraid of the consequences? What if the truth comes out? You know I agree that slavery is a dishonorable trade. But what if your name were to be connected with the campaign of terror that has already cost the slavers so much? You have so much to lose!"

"I have *nothing* to lose."

With a twisting flash of metal, Nathaniel's sword suddenly left his hand and went skittering across the floor as the tip of his friend's saber was suddenly pressed against his chest. The gallery exploded with cheers.

"Five new ships, Nathaniel! Confiscated by my own men and anchored in the Channel off Gravesend. They'll be there, ready for you, at dawn next Friday."

"It goes against all of my training to destroy so many fine

British ships." He pushed the weapon away with a gloved hand and wiped off the sweat on his face with the back of his wrist. "But, by Gad, 'tis for a good cause. And besides, our fleet certainly *does* need the target practice!"

The clap on his shoulder was friendly. "You are a fine man, Nathaniel, despite your weakness for the low parry."

"And you, Stanmore, do have a heart!" With a wry grin, he accepted the sword from the servant. "But wouldn't that be a shock to the legion of women who swear that you haven't one?"

Philadelphia

Standing in the darkness of Strawberry Alley, Rebecca shivered and pulled her shawl tightly about her. The evening was chilly, but it seemed to her that she was the only one who noticed.

The door to the Death of the Fox Inn stood open, and the sound of a fiddle and singing voices spilled out into the muddy street around her. She could see the tables filled with tradesmen and travelers, tankards and cups of beer and cider in every hand, swinging to the rollicking rhythms of the old tune. As she watched, Annie entered from the summer kitchen out back and worked her way through the revelers, plates of mutton stew balanced expertly along her arm.

The sign above swung slightly in a light breeze, and Rebecca looked up at the painted depiction of the fox, its back to a tree, cornered by a pair of hounds. Taking a deep breath, she forced herself to climb the three stone steps to the doorway.

"Mrs. Ford!" The wife of the innkeeper was quick to notice and come to her as she stepped in. "Is everything all right? Has Molly gone to labor?"

Having served as a midwife in her younger years, Nellie Fox was still called on from time to time by those living along the alley.

"No, she is well, and it is not time yet," Rebecca said quietly. "I am here to see a gentleman from England. I was told he is staying here. Sir Oliver . . . Sir Oliver Birch."

The woman's eyes brightened at the name. "Aye, he's here. A

fine paying customer, too. In fact, the gentleman just retired to his room not long ago. I didn't know he was any relation of yours, Mrs. Ford."

"He is no relation. We have business together." She stepped to the side to allow two of the patrons to walk out. Both men nodded to her respectfully. "Would it be too much trouble, Mrs. Fox, for you to send someone to the gentleman's room and tell him that I desire to speak with him?"

"Nay, not at all, Mrs. Ford." The woman immediately turned to one of the serving lads and told him shortly to do exactly as Rebecca had asked.

With a word of thanks, Rebecca moved to the closest table by the door and sat down uncomfortably on the edge of a bench standing against the wall. She didn't want to think for fear of losing her courage and walking out of the place.

On the far side of the tavern room, Efraim Fox was standing by the square storage space that had been built into the corner. Through the wooden bars rising to the ceiling, she could see the casks stacked against the wall and the smoked meats hanging from hooks. The innkeeper was pouring cider from a large pitcher into a couple of leather cups and watching the fiddler, who was playing merrily by a side window.

Other than stopping in every now and then for one of the local meetings held at the inn, Rebecca was not a frequent visitor to the place. But having lived in this neighborhood for as long as she had, she knew the innkeeper and his wife (and more than a few of the revelers) well enough to feel quite safe sitting in the tavern alone. As she waited, the fiddler finished his tune, mopped his face with his sleeve, and sat down at a table where Annie had laid his supper.

Rebecca had rehearsed in advance all that she wanted to say to the lawyer, but when she saw the tall, older man enter on the heels of the serving lad, she felt fingers of panic gripping her throat.

"Mrs. Ford, I am in your debt. Thank you for coming to meet me on such short notice."

Rebecca rose to her feet and nodded hesitantly. The dim light of the stairs to her rooms had not afforded her a very good look at the man. Here in the inn, she had a much better view of the lawyer's features. Sir Oliver was younger than she had originally thought. His gray eyes were gentle and not unfriendly. He extended a hand, inviting her to sit down again. Once she had seated herself, he took the chair across from her.

"To begin, madam, I sincerely hope that you will accept an apology for the reckless manner in which I approached you this afternoon. Doubtless, I should have sent a letter of introduction around first." The lawyer paused, continuing when she nodded. "You see, Mrs. Ford, I am fully empowered to act on behalf of Lord Stanmore, and my primary aim is to accomplish fully the undertaking his lordship has entrusted to me. And I should say immediately, that includes expressing his lordship's gratitude for the manner in which you have cared for his son. Allow me also to explain his desires with regard to his son, and speak briefly of the reward you might expect for your—"

"Let me make something clear to you right now, Sir Oliver. What I have done for Jamey these past years—what he has meant to me—it is not something that I ever expect to be rewarded for, beyond what I have already received." Rebecca tried desperately to fight back her surge of emotions. "I have loved Jamey as my own son, and I am the only mother he has ever known. There is *nothing* that you could ever pay that would replace the joy he has brought into my life."

The lawyer stared at her, a thoughtful look gradually working across his face as she continued.

"Now, with regard to your client's desire . . . I must tell you straightaway that as yet I have seen no proof to support your claim that Jamey is the Earl of Stanmore's son."

"I should be more than happy to provide you with documentation, if you wish to see it," he responded quietly.

"Later, if you please, Sir Oliver." Rebecca nodded. "I will tell you that I see no reason why anyone would make such a claim if there were not some basis for it in truth."

She paused as Annie approached the table and offered drink to the two of them. Rebecca declined anything for herself with a shake of her head.

"Please continue," Sir Oliver encouraged brightly, obviously pleased with the turn in the conversation. "I must say that when I left England, I harbored grave concerns as to the kind of people I should find in the colonies. You have no idea, madam, how reassuring it is for me to find someone of your . . . well, your level of understanding."

"Be that as it may, Sir Oliver, the puzzling matter for me . . ." Rebecca paused as Annie quickly returned with a pewter cup of ale and placed it before the lawyer. "Perhaps you can enlighten me as to why it took the good Earl of Stanmore nearly ten years to seek the return of his son?"

"His lordship did not know of his wife's death, Mrs. Ford, or he would have sent for his son sooner, I assure you."

The man's matter-of-fact answer jarred Rebecca momentarily.

"If I might pose a question for you, madam . . . if you knew the deceased traveler was Lord Stanmore's wife, could you enlighten me as to why in ten years *you* have not returned his son?"

She felt heat rush into her face. "Why, I did not know anything about Lord Stanmore. I fear I had no chance of knowing the lady."

His eyes studied her face carefully. "Then how was it, madam, that you came to take possession of her child?"

"I . . ." She tucked her hands in the folds of her skirts to hide their trembling. The gentleness in the man's gray eyes was gone now, replaced with a look of close inquiry. "A kinswoman of mine was traveling on that ship. As far as I know, there was no one traveling with the mother, not even a single servant. You certainly can understand, sir, that no one would have imagined that a woman traveling alone might be the wife of an earl. When she fell ill and died on that ship, there was no one to take the child."

"I see." The lawyer's long fingers reached for the cup. "May I ask if you were already married before James was brought to you?"

"I had already been promised. So I knew I would soon be."

"And did not this frighten you?"

"Certainly not! I asked for the child. And Mr. Ford and I were delighted to have him . . . it was just so sad that my dear husband passed away so soon after our marriage."

"Raising a child alone! Did it not cross your mind even once to try to find the child's proper kin? Perhaps sending a correspondence by way of the ship's master. Would it not have been . . . ?"

"As I said, the lady was traveling alone." She let her temper boil to the surface. "All that the ship's master knew was that the good lady had arrived on his ship when the babe was still a newborn. Now, Sir Oliver, I desire that you place yourself in my position for a moment and answer this. What kind of a husband would a wife run away from with so young an infant to care for?"

"You assume, of course, that she *was* running away."

"Very well. But if she were not running away, why would her husband wait ten years before even inquiring after his wife and son?"

The lawyer was clearly put off by the frankness of her question. "I must tell you, madam," he said finally, "I am not at liberty to answer all your questions."

"Then we are at loggerheads, Sir Oliver, if you will pardon so plain a term. Though I openly admit that I did not bear Jamey, I tell you now that I will not allow my son to be taken by a stranger to an unknown father, no matter what potential advantages this new life might hold for him."

She rose to her feet.

"Please sit down, Mrs. Ford." He, too, rose and gestured to the seat. His voice was calm and conciliatory. "The last thing I care to do is to alarm you more than I did this afternoon. I shall explain as much as I can. And please accept my apologies for placing you on the defensive regarding what you did or did not do so many years ago." Sir Oliver's eyes gentled again. "I have seen James. I am aware of his—well, if I may be so blunt—his physical deformity. At the risk of being presumptuous, madam, may I say that your abilities as a guardian are, in my mind, quite remarkable."

Rebecca sat down again on the edge of the bench. She could feel her face still burning. Her entire body felt as tightly strung as the instrument the fiddler was taking up again across the room. She waited for the lawyer to continue.

"Searching the world for a wife and a child is not an easy task, Mrs. Ford. Until recently, the Earl of Stanmore had no knowledge of where his wife had fled. You see, he was away at the time of James's birth."

This did nothing to soothe Rebecca's concerns about the man.

"I will confide something in you, Mrs. Ford, that normally I would not. But under the circumstances . . ." Sir Oliver lowered his voice. "The scandalmongers in London at the time of her disappearance had a delightful time spreading the story that Elizabeth Wakefield had run away with . . . well, with a lover. No husband, I should think, could be expected to recover readily from such scandal."

At that moment the fiddler struck up a tune, saving Rebecca from giving herself away. She'd been ready to speak on the behalf of the deceased woman, in spite of knowing that her safety lay in remaining silent.

"You said that you are aware of my son's physical condition. Does his lordship know of it, as well?"

"His lordship does, indeed, know about James's hand. He was informed when he arrived home by those in attendance at the time of the birth."

"Does he also know . . . ?" Rebecca added quickly. "Does his lordship know that Jamey is also hard of hearing?"

The lawyer's gray eyes showed surprise for the first time. "But today . . . today he seemed quite . . ."

"Jamey hears the words if he is looking at the speaker's face. I believe he is entirely deaf in the right ear and can hear only a little in his left." Oliver Birch's silence reinforced Rebecca's anxiety. "Knowing what you do now, can you swear to me that your client is compassionate enough to look past the boy's shortcomings and accept him as his son?"

The look that immediately came into the lawyer's face spoke volumes about the high regard he held for his client. "I can assure you, Mrs. Ford, that the present Earl of Stanmore is a most honorable man. He is an esteemed and active member of the House of Lords. His character is noted throughout England for his sense of fairness and justice. I have known him personally for over twenty years. No matter what James's difficulties, I would stake my life that you'll do very well by the boy in sending him back to England and to his father."

As he finished, Rebecca felt her very life slowly draining from her body. Words of reason kept forcing themselves over and over into her awareness. *He would be better off in England. He will be happier there. He will have title and wealth and position.* But she didn't want reasonable. Or logical. She wanted Jamey. Panic began to rise again within her. Thoughts of running from the inn and hiding, of taking Jamey west with some group of settlers popped into her head.

"Perhaps such words sound hollow and insubstantial." The lawyer pushed the cup away and folded his long fingers together before him on the table. "Knowing now the full extent of James's difficulties, I truly understand your concern regarding how he would fare on this journey. I sense quite clearly that you are also concerned how well the lad will adjust, once situated in the household of his father."

She nodded, forcing herself not to think even for an instant how devastated she herself would be once Jamey was gone. Sir Oliver's thoughtful gaze lingered on her face.

"Mrs. Ford, allow me to make a suggestion that might ease the situation for all parties. If all had gone as I had planned—and you had parted with James as I had hoped—I would have employed someone to accompany us on this journey. Being a confirmed bachelor myself, I do not have much experience with the needs of a lad his age. What I am suggesting is this, Mrs. Ford. Why not accompany the boy and me back to England?" Rebecca knew she must have looked startled, for he quickly continued. "As an honored guest, naturally, of the Earl of Stanmore . . . and myself."

The same fear that had gripped her when Molly had suggested such a thing once again took hold of her body. Rebecca could feel the noose tightening.

"This is the only solution that makes sense. And there is nothing that you need to concern yourself with while you are away. I shall make any arrangements that are required."

Rebecca pressed her fingers to her temples briefly, trying to soothe the pounding ache that wouldn't go away.

"I understand your concerns, Mrs. Ford. Your doubts and fears are quite real, and I admire you for having them." Oliver Birch's voice turned gentle. "Though you do not know me, I ask that you trust me, my dear. Trust me that this journey shall prove to be entirely advantageous to both you and your son. Come to England and see for yourself that the lad is satisfactorily settled."

Rebecca swallowed hard, forcing down the knot in her throat. She rose slowly to her feet.

"Please tell me that you will at least consider the offer." Sir Oliver stood, as well.

"I do not have to consider the offer, sir," she managed to whisper. "I have no choice but to accompany you."

Chapter 6

Sir Nicholas Spencer tossed his overcoat to the footman and scrutinized his appearance in the mirror. Ignoring the fresh cut above his right brow and the darkening bruise on his prominent cheekbone, he focused instead on his cravat. Satisfied, he stood back, cocked his head critically, and smoothed the lapels of his new satin coat. An old house steward hovered patiently a step away.

"Good morning, Philip," Nicholas said, turning. "Did you and your master have a pleasant time down at Solgrave?"

"Indeed, sir. Lord Stanmore is in the library, sir."

Nicholas fell in step with the steward.

"Did his lordship fall ill while you were in Hertfordshire?"

"No, sir," the tall, angular steward responded with a turn of his head. Together they ascended one of the grand staircases that curled, like great marble arms, around the immense entrance hall.

"Then did he suffer a fall from his horse? Sprain an ankle?"

"No, sir," Philip answered in his immutable monotone.

"Hmm. A new colt then has been added to the stables?"

"No, sir."

"It must have been a beautiful woman. Out with it, man."

"No, sir."

"Then, it had to be an orgy of wantonness! That rogue master of yours has secretly assembled an entire harem of women down there! Is that it, Philip?"

"No, sir."

"Has your brother, Daniel, burned down Solgrave, yet?"

"No, sir."

Nicholas paused on top of the stairs and looked sternly into the steward's bland expression. "Then tell me this, Philip. Does anything *ever* make you smile?"

"No, sir."

Nicholas turned and strode through the massive, elaborately detailed doors into the library. As the door closed behind him, he spied his friend writing at a huge desk by the window.

"Your steward," he began without a greeting, "is by far the most miserable old bugger I've ever had occasion to know in all my life."

Samuel Wakefield looked up from his correspondence and smiled at his friend. "Of course! Philip is Philip. You shall only be the more miserable for it, if you think you can change him."

"That has the ring of a challenge to it," Nicholas growled with a toss of his head toward the door. "Your majordomo, my friend, has only known me for the last twenty years or so. Don't you think he could greet me with a 'good morning'? Or, 'what a fine day it is outside, sir'? Or, 'whatever was the cause of that nasty cut on your handsome forehead, Sir Nicholas?' The problem with the world today is that no one asks the *right* questions!"

"Why, that *is* a fine mark on your brow, Nicholas. Who was it this time?" Stanmore pushed aside the work on his desk and leaned back in his chair. "No, never mind that. I wouldn't know your cohorts anyway. Tell me, though, where you acquired such a finely wrought crest?"

Instead of answering his friend's question, Nicholas picked up the copy of the *Morning Chronicle* from the earl's desk and pointed to an article on the front page.

"Here is perfect proof for my argument. Imagine, this rag of a newspaper giving that John Wesley fellow all the credit for those five new ships being sunk last . . . well, whenever it was."

"Friday."

"Exactly. Do they ask *how* some religious zealot managed to get those slave ships out there where they could be blasted to splinters by His Majesty's Navy?"

"Do they?"

"Hardly."

"Well, Wesley *is* a strong voice against the slave trade."

"Even so, Stanmore, you cannot tell me that prayers and good intentions were enough to steal those ships *after* they were paid for and *before* they could go south on their hellish business." Nicholas eyed his friend wryly. "Such a trick would take a great deal of planning and finesse . . . and money, too, I should think."

"Very well, I concede your point . . . about the questions, that is. But tell me, Nicholas, about the wound you bear so handsomely. Where did you get this one?"

"If you must know, 'twas at Wimbledon." Nicholas dropped the paper on the desk and touched the cut on his forehead. "These deuced country fairs are not what they used to be. And before you start your lecturing, m'lord, you should know that I was an innocent bystander . . . until I was pushed into the ring. From there on, it was self-defense."

"Pushed? Ha!" Stanmore pointed to a chair. "I have yet to meet a man—or a woman, for that matter—who can push Nicholas Spencer into anything."

"Yes, well, while we're on the subject of being pushed"— Nicholas seated himself across from Stanmore—"I certainly hope you were not spending piles of money down in St. Albans."

"What are you driving at?"

"Very well. Straight to the point, then, and with just the right question. During your absence from London, the latest paramour of yours was quite distressed. The word about town—not that I ever listen to it, of course—but the word is that this same lady has consoled herself by losing *immense* sums of money at a variety of gaming establishments this past sennight . . . far more than usual."

"Louisa and I have an agreement. I refuse to support her gambling habits."

"Say what you will. But be warned, my friend, the siren is, I believe, a bit desperate."

"Is this all you have to do, Nicholas, spread gossip?"

"Why, no! As a matter of fact, I have quite a full schedule. Just today, for example, I will be extremely busy exercising my new pair of very handsome grays before dropping in on a little soirée over at Lady Mornington's. Then I shall do my best to keep up appearances as a man-about-town by losing money at either White's or Brooks's . . . I haven't decided which. Later on, of course, I must spend the requisite hour in the pleasure gardens. . . . What do you think, Stanmore, Vauxhall or Ranelagh this evening? And then there is the sporting—but wait." Nicholas stretched his long legs out before him and studied his friend's serious expression. "There is something else troubling you, isn't there? And if I am not mistaken, Lady Nisdale's gambling is not the source of it."

Stanmore rose to his feet and walked to the large window overlooking Berkeley Square. "Your acute powers of observation are not diminished by your roguish style of living, Nicholas."

"The devil take my life, Stanmore. I've known you too long. Tell me what is wrong."

"I received news of Elizabeth while I was away."

Nicholas straightened in the chair and stared at his friend's grim profile.

"Oliver Birch was indeed able to track her." The earl's glance in his direction was brief and hard. "He sent me a letter from New York bearing the news."

"So Elizabeth *has* been living in the colonies for all these years."

Stanmore turned sharply and faced him, "She died on the journey across, ten years ago."

Nicholas knew better than to offer any sympathy.

"Oliver managed to find the ship that took her across."

"What of the lad?"

"He wrote me that the infant, it appears, survived the journey."

There was no look of happiness on the earl's face. Nicholas could not discern even a hint of relief there, as he would have expected in his friend's countenance. After all, Stanmore had just told him that his own lost son might possibly still be alive.

"Oliver's letter concludes with his intention of traveling to the Province of Pennsylvania. The last anyone saw of the lad, he was in the care of a woman who had accompanied Elizabeth during the crossing. The woman's destination was apparently Philadelphia."

"Does Birch know who the woman is?" Nicholas watched his friend walk away from the window and move toward the large fireplace dominating one side of the room. "The way I remember it, none of the servants went with Elizabeth, and no one in her family or in her circle of friends had even been contacted when she disappeared that night."

Stanmore stood erect, staring up at the portrait of his father, the last Earl of Stanmore, hanging above the mantel.

"You remember the details correctly," he said after a long moment of silence. "I do not know who the woman is."

Nicholas followed his friend's gaze. "So what is your plan?"

"I wait to hear again from Oliver. In the meantime, there are announcements and arrangements that need to be made regarding Elizabeth."

"Of course."

After a few moments, Nicholas joined his friend before the portrait.

"You know that you are now fair game . . . a 'catch.' "

"A catch that has no intention of ever again being netted."

"Nevertheless a challenge in the eyes of every eligible female."

"They can all go to the devil."

"A shocking attitude for a peer of the realm." Nicholas shook his head disapprovingly. "You have to remember what the old man had in mind for you. A title and wealth—which you have. Respect—which you have earned. A beautiful wife—which you had at one time and will certainly have again. But most important, a son. An heir. It all came down to that, didn't it?"

"More than you know," Stanmore said grimly. "But there *is* already a son and heir, and Oliver Birch will bring him back to England soon enough."

Chapter 7

The sun was warm on his face, and the pungent tang of tar and sea and wood smoke filled his lungs. Listening to the sounds of sailors and longshoremen, Stanmore considered that these were the very smells of a glorious past—of the England of Drake and Raleigh and Hudson and Smith—and also the odors of a less than glorious present.

Stanmore gazed out the window of the rooms that Birch had taken in the inn on Broad Quay. Below him at dockside, sledges piled high with tobacco, sugar, and cotton formed a steady stream of traffic along the timeworn cobbled street. The countless number of ships moored along the miles of Bristol's docks stood so thick together that it resembled a tangled forest of masts and spars and lines for as far as he could see.

By a trading ship directly in front of the inn, a line of Africans sat in chains while the slavers prepared to load them for the voyage to the sugar plantations in the Caribbean. The sight sickened him, and—looking up at the massive square steeple of St. Mary Redcliffe—he swore inwardly that he would never give up his fight against the barbarous trade.

The sound of the door opening behind him brought Stanmore around, and he watched Sir Oliver shake his head as he walked back inside the room.

"Sorry to make you wait. But there is no sign of them in their rooms. Since it is such a beautiful day, Mrs. Ford must have taken young James for a walk. I left word for her to come here as soon as she arrives."

Stanmore turned his attention back to the quay.

In the distance, beyond a pier piled high with casks of Madeira, a young urchin of a lad was running in wild circles around his mother. The worn blue breeches, the shabby red waistcoat, the untamed hair riffling in the breeze—all tokens of the careless and yet natural freedom of a child of the lower classes. Stanmore frowned. It was a manner that he himself had never been allowed to enjoy, and neither would James. He watched the gray-cloaked mother, opening her arms and catching the boy as he threw himself roughly against her. The two toppled, and he watched with dismay as they fell laughing against an empty sledge.

"She is not what you are expecting."

Stanmore rested a hand on the open window as a few passersby blocked his view of the two. He did not turn to look at the lawyer. "And what is it exactly that I am expecting?"

"It is clear, m'lord, that you are expecting someone who can be bought off. I mean no disrespect, but you are quite off the mark in your assumption that Mrs. Ford is here because I failed to offer her a large enough reward in Philadelphia for the services she has rendered."

"We shall see how 'off the mark' I am, Oliver."

He continued to peer out until the people blocking his view moved on and he could see the two again. The woman was crouched before the boy. The hood of her cloak had fallen back in the chaos of the moment, and flowing locks of golden red hair now caught the bright sunshine. She had her back to him, but Stanmore could see the way her hands were cradling the boy's face. He assumed she was scolding the lad, but all the love in her gestures spoke differently. A moment later, the boy placed his arms around her neck, remaining in the mother's embrace for several moments. In spite of the openness of their public display of affection, a sense of intrusion on something private stirred in the pit of his stomach, and he averted his eyes.

Birch's furrowed brow greeted him as he looked across the room.

"Speak your mind, Oliver, for God's sake! You look as if you're being led to the gallows."

"I had the pleasure of spending some time in Mrs. Ford's company on the journey over, m'lord. I must tell you that despite the pressures of being a widow without resources endeavoring to raise a child, she manages to maintain a remarkable attitude of poise and grace. Despite her simple attire, she possesses exquisite manners. Numerous times during our journey, I witnessed instances where the woman's kindness and lack of pretension won the approval of men and women alike. She is no rustic, m'lord, and she possesses that quality that—without any conscious effort on her part—elicits people's respect."

Stanmore's dark gaze fixed itself on the lawyer. "Come to the point."

"I have already come to the point, m'lord. She is simply not a woman who will be bought." The man's voice expressed his conviction. "Mrs. Ford has acted in the capacity of James's mother for nearly ten years. And I must say that her affection for him—her relationship with him—well, it is of the type not generally found among the *haut ton*."

To hide his growing irritation, Stanmore strode away from the lawyer, taking a survey of the room's sparse furnishings. By a small fireplace between two windows, he picked up a slightly bent poker.

"I encourage you to listen to her recommendations and her concerns regarding the lad before dismissing her. On the journey over, she enlightened me with—"

"You appear to have spent a *great* deal of time in each other's company during this crossing."

Color crept up the lawyer's neck. "It is not what you think, m'lord. We did, however, have reason to converse from time to time. Quite reasonably, I should say, Mrs. Ford had questions about James's future . . . concerns about where the lad was to live and how much time he would be spending in your lordship's company. She has definite opinions about the importance of living in the country versus the city and . . ." He looked away under the pressure of the earl's gaze.

"I must say that you sound like a man smitten, Oliver." He waved off the lawyer as the man started to object. "Don't take me wrong. You know I am the last man to meddle in another's affairs."

"You are misconstruing my motives in speaking on her behalf,

Lord Stanmore. Your son's welfare was the point of our discussion on the journey and—"

A soft knock curtailed any further explanation. Stanmore nodded toward the door, and Sir Oliver moved to open it.

Standing with his hand on the latch, he looked into the earl's eyes. "You pay me to advise you, m'lord. I advise that you give the woman a fair hearing."

Standing in the corridor outside of the rooms taken by the earl, Rebecca tried to reassure herself that Jamey was fine. The cheerful Irish serving woman who was helping him clean up and change into his best clothes reminded her of an older Molly Butler, and Jamey obviously felt comfortable with her. He would be ready for his appointment with his father.

She herself had not even bothered to shed her cloak before directing her steps to Lord Stanmore's rooms, for the message from Sir Oliver had said that his lordship wished to speak to her first.

Cold dread washed through her as she raised her hand to knock. She had tried. Lord knows, she had tried to tell Jamey the truth of his parentage. When they were walking along the quay, she had once again failed to find a way of telling him—just as she had failed each time she'd tried on the ship. The simple truth was that she just couldn't cut the bond between them before he'd had a chance to form a new one. She couldn't leave him alone and vulnerable—not until there was another to take her place.

She prayed for some understanding and compassion on the peer's part on her failure to do what was right. She desperately hoped that a solution might even be suggested by Jamey's father. She lifted a trembling hand to the door again.

A flushed Oliver Birch opened the door.

"I'm very glad you are here, Sir Oliver," she started in a low voice. "I wanted to make certain that I received the message correctly. His lordship wishes to meet with me before he meets with James?"

"That is correct, Mrs. Ford."

As Rebecca listened to the lawyer's quiet words, her gaze was drawn to the broad back of the man in riding clothes who moved to look out the window across the room. He was slightly taller than the lawyer, but something in his build, in his wide confident stance, in the way the black jacket hugged his back, made him appear larger than any man she'd ever known.

"What of James? Shall I have him brought here after a short while?"

"Don't concern yourself with that just now, ma'am."

Rebecca shot a quick look at the lawyer's face. His eyes flickered away, and she felt a chasm open in the pit of her stomach. She turned her attention again to the earl's unmoving back. Dark, unpowdered hair, the color of night, tied neatly in the back was all she perceived.

"But before I can . . ." She hesitated. "It is important that his lordship meet his son before . . ."

"Please come in, Mrs. Ford. His lordship has been waiting. I shall go and look in on James shortly."

Lord Stanmore turned and faced them.

For a long moment, Rebecca stood perfectly still, stunned and staring, unidentifiable thoughts flitting through her head. This was not the man she had envisioned . . . not the man who had driven his wife away.

Strangely, the face had no flaws. High, firm cheekbones. A strong, determined jaw. A straight and perfect nose. His eyes, curtained by lashes long and dark, were fixed on the floor between them. The Earl of Stanmore was a dangerously handsome man.

And his son, Rebecca thought, looked nothing like him.

"Please come in," Birch repeated the invitation and stood back for her to enter. "Your lordship, may I present Mrs. Ford?"

Stanmore fixed his gaze on her. He had heard Birch's introduction, but he suddenly found himself struggling to regain his composure. It was the same bloody woman he'd been watching from the window. At least, the cloak and the windblown red hair looked the same. Indeed, it was certainly the same woman.

But her face! Though he could not see it when she was walking on the quay, he could easily see now the reason for his lawyer's obvious enchantment. She was really quite beautiful . . . in an unexpected way.

Her gaze was averted, and he had glimpsed those clear, unusually blue eyes for only an instant. It was enough, though. And the pull of attraction he was feeling only served to anger him more.

"If you will excuse me, m'lord, after looking in on James . . . I will be down in the coffee room . . . er, making arrangements."

Birch slipped out the door, and Stanmore noted the anxious gaze the woman directed at the lawyer as he made his escape. The earl waited for a moment, allowing the silence to build. Finally, he broke it.

"Did you have a pleasant journey over, Mrs. Ford?"

"We did, m'lord."

Her voice was trembling slightly. He watched her eyes search the room with alarm. Her hands were fisted tightly at her sides. Her very stance conveyed the image of a doe brought to bay.

"And your week in Bristol has not been a hardship, I hope."

"No, m'lord."

He clasped his hands behind his back and tried to not focus on the tendrils of fire that framed the pale face. "I have a number of engagements awaiting me in London, so it would be best if we get down to the reason for my trip to Bristol." He started pacing. "Before I present you with what I believe you will find to be ample compensation for your service to my family, I want you to know, Mrs. Ford, that you are welcome to remain in England as my guest for as long as you wish. Your expenses—"

"Compensation, sir?" she interrupted, her sharp gaze stopping him dead. "I was under the impression that I was invited here to speak to you about your son."

"You are mistaken, ma'am. I have asked you here so I can finish what my lawyer failed to do . . . in spite of my clear instructions to him."

"Sir Oliver made a very generous—though misdirected—offer of money in Philadelphia, m'lord. Please be assured that the sum he offered had nothing to do with my refusal. But I must tell you that such a discussion is pointless."

"Mrs. Ford . . ." He crossed his arms over his chest. "Madam, you *shall* be paid for your—"

"M'lord, I must insist that you consider the matter of this compensation *closed.*" The change in her demeanor was immediate and remarkable. The hounds might have her at bay, but she was not ready to lie down.

"My family has incurred a debt to you. Until you accept what is rightfully owed to you—"

"You owe me nothing, m'lord. There is nothing owed, for there was no debt—no bartering—no contractual agreements of any kind. I did not take James into my care with any expectation of monetary gain. And, to be perfectly blunt, I refuse to demean my affection for your son by allowing you or anyone else to quantify its worth."

"Mrs. Ford . . ."

"I beg you, Lord Stanmore, to cease this line of discussion."

Stanmore stared at her for a long moment. There was more demand in her tone than begging. She *was* a fighter.

"Thank you, m'lord. Then since we have concluded our discussion of what you wished to address, I have some business that I should like to discuss with your lordship."

"*You* have business to discuss, madam?"

"It has to do with the welfare of your son."

"Ah, yes. Well, the lad is back where he belongs. His welfare is no longer your concern."

"I beg to differ, m'lord!" The anger that brought color instantly to her cheeks was also evident in her tone. "I am the only parent that he has ever known. He remains my concern."

"That was a mistake that we have rectified."

"Mistake?" Blue eyes flashed hotly in his direction. "It may have been a mistake that you lost a wife and a son. It may have been a mistake that you took nearly a lifetime before searching after them. But, for me, finding and raising James has been a blessing from heaven. And no matter how difficult this situation might appear to your lordship right now, my concern . . . nay, my love for him will *not* be called a mistake."

Stanmore felt his back stiffen, and Birch's warning came back to him. The lawyer was correct. Mrs. Ford was not at all what he had expected.

The two measured each other in silence for a long moment, and then she turned her head.

As he watched her, he felt his perception shift slightly . . . and he cursed himself silently. But it was true, the woman had a natural right to be protective of the lad. Nonetheless, he could not allow her display of raw emotions to affect his judgment—not while James's future was the topic of discussion.

"You misunderstand my intentions," he said finally.

"Then perhaps you have misspoken them, m'lord."

Clasping his hands behind his back again, he sent her a sharp glance and began to pace before the fireplace. He didn't need to explain anything to her. He had the power and the legal right to dismiss her and to do exactly as he'd planned. But the recollection of the young boy throwing his arms around her—the nagging thought of the bond that obviously existed between the two—these things gave him pause.

"You must understand that you are not tossing the lad to the wolves, Mrs. Ford. We both have James's best interest in mind." He tried to gentle his tone as he paused before the small hearth to face her. "I assume your concern pertains to the lad's immediate welfare, and my plans have been formed to see to it that he is provided for and cared for . . . so that he is prepared to assume his rightful position. Our goals are not so different."

He waited for an argument, but she gave him none, so he resumed his pacing as he delivered his lecture.

"For a boy of James's age and lineage, the most critical step will be for him to acquire a solid foundation for his education. And this is what I have planned for him now that he has arrived."

He gave her a quick glance. Despite her travel-worn attire and her rather untamed hair, she looked quite regal standing there, listening intently to him. Even the flaming color in her cheeks had begun to subside.

"James will be sent to Eton. For generations, all the Stanmores have been Eton men. It is a fine school. Sir Oliver has warned me already of the lad's difficulties. To be blunt, he has informed me of the lad's deafness."

"He will not fit in."

"He will with time. I shall see to it that James will receive all the proper assistance."

"You know nothing of the assistance he will require."

"Beg pardon?"

"When is James being sent there?"

"Immediately, of course."

Shoulders raised. Head high. Eyes again flashing with challenge. He watched the fists form again at her sides. "Why, m'lord?"

"Are you questioning the importance of education?"

"Hardly. I am a teacher myself. I would *never* question such a worthy course of action. But I do question the timing of his departure. The month of June will soon be upon us."

"He will need to attend during the summer in order to catch up with the rest of the boys who will be returning in the fall. The arrangements are—"

"And how much would he suffer if you were to delay your plans and send him there *with* the rest of the students in the fall?" She took a step toward him. "More importantly, though, I wonder if you have considered how much he would suffer if you proceeded with such a plan. Put yourself in his place, m'lord. If you were sent to a strange school, among unfamiliar people, having just been separated from the only family you have ever known, how would you feel? Compound that with the brutal knowledge that your newfound father has shown no interest in even becoming acquainted with you." At his silence, she pressed on. "I wonder how you, or anyone, would feel, m'lord."

"He will adjust."

He saw her close her eyes and take a calming breath, no doubt to cool a temper that was blistering beneath the skin.

"But is there any reason *why* he should be forced to adjust so abruptly?" She did not wait for an answer, shifting her gaze to the floor at his feet. "Blame me if you will, m'lord, but your son is different than other English boys . . . in so many ways." She appeared to be measuring the distance that separated them. "In wealth and comfort, there has not been much that I could give him while I have had him, but he has never wanted for affection or love. I have always been prepared to fight his battles with him when other children laughed at his deformed hand or when adults screamed at him cruelly, thinking him ignorant rather than simply hard of hearing. I fought for him, and I taught him how to fight for himself. I taught him to draw strength from the goodness that he carries within, and never surrender to a hardship that burdens him. I taught him that burdens make us strong. But for all of that, m'lord, he is still only nine years' old and far too young to be facing a whole new world of obstacles on his own."

Stanmore had never harbored any intention of ever allowing compassion to affect his dealings with the lad, but the woman was proving quite adept at eliciting his sympathy. *Damn me,* he swore silently, turning sharply toward the window and staring out.

"I ask you, m'lord, to reconsider your decision. I implore you to give him a chance—to get to know him—even if just for now. When the fall comes, there will be ample time for you to decide what must be done. I only ask that you allow him to adjust to his new life in steps. Let him feel accepted by you . . . before I leave him."

The last words caught in her throat, and he did not have to face her to know she had tears in her eyes.

Damnation! He shut his eyes and forced himself to master his anger. The woman had no right to question his decision. She knew nothing about his past. She knew nothing of the torment he'd endured or the willpower he'd exerted to make himself come even *this* close to the child.

She also knew nothing about the promise he'd made.

Stanmore opened his eyes and stared out at the cobbled stones where he'd seen them first. The quay seemed strangely empty and idle.

He turned sharply and faced the woman waiting quietly for an answer.

"Two months at Solgrave, my home near St. Albans," he pronounced gravely. "A private tutor will be sent down to work with the lad as soon as he settles in." He paused, frowning deeply. "And you would do me the honor of accompanying him there . . . if you wish it."

The instantaneous change that swept over her was most diverting to observe. She closed her eyes for an instant, and he saw her lips move in silent prayer. More so than in almost anyone he had ever met, Mrs. Ford's face was an open window to her soul.

Finally, she nodded and took a step backward toward the door. "Thank you, m'lord."

"Mrs. Ford," he found himself calling after her.

She paused with a hand on the latch.

"I meant what I said in asking you to remain at Solgrave as my guest." Stanmore looked out the window. "However . . . well, since there is no delicate way to put this, I will just say that you will find that the attire that is apparently suitable in the colonies is hardly suitable here. Mrs. Trent, my housekeeper in St. Albans, will see to it that you have everything that you need."

Escaping the room as quickly as she could, Rebecca paused in the empty hallway and pressed her icy hands to the feverish skin of her face. She felt shaken, spent, and in total chaos over a battle that she appeared to have won. But why was it, then, that she felt so wounded?

The sounds of footsteps on the stairs jarred her from her momentary lapse. Hurriedly, she moved down the dim corridor and slipped into the first of the two rooms that she and Jamey were occupying. A door between the chambers was ajar, and before joining the lad, Rebecca untied the knot of the cloak at her neck and laid the garment on a chair. On the wall in front of her, a small mirror caught her reflection.

A gasp of astonishment accompanied the sudden flush of color that sprang to her cheeks. She stared in shock and dismay at the rippling waves of hair dancing in every direction. Taking in the well-worn dress, covered with splotches of mud where Jamey must have held her when the two had fallen down, she realized she looked more like a strumpet than a prim tutor fit to preach tolerance and compassion.

No surprise that the arrogant Earl of Stanmore had no qualms about telling her that she was unsuitably attired for a stay at his estate. She sighed deeply and bent to the task of creating some sense of order out of the wild locks of flaming hair.

"You're back, Mama!"

Jamey's delighted cry from the doorway and the excited bounce in his step as he came forward, stopping in front of her, made Rebecca immediately sweep her troubles aside.

He gave her a formal bow. "Have I cleaned up properly, ma'am?"

She gave him a full curtsy. "Aye, Master James. I'd say you look absolutely stunning."

Rebecca blinked back tears and opened her arms as Jamey moved into her embrace. She kissed his freshly brushed hair and looked up to find the serving woman smiling warmly at the two of them.

"Is there anything else you'll be needing now, Mrs. Ford?"

Rebecca shook her head. As soon as the woman had left the rooms, though, Jamey started to bombard her with questions.

"Now, who is it that I have to be meeting this afternoon?"

Rebecca looked down into the young boy's upturned face. "The Earl of Stanmore."

"And what is he to you?"

She took a deep breath and tried to calm her jittery stomach. "He is no one to me, but—"

"Very well!" He shrugged and pulled out of her embrace, walking to the open window. "If he is nobody to us, then maybe you and I can take another walk down the quay."

"Jamey . . ."

"This time, I am going to count the number of ships we see. I know George won't believe me when I tell him that there were more ships here than we have at our wharves in Philly."

"Jamey . . ." Rebecca moved next to him at the open window, knowing in her heart that she wouldn't be able to find the courage to repeat what she was about to say. Once would be crushing enough. She wanted to be certain the young boy heard her clearly.

"When do we go back home?"

Rebecca heard a note of sadness in his voice and she caressed his hair. "We just arrived, my love."

"I don't like it here. I want to go home."

She lifted his chin and found tears glistening on the rims of his blue eyes. "Tell me what's wrong, Jamey."

"I don't like the way these people treat other people."

She hesitated, trying to remember what they had seen—what Jamey might have noticed that had escaped her own attention.

"What do you mean, my love?"

He pulled his chin free, and Rebecca followed the direction of his gaze. She spotted a line of Africans in chains being boarded onto a ship at the quay in front of the inn. She frowned and took a deep breath.

"Isn't it wrong to treat people like that?" he said, looking up at her.

"Of course, it is wrong. Those people were stolen from their own families and homes and brought here against their will." In Philadelphia, because of constant efforts by many of its residents, led by the Quakers, many slaves had already been given back their freedom and were living side by side with whites. In fact, she'd heard that a man named Benezet was about to open a school for blacks this very year.

Rebecca could understand the lad's uneasiness, though. The number of slaves Jamey had seen this week, the way most of them were shackled and handled, was not like anything he had ever seen.

"Do they treat them like this because they are different?"

"I think they treat them like this because some men are greedy and cruel and lack the belief that we are all God's creatures . . . equally."

"Will they treat me like this because I am different?"

Rebecca realized Jamey hadn't heard her last words. He was now staring at the two fingers of his deformed hand poking through his sleeve. She took hold of his hand and brought it to her lips. Tearful eyes followed her movement.

"You are perfect as you are, my love. In God's eyes, we are all perf—"

"Then why?"

She shook her head. "I cannot answer that. But I do know that we should never be ashamed of who we are. Instead, we should work hard to teach and change those people who value money above compassion. Those who are ignorant simply don't know any better."

His trust in her words was clear as he blinked the tears away. She kissed his fingers, wiped a tear from his cheek, and caressed his face with the warmest smile she could summon.

"Now, about this meeting you will be having with the Earl of Stanmore. I have something very important to tell you." He watched her. Waited for the words. Rebecca took a breath and pushed herself to say the words. "It is something that you must know before he sends for you. But what I am about to tell you, my love, changes nothing between us. It does not change how much I love you. It . . . it . . ."

The sound of shouting and the clattering of a horse's hooves on the cobbles below stole Jamey's attention from her, and her shoulders sagged a little as the boy leaned out the window.

"Jamey, I . . ." Rebecca stopped as she saw what was happening.

"Look at that, Mama. Isn't he a stepper!"

Amid the activity of the busy harbor front street, a beautiful chestnut-colored stallion was prancing and pulling at reins held somewhat tentatively by a stablehand. Before Rebecca could say anything, though, the Earl of Stanmore strode out the front door of the inn and into view.

As the two of them watched, the nobleman took the reins and spoke curtly to the steed, which settled down immediately at the sound of his master's voice. Stanmore swung up into the saddle easily and turned to say a parting word to Sir Oliver Birch, who also came out from the inn.

Standing with her hand on Jamey's shoulder, Rebecca felt her heart sink. All the courage she'd built up drained out of her in an instant. There would be no meeting, after all, between father and son this day.

"Who is the man on that beauty? Mama, look at the way he sits."

Involuntarily, Rebecca's fingers tightened on Jamey's shoulder as she prayed for the earl to look up to the open window.

With a final nod at Sir Oliver, Lord Stanmore did finally look up. But Jamey was not the recipient of his parting glance.

His piercing gaze fixed only on her face for a moment, and then he was gone.

Chapter 8

One could always count on a capital dinner at the Duke of Gloucester's, on cigars of the finest quality, and on port that would make a Madeira monk puff up with pride. The ladies had long retired to the drawing room and the duke was gesturing for his fourth glass when Stanmore turned to Nicholas to voice his displeasure with his friend.

"Just assure me, my fine-finned gudgeon, that bringing Louisa as your guest tonight was done purely for your own entertainment."

Nicholas took the cigar out of his mouth and looked at him as if he'd sprouted an extra head. "My good man, you certainly know me better than to insult me this way. You know I like my women beautiful but unpretentious. I like them innocent, or at least with the ability to put on a good show of it. But the truth is, Stanmore, that since I have yet to meet my ideal woman, I find that I also prefer to wile away my time with the rich ones. And by that I mean far richer ladies than Lady Nisdale and the paltry ten thousand a year her dearly departed husband left to her. Why, she can go through that—without anyone's help—in six months' time."

Stanmore waved off the passing butler, but Nicholas accepted another glass.

"The lady you have referred to came here tonight as my guest because she gave me the distinct impression that you wanted her to be here."

Stanmore's glare was withering.

"I did not say that I believed her. But seeing the foul mood that has laid claim to your disposition—a disposition that has been steadily worsening since your return from Bristol—I thought it might just prove diverting for you." Nicholas fit the cigar between his lips and studied the brooding expression of his friend over the smoke. "I have not asked you what went wrong in Bristol, for I know you will tell me only if it pleases you. But I know the value of a willing woman when it comes to improving a man's mood . . . even if the woman has been complaining openly of late about being neglected and privately hinting of her fears of having offended somehow."

"It never ceases to amaze me how indiscreet Louisa can be."

"You are the one, my friend, who chose her as a paramour, and if I remember correctly, a month ago you were not quite as sensitive about the lady's lack of discretion."

An image of Louisa's bright smile and warm greeting when he'd arrived at the Duke of Gloucester's tonight came back to him. He was fairly certain he'd been civil in his greeting, albeit perhaps a little distant. What else was to be expected? He'd been both surprised and displeased to see the damned woman.

And what of it if his disposition was a bit surly these days? Stanmore wished he knew why he'd been feeling so damnably off lately. No, that wasn't entirely true, he thought, watching the blue cigar smoke hang over the table.

It was that woman . . . that blasted Mrs. Ford. It was the look of her . . . the wounded way she'd looked at him out the window as he'd prepared to leave Bristol. That was an image that he simply hadn't been able to shake. He scowled fiercely, downed the port in his glass, and turned his glare on Nicholas.

"You brought Louisa here tonight," Stanmore growled, "and I expect you to accompany her home."

Before his friend could answer, a footman whispered that Lord North desired to have a word with Stanmore. The earl turned and waved to the new prime minister, who was gesturing to him from a small group gathered by one of the tall windows. It had been at Lord North's encouragement that Stanmore had agreed to attend tonight. The minister's promise of lending an ear on the issue of the slave trade made attendance at the dinner worthwhile—no matter how uninterested Stanmore was in such entertainment these days.

He had a parting word, though, for Nicholas before he started

across the room. "I value your concern, but don't disregard our rel-
ative positions. You have always been the rogue, and I the responsible man. You've always caused strife, and I have always endeavored
to resolve it. What would become of the world if we were to change
places? Do you wish, scoundrel, to become *answerable*?"

"Dash it, Stanmore, I see your point. Disregard anything I've
said."

She had spoken quietly and steadily until she could say no more.
Jamey simply stared. His lower lip quivered. His young face
flushed red from emotions that were, no doubt, churning in his
breast. His blue eyes showed his distress and confusion as he struggled to take in her words. In them, she could see his doubt and his
desire to deny what she was saying. Finally, he simply turned away
and stared out the small window of the carriage, watching the countryside rush by through a veil of tears.

The sobs crowding in her own chest threatened to rise into her
throat and choke her, but she continued. She had no choice but to
tell him as much of the truth as she could—at least as much of it as
she'd dared to divulge to Sir Oliver when they'd been in Philadelphia. Rebecca spoke as long as the words carried her, but Jamey's
continuing tears and the sense of utter despair afflicting him soon
checked her.

She knew that these moments in the post chaise and four that Sir
Oliver had arranged to take the two of them east might be the last
private time they would have together. And in a place as large as
Solgrave, she simply could not afford to delay any longer what
Jamey would inevitably discover once they arrived there.

He had to learn the truth from her and no one else.

The carriage lurched roughly, and Rebecca put a protective hand
on Jamey's knees to stop him from sliding off the seat. He didn't
flinch away at her touch, and she silently sent a prayer of thanks
heavenward. Summoning up her courage, she moved to the seat
across from him.

"Jamey!" she said softly to him, taking hold of his chin. He
turned his weepy eyes from the window and looked into her own
face. "Jamey, please talk to me."

He wiped off his face with his sleeve. "How long?"

"We should be there shortly."

He shook his head and entwined the fingers of her left hand in his own. "How long will you stay at . . . at this place with me?"

She had expected his questions to be about the father. Yes, more than anything else, she had hoped he would want to know about the man who had supposedly been searching for years for his lost son. This had been the version of the story that she'd conveyed to him. But his question—the anguish that she could so plainly see in his face—had to do with her.

She forced herself to look truthful as she reached deep for another lie.

"I'll stay as long as you want me to stay. I can find a job in a village near Solgrave. Later, when you are sent to Eton, I can come and live in the town. Or at Windsor, that's just across the Thames and very near the school. You are not losing anything that you have right now, Jamey. You must see this change for all that you are gaining. For all that Lord Stanmore . . . that your father is offering you."

His face showed how unconvinced he was, and Rebecca felt vaguely ill, knowing that she herself lacked conviction on that score. If only the Earl of Stanmore had shown some warmth toward Jamey! If he had shown any sign of welcoming him!

The driver of the carriage called out, announcing their approach into St. Albans. Out the window, Rebecca could see a busy brickworks and the spires and roofs of the town beyond. Under different circumstances, Rebecca would have taken joy in sharing with Jamey what she had read in her youth about the ancient town. But right now all she could do was fight down the growing knot in her own throat and silently utter a prayer. They drove on through the narrow winding streets, passing finally the pointed arches of St. Albans Cathedral.

A few moments later, the carriage was rolling north from St. Albans over a less reliable road than the coach road from Bristol. Then, two miles farther on, the driver turned into a well-kept drive bordered by tall, handsome trees.

Rebecca clutched Jamey's hand. "It shan't be long now."

On through a large deer park the carriage rolled. At times the trees opened into sheep-dotted meadows that gave the travelers beautiful views of the surrounding farms and countryside, and Rebecca realized that they were climbing in almost imperceptible grades onto higher ground. At one vantage point, they could see in the distance a small village huddled along the sides of a meandering river.

Finally, as the chaise topped a wooded hill, the drive turned and ran along the crest of a grassy knoll.

"Jamey, look!" Her attempt at cheering the boy was answered with an indifferent shrug.

To the left of the carriage, the trees opened onto a broad valley. On the far side, nestled among the wooded hills that rose up behind it, a finely built rambling house of red brick sat comfortably amid orchards and gardens and fields. From the style of its architecture, the house must have been built in the time of Queen Elizabeth. Ancient, but solid and tasteful and unpretentious. Before it, wildflowers of purple and white colored a rolling meadow that ran down to a broad lake. There was a "natural" quality to the house and setting that welcomed a traveler. Rebecca had never seen a place quite so beautiful.

"You will love your new home." Her whisper was answered by another of Jamey's shrugs. As the chaise crunched to a stop on the gravel of the impressive courtyard, the young boy sank deeper into the cushioned bench and closed his eyes to the few servants awaiting in greeting outside.

"Jamey." She held his chin and encouraged him to open his eyes before the door of the carriage was opened by the groom. Frightened blue eyes opened and pooled immediately with tears. "I am here with you. I love you today the same as I loved you yesterday, and I will continue to love you forever."

"But I am not your son."

She flattened his hand against her chest. "You are my son in here, and that will never change."

He shook his head. "But . . ."

"Don't mourn a loss where there is none, Jamey," she pleaded. "Don't torment yourself or me by acting as if I were already gone."

There were more tears, and Rebecca forced back her own bursting emotions as the young boy wrapped his arms around her.

"I'm afraid. These people . . . I don't know them."

She pulled back just enough to use a handkerchief from her own sleeve to wipe his face clean. She then smiled into his face and clutched his hand tightly in her own. "I'll give you my strength, and you give me some of yours. Let's go and meet these good people together."

The sky was edging from black into gray, and Jamey knew that storm clouds would not delay much longer the coming morn. Kneeling on the wide windowsill with his forehead pressed against the cool panes of glass, he watched the shapes begin to form outside. Indistinct at first, and then growing clearer, a pair of monstrous giants changed into a grove of plane trees. A strange, horned head of some huge decapitated beast turned out to be only the stables.

Beneath his window, a small formal garden gradually became more distinct, and he looked out past its well-kept paths and beds to the meadows and the gray lake. The drive leading out of the estate and back to the St. Albans road wound over the small stone bridge at the top end of the lake and up the far side of the valley. He stretched and frowned. He had been kneeling at the window for the past few hours, hidden behind the thick draperies, and watching.

They'd only arrived yesterday and he already knew he didn't want to be here. The room they'd given him was larger than the two rooms he and his mama had occupied in Philadelphia. And the bed was so huge that all four of the Butler children could have slept in it and there still would be room for more.

He hated this room. He hated his bed. He hated the people who wore all those proper clothes and spoke correctly and tried to not stare at his hand and kept calling him "Master James." He hated the fact that he was separated from his mama and that she no longer wanted him for a son.

The things she'd told him yesterday. About his real mama dying years ago and how it was time he started spending time with his real father. It couldn't be true. Someplace deep in his chest, Jamey knew that he had to be her real son. He loved her so much. Just the thought of her going away made him hurt to the point of bursting.

Even now he could feel the ache in his gut. He choked back the knot in his throat and peered past the curtains toward the closed door. She was sleeping in the room next to his. But what if she'd decided she didn't love him anymore and left him during the night? There were many doors to this place. And what if the carriageway he'd been watching wasn't the only way off the estate?

Once, not long after moving to the window, Jamey had seen someone crossing the property, carrying a lantern and a cudgel. A huge dog had ambled along beside him. A watchman, he'd decided.

He hadn't been the best of boys last night. He hadn't touched his dinner. He'd pretended he couldn't hear anything anyone said. He'd even been rude to Mrs. Trent, the heavyset housekeeper, flinching when she'd put a friendly hand on his head while she'd been showing him his room. That had really put his mama out. She hadn't said anything, but he could tell it from her eyes. Her eyes told everything.

He had a scolding coming, no doubt. But, sitting in the window, he realized that even this was a good thing. It gave him as good a reason as any to go and wake her. And make sure she was still here.

Jamey pushed the curtains back and dressed quickly.

There was something strange about the hallway, Jamey thought, as he stepped out of his bed chamber. He'd been too stubborn last night to show any interest. But now he stood staring.

The people in the paintings on the wall—the men and women in fancy clothes, and some even in armor—were staring back at him. Vaguely, it occurred to him that some of the servants must be awake, for there were two newly lit candles on a couple of the tables along the wall. He glanced in the direction of his mama's closed door, but then his attention was drawn back to the paintings. Next to a picture of an angry-looking man holding a book and wearing a sword, there was a picture of another man standing before a beautiful dappled gray hunter. Around him, servants were holding a hunting lance and tending to a huge stag he'd obviously just killed. Jamey had never been hunting himself, but Tommy Butler had told George and him plenty of stories about it.

These people, though, looked to be much fancier in their dress than any who would go hunting in the woods along the Schulkyll, Jamey thought. Walking down the hall, he continued to look up at the uniformed men and elegantly dressed women sitting in the portraits, or depicted on tall horses with scenes of hunts in the background. More than one had this house pictured. One had a castle in it.

"All this fuss over such a wee lad."

"Mind your tongue, Bessie. . . . The master's son. . . . Whatever we can do. . . . Worth the fuss, as you call it. . . . Away for as long as the wee one has. . . . 'Tis a shame we cannot do more."

"Well, I don't know. . . . If Cook burns that porridge this morning, I don't know but that I'll . . ."

"Hush, you vixen . . . be waking the household. How'd you like to be put out on your . . ."

Pausing by an open door, Jamey listened hard to comprehend the snatches of talk between the two women. The two servants were busy working in a huge chamber. If he turned his good ear to it, he always heard much more than people thought he did. But he'd always kept this secret to himself. It was a special thing to have his mama think she was the only one who could say anything to him and he could hear. It wasn't a lie, he reminded himself as he slipped by the open door and stopped to look at a painting just beside it. It was a way to get good attention from those he liked . . . and to ignore the people that he didn't.

"This wom . . . Ford . . . the lad's nursemaid?"

At hearing his mama's name, Jamey's gaze dropped from the painting and riveted on the open doorway. He moved to the door.

". . . I heard Mrs. Trent say in the kitchen last night, that's about what she's been to the lad for all these years."

"If she is one of us, why did they have her placed in this wing?" The younger woman's voice turned peevish.

"She ain't one of us. She's quality . . . you can see that from her manners plain enough."

"Perhaps so . . . but you couldn't tell from her clothes."

Peeking around, he saw the maid he assumed to be Bessie shaking out a blanket and folding it again.

"That don't mean anything, you fool. They've just come from the colonies . . . from Pennsylvania."

"Well, she's in England now. Why, you should have heard Helen going on this morning in the washroom about this Mrs. Ford being put just down the hall from the master's rooms. And she had a point, too, if you ask me."

"I'd know better than to ask a goose like you . . . or Helen."

"Well, 'tis just a good thing he is not here yet, or folks would start to talk."

"Start? Ha! You and the other idlers are already talking, it seems to me," the older woman chided, going around and closing the windows. "From all we know, the woman has a husband waiting in the colonies. Mrs. Trent says that she's only staying a short while. So the way I see it, she may very well be long gone before his lordship comes down from London."

"Going? And pray, who's to be taking care of the wee master? It shan't be me, I tell you . . ."

A slight noise by the doorway drew both women's gazes, silencing them immediately. Bessie moved quickly to check the hall, but she saw no one. Listening carefully, though, she thought she could hear someone running in the distance, down the servants' stairs toward the kitchen wing.

"And to conclude, m'lords, I say to you that a tide of moral authority is rising in this land of ours. We who sit in this Palace of Westminster today have a solemn duty. The time has come. Though we have done perhaps irreparable harm in the past . . . though the blood of so many stains our hands . . . it is our duty to put things right. The barbarous iniquity of slavery *will* be washed away, and it is our duty to see that all vestiges of this evil are cleared from our great houses, from our towns, from our ports. We *must* wash this evil from the very shores of England."

As the Earl of Stanmore sat down, many of his fellow members of the House of Lords responded with calls of "Hear, hear!" From others, however, his speech brought only stony looks and silence.

As the next speaker rose, a page appeared at Stanmore's elbow.

"M'lord," he whispered. "Your presence is urgently desired in the lobby."

Pulling his wig from his head, the earl strode quickly from the chamber to where a footman wearing Stanmore's own livery waited anxiously.

"I've just come up from Solgrave, m'lord." The footman bowed and handed him a letter. " 'Tis urgent."

Glancing quickly over the crabbed handwriting of his Hertford-shire house steward, Stanmore cursed fiercely before storming from the palace, the footman in tow.

The last golden vestiges of afternoon sun were just fading as the two serving men carried branches of candles into the suite of sa-loons on the first floor of Lady Mornington's palatial home. On a brass perch in one room, a brilliantly colored macaw shuffled along the bar and crooned noisily at the closest servant.

The saloons were still quite busy, and voices and laughter filled the air. Two dozen or so ladies remained, many plying their skills at the variety of gaming tables their hostess was kind enough to pro-vide. While some were seated around tables, intent upon the cards the faro dealer was turning up, others sat in pairs playing piquet. Still others, finished with their gambling for the day, gathered in small circles or roamed from this group to the next, eager for the latest bits of gossip.

Louisa Nisdale stood by one of the tall windows that looked out over Grosvenor Square, hardly pretending to listen to the group that had gathered around her. She'd lost another five hundred guineas at piquet this afternoon, and though she knew that she was frowning, she really didn't care much at this point. As it stood now, she couldn't request an extension to her credit in Lady Mornington's establishment without some kind of encouraging news from Stan-more. If she were refused, word would quickly spread and her presence would be unwelcome at every gaming house in London.

She frowned more deeply as the topic of the conversation caught her attention. If Stanmore's sudden disinterest in spending time with her weren't distressing enough, it was obvious that everyone in London seemed to be intimately familiar with the earl's private affairs. Everyone but her.

". . . and you could be quite correct in that, my dear," Mrs. Beverley was saying in her annoyingly conspiratorial whisper. "My milliner told me that all of Kensington is simply abuzz with the news. She told me that she has it on the very best authority that fifteen dinner invitations were delivered to his lordship last week alone."

"With Elizabeth's name finally put to rest," Lizzy Archer chimed in, "it only follows that there should be a mad rush for Lord Stanmore's attentions."

Mrs. Beverley gave a knowing laugh. "To think all those fathers who have suffered so to keep their daughters clear of Stanmore's path for all these years! Now that they've a chance at matrimony, they're gladly throwing their lambs to the wolf."

"If I may say, ladies . . . the devil take matrimony, for I'll gladly don sheep's clothing myself. *That* wolf can have me whenever and however he chooses."

Louisa carefully unclenched her jaw as the laughter rippled through the group. She put on an air of indifference and turned, sending a cutting glance Lizzy Archer's way. The young woman's large white bosom, so artfully spilling over the top of her dress, was already heaving at the very possibility of bedding Stanmore—no matter how unlikely the possibility.

"Why, Louisa!" the diminutive Lizzy gasped with feigned surprise. "I had no idea you had given over your game of piquet. Did your luck run out?"

"Why, Lizzy!" Louisa said breathlessly in the same counterfeit fashion. "I had no idea you had given over Lord Archer after less than a year of wedded bliss. But you know, my dear, sometimes we are just not lucky enough to recognize what we have. Take, for example, your Archie . . . not just energetic but talented, too. Why, I was telling him the other night that his technique is quite commendable."

With a flourish, Louisa patted the red-cheeked woman on the hand, turning her back on the astonished onlookers before making her way toward her hostess, Lady Mornington. The older lady's wry smile told Louisa that she had overheard the little discussion.

"I give you a lot of credit, Louisa, my dear. Your luck may have been out today in cards, but when it comes to protecting what is yours, you have an unnerving ability to break the bank every time. Come and sit with me."

Louisa seated herself beside Lady Mornington and cast an impatient eye over the faro table across the room. "What is mine appears to be a subject that is questioned more often than I desire these days."

"Then perhaps you should be more persuasive." Lady Mornington inclined her head toward her young friend. "Perhaps it is time to press your advantage, my dear."

"With Stanmore?" Louisa tucked a strand of her powdered hair in place before turning her pouting face away. "One must be very judicious when it comes to pressing his lordship. But believe me, I have devised my strategy . . . and the cards look quite promising."

"Does this strategy perhaps involve a certain close friend of the earl . . . a certain man of the town?"

One of Louisa's finely penciled brows lifted with admiration. "You keep yourself well informed."

"I do . . . and I must say that I don't approve of your plan." Lady Mornington's scowl was genuine, deepening Louisa's surprise. "Sir Nicholas Spencer might play along with your charade, but he would take a bullet in the head before being party to anything that will adversely affect his friend's well-being."

"I assure you that I have Stanmore's well-being in mind, as well."

"Perhaps, Louisa, but do not expect Sir Nicholas to do anything that will compromise his friendship with Stanmore."

"What I am considering is completely harmless to all concerned," Louisa was quick to explain. "Sir Nicholas is as fond of gaming as I am, so it is quite natural for me to cross paths with him when he is in town. Pray, madam, is it so inappropriate that I should strive to remain apprised of Stanmore's whereabouts and doings? Nicholas is good company, and he freely provides me with such information."

The older woman's gaze swept the room before turning to her. "And have you learned anything of value, my dear, from your association with Sir Nicholas?"

"Indeed!" Louisa smiled as brightly as she could manage. "I have learned that Stanmore's absence from my side has purely been the result of his efforts to settle his son."

"Were these Nicholas's words?"

She fought back an embarrassed rush of heat in her face. "Though he has not used those exact words, it is the only logical answer. Stanmore has not been seen in the company of anyone else."

Lady Mornington smiled knowingly. "Then I assume that you have already been practicing ways to charm a lad of his age."

"You may be certain that I have every intention of forming the warmest of connections with James Samuel Wakefield." Louisa smiled back at her hostess. "Only a fool would forgo seizing such an opportunity, and you know that I am no fool. You may safely bet on it . . . I will have Lord Stanmore for my own."

Chapter 9

The Chiltern Hills, shrouded in mists, loomed dark and ominous over Solgrave, but the mud-covered rider took no time to spare the ancient ridge even a glance.

The threatening clouds overhead had more than once made good their threat in the past several hours, deluging the roads from London with cold, stinging rain. The treacherous byways had required the rider's utmost skill. But now, as Stanmore pushed his exhausted horse ahead, the end was in sight. Racing across the rain-soaked meadow, the earl rounded the lake at a gallop, pounded across the stone bridge, and reined up at the front door of the mansion.

At first glance he could see that the entire estate was in turmoil. Dismounting from his steed, Stanmore strode through the huge doors into the entry hall. Daniel, the house steward of the family's country seat, dogged his heels, his apologies and explanations tumbling out breathlessly.

". . . and Mrs. Ford discovered Master James was missing first thing in the morning, m'lord. We searched everywhere . . . we turned the house all akilter . . . and searched the grounds immediately surrounding . . . and the stables—you know lads love horses—and the servants' quarters. I am dreadfully sorry, m'lord. When we could find no sign of the lad, I sent for you."

Stanmore discarded his sodden coat and handed it to a footman before heading toward his library in the new wing. "Have you sent someone to Knebworth?"

"Aye, m'lord. Porson took six men from the stables. They spread out and stopped at every cottage from here to the village. No one has seen the lad."

Stanmore stalked into the library and immediately found himself looking at the lake through the large windows of the room. He stopped abruptly, a mysterious tightness gripping his chest. Two years ago, the son of one of the servants had drowned in the lake. They'd found his body a week later by the dam at the old mill. His steward spoke quickly, obviously reading the frown on his face.

"We . . . we haven't started searching the lake, m'lord."

An image of a red-haired woman embracing a child on a dock in Bristol immediately came before him. He could see the blue eyes that had looked at him beseechingly, the lad standing beside her in the open window at the inn.

"Bring Mrs. Ford to me."

He turned his back on the steward. As Daniel quickly retreated, Stanmore's attention again was drawn to the waters of the lake. Two miles in length, the narrow band of water formed a crescent across the estate, ending at the old mill above Knebworth village. Over the years, the deep, clear waters had brought grief to a few families living near it. He watched two of his gardeners hurry down from the house and turn to follow a path along the water's edge.

James drowning on his return . . . no, on his first coming to Solgrave. It was just not possible. Fate would not deal such a cruel hand.

He saw a half dozen men emerge from the trees at the far side of the valley, converse for a few moments, and then disappear into the wood again as the rain began to come down in sheets, obscuring even the far side of the lake.

He cursed himself silently. The devil take him if he hadn't tried to keep the promise he'd given at the old man's deathbed. He'd brought the lad back. And that was all that was expected of him. He would do his duty, and the family line and good name would be preserved.

But now this. Life seemed to hold nothing but twisted luck for him . . . and for the boy, as well, it seemed.

The sound of footsteps behind him turned Stanmore around. Daniel stood in the doorway, looking for the world like a gallows bird, and Mrs. Trent stood beside him, wringing her hands.

"Mrs. Ford is still out there searching, m'lord." The housekeeper cast a nervous glance at the window and then looked down at her hands.

"What do you mean, she is out there searching?"

"I told her to stay put, m'lord," Daniel mumbled desperately, cutting an accusing look at the portly woman.

Mrs. Trent shot the steward an answering glare before speaking. "She was beside herself, m'lord. Anyone taking a step out or coming back . . . and she was rushing after them. She was near mad with worry. There was no holding her back, try as we may!"

"*When* was it that she went out?"

Embarrassment colored the housekeeper's face. "She set out on foot . . . a little before noon, m'lord."

"That's hours ago," Stanmore spat as he started for the door. "Which direction did she go? What does she know about where a boy could get lost around here?"

"M'lord, she was even wilder than Maire when she'd lost her Johnny two years ago." The housekeeper nodded toward the rain pelting the windows. "There was no stopping her. 'Twas as if she was missing her own son."

"For God's sake, how *else* was she to feel?!"

Stanmore stalked to the windows, his mind racing. He'd met Rebecca Ford only once, but the woman's affection for the lad was something that he didn't think he would ever forget. In fact, there were a few other things about the woman that continued to linger in his memory. But this was no time for thoughts of that nature, he thought, scowling. Why, she could be in the damned lake, herself!

Whirling to face them again, he began barking orders on his way out of the room.

"Daniel, send someone to the village looking for Mrs. Ford. Mrs. Trent, question whoever attended her this morning. See if they might have mentioned any place that she might have gone to search. Something that might have been said to induce her to set out on foot."

Striding down the long servants' corridors and into the kitchens, Stanmore found himself surrounded by the anxious faces. House servants, grooms, gardeners—everyone not already out on estate grounds—were immediately organized into search parties and quickly dispersed.

A dry riding coat was waiting for him by the time he reached the front door. A fresh hunter stood prancing on the graveled yard.

Obviously challenged by the mere glimpse of a dry coat, Zeus himself took a hand in the proceedings. The storm seemed only to worsen, the wind rising as flashes of lightning illuminated the Hertfordshire landscape.

Stanmore spurred his mount across the lawns and meadow to the path around the lake. One of the upper maids had apparently been stupid enough to mention Maire's lost boy to Mrs. Ford. She had even told her of the mill and how they'd found him there.

The wind and rain stung his face as he made his way along the shore, but Stanmore's mind was focused on finding the lad . . . and Mrs. Ford.

Rebecca.

Even as the woman's name occurred to him, anger suddenly flooded through his veins. Why he felt any concern for her at all was beyond his understanding. She was the cause of all of this. If he had not allowed himself to be taken in by her pleas, if he had simply stuck to his original plan, the boy would be at Eton even now.

The foolish, stubborn, meddling woman. He cursed into the wind as he continued on along the lake. As he rode, he continually swept the trees with his gaze for signs of anyone taking shelter there.

The storm was nearly a gale by the time Stanmore spotted the old mill in the distance. Coming out of a grove of trees, though, he saw her through the pouring rain. The gray-cloaked figure, her back to him, had just fallen on the muddy bank and was struggling to get her feet beneath her. He spurred his horse toward her.

"Mrs. Ford!" he called out.

The woman straightened up and turned toward him. The wind whipped the long wet hair across her eyes, and she clawed it out of her face. The dark cloak and the dress beneath it were stained with the mud and rain, and torn from the brambles she had been traipsing through. A look of hope flashed across her muddy face.

"You've found him!"

Though the mud dragged at her sodden shoes as she started toward him, he could hear the note of relief in her cry. As he reined up beside her, he was struck by the paleness of her face beneath the smudges of dirt.

"No. They have not found him."

The blue eyes fell and her face immediately took on a haunted look. He saw her thin frame waver in the force of the wind, and he leaped to the ground, thinking that she was about to fall. But she turned away from him without another word and began slogging through the storm toward the dam.

"Wait!" he ordered abruptly, pulling his horse behind him. "Where do you think you are going?"

Her gaze was directed ahead toward the dam and the old sluice leading to the mill wheel. She looked like a madwoman.

"There is nothing you can do that we cannot do better—nowhere that you can search that my people cannot cover more thoroughly than you."

She was deaf to his words and did not even look up as a bolt of lightning lit the sky. Stanmore's horse, however, reared nervously, and he turned momentarily to steady the animal.

"This is madness, woman!" he shouted just as her feet slipped from under her. He cursed under his breath as she slid down the embankment to the edge of the water, and moved as quickly as he could to her aid.

She wouldn't accept his outstretched hand as she stubbornly clawed her way up again. Covered now in mud from head to toe and shivering like a leaf in December, she was perhaps the most pathetic-looking creature he'd ever encountered. But nothing about her situation seemed to dampen in the slightest her will to go on with her search.

"If this is not the most absurd . . ." He found himself trailing after her as she continued on without giving him even a look. "Mrs. Ford . . . Rebecca. Don't you see that I am losing time chasing after you when there is a graver matter at hand?"

Again she ignored him, and Stanmore found himself becoming

genuinely angry at the mulishness of the woman. Catching up to her, he took hold of her elbow and turned her around.

"You must return to the house this instant."

She pushed the wet hair out of her face and her eyes flashed with fury.

"Let me be."

The words were spoken through clenched teeth, but he paid no heed to her temper. "I cannot. Like it or not, you are my guest at Solgrave. I am responsible for your safety."

"Save your concern for one who truly matters." The look in her eyes changed, and tears mixed with the rain on her face. "Your son is missing. Do you understand that?"

"And you blame me?"

"I do!" she cried. "James is missing . . ."

"Has run away, you mean!"

". . . because you failed even to introduce yourself to him or acknowledge him when you had a chance. He's run away because he was afraid. If you had listened to anything that I told you in Bristol . . . if you had taken into consideration his age . . . his condition . . ."

"Have you considered, madam, that perhaps your own shortcomings in raising him with some sense of discipline—"

"Don't you *dare* criticize me. He has grown and thrived in my care."

"A weed thrives on the roadside with very little tending."

"Insult me as you wish." She jerked her arm free. "But let me go. By God, I will find him. And when I do, I am taking him back with me to Pennsylvania. It is obvious to me—and to James—that you have no real wish for him to be here. Only . . . damn me, but if I had known that sooner, I never would have allowed you to uproot that child."

She struck off in the direction of the old mill again, leaving him cursing himself bitterly for unleashing his temper at her. In so doing, he had let her take charge.

"Mrs. Ford!" he called, going after her.

She trudged on, giving no indication of having heard him.

"Rebecca!" he shouted, reaching her side with a few long

strides. This time as he took hold of her elbow, he spun her around and grabbed her other arm, as well. He wasn't forcing her to stay put, he reminded himself, but he would damn well intimidate her if that's what it took to hold her long enough to make her see reason. She turned her face away, refusing to look at him.

"I was . . . I was rash in my words. I have no right to criticize you for what you have done for James."

"I have no time for your apologies, either." She tried to pull out of his hold, but Stanmore only tightened it. His fingers dug into the soaked fabric of her sleeves.

"And I have no time to drum up an argument. We are both after the same thing." He motioned toward the darkening sky. "It soon will be night, and I am wasting time not helping with the search."

"Then go," she cried out, twisting toward the mill.

"I cannot. Not when you are running around in this storm, endangering yourself without purpose."

"I am not the one that you should concern yourself with. It is James who—"

"It is James who will be needing you when he is brought back," he interrupted, shaking her once. He didn't want to think about the gray water beside them. About the possibility of a boy gone forever. He needed her back at the house, where her situation would not prey on his mind. "Have you considered the predicament you may be creating? What happens when James is returned and you are not there to greet him? You are the only one that he really knows. The only one who will be able to comfort him."

Her body sagged slightly in his arms. "But I . . . I just cannot stay there . . . waiting. I feel so . . . so helpless. I . . ." She looked up at him with tormented eyes set in a face suddenly showing her weariness and vulnerability. The wind blew wet strands of hair across her pale cheek.

"Think of *him*! Think of how you can help him most," he said reasonably. He finally had her attention. "Let me take you back to the house. I was raised in this place. I know every hiding place where a boy of his age can go. I know how far he can run and in which direction. I'll go after him myself . . . but I need you at the house to care for him when we bring him in."

She didn't answer him, but Stanmore took her silence as a sign of assent. Wrapping his fingers around her wrist, he pulled her toward his horse. Her steps were heavy, resignation written in her every movement. He removed his coat and wrapped it around her shoulders. Although wet, he hoped the warmth of his body would offer some comfort.

He didn't trust her to hold on, seated behind him. So instead, he lifted her easily onto the back of the giant animal and swung up behind her.

She didn't utter a word as Stanmore wheeled the hunter around. She held herself rigid, away from his chest, her eyes searching in the distance. The hands clutching the mane of the horse were nearly blue beneath the mud, though, and he could see the shiver trembling uncontrollably on her lips. Wrapping a hand around her waist, he pulled her against the warmth of his body.

"We'll be there soon." His chin brushed the soaked strands of hair, and he frowned at the unsettling feeling of protectiveness that coursed through him. "Let Mrs. Trent see to your needs when you get back. Dry clothes. A cup of wine. You cannot allow yourself to become ill . . . not when he . . . well, not when the lad needs you most."

Silence was her only answer. In a few minutes, Solgrave came into view, standing solidly against the storm. The lamps had been lit, and Stanmore pressed a hand against her shoulder, drawing her more tightly against his chest to protect her from the whipping rain.

Certain things were starting to make sense now. Birch's immediate liking of this woman, for one. The trust that the lawyer bestowed on her. This was a totally uncharacteristic response in the old bachelor. Stanmore could see that there was something about her that spoke of strength—an independence that was not based on position or wealth. Added to that, the woman had compassion and intelligence . . . and she was as obstinate as a rock. And yet, right beneath the pale skin and stormy blue eyes, there was a vulnerability that he doubted everyone saw.

He hadn't even dismounted from his horse when Daniel and several of the grooms and footmen rushed out into the rain. He handed the soaked woman down from the mount.

"Any news?" he asked of his steward.

"Some of the men have come in and gone again. They've talked to most of the villagers, m'lord. It appears fairly certain the lad did not go to Knebworth." The steward nodded toward the lake. "Shall I put together a party with hooks and lines to—"

"No!" Stanmore interrupted the steward with a warning glance. "We've more places to look yet. See that Mrs. Ford is attended to."

Rebecca held his coat up to him. He reached for it, and their gazes met in the pouring rain.

"You will bring him back."

"I've said I will."

Chapter 10

The darkness that descended was complete and broken only by occasional flashes of lightning. The wind and rain still lashed at him as he rode, but Stanmore sensed that the gale was beginning to blow itself out. Dashing the rain from his eyes, he reined in his mount at the edge of a small meadow, peering through the dark for the ruined cottage that he knew was nearby. It was one of the last places he could think of to look. He frowned at the thought of going back empty-handed.

The hut had been a tumbledown affair even when Stanmore had roamed the woods as a boy. As he nudged his horse into the clearing, though, he realized he had not been out in this area for fifteen years, at least. The cottage had once been inhabited by gamekeepers of the estate, but no one had lived there in decades.

Another flash of lightning showed him that his memory was not so bad, after all. Framed by tall plane trees and a few ancient oaks, the cottage sat at the far edge of the meadow. Even at a glance, Stanmore realized that the hut was far more decrepit than he recalled.

But the condition of the place would mean nothing to a boy seeking shelter from the storm. The forests that covered the rolling hills and valleys for the next mile or so would soon give way to farms and then the park belonging to Squire Wentworth's Melbury Hall, but James wouldn't know that.

Stanmore dismounted before the hut and secured his horse to a low stone wall. Taking a step toward the low door, he stopped and eyed the shelter warily. Even though half of the thatched roof had fallen in years ago, the place did not have the feeling of being totally deserted. Branches, broken to a uniform length, had been stacked against the stone wall. The leather hinges that once held the door in place had long ago given way, but someone had fairly recently pulled the stout wooden planking up against the narrow opening. The single window even appeared to have a hide tacked across the inside to keep out the weather.

And as Stanmore stood there, the shifting wind brought him the smell of a wood fire. Man or boy, he thought, someone was in that cottage.

Just to be sure, the earl circled the place. Gypsies regularly came through the area, though usually in the fall, but they rarely camped in this part of the estate. An escaped convict or a wandering beggar was not likely to have wandered so far from the roads or from the farms, either. More than likely, it was simply one or more of the children from his estate or from Melbury who had been doing the minor repairs. They had always been drawn to the hut. When he himself was young, he had played "storm the keep" in this very place. How many times he led his "army"—composed of the woodcutter's sons and the Trent boys—to victory against some of the farm lads from Melbury.

The flashes of lightning told him that no serious repairs had been made to the cottage. A stream of water was running from a small gap in the crumbling wall at the back of the hut. Deciding that discretion was probably in order, though, Stanmore crouched and peered through the small opening. The fallen thatch blocked his access, but he could see the light of the small fire flickering on the wall across the small space.

As he watched, he saw a young hand reach over and carefully place a broken branch on the fire. Obviously, the occupant had not heard him approach, for there was no nervousness in the boy's movements as he added another branch to the fire. This time Stanmore caught sight of the lad's other hand.

It was James.

Stanmore's lips twitched, and a feeling of relief swept through him, its intensity surprising him and causing his face immediately to crease into a frown. He remained where he was for the longest moment and just stared at what he could see of the boy. His back was turned, and the earl could only see the extended arms and mud-died knee breeches and the bare legs and feet. Although late in May, the chill night air lacked the feel of summer. But still, on this stormy night, James had chosen the discomfort of this ramshackle cottage over all the luxury that had surrounded him at Solgrave.

Stanmore pushed himself wearily to his feet and made his way around the cottage to the door and the slab of wood propped against it. He considered for a moment and then took a step back toward his horse.

"Holloa! Is anyone in there?" he called loudly over the sound of the storm.

Moving forward, he carefully pushed the door aside and peered in. The fire was still burning, but the lad had disappeared. He ducked his head and entered the cottage. On the far side of the hut, two muddy feet protruded from beneath the fallen thatch.

As Stanmore looked at the boy, the rain began to come down again in earnest through the broken roof. He studied the low and unsteady rafters and then crouched before the boy's hiding place.

"There is no point in running away or hiding. You must be soaked to the skin now. At this rate, you'll probably come down with a fever and die within a fortnight."

James didn't move from his hiding place, so Stanmore glanced up at the inside of the place. Someone had indeed been spending time in here recently, for there were telltale signs throughout the space. The ashes in the fire indicated that more than a few meals had been cooked there, and the bones of rabbits and squirrels in a small pit by the wall told him that his deer park was at least feed-ing someone in the neighborhood. With a wry smile, he turned his attention back to the boy who was stubbornly continuing to ignore him.

"Come, James! I can see you, lad."

There was still no movement, and he remembered what Birch and Mrs. Ford had told him about the boy's difficulty in hearing. He stood up and heaved a pile of thatch to the side, revealing the boy.

He had Elizabeth's eyes. And her coloring. And the same blond hair. And he was shivering slightly from the rain . . . or from fear of him. The earl stretched a hand out to the boy.

"It is time for you to return to Solgrave."

The lad made no move to accept the proffered hand. He just continued to stare at him with a piercing glare that Stanmore also recognized.

"You've put the household in complete disarray today. Now, I know you don't care a rush for my people's concerns, but there is one person there that I know you *do* care for." He crossed his arms over his chest. "Mrs. Ford was so upset that she went out in this storm searching for you . . . alone and on foot. We were able to bring her back to the house for a short time. But if I don't take you back right now, then she will be going out again."

Stanmore jerked a thumb toward the dry corner of the hut.

"I doubt she'll be as lucky as you to find a place to dry out or a fire to warm herself. She will be coming down with a fever, and it will be your fault. So if you care nothing for her . . ."

James rose to his feet, but said nothing.

With a grunt, Stanmore used his boot to put out the fire while the boy went and stood by the door waiting. When the earl motioned for James to go out ahead of him, he was amused to see the boy replace the slab of wood across the front of the door.

The two walked in silence through the rain to the waiting horse. Stanmore, lifting the child onto the back of the animal, was amazed to realize that—even soaking wet—James weighed almost nothing.

There was a great deal that Stanmore knew he himself had to say to the lad. Some explanation for the past perhaps. Some greeting or introduction, he supposed, this being their first meeting. Still better, the boy deserved a good tongue-lashing for the trouble he had caused Solgrave's servants.

But he said nothing. Instead, the ride back to the house was made in absolute silence, broken only by the rumbling of thunder receding in the distance.

The bed remained untouched. The household had finally settled after the ordeal of the day and night. Rebecca sat quietly in a chair in her bedchamber and pondered the emotional sleigh ride she had experienced in the last twenty-four hours.

She had never been more saddened or crazed than at the moment when she'd discovered Jamey missing this morning. And she could not recall a moment of greater joy than she'd experienced tonight at the sight of him descending safely from his father's gleaming horse. She had rushed into the rain and had cried as her boy had run into her arms and buried his face into her neck—mumbled words of apology nearly drowned out by the sound of the earl issuing directives to his servants. After a moment, though, she had to draw back and release Jamey, allowing the housekeeper and the steward to take charge of him.

Overseeing their efforts from a distance, she had seen them do everything she would have done and more. Drying him. Dressing him in warm clothing. Feeding him. Putting him to bed. She had nodded encouragingly when he had directed his soulful gaze at her.

He was James Samuel Wakefield, the heir to a vast fortune, the next Earl of Stanmore. And Rebecca knew—as difficult as it was for them both—she had to hold herself back and allow Jamey to learn to deal with these people who were a part of his future.

Earlier, when she had returned to the house and was waiting for news of him, Rebecca had found plenty of time to think over what the Earl of Stanmore had said to her. It was the truth. It was *her* fault that the young boy had acted so hastily this morning. Her lack of experience in bringing up a child—her years of excessive protectiveness—had led to Jamey being so dependent on her, so attached to her. Now, she had to do her best to help him become more independent . . . to acquire what he needed to take his true place in the world.

She brushed away the tears on her face and pressed a hand to the ache in her chest. It was no help. She was an unholy mess, but she was truly missing him already.

Rising to her feet, she tightened the belt of the robe Mrs. Trent had given her earlier and walked toward the door. She had said good night to him, gently refusing to sit with him when he was finally put to bed. But now, a couple of hours later, she knew he would be asleep. And she had to see him. She had to at least look at him and try to soothe her aching heart.

The hallway was quiet when she stepped out. As she approached his door, she had a moment of panic. What would happen if he were missing again? But her mind was quickly put at ease when, upon opening it, she saw him sleeping peacefully, as if nothing had ever been amiss in the world.

Rebecca stepped in and quietly closed the door behind her.

The curtains were open, and a soft blue light imbued the room with a pervading sense of serenity. The rain had stopped, and a bright moon had somehow worked its way through the clouds. Outside, the countryside glistened beneath its white beams.

Rebecca stood for the longest time with her back against the door, watching the young boy sleep.

Jamey! Only a short time ago, she had thought her life so complete. She had been a mother to someone who needed her. She had been fulfilling a promise she had made long ago, and in so doing she had filled up her own life with joy. She brushed away a tear and walked toward the bed. Leaning over him, she pulled the blanket up to his chin. She touched his unruly hair and brushed a soft kiss over his brow.

Straightening up, her heart leaped in her chest.

The Earl of Stanmore, sitting in a chair in a shadowy corner, was gazing at her intently. He obviously had been watching his son sleep, but now his gaze was fixed on her. It was a strange, unsettling look. It was like looking into the eyes of a great cat.

Embarrassment, guilt, emotions that she somehow couldn't put a name to surged inside her. She took a step back, but found the earl's piercing gaze following her. With one quick look toward the sleeping Jamey, Rebecca turned and—as calmly as she could—escaped the room.

She was down the corridor, nearly to her own door, when the sound of the earl's tread made her pause.

"Mrs. Ford."

Rebecca wished she could stop the strange fluttering of her pulse, curtail the heat rushing to her face. She turned around to face him. They were alone in the semidarkness of the hall corridor, the dark portraits of his ancestors looking down on them. Her gaze fleetingly took in the topboots, the tight buckskin breeches, and the white shirt carelessly left half buttoned. She found herself staring at the dark skin and the corded muscles of his neck.

"I see you were not able to sleep, either."

She forced herself to look up into the chiseled face and the dark eyes. The way his gaze traveled from the tip of her bare toes to the wayward curls hanging to her shoulders caused Rebecca to swallow hard. She pulled the folds of the robe tighter around her neck.

"I had hoped to speak to you tonight, as I need to return to London for a short while. Parliament will be rising, but I must attend to a few private matters, as well."

Like a fool, all she could do was nod. Something about him had taken hold of the very breath in her chest.

"I wanted to tell you that you were correct in recommending that James come here for a time before he was sent to Eton."

"Are you trifling with me, m'lord?" she managed to get out.

"Not at all. What he did today—running away—could have had far more serious consequences in a public place like London, or at school."

For the first time since arriving in England, Rebecca felt a ray of hope about Jamey's future. The Earl of Stanmore did appear to care about his son.

"Having activities to occupy his mind—getting him involved in life here at Solgrave—these things will perhaps improve his disposition toward his new life in England."

"I agree."

"I have instructed my steward Daniel to hire a tutor for James. I would like you to oversee his selection, though. I recall Birch telling me that you were a teacher yourself in the colonies, so your approval will, naturally, be highly valued."

"I am honored," she murmured, again finding herself unable to maintain eye contact with the earl. Fighting him over James had been easy, but facing him alone and . . . well, dressed as he was, made her tremble strangely. And what made it worse was that he was being so agreeable!

"I know it is late, but I am going to the library for a glass of wine. If you care to join me, perhaps you can tell me anything else of importance that my people should be aware of in dealing with James?"

Rebecca felt her face grow warm again as a rush of sensations suddenly filled her. The feel of the earl's strong arms as they had held her in place on his horse, the occasional brush of his chin against her wet hair, the warmth of his coat, the smell of night and forbidden desires—all of these things set her heart drumming wildly in her chest. And then a fear ten years old took hold of her. She shook her head, panic and desire at odds within her.

"I . . . I am very sorry, m'lord. But it is late and . . . and it has been a tiring day." She took a step backward toward her door.

He nodded with a look of perfect understanding. "I have been remiss in not even inquiring after your health. After the hours that you spent in the rain yourself, you—"

"I am fine," she said convincingly, taking another step back until her hand rested on her door. She needed to get out of this corridor. Away from him. In his presence, something she could not understand took control of her senses. It was as if she was losing control of her body. Her reaction to him was absolutely appalling. What was happening to her? "I . . . I am quite well. Good night, m'lord."

"Mrs. Ford!"

His call kept her from escaping into her room.

"I believe you should stay. I invite you to stay as long as it takes for James to be perfectly settled in Solgrave."

"Thank you, m'lord."

She slipped through the door and closed it behind her. Placing her fingers on her fevered cheeks, she stared with unseeing eyes into the darkness of the room. Standing there, Rebecca wondered if the earl's invitation had been for Jamey's sake . . . or for some interest of his own.

Chapter 11

Sir Oliver Birch was both surprised and disturbed by Stanmore's questions.

Summoned to the earl's Berkeley Square town house on a Sunday evening, the seasoned lawyer had come sensing trouble. Now, sitting in the comfortable chair in the spacious library and watching Lord Stanmore talk and pace, he knew it.

"If I may repeat what you just told me of this woman," the earl said thoughtfully, his hands clasped behind his back, "you are absolutely certain she accompanied Elizabeth on the journey to America."

"Not absolutely certain. But according to the physician who was on the ship, and who is now residing in New York, a woman named Rebecca traveled with her. Our Mrs. Ford certainly fits the description that he gave me. In fact, he was the one that recalled her traveling on to Philadelphia. He told me he only happened to overhear her making her arrangements."

"Indeed." The earl stopped by the marble fireplace, a frown creasing his brow. "Why did he 'happen' to recall all of this, Birch, ten years after the fact? Didn't he trust her?"

"I cannot say, for certain." The lawyer swirled the fine claret in his glass. "But she is . . . er, was an extremely attractive young woman." Feeling Stanmore's fierce glare upon him, the lawyer quickly continued. "Not to mention that she was traveling on to Philadelphia with only the child."

"How could she get a coachman to take her, unescorted?"

"Things are quite different in the colonies, m'lord. Women apparently travel unescorted as a matter of course." He hesitated. "But you should have no fears with regard to her reputation. Whether we are speaking of ten years ago or ten days, I am quite certain—and I say this from my own journey with her and from all I heard in Philadelphia—Mrs. Ford has a strict code of conduct. Quite refined, in fact . . . though thoroughly unpretentious. Her life in the colonies has made her perfectly at ease in her dealings with men, but she also demands propriety at all times from everyone. Why, even the sailors treated her with the utmost respect. I find the woman quite remarkable, really."

Birch noted the fleeting look in the earl's dark eyes, but he did not want to hazard a guess as to the meaning behind it. He watched Stanmore move to one of the large open windows and stare out into the park that graced the square. There was no doubt in the lawyer's mind that this summons had to do with his lordship's brief but sudden sojourn to Solgrave yesterday.

"Is there a chance that she might have made Elizabeth's acquaintance in London?"

"I seriously doubt it. You know the social set to which your wife belonged." Birch shook his head thoughtfully. "Though Mrs. Ford is obviously well-educated and has a disposition that speaks of gentility in her upbringing, she isn't a member of London society. I believe they must have met during the initial crossing. I, for one, can understand why Elizabeth saw reason to entrust her with the care of James."

"Can you, Oliver? Then can you think of any reason why this woman has chosen to hide her connection with Elizabeth? From what you said of your first meeting in Philadelphia, she lied to you about it there, and she has yet to admit to knowing her."

The lawyer glanced thoughtfully at the earl. "It could simply be that her secrecy stems from a lack of trust. Mrs. Ford is obviously devoted to your son. She may well have been as devoted to your wife. Why else would she have accepted the responsibility of raising the child? She obviously had no intent of personal gain."

The earl nodded.

"Her loyalties lie with Elizabeth and with James, m'lord. You and I have yet to earn her confidence." Birch shrugged his shoulders. "But on the other hand, all of my assumptions could be incorrect. Perhaps everything she says is true. We could be mistaking her for someone else who *was* on that ship with your wife."

Stanmore stood for a long moment, apparently considering this possibility.

"Tell me what you know of this husband . . . this Mr. Ford."

"I know very little," the lawyer said, relieved that they were moving past Rebecca's possible fabrication. "They must have married soon after she left New York. He has been dead for some years, though, according to those I questioned in Philadelphia."

"What else? What did he do for a living?"

"There was very little that anyone could add, for certain. Some thought he was a carter, others believed he had been a soldier. Whatever his position in life, he obviously did not leave much behind for his wife. From what I was able to establish, for virtually all the years Mrs. Ford has been in Philadelphia, she has been living on the fruits of her own labors and supporting James and herself fairly successfully."

"So there were no other children."

"None that survived, at any rate."

As Stanmore turned to face the lawyer, his dark gaze was probing. "Anything else about her? Anything about her parentage? Where she was born and raised?"

"The only information I was able to establish with any certainty pertains to the years that Mrs. Ford has resided in Pennsylvania. If I were to hazard a guess, I would suggest that she may have been the daughter of a cleric . . . and raised in a town not so remote or rustic, either. As I mentioned before, she either had excellent tutors or was sent to a fine school as a girl, for she is certainly learned in a variety of subjects. In Philadelphia, there were many who spoke of her proficiency as a teacher."

Birch crossed his long legs as the earl turned to the window again. He knew that one never questioned Stanmore. Even so, the lawyer was very curious about the nature of the trouble yesterday.

"If I may say, Mrs. Ford struck me as a refreshing change from many Englishwomen of the same station in life. And aside from one small misrepresentation regarding her past, I believe she is perhaps the most honest and straightforward woman I've ever met."

Watching the peer carefully, Birch saw no disagreement in Stanmore's attitude. The lawyer let out a silent breath of relief, as he had every intention of keeping Mrs. Ford in Stanmore's good graces, if he could. In fact, though he would never admit it openly, Oliver planned on finding some excuse to visit Solgrave in the near future. And it wasn't for the country air that he wished to visit Hertfordshire.

Mrs. Ford might be a pauper, but her lack of wealth was no hindrance as far as Birch was concerned. For the first time in his life, the woman had awakened in him thoughts of matrimony and children. Though he was entirely inexperienced in matters of the heart, the way he saw it, all that was required of him now was spending some time in her company, making his intentions known to her, and receiving some encouraging response from the lady. After that, it was simply a contractual matter, putting the entire affair back in the arena where he operated the most comfortably.

"Do an inquiry this week regarding Lady Nisdale's finances. In particular, I want to know the total of all her outstanding debts."

Jolted from his own line of thinking, Birch raised a dark brow at the earl's comment.

"I can already tell you that it will be a large sum. Dame Fortune has not been smiling on Louisa for some time."

"You will pay off all of her debts, including her gambling debts." His lordship's manner was relaxed, almost indifferent, as he crossed the floor to the fireplace. "Send word to the house when the notes have been collected. There will be a letter waiting here to be delivered to Lady Nisdale when the task has been completed."

"She should be grateful for such generosity, Stanmore."

"She'll be incensed that I am ending our liaison."

This was just the latest of a number of partings of the ways that the lawyer had handled for his wealthy client. In previous situations of this type, Lord Stanmore's openhandedness had always helped to dry the tears shed afterward. In this case, however, knowing Louisa's temperament, Oliver was certain that he would have to handle the delicate matter with all the diplomacy and finesse at his command.

"Your timing might be quite good, however," Birch responded

carefully, watching Stanmore's straight back as he paused before the portrait of his father. "In what I believe might simply be a bid for your attention, I regret to tell you that last night—after attending the opera in Haymarket—Lady Nisdale was observed gracing a certain gentleman's arm in Vauxhall Gardens."

"Louisa might do well to pursue that course of action. I no longer have any interest in the woman's indiscretions." He turned away from the painting and moved to the large desk. "I have some appointments tomorrow, but on Tuesday I plan to return to Solgrave for a fortnight . . . at least."

Birch straightened in his chair.

"Mrs. Ford made some very sensible recommendations to me in Bristol . . ."

The earl continued to speak, but Birch's mind was racing in a number of directions at once. And then, suddenly, everything made sense. The ending of the affair with Lady Nisdale. The endless questions about Rebecca. Oliver knew Stanmore didn't give a rush about spending time with his son. He had said so himself, many times, before and even after finding James. It was Rebecca herself who had caught his lordship's eye, he thought bitterly.

"Leaving London, m'lord? With the King's Birthday just a fortnight off? There will be great disappointment among the *ton*, I should say."

"With the Parliament rising yesterday, my time is my own." Disdain was etched clearly on the nobleman's face as he seated himself behind the desk. "Being considered a *catch*—as our friend Sir Nicholas so indelicately refers to it—was not a comfortable role prior to my marriage to Elizabeth, and it is not now. My friends will understand and the rest may be damned." He picked up some correspondence and laid it down in front of him. "I have another task for you, as well, Oliver."

Birch sat forward on the edge of his own chair, hiding his distress. For the first time in his life . . . ! And now, Stanmore for a rival . . . ! Bloody hell!

"I want you to assume that Rebecca Ford—or whatever her name is—boarded that ship with Elizabeth ten years ago. I want you to find out her true name if need be, her parentage, her reason for going to the colonies. I want to know why she decided to stay instead of returning to England with the boy."

"That could take months, you know."

"I have faith in you, Oliver."

Well, there was no sense in arguing the difficulties involved in finding out these things. They both knew that if there was anyone in England who could ferret out such information, it was Oliver Birch of the Middle Temple . . . and his bloody connections. After all, he'd been able to find Elizabeth, and later, James—a task that had been considered impossible by a number of his associates.

"Bring me the truth, Birch. I need to know everything about her."

As the lawyer rose to his feet, he couldn't help but feel the icy fingers of defeat around his heart. Lord Stanmore was a very handsome man. And a generous one. Why, if the most beautiful—and the most worldly—women in London could not withstand his allure, what chance could Mrs. Ford have against him? There was no denying the earl's desires; he simply took what he wanted.

And now Stanmore was returning to Solgrave—and not to spend time with his newly discovered son as he would have London society believe. He was returning to his ancestral home to . . . to dazzle a defenseless woman!

Bloody hell, Birch cursed as he stepped out of the earl's library. Why couldn't he leave this one woman alone? Rebecca Ford had none of the experience of Stanmore's other liaisons. The lawyer was certain of that. And she could have no idea how dismal her life would be when he eventually cast her aside. He only prayed that she was sensible enough to know that there could be no permanent place for her in the life of Lord Stanmore.

Indeed, it was her only hope.

The patch of sunlight brought out the golden streaks in Jamey's mop of hair as the boy sat quietly listening to the new tutor's instructions. Watching from the large windows of the gallery overlooking the walled formal garden, Rebecca felt immensely relieved at Daniel's choice of Mr. Clarke, formerly of Eton.

Now retired, the teacher had told Rebecca that his long career had concluded just a year earlier. Beekeeping—and the care of his aging mother—were now the only things to "f-f-f-f-fill my t-t-t-time." Hardly enough for a man with his energy, however, for Mrs. Clarke, his mother, was eighty-four-years old and in "p-p-p-perfect health." So the arrangement that allowed him to ride over to Solgrave several mornings a week from their cottage near the village church suited him immensely.

Daniel had suggested him, and Rebecca had approved his choice. Standing now in the gallery, she smiled at the sight of the teacher's wild hair sticking out in all directions from beneath the old-fashioned bagwig. There was nothing that was intimidating about this man, she thought, and her observation of Jamey's reaction to the scholar now reinforced that perception. Small of stature, with bristling eyebrows above kindly gray eyes, Mr. Clarke was the perfect person to introduce Jamey to his new home and his future life at Eton. The stammer, it appeared, only came out when he was addressing women. Why, even his surprising decision to hold their first lessons outside was a mark in his favor!

"Mr. Clarke will not be leaving the boy alone, Mrs. Ford. And Daniel has a footman keeping an eye on them."

Rebecca turned and smiled at the housekeeper standing by her side. She hadn't even heard the woman approach. "I'm not overly concerned, Mrs. Trent. I simply wanted to be certain that all was going well. I believe James likes him, but what do you think?"

"Of course, he does!" the woman spoke brightly. "Mr. Clarke is a bit odd, perhaps, but all those bookish types are, from what I've seen. But certainly a good fellow, I'd swear. I've known him since we were children. I've come to tell you that the dressmaker from St. Albans is waiting to see you, Mrs. Ford. I've set her up in the sewing room in the east wing. And the woman has already seen to the new shirts you wanted for Master James."

"That all sounds very well, Mrs. Trent. Will you thank her for me?" Rebecca asked as her gaze again returned to Jamey. To her delight, he was actually speaking to Mr. Clarke, who was nodding his head vigorously at the boy's responses.

"I'm afraid that won't do, Mrs. Ford. Won't do at all!"

The housekeeper's emphatic reply drew Rebecca's attention

again. For the short time that she'd been here, Rebecca had already noticed that, good-natured as she was, Mrs. Trent was generally quite emphatic about the way that things must be done. A positive quality, she knew, for someone with such important responsibilities. Managing a country manor like this one was not a task for the indecisive.

"When his lordship left us for town," the housekeeper went on, "he made a point of reminding me that I was to see to a new wardrobe for you. Now, I am not one to be reminded of my duties, Mrs. Ford. When we sent word in to St. Albans yesterday morning about the shirts, I also sent along a girl with specific instructions. A girl just about your size—"

"I am quite happy with what I have, Mrs. Trent. I don't believe that I need to be burdening Lord Stanmore with such unnecessary expenses."

The housekeeper shook her head, frowning as she surveyed Rebecca's gray dress.

"There is plenty of wear left in this dress, Mrs. Trent."

"Aye, ma'am, but it will not do, not even for a country dress." The woman's face showed that there would be no further discussion. "Mrs. Ford, you are in England, now, and a guest of his lordship. We mustn't allow your good heart to interfere with what must be done. With your help or without, I will simply have to order at least a dozen dresses for different times of the day, and for the occasions that will present themselves during your stay. You won't be dancing in any dress that is suitable for winter in the colonies, I can tell you."

"Dancing? Mrs. Trent, I have no plans for such socializing while I am here."

" 'Tis my duty to see that you are prepared, Mrs. Ford, and that's all there is to say on the matter."

"But, honestly, I—"

"His lordship will brook no 'buts,' ma'am. You don't want an old servant like me put out for shirking her duties, do you?"

"No, of course not! But I—"

"Very well, then." The housekeeper patted Rebecca's hand. "We shan't overdo things. You'll see."

Rebecca sighed resignedly, and Mrs. Trent smiled.

"In the good old days, when we'd have folk in for dinner parties twice a sennight, at least—with a garden party on the weekend and a ball here and there—I would never have recommended a dress from a shop in St. Albans." The housekeeper glanced nostalgically at the portraits adorning the walls. "In those days, Daniel—or his father before him—would have been calling for a coach and grooms to take you to Oxford Street in London for your shopping. Why, we'd visit every dressmaker's shop and clothier's warehouse in the city. But if you went *now*, I would be asking you to stop at Wedgewood's place on Great Newport Street. His Etruria Ware is all the rage, you know!"

"No, I didn't know," Rebecca replied, suppressing a smile.

"From what I hear, he has a great room in which they deck out the cabinets and vases, and set the places at table . . . just like an elegant dinner party! Why, every few days they alter everything . . . so the ladies fancy going back quite often." She let out a longing sigh. "It has been a very long time since I was blessed with making the arrangements for a party!"

"The earl's wife must have been fond of them."

The housekeeper frowned deeply. "I suppose she was . . . not that I'd know, mind you. After all, we were not good enough here in the country to put on a party for *her*. She would entertain up in London . . . or at his lordship's other homes in Bristol, or in Bath. Aye, she was sure to choose anywhere over Solgrave, though I don't know why, I'm sure."

There were so many questions Rebecca had about Elizabeth—questions Mrs. Trent might be able to answer. But seeing the housekeeper's obvious disapproval of the late Lady Stanmore—the grudge that clearly had not diminished even after so many years—she decided not to press for information right now.

"Now, his lordship's mother . . . now, there's a lady who was famous for her entertaining. Why, the grand parties she presided over here at Solgrave! My dear, I could tell you stories. . . ."

Mrs. Trent's voice trailed off, lost for the moment in her happy thoughts, and Rebecca turned her attention to her favorite view, outside. Jamey was leaning over Mr. Clarke's shoulder and looking at a book the teacher had open.

"Mrs. Ford, you are surely a good-hearted woman. We've not had a guest like you at Solgrave in a dog's age." Clearly, all thoughts of fashionable tableware and parties were now forgotten.

"I am not having a dozen dresses made for me, Mrs. Trent."

"Truly, I know you wouldn't want his lordship beating an old woman like me over something so easily resolved now, would you?"

She turned and met the housekeeper's forlorn look. Rebecca couldn't stop a smile from breaking across her lips at this new tactic.

"I knew you'd see it my way. We don't have to argue over numbers, ma'am. You just be a dear and come with me."

Reluctantly, Rebecca found herself being led toward the east wing, where the seamstress and her assistant were no doubt lying in ambush.

"Now, don't be alarmed when you see what they've brought along. What, with the King's Birthday celebrations not far off, the woman has been busy as can be, but she dropped everything to put together a few things that may just fit you . . . with a tuck here or there."

Rebecca came to stop. "Dresses already made?"

"If they fit—and I think they will—and if you fancy them, you'll be doing this hardworking seamstress and her three young ones a great favor."

"Mrs. Trent . . ."

"No arguing, my dear." The heavyset woman nudged Rebecca with her elbow. "If you won't do it for yourself, then do it for Master James. Knebworth Village belongs to his lordship, you know, and during the King's Birthday festivities, the entire household will be going down there. Mind you, there'll be many an eye clapped on the lad and on the mysterious lady who's been taking such good care of him for all these years."

Rebecca stared down at the tips of her worn shoes and stifled the urge to say that she'd prefer to stay behind.

"Picture it, ma'am. You walking to the village at the lad's side, proud as a mother hen—as you should be—and dressed the way a lady of your position should be dressed. Seeing you, everyone will know that Master James was brought up proper, and all's well! But if you don't do as I bid, the poor dear will suffer the barbs of those wagging village tongues for years!"

Rebecca *wished* she could argue against the housekeeper. She herself had been raised alongside girls from some of the finest families. She well understood the need for such display in certain situations.

Scolding herself for not seeing to this before leaving Pennsylvania, she followed Mrs. Trent to the door of the sewing room. It would have been a great deal more reasonable to have a dress or two made in Philadelphia than what it would be here. She hated the thought of owing anything to Lord Stanmore. She had no wish to be paid for her efforts on Jamey's behalf.

The dressmaker, Mrs. Pringle, turned out to be a very thin and energetic woman with the face of a person who was perpetually harried, as if the sky were about to fall at any moment. By the time Rebecca and Mrs. Trent entered, the woman and her silent assistant had already laid out at least a half dozen dresses for daily wear and for wear in the evening, several styles of chemises and hooped petticoats, three different pinafores (plain or with lace and bows), two wide-brimmed straw hats (that she had taken the liberty of picking up from her friend Mrs. Grant, a neighboring milliner in St. Albans), and a dazzling array of ribbons, bows, gloves, linen scarves, and other accessories.

After Mrs. Pringle had cast a professional eye over Rebecca, her thin lips turned up in a momentary smile.

"I just knew, Mrs. Trent. I just knew. Mrs. Ford, these dresses will look beautiful on you. I took one look at that girl you sent in, Mrs. Trent, and I said to my husband—he's the tailor in St. Albans, don't you know! 'Mr. Pringle,' I said, 'we'll make up some dresses that'll look beautiful on this Mrs. Ford.' And here, I was right. Why, just look at them!"

Rebecca watched uncomfortably as, one after the other, dresses of muslin and embroidered linen in prettiest shades of peach and cream, green and blue, were laid out before her. Each was adorned with fine lace, and every one was prettier than anything she'd worn since leaving Mrs. Stockdale's school in Oxford.

A vague queasiness settled in the pit of her stomach.

Modesty, chastity, virtue. The words came back to her. *Draw no attention to yourself, Rebecca Neville. Modesty, chastity, virtue.* Her schoolmistress had been tenacious in preaching the value of virtue to the young Miss Neville. Then, without warning, the thought of Sir Charles Hartington in the library in London suddenly emerged from the dark recesses of her mind. Even as she fought back the bile rising in her throat, Mrs. Stockdale's words continued to ring in her ears.

Thoughts of those last days in London so distracted Rebecca that she suddenly found herself standing on a stepstool, as Mrs. Pringle and Mrs. Trent busily discussed which dress should be tried on her first.

Rebecca blushed fiercely as the dressmaker unbuttoned the gray wool dress, helped her to step out of it, and then without ceremony cast it aside. In a moment, she was standing in a dress the color of ripe peaches and looking at herself in a mirror held by Mrs. Pringle's assistant.

"I believe you are right, Mrs. Trent," the dressmaker was saying. "This flowered sprig muslin is very becoming to her. Just dark enough to bring out the color in her hair and accentuate her complexion. Don't you agree, Mrs. Ford?"

As the two women chatted away, holding up pinafores and scarves and ribbons to the dress, Rebecca gazed at the low neckline; at the yards of lace that were layered in the sleeves and the full skirt. Before she could voice an objection though, Mrs. Pringle pulled the pins out of Rebecca's hair. Rich waves of red and gold cascaded down over her shoulders.

"Oh, my!"

Mrs. Trent's exclamation was silently seconded by the delight in the eyes of the girl holding the mirror.

"I declare, Mrs. Ford," the housekeeper said brightly, "if we work in a ribbon here and there, you will match the most beautiful lady ever to pass through the gates of Solgrave . . . and this is just a day dress!"

"'Tis true, ma'am," Mrs. Pringle said emphatically. "St. Albans would close up shop and put on an assembly for you, if you were to come to town."

"I believe you're on to something, Mrs. Pringle!" The housekeeper's gray eyes were shining with excitement. "Indeed, I shall speak to the earl about giving a ball in honor of Master James . . . and to introduce Mrs. Ford to the neighborhood."

She circled the stepstool and stood before Rebecca, a happy smile deepening every crease and wrinkle in her face.

"We simply must start showing you off, my dear. You are absolutely too lovely to be keeping yourself hidden as you have."

For a lifetime, Rebecca had trained herself to look plain. Always, she had striven to look severe, to appear much older than she was. From the set of her mouth to the expression in her eyes to the binding of her mane of unruly flaming hair, she had tried to fade into the background . . . to go unnoticed. From the time she left London, she'd always been fairly successful.

Rebecca now stared at the reflection of a stranger in the looking glass and felt her stomach turn.

Chapter 12

Carrying a basket of food between them, they walked to the old mill for a picnic.

Jamey had been the perfect child for all of the morning, paying attention to Mr. Clarke's instruction, and later spending some time with Daniel, learning his way about the large house. Regardless of the complimentary words and the obvious relief on the part of the steward and the housekeeper, though, Rebecca had taken one look into those restless blue eyes and she had known it was time to give the lad a chance to break loose for a while.

Coming from the less formal life that they'd led in Philadelphia, things at Solgrave surely must appear quite restrictive to Jamey, Rebecca realized. Every moment of the day seemed to have some significance. Rebecca knew she would have to combine the "business" of the boy's new life with some opportunity to play and to run.

The two of them found a stretch of soft grass near the ruined mill. She put down the basket near a clump of willow trees, delighted to see the look of mischief in his eyes.

"May I ruin these new clothes?"

"You certainly may not ruin them." She smiled at the upturned face and undid the ribbon of the straw hat Mrs. Pringle had forced her to wear with the new dress, "Though I don't believe a bit of dusting would hurt . . . but give me that jacket!"

Shedding the garment, the boy threw himself with a loud whoop on the grass and rolled down the long slope toward the lake. It was too late to mention that stains from the grass were a little different from a bit of dust, so she just sighed and then laughed at his antics.

Rebecca pulled a small blanket from the basket that Mrs. Trent had sent with them and spread it on the grass. Kneeling down, she began taking out the food and watching Jamey as he climbed on a boulder at the edge of the water.

She sat back on her heels, frowning. Rebecca had not questioned Jamey about what he had done and where he had gone three days earlier. Hearing his murmurs of apologies and sensing his fears of being left alone, she had made a pact with herself simply to look ahead and to continue to encourage him during the adjustments he had to make. He was only a boy, and running away was the most natural thing to do in a moment of stress. After all, hadn't she herself done the same thing so many years ago?

And yet, here she was, back in England—the one place she had sworn she would never return to.

"Can I go swimming?" He had doffed his shoes and stockings, and was standing in the water.

"You cannot. The lake water is too cold."

Jamey gave Rebecca a wry look and then ran up the slope, throwing himself in her arms. The two sprawled on the blanket, her straw hat flying into the grass. His sleeves were already wet.

"I'm sweating, and the water's fine. Please, Mama . . . please let me go in! You know I'm a good swimmer."

It was true. Thanks to the Butler boys, Jamey had been swimming in the Delaware River for the past four summers. Those boys spent a great deal of time down at the waterfront, leaping off the piers and playing.

"Come and feel the water yourself, Mama. Come and see. It's really warm."

Rebecca let him pull her to her feet, but went no closer to the lake. Dressed as she was, she had no intention of walking back to Solgrave in ruined clothes.

"Come and check the water yourself," he wheedled. "It's much warmer than dockside . . . even in July."

Rebecca tucked a strand of her hair that had come loose from its ribbon behind an ear. She unpinned the lace-edged scarf she'd been wearing around her neck and placed it on the blanket. She then walked with him to the edge of the lake. The water, so gray and muddied a day before, now ran clear. Along the shallow edges she could see tiny fish flitting along a sandy bottom.

"Please, Mama!" he tugged on her arm. "I have been the best lad. You saw it yourself. I gave no trouble to Mr. Clarke, even though I was sorely tempted. Please!"

Rebecca couldn't resist the upturned face. The eyes turned mischievous when he saw that he had her convinced. He knew exactly how to melt her heart.

"I have nothing to dry you with."

He quickly began stripping off his clothes. "Never mind about that. You just sit up on the blanket. I can use that . . . or I'll just lie in the sun until I'm dry."

"What about all the food we've carried down here?"

"We'll eat it later. Turn around, Mama!"

He paused until she had turned to go back up to the blanket. In a moment, she heard him splashing into the deeper water.

"You be careful . . . not too far out!"

Spurring his fresh hunter along the lake, Stanmore's irritation only grew sharper. He had pushed his favorite bay gelding harder than he should have on the ride from London, but that vague sense of impatience nagging at him had been unsettling, to say the least. Why, he'd left Philip and the entourage of servants in his dust long before they had even reached Marylebone.

Upon arriving at Solgrave, the earl's first question had been about Mrs. Ford, and Daniel had hastily informed him that she and James had gone off on their own toward the old mill.

He'd dreamed about her again last night. Rebecca had come to him as he'd seen her in James's bedchamber three nights ago. She'd come to him—at first modest and ill at ease—presenting herself as she had on every occasion that they had met. But as the gauzy fabric of his dreams continued to weave, he'd peeled her reserve. He'd awakened this morning feeling restless and anxious to see her.

Physical attraction to a beautiful woman was nothing new to a man of Stanmore's age and experience. But the realization that Rebecca Ford was, at the very least, hiding any interest she might have in him and perhaps even fighting it, aroused his curiosity. The fact that she obviously had no intention of pursuing or encouraging him, as other women so often did, only aroused his curiosity that much more. There was an innocence in it. The quality she possessed was not the childish, annoying coyness found in so many young women of the *ton*—but a charming, honest kind of struggle.

Despite her modesty, though, she was attracted to him. He had seen the gentle blush, the trembling hand, the way her stormy eyes had studied all of him that night outside her room. There were definitely enough telltale signs to tease him and unsettle his dreams.

As Stanmore rode toward the abandoned mill, it occurred to him that his interest in Rebecca Ford conflicted with his plans for James. True, his expectations of the boy had been quite different than the reality. He'd had every intention of ignoring James, of sloughing him off to school. The lad would be comfortable enough amid the accommodations provided for the children of England's wealthiest class. But James's defiance—the lad's obvious desire for independence—had certainly surprised him.

This had been the reason for his visit to the boy's room that night. Stanmore had wanted to look into that face and be reminded again of Elizabeth. He'd wanted to wash away the growing confusion and focus on his wife's cowardice, on her lack of honor. But he hadn't been able to see any of that in the sleeping face. The mother and son shared so much in their features, but there was a different spirit at work beneath the surface.

The ruins of the old mill came into view, and he spotted the bright flutter of the woman's dress dancing in the wind. She was walking to the edge of the lake, her back to him. A few strands of golden red hair had already escaped their confines and were teasing her slender neck. As he drew near, he let his eyes appreciatively take in the new dress. He would be sure to thank Mrs. Trent for arranging for this new wardrobe. Somehow, he had a feeling that it couldn't have been an easy task.

She must have heard the horse's hooves on the path, for Stanmore saw her raise a hand to her eyes to block the sun as she turned in his direction.

He reined in the hunter and tethered him to a dangling willow branch. "I hope you don't mind the intrusion, but it is far too warm a day to be spent indoors."

She shook her head and cast a quick glance at the lake. "I . . . I didn't know you were coming down from London today, m'lord, though we're glad you are here. If you are hungry, I believe there is enough food in that basket to . . . to . . . feed a . . . regiment."

Her faltering stammer indicated that she must have noticed his silent but admiring appraisal of the way she looked. Stanmore saw her gaze flit to a lacy scarf that she'd discarded on the blanket near the top of the slope. She modestly crossed her arms over her chest, and his gaze was drawn to the perfect swells of her ivory breasts above the neckline.

He found he was indeed feeling hunger, but not for anything in the picnic basket. He knew that he had to curtail this growing obsession with her. Rebecca Ford was no Covent Garden whore. Nor was she one of the easy ladies of the London *ton*. She was a prize worth savoring, and he had no intention of frightening her away.

"Plenty of food, you say. Well, Harry—my cook here at Solgrave—was one of twenty-one siblings." He walked casually toward her. "He is generally known for valuing quantity over quality."

She gave a little shake of her head in disagreement. "You are being unjust, m'lord, Your cook is a fine one, indeed. I've been very impressed with the quality of everything I have been served."

"And you are simply being a gracious guest. But considering the slenderness of your figure"—he kept his eyes fixed on her face—"and the perfection of your manner, you might be starving here, and you would say nothing in protest."

A pretty blush crept into her cheeks, and she looked away, robbing him of the pleasure of seeing the blue of her eyes.

"I assure you, m'lord, my stay at Solgrave has been the most enjoyable."

"I am very pleased to hear that, ma'am." He spoke the words gently, stopping only an arm's length from her.

Wisps of her hair danced in the breeze, and Rebecca tucked them behind a delicately curved ear. So near, he could feel her skittishness. Stanmore turned to look at the lake, the sky, the stretch of the trees curving up and over the crest of the hill on the far side of the valley. Moments later, though, he found his gaze had already returned to her face.

"Daniel tells me that James began his lessons with a tutor this morning."

"He has." She smiled, but a second later a fearful gasp escaped her lips as she stepped sharply toward the lake. "Jamey!"

Stanmore followed the direction of her gaze and stared at the calm waters of the lake.

Forgetful of the shoes and dress, Rebecca took a step into the still waters. *"Jamey!"*

"Where is he?" In an instant, Stanmore had shed his jacket and vest and stepped in after her.

"In the lake. He was . . ." The boy's head bobbed to the surface for an instant some fifty yards from the shore and immediately disappeared again.

Stanmore ran a few steps into the lake and dove into the deeper water.

"No, m'lord!"

He heard the cry from the shore, but he did not turn. He knew where the boy had gone down. He immediately dove again, gliding along just beneath the surface of the water toward the spot. He'd swum the length and breadth of this lake from the time he was just a lad. And he knew very well that the shallows around the shore had deceived many in the past. The sandy edges dropped off so quickly and so deeply that the lake seemed to have no bottom in places.

His strokes were strong, and he reached where he'd seen the lad only moments ago, but the calm surface of the lake lay unbroken. He took a deep breath and dived downward.

The water become painfully cold only a few feet beneath the surface, and Stanmore looked about him wildly for any sign of the boy. There was nothing. He surfaced again, and took another deep breath, but this time—as he started to dive again—he glimpsed a splash of water thirty yards or so closer to the dam.

He swam furiously in that direction, but again found no sign of James beneath or on the surface. He dove again, directing his strokes closer to the dam. Nothing.

Stanmore treaded water for a moment, suddenly fearing the worst. His heart hammered in his chest. He glanced toward the shore. There he saw Rebecca had stepped back from the water's edge and was waving in his direction. Before her, near the shore, he saw the scrawny body of a naked boy stand up in the shallows. The water splashed around him as the lad ran toward the woman.

He did not know whether it was due to the cold of the lake water or the scare of James's disappearance, but an angry pounding began to drum in his temples. Thoughts of thrashing the boy's skinny, white behind ran pell-mell through Stanmore's head. He was angry enough to do that, he was certain. He started for the shore.

Rebecca must have sensed his state of mind, though, for as he swam toward them, Stanmore saw her hand James a bundle of clothes, wrap him in her own scarf, and send him running toward Solgrave.

Each of his boots weighed at least fifty pounds. His shirt and breeches clung to his body as Stanmore finally stepped out of the water. Glaring at the boy as he disappeared into the trees, he growled a curse under his breath and focused his anger on Rebecca. She had picked up the blanket from the grass and was holding it out to him.

"You told him to run away, instead of facing the consequences of his actions."

He saw her take a step back as he stalked up the slope.

"He was cold . . . shivering like a leaf . . ."

"He saw me swimming after him. He could have waited and told me he was in no danger."

"He is a boy. He just thought it was a game." She tried to give him a weak smile, but his fierce frown caused it to fade immediately. "It was my fault. I tried to stop you, but—"

"You have raised a *coward.*"

"James is *no* coward." Rebecca raised her chin in defiance as her temper flared. She shoved the blanket into his chest. He let it drop to the grass and took another step forward . . . only to have her take two back. Her gaze traveled down his chest before fixing again on his face. "It was just a mistake. He went to the house . . . to change. He was dripping wet . . . as . . . as you are . . ."

As her voice trailed off, Stanmore felt the heat of his anger turn to desire. He continued stalking her, and she continued to back toward the mill.

"I cannot let this pass. When he ran away, I did nothing, but not this time. He needs to learn the meaning of responsibility. He needs to know that there are consequences."

"He didn't know he was doing anything wrong. He is a good swimmer. In fact, an excellent one. If anyone is to blame . . . it is I." She stopped abruptly as she backed against the wall of the old mill. "I . . . I overreacted."

"Stop protecting him, Rebecca. He needs to—"

"It was I," she pleaded. "This time, *I* am the one at fault."

He watched her rapid breathing. He took a step closer and allowed his gaze to roam, to caress the beautiful column of her neck. His eyes lingered on the wild beat of her pulse against the translucent skin of her throat and moved lower to admire the rise and fall of perfect breasts to the uneven rhythm of her breathing. He still moved closer, his gaze focused on her full lips. He almost smiled as they parted—a gasp escaping them—as his cold, wet body came in contact with her warm one. He focused on her blue eyes, suddenly lost in the storms of passion raging in them.

Rebecca saw his eyes darken. Her breath hung suspended in her chest. Her head, her back, her palms—all pressed against the hard, stone wall behind her—could create no distance. Even if she could have moved back, the pressure of his hard, wet body in front told her that he would follow. Even if she were able to move mountains at this moment, she knew he would come after her.

His mouth descended upon hers, and her eyes closed. His lips were hard, almost bruising in their insistence. Then, just as Rebecca felt fear beginning to crawl up her spine, Stanmore's mouth gentled, and she was jolted by a strange, molten heat uncoiling in her middle.

Stunned at first, she stood still, trying to understand the sensations racing through her. She was even shocked to find that she loved the feel of his fingers on her skin as he held the sides of her face. She hesitantly opened the eyes that she had shut so tightly and saw the sharp angles of his handsome face as he drew back briefly before lowering his head again to nip and suckle her bottom lip.

She couldn't move—couldn't breathe—but her heart was beating so hard that she was afraid it would explode in her chest at any instant. And still, the undulating mass of molten sensations was threatening to set her insides on fire.

"So beautiful," he murmured against her lips, and Rebecca found herself staring into specks of silver deep in his dark eyes. "Kiss me, Rebecca."

His fingers dug into her hair. She felt the ribbon loosen, the thick waves sliding down onto her shoulders. His lips again lowered to hers.

Rebecca's startled hands jerked away from the wall, clutching at his back as the pressure of his mouth increased, and his tongue started teasing the seam of her tightly closed lips.

"Kiss me, Rebecca."

She opened her mouth to tell him of her ignorance in such matters, but no words came out. It wouldn't have mattered. His lips descended again, and he thrust into the opening . . . sampling, rubbing, exploring her mouth.

Bolts of lightning shot through her with a scorching heat that she thought might kill her. His tongue rubbed against hers, and Rebecca vaguely felt his hands move down her back and encircle her waist. He pulled her even tighter against the solid strength of his chest. She no longer felt the wetness of his clothes, but only the incredible heat that seemed to possess them both. Her lifelong fear of intimacy suddenly transformed into an eternity of desire.

Rebecca became almost frantic to satisfy this sudden hunger for him. Her hands traveled down his back. She could feel the powerful muscles beneath the clinging linen of the shirt. It was almost miraculous, the way her body felt, softening and molding itself to the contours of his body.

Through a haze, she heard his low growl of pleasure. And as he pressed her into the wall, she felt something else. The thin buckskin of his breeches could hardly be expected to conceal the presence of the aroused manhood pressing intimately against her body.

Clarity and sanity returned instantly as a series of images sprang

up before her eyes. Images razor sharp and horrible. A library in
London. A man aroused. A man willing to violate the body of another. A murder.

The same hands that had been struggling to pull him closer, now
wedged themselves between their bodies. Rebecca turned her face
and shoved at his chest. To her surprise, he immediately released
her. She felt light-headed and awkward, as shame and embarrassment quickly drained her of her strength.

"I . . . I am so sorry." Her cheeks burned. Her entire body trembled as she edged herself away from the man and the wall. She
stumbled backward toward the basket of food spread on the grass.
"I shouldn't . . . I was wrong. . . . This is all . . . all my fault."

"Rebecca!"

The sound of her name, uttered clear and low, felt like velvet in
her ear. She took another step back before hesitantly looking up.

"I am so sorry."

The embers of passion glowed deep in his eyes. A flickering
movement in his jaw told her of the battle that was waging inside
him. But he had not moved. He wasn't coming after her.

And suddenly she knew. This man would not hurt her to appease
his lust. Even stronger feelings of shame washed through her at the
thought that she had compared the Earl of Stanmore to Sir Charles
Hartington.

Nonetheless, he was still very much a man.

"I started this." His words spoke of his conviction. "There is
nothing wrong with—"

"No!" She raised a hand to silence him and shook her head before taking another step back. "You are not to blame, but this is very
wrong. This will not happen again."

Turning, Rebecca ran as fast as she could toward the path. At the
crest of the hill, though, she cast a quick glimpse over her shoulder
and then stopped, her breath caught in her throat. Lord Stanmore,
shirtless and barefoot now, was striding into the cold waters of the
lake for another swim, the powerful muscles of his broad back rippling in the summer sun.

Chapter 13

By the time Jamey reached the cottage in the woods, the loose-fitting shirt on his back was nearly dry. Putting down his mother's scarf and the shoes and stockings he'd tucked under his arm, he pulled the makeshift door open a little and peered inside.

"Israel! Are you in there?"

The inside was dark and cool, and he could feel the dampness that still lingered in the hut. A small movement by the fire caught the boy's eye.

"Israel?" His call was louder this time, and he pulled the door open farther to let more light in. "Israel . . . are you here?"

"Aye, sir." The voice was familiar. "No place else to go."

A grin broke over Jamey's face as he saw his friend huddled in the darkness. The other boy was pushing himself into a sitting position.

"What were you doing? Sleeping?" Without waiting for an answer, Jamey stepped out of the cottage and picked up his shoes and his mother's scarf. While he was out there, he filled his arms with some branches for a fire.

The day he'd run away from Solgrave, he'd walked in the pouring rain for hours through the woods and meadows of the park before coming upon a hollow trunk of a huge and ancient oak tree. Thinking it might be a good place to find shelter, he had been more than a little surprised to find himself face-to-face with a boy of exactly the same size and age.

When the boy made room for him, Jamey knew he'd found a friend. Huddled beside Israel in the tree, he had told the boy that he was running away from his new home. Israel had mentioned that he really didn't think of the place where he ate and slept as his home. So now, he was working on a new one for himself in the woods.

Jamey told him that he'd been happy all of his life until yesterday, when his mama had told him that he was a nobleman's son. He didn't want to be any stranger's son. He had been perfectly happy with only her.

Israel said that he never remembered having a mama or a papa. He'd had to work with the woodcutter for his food. And he always looked down and never talked back when the white people at Melbury Hall addressed him, because he was a slave. He supposed his skin made him different.

Jamey had simply shrugged his shoulders at the news. He told Israel that where he was from, a lot of people didn't hold with owning slaves, and that a great number of people whose grandparents had come from Africa and from the Indies were free.

This hadn't really seemed to make much of an impression, but when Jamey had told his new friend that he too was different in his own way, Israel had raised a curious eye. Then Jamey had pulled up his sleeve and shown him his claw hand.

Israel had been quite impressed by the looks of the hand and, when the rain eased up a little, had asked Jamey if he wanted to come and see the home he'd been working on.

A couple of hours later, as the two had been sitting and eating some of Israel's food, they had decided that together they could fix up the place better than Israel could alone. And since Jamey wasn't going back to Solgrave, he could be keeping an eye on things when Israel was working with the woodcutter. The pact was sealed with a handshake.

Jamey walked inside the cottage with his arms full.

"You were gone when I came back the other morning."

He dropped his load on the floor and started stacking some of the sticks on the pile of ashes. "He came after me."

"Your papa?"

"The earl, and I still say he is no relation to me," Jamey corrected him, glancing at his friend's bare feet. Israel's callused hands were dangling around his bare legs, and that was all of him he could really see in the dimly lit hut.

"Did he ask any questions . . . about this place . . . and the fixing up of it? We're on his lordship's land, you know. Biddle the wood-cutter told me everything from the ridge over belongs to Solgrave."

Jamey snorted, shaking his head. "He didn't ask a thing! He doesn't care anything about it . . . or about me. He didn't even look twice at the place."

Falling silent, he finished piling the wood. "I thought I'd make a fire. I went swimming in the lake, and my clothes are wet. My breeches are stuck to my arse something fierce."

"Aye, there is dry kindling over there, and here's my flint."

The flint dropped on the ground beside the ashes. Jamey pushed himself to his feet and went for the kindling. "Are you planning to do any work about the place today? I can stay awhile and help. They shan't be looking for me for hours."

"Nay, I don't much feel like . . ." Israel's voice was so hushed that Jamey didn't hear his final words. He picked up the flint and turned to his new friend.

"I'll need a bit of steel . . . or a knife if you . . ." He stopped, getting for the first time a good look at the other boy's battered face. "Israel?"

He moved closer and saw the bloody shirt. Panic twisted a knot in his belly, but Jamey moved and crouched next to his friend. Using his left hand, he touched the fresh blood on the worn sleeve of the shirt. There was more on the back, but as Jamey tried to pull him forward to look, the other boy winced in pain.

"Your face . . . all this blood . . ." Jamey felt his stomach lurch at the sight of Israel's face. One eye was swollen shut. There was a lump on his forehead. A cut was still bleeding on the puffy lips. "My Lord! What did you do?"

"I am a slave, remember?"

"They can't just beat you for nothing. Who did this to you, Israel?"

"No one cares who did this to me!"

"I care," he cried. "I shall go right now and give them some of the same."

Israel shook his head, and Jamey could see he was in pain. "They are far bigger."

"Then I can . . . I'll throw rocks at them. I *will* make them pay for this."

The other boy dropped his chin to his chest again.

"Someone has to teach them a lesson."

The slumped shoulders spoke of defeat, and Jamey had a sickening feeling that this was not the first time Israel had faced a beating.

"Size is not everything, you know," he started hopefully.

"I know. Color is."

Jamey swallowed a knot in his throat and fought back the tears that were burning his eyes. He sat down in the dirt next to his friend and pulled his knees up to his chest. In his mind he saw the Africans he'd seen in shackles in Bristol.

"You are different only if I am different," he said a little while later. "But I've had someone to protect me. My mama has looked after me since forever. You need a protector . . . until . . . you get strong and can take care of yourself."

Israel didn't say anything, so Jamey laid a hand gently on the boy's knee.

"I am not brown-skinned, but people try to hurt me, too." His friend continued to look down. "One day, two summers ago, my friend George and I were coming back from fishing down by the docks in Philadelphia. This sailor started yelling at me for throwing something at him, and I had done no such a thing. And then, before I knew it, he had me by the ear and was cursing at me pretty fiercely, yelling about how he was going to break my other hand so I would have two crippled hands. Now, I really hadn't done anything wrong. He just didn't like me . . . maybe because he thought I was weak. Maybe because he could see I was different than him."

Jamey remembered how scared he'd been. It didn't matter how much he squirmed or what he said, he had been sure that he was going to have his good hand broken.

"Then, just when I thought I was done for, my mama showed up. She is just a little thing, you know. But how she faced down that son of a bitch! She just walked right up to him and lit into him, scolding him like a schoolboy. Why, she looked to be about ten feet tall."

Jamey felt himself fill with pride at the memory. He saw Israel lift his head and wipe at the bloody corner of his mouth with a dirty sleeve.

"Wait!" Jamey put a hand on his arm before scrambling to his feet and fetching his mama's scarf. Carefully, he laid it on the other boy's knees. "Use this. She won't mind. I know anytime I've ever been hurt, it's made me feel better to hold something of hers."

Israel stared at the fine linen on his lap.

"I can't touch this. They'll hang me, for sure, for stealing it."

"They can't. I gave it to you."

After a moment, Israel touched a corner. Then he brought his head near it and, closing his eyes, he breathed in the smell. Jamey knew the smell. Lavender. He watched the bruised face, the sad expression.

"So this is what having a mama is like."

Tears sprang into Jamey's eyes, but he tried to fight them back. "No one would dare to beat you again if my mama took you as a son."

"That's not the way things work." Israel tried to open his eyes. The left eye was now completely swollen shut. The good one had tears in it. "And if you are my friend, you will forget all of this. If he hears that I complained, then I shall be far worse for it."

"Who?" Jamey asked again.

"Never you mind. In fact, it'd be better for both of us if you didn't even see me today."

Leaping to his feet, he stumbled out of the hut. Jamey followed him across the meadow and then stopped as Israel ran off into the woods, the linen scarf clutched tightly in his hand.

There was no getting around it. Stanmore knew it. Everyone knew it. The first day in the country at Solgrave was hell. It always had been. It always would be. It was just a good thing for them that the two stewards were so damned capable at running his households.

Nonetheless, waiting for the two brothers to work through their inevitable routine always managed to try Stanmore's patience. It was like watching two mastiffs circling each other—growling and snapping, their heads low, shoulders hunched, each one looking for the opening that would give him ascendancy over the other.

Daniel was house steward for Solgrave. Philip was steward of the London house and the elder of the two by ten years. Therefore, based on some idea of primogeniture, even in service, the dour-faced Philip felt it was his duty to criticize and to "guide" his brother on matters Daniel had been seeing to at Solgrave quite competently for over twenty years. It didn't matter that Daniel's responsibilities and the number of people who reported to him far exceeded Philip's. It was simply a tradition that they should bicker for the first twenty-four hours, and Stanmore had long ago learned just to stay out of the line of fire and out of the servants' wing.

Besides, he often thought with a grin, the two would be dreadfully hurt if he ever decided to leave Philip in London.

By the time Stanmore returned from his swim down by the ruined mill, the carriage conveying his steward and his own personal servants from London had arrived and the household was bustling with activity. Determined to avoid his stewards, the earl retreated to his own chambers to clean up and dress. As a result, he asked no one about Mrs. Ford's whereabouts, including his valet, who retired quickly from the dressing room with Stanmore's wet clothes and boots.

What they had shared in the shadow of the old mill had happened quite unexpectedly. And yet, his arousal had been so potent that even the second dunking in the lake had not completely cooled his ardor. As he stood gazing out his windows at the stables beyond the grove of trees, though, he realized that it was incumbent on him to speak to Rebecca and make her understand that there should be no apologies for what had taken place. They were both adults. Both had past marital experience. Indeed, with a woman like her, candor—or something akin to it—was the best course of action. Just because their stations in life differed substantially, there was no reason why they should not act on their mutual and quite obvious attraction. So long as they maintained a modicum of discretion, so long as she accepted the fact that there could be no permanency in their liaison, what could be the harm in it?

The knock on the door brought him out of his reverie. Daniel entered with Philip on his heels.

"I see there is to be no escaping you two today."

"Beg pardon, m'lord?" Daniel replied after bowing.

"What is it?" Stanmore watched Philip circle the chamber, inspecting the furniture for dust or any other sign of expected negligence.

"M'lord," Daniel continued, frowning but determined to ignore his brother. "Mr. John Clarke, M.A., is waiting in the library, as your lordship requested."

"And drinking your port, more than likely," Philip muttered as he smoothed an imaginary wrinkle from a perfectly starched linen covering a table by the window.

"Philip, kindly tell Mr. Clarke that I'll be down shortly." He paused as the two began to bow themselves out of the room. "And Daniel, see that the new tutor is offered a glass of our best Madeira."

John Clarke had not changed much in the almost twenty years since Stanmore had last seen him. When young Samuel Wakefield had been a student at Eton, Mr. Clarke's old bagwig with the locks of unruly hair sticking out from beneath it had been legendary. And if the man had grown partial to his wine, he didn't appear to be any the worse for it. After greeting the old scholar and exchanging a few general pleasantries, Stanmore immediately focused his questions on what he wanted to know.

"From what you have seen of James this morning, Mr. Clarke, do you believe he will be ill-equipped to attend Eton in the fall?"

"Why no, m'lord." Clarke bowed slightly, a habit Stanmore noticed him doing after nearly every sentence he spoke. "I would say that Master James is a shy lad. But that's to be expected, I should think. Of course, that may perhaps hinder him somewhat in making friends. But that is not uncommon in a first-year boy."

Stanmore moved away from his desk and sought the sunshine pouring in through the large windows looking out over the lake. "How much is he lacking in his studies, compared to other lads of his age?"

"From what I can see, Master James needs work in the classics.

But outside of that, m'lord, he appears quite proficient in his reading, writing, and arithmetic. I even noted the lad speaks a bit of French when prompted." The scholar clasped his hands behind him and rocked on the heels. Stanmore had seen him do that a hundred times in the classroom and knew that the man was feeling more comfortable. "Of course, I have had only a morning with him. But as we spend more time together, I can assure you that I will see to it that he will be well prepared, by the time fall term starts, in *all* areas of study."

The earl turned his gaze out over the water of the lake. He wondered if Rebecca had returned to the house. Finding that he had to push aside the enticing image of her entwined in his arms, he turned again to the teacher. He couldn't allow himself to become overly absorbed in this affair.

"What of his hearing?" he asked, frowning. "What difficulties will arise when he is thrown in with other lads at Eton?"

Mr. Clarke's eyes were focused on the colorful pattern of the Persian carpet. Finding his answer in the man's hesitation, Stanmore turned back to the window.

"M'lord, that is a difficult q-question. He wouldn't be the first Etonian to have a hearing p-p-problem. In my judgment, m'lord, Master James—"

A soft knock on the door drew both men's gazes. At Stanmore's call, Rebecca hesitantly opened the door, took a step in, and looked about the room.

"I must apologize for the intrusion, m'lord," she said quietly.

The thought occurred to him that there was something quite charming in the fact that she had not gathered her hair up on top of her head since he'd set it loose by the old mill. The thick waves of red silk tumbled appealingly over her shoulders, bright against the ivory skin and the new dress.

"Your presence is always welcome, Mrs. Ford."

She curtsied shyly to Stanmore, but refused to meet his gaze. She turned to the tutor. "Mr. Clarke, by any chance were you planning any lessons for Jamey . . . for James this afternoon?"

"I . . . I th-th-thought . . . the . . . the . . . m-m-morning lesson was enough, m-madam."

Stanmore turned with surprise to the stammering scholar, who stood blushing fiercely and bowing with every word. A rival, the earl thought, his amused gaze shifting back to Rebecca. He couldn't help but admire how compassionately and attentively and politely she behaved in the face of the man's suffering.

"Then, you have no lessons planned for this afternoon?" she asked gently.

"N-n-no, madam. As we d-d-discussed earlier, n-n-not f-for the f-first day."

The hint of anxiousness that flickered across Rebecca's face at Clarke's answer did not go unnoticed by the peer. He noted the way her knuckles went white as she clutched the fabric of her dress.

"Thank you, Mr. Clarke. M'lord." She backed toward the door. "I'll take my leave of y—"

"Mrs. Ford!"

She paused with a hand on the latch, her face paling visibly.

"Mr. Clarke, leave us."

The tutor mumbled his hasty farewells before departing from the room. After stepping to the side, she stood motionless by the door, but Stanmore could see a storm brewing in the blue eyes.

"Kindly close the door, Mrs. Ford," he asked gently.

She shook her head. "I should prefer not to remain, m'lord. I was on my way—"

"Mrs. Ford, I am not about to ravish you in this room. Close that door."

At her hesitation, Stanmore strode to the door and closed it himself. Turning, he took her hand in his and led her away from the door. The fingers were icy, her expression clearly nervous. She did not try to remove her hand, but her anxiety was palpable.

"What is wrong, Rebecca?"

Her head lifted, the troubled eyes meeting his. He saw the small trembling of her chin, and Stanmore had to garner every ounce of his control to keep from pulling her into his arms. His thumb caressed the back of her hand, but she quickly pulled it out of his grasp.

"James has run off again. Is that it?"

She took a long moment before finally giving a nod. This confirmed that her nervousness had nothing to do with the intimacy they'd shared by the old mill.

"Put your mind at rest, Mrs. Ford," he said matter-of-factly. "You are not in Philadelphia. This is a large estate with many attractions for a lad of his age. Just because you cannot see him every moment of the day, you need not think that he is in any danger. There are many who work here, in the house and in the stables and on the farms, and all of them consider it their foremost responsibility to look after the lad. While the lake has its dangers, the boy has made it patently clear that we needn't worry about that. In short, you can cease your fretting."

A deep blush colored the skin of her neck and her cheeks. "I am sorry to appear so foolish, m'lord. Old habits are difficult to break."

"There is no need for an apology, Mrs. Ford."

Stanmore caught her impatient look toward the door.

"If you will forgive me, m'lord." She tried to go around him, but he took hold of her elbow.

"When was the last time anyone saw the lad? And what is it *exactly* that has you so alarmed?"

She gave him a grateful look. "We . . . I was the last one. I have already spoken to a number of the servants, and it appears that he didn't come back here after he left the old mill. He is probably still running around in his wet clothes and . . ."

"The day is warm and pleasant. I assure you, he will not suffer from being outside." His words sounded patronizing, even to his own ears.

"I can see that my shortcomings as a parent are readily apparent to you, m'lord. However, I am making every attempt to hold back and allow those who will be very much a part of James's future to take an active part in his life." She took in a half-breath and stared at some invisible mark on his coat while moving slightly to detach her elbow from his grasp. "Nonetheless, my good intentions and my love for your son are separate matters entirely. I fear I will never be able to sit idly when I think he may be in danger. Good day."

It took only a few strides to overtake her at the door. Stanmore knew this was not the time to engage Rebecca in a discussion of love versus attachment. Personally, he seriously doubted that such a thing as love really existed. He'd never been the recipient of it in his life, of that he was certain. He had felt passion, but that was another matter entirely. And he'd never harbored any feeling that he might confuse with love. Attachment, though, was a much simpler matter to deal with. James had lived with her for many years, so naturally she was attached to him. And as these things went, once Rebecca and the boy were separated, they would both adjust. Presently though, he preferred Rebecca to stay at Solgrave, so winning the point would hardly be in his own best interest.

"Allow me," he said, opening the door and following her out. "I assume you plan to go in search of him."

"I . . . I was planning to take a walk. The deer park is extensive, but there is a chance I might cross paths with him."

"Do you ride, Mrs. Ford?"

Still avoiding his gaze, she shook her head. "No, m'lord. I think this is hardly the time—"

"Then I shall arrange for you to learn while you are here at Solgrave. It will facilitate chasing after James immensely, I should think."

She nodded politely.

"I have a proposition for you, Mrs. Ford." He turned, finding her startled eyes upon him. "I will go after James. I know where he is."

"You know?" she cried in disbelief, stopping and facing him.

"Well, I should say I have a strong suspicion that he has returned to the same ruined cottage where I found him two nights ago."

"Then you don't believe he has run away again."

"I do not." Stanmore turned and moved off a few steps, motioning for a footman to bring his gloves.

"Have a horse brought around," he told the servant before turning back to Rebecca. "I believe he has found a refuge of sorts in it. He probably sees it as a place to play . . . as I assume most young boys would."

"But is this cottage not far off?"

"I'll ride over myself and make certain he is there. However, getting back to my proposition." He paused again. "I am planning on staying at Solgrave for a while. I will not be returning to London for a fortnight, at least."

She blessed him with a smile that nearly stunned him with its beauty. Rebecca Ford was a woman who needed to smile more, Stanmore thought, forcing himself to move toward the door.

"This is exactly what James needs," she continued. "Time spent with your lordship will surely settle him."

Spending time with the boy was hardly the reason for Stanmore's extended stay. Still, though, the warm approval in her expression caused him to withhold the truth. "Mrs. Ford, I *will* spend time with him. But in so doing, I would like to rely on your help, your guidance. I make no claims to any knowledge of how to parent a boy like him. I would like to be sure that I am proceeding as I should."

Her pretty head bowed with modesty. "I am no expert, m'lord,"

"Kindly do not require that I deliver one of your own lectures back to you." He arched a brow in challenge and then hid a smile as she bit back her response. "Very well, then! I'm happy you have decided to see things my way."

The shipmaster's cottage sat nestled into a grassy knoll overlooking the sparkling gray-green waters of Bayard's Cove in Dartmouth.

Sitting on the wooden settle opposite the retired seafarer, Sir Oliver Birch listened carefully to the meandering recollections of a journey undertaken ten years earlier. The stem of the clay pipe he'd been offered was smooth and warm between his fingers, and he noticed that the sailor—blue smoke hanging like a cloud around his head—held his pipe by the bowl, his leathery fingers seemingly insensitive to the heat as he puffed away at the tobacco.

"I recall it as if 'twere yesterday. My ship, the *Rose*—and a finer ship ne'er sailed the western seas, I'll warrant ye—she'd just had her hull scraped at Shadwell's. Eager we were to be out on the open seas again. Time and tide waits for no man, they say."

"So I understand, sir," Birch said, trying to keep his impatience out of his voice.

"Aye, well, after taking on cargo and a handsome lot of passengers, my first mate sailed her down from London to Dartmouth. 'Twas in the month of July, I recall. That's where I joined my crew and we set sail for America. But 'twasn't afore Dartmouth that ever I clapped eyes on the lass or the lady or any of 'em."

Through the open window, Sir Oliver watched a fishing boat pass along the bay beneath the cottage.

He nodded encouragingly at the seafarer. "Please tell me anything you recollect. Anything at all."

"Aye, well . . . she was quality, that's certain enough." The captain cocked his head and pointed the stem of his pipe at the lawyer. "They were both quality, but one of them, the mother, was definitely the one with means."

"Her name was listed on the ship's books. Why not the other's?"

The old man shrugged and puffed at the pipe. "Over the years, more than a few folks have paid their passage without putting down a name on the manifest. Some've had good reason, I suppose. One of the mates told me when the two women come aboard off a boat from Wapping Stairs, her ladyship paid extra, she did, to put no name down for the other."

So they did know each other prior to that journey, Birch thought, remembering Stanmore's suspicion that Rebecca and Elizabeth might have been acquaintances prior to embarking for the colonies.

"Did you meet the mother? Did you talk to her before her death?"

"Aye." The man nodded and started refilling his pipe. "I went in to her when Miss Rebecca saw the trouble the other one was facing. Wanted a doctor, she did."

"Miss Rebecca?" Birch asked. "That's all you remember of her name?"

"Aye! And that I learned only because that was the name the sick woman kept calling her. We happened to have another passenger, a doctor he was, and I went in with him to see the unfortunate woman." The old sailor shook his head. "The lass had no chance. She was sick from the birthing. He bled her, but 'twas no use. By then, everything was in the Lord's hands."

"Did she tell you anything before she died? Anything about the infant? To whom he should be sent?"

The sailor shook his head again. "She knew there was no hope, and the whole time we were there, she was clutching Miss Rebecca's hand, she was. Any fool could see the arrangements had all been settled between the two women."

Birch watched the sailor's weathered face as he relit his pipe. "What else? What can you tell me about this Rebecca?"

"Afraid the barrel's empty, sir. I had a ship to sail, I did, and she had a baby to keep. Saw nary a glimpse of the lass for the rest of the trip. When we dropped anchor in New York, the woman went ashore with all the rest of the passengers, and I ne'er saw her again."

Frustration poked at Birch's insides. "But there must have been something else. Think, man. Did she make any friends while she was aboard? Talk to anyone?"

The sailor shook his head. "Don't believe so. She was grieving at the death of her friend, I should think. I believe everyone left the lass to herself."

"Try to recollect," Birch pressed, changing direction. "Was there anything about her that made an impression on you? Perhaps something that she might have left behind—a locket, a handkerchief— anything that might have given you a hint about her real name."

"That was a long time ago." The man's gray eyes narrowed to slits as he considered. "She was a pretty lass, as I recall, with hair the color of gold and fire. She had eyes that matched the blue of the sea off of Bermuda, she did. Aye, she's a woman I'll not forget . . . unless I'd be mixing her with that barmaid at the Pelican Inn at Port Royale. But nay, I wouldn't be doing that."

Birch stood up in defeat and walked toward the open door. Of anyone on the *Rose*, his greatest hope had rested with the ship's master.

Looking out beyond the worn path leading from the cottage, the lawyer could see cobbled streets snaking down past old stone houses and shops. As his gaze drifted vacantly to the numerous masts of ships anchored in the bay, Birch carefully tallied again the sailors who had been on that ship and were now living in Bristol. Three. Not much to hope for. Nonetheless, he would ride to the city and search out those men. One of them might have learned something about this Rebecca. It was impossible for her not to have left behind some hint of her history.

"Ye are paying good money to hear facts, ye are, sir. I don't suppose ye'd be interested in gossip I heard some time later."

Birch turned sharply. "There could be gold in gossip, as well, sir."

"She struck me as a right good woman."

"I am well aware of her virtues," Sir Oliver said a little snappishly.

"Ye know her?"

"Never mind that, sir. I am paying you for answers."

The sailor's eyes narrowed for a long moment while he puffed on his pipe. Finally he nodded in understanding. "As ye say, Sir Oliver. 'Twas not till the next summer, and we were anchored in the Thames off Limehouse that I heard the rumors just by chance."

It was difficult to be calm, but Birch waited.

"The word was that a month or so after we'd weighed anchor for the colonies, a gentleman was making the rounds of every ship's company, dock, and tavern from the Tower to Dugby's Hole. Offering gold, he was, and questioning every sailor, mate, and ship's master he could lay hold of. This gentleman was looking for a certain woman."

"How do you know there was any connection to your passengers?"

"The description fit her. Hair. Eyes. Age. Build."

"Any names?"

"Aye! The first name was the same, too. Rebecca . . . Rebecca something."

"Do you remember anything of the last name?"

"N . . . something. Nipper . . . or Netter . . . or . . ." He shook his head. "Names don't stay the way faces do."

"Why didn't you go and find the gentleman and offer what you knew?"

The man shrugged. "Too much trouble, perhaps. Don't know. Maybe I didn't see the need at the time. Made a good living by the sea, and my pockets had coin enough in 'em." His gaze narrowed. "Besides, I recall it seemed to me then that if the lass wants to go to the colonies and start o'er . . . then what gives some old sailor the right to spoil her plans?"

"How about the gentleman's name? What did you hear about him?"

The next shrug only served to frustrate Oliver more than the last one. "I'll be no help to ye there, either. I told ye, I never talked to the man. All of it might've been just gossip for all I can tell. I judged ye to be curious enough to hear all of it."

Birch walked to the table by the window. Reaching into his pocket, he started to add to the money he'd already put there. Pausing, he held the coins over the others.

"You said the gentleman spoke to a number of people in London. Can you tell me the names of anyone who might still be there? Men who are not already dead or at sea for most of the year? A tavern keeper, perhaps?"

The shipmaster's keen gaze shifted from the coins to the lawyer's face. "I reckon that's something I can help ye with."

Chapter 14

Jamey stopped in the path and looked up into the faces of the approaching horse and rider. The chestnut-colored stallion was a magnificent animal, though the earl sitting atop his back was obviously the master. Lord Stanmore had changed out of his wet clothing, the young boy realized, watching the dappled sunlight filtering through the leaves of the trees play on the short black coat that matched the rider's breeches and topboots.

He stared into the man's face to gauge his lordship's temper. His mother hadn't had to warn him when he had come out of the lake earlier. Though, in a way, Jamey had wanted to impress the earl with how well he could swim, it took only one look at his mother's face for him to know that Lord Stanmore was not too happy about coming in after him. Well, no one had asked his lordship to dive in after him!

Those thoughts aside, Jamey wondered if he was in for the kind of beating that someone had meted out to Israel. If that was the way things were done here, it would take only one beating to send him packing. And he wouldn't stop at the cottage, either. He'd walk back to Bristol, if need be, and sign on as a cabin boy on the next ship sailing.

One look at the earl's indifferent gaze, though, and he knew the man didn't care enough for him even to get angry, never mind beat him.

"Your shirt and shoes are missing."

The words were a statement and nothing more. Stanmore reined in the horse beside Jamey. Rather than watching the man, the boy's attention was focused on the horse's black eye as it rolled toward him. With great interest, Jamey watched the flicker of the animal's ear. He couldn't help himself but to extend a hesitant hand and touch the top of the horse's nose and then his neck.

"Do you like horses?"

Jamey didn't say anything, because he'd made a pact with himself to answer nothing the earl asked him.

"Perhaps you'd enjoy riding one, yourself. I can have one of the grooms find a gentle pony. You can begin learning anytime you like."

He really wanted to ride. He really . . . really wanted to learn how to ride a pony. No, he thought, he wanted to ride a horse as big and beautiful as this one. He stroked the powerful neck of the steed. He was softer than velvet. But again, his own vow kept him from showing any enthusiasm. He might be only nine years old, but it wasn't too difficult to figure things out. As soon as his mama thought Jamey was getting along here, she would disappear from his life, forever. Of that, he was certain.

The horse pawed the ground impatiently, and Jamey stepped back, only to find the earl's hand extended toward him.

"Come, I'll give you a ride back to Solgrave."

He could have walked back to the house on his bare feet and without any help from his lordship, but he'd really liked the feel of the horse under him the other night when he'd ridden to the house, mounted behind the earl. Jamey looked for a way to climb up on the horse's back without accepting Lord Stanmore's help, but there wasn't one. He took the proffered hand and fairly flew off the ground, landing gently on the animal's back.

The earl half turned in his saddle. "From now on, you will tell someone at the house when you decide to disappear for a few hours. You may think you are quite the independent lad, but Mrs. Ford has been worrying about you for too long, now, to change her ways so quickly."

Jamey said nothing in response, but he did feel a pang of guilt that his mama had been troubled. She had always been agreeable when he and the Butler boys went off together in Philadelphia. Perhaps he just needed to make her see that there was far less trouble that he could get into here at Solgrave. Maybe if he were to tell her about Israel. He thought about that for a moment, deciding in the end that he couldn't. He'd promised his new friend that he would say nothing to anybody about him.

The man and the boy rode back to Solgrave in silence. As the chestnut stallion cantered easily along forest trails and over rolling meadows, Jamey's mind drifted back to the little cottage in the woods and how defeated his friend Israel had been. It hurt him to see how sad Israel had been . . . and how fearful.

There was something very wrong on the neighboring estate, and Jamey wondered if there was anyone at Solgrave who could help him to help his friend. Maybe he couldn't avenge the beating Israel had taken, but somehow the evil ways of Melbury Hall had to change.

And he needed to find the person who could make a difference.

The cup and saucer hit the wall with a violent crash. Another sweep of an arm, and the table was nearly laid bare—with puffs, powders, patches, and one practically new prayer book flying across the dressing room. The crumpled letter bounced against the mirror and dropped harmlessly onto the table.

"Is his messenger still downstairs?"

The serving girl took a step back toward the door and shook her head. "Nay, m'lady. This was delivered early this morning."

As Lady Nisdale's hand reached for the heavy jewelry box of tortoise shell and ivory, the young woman hastily escaped her lady's dressing chamber. A moment later, the sound of the box splintering the wood of the door echoed through the entire second story of the town house.

"*Bastard!*" Louisa screamed, pouncing on the letter and tearing it to pieces.

Her rage cried out for release, and nothing was safe in her path of destruction. A robe of sheer silk lying at the foot of the bed was ripped in two. Heavy bottles of perfumes adorning the high chest joined the jewelry box at the base of the door. Too angry to hesitate, too frustrated to think, she tore through the chamber, upsetting tables and chairs, laying waste to everything within reach until she finally faltered breathlessly by the window, clinging to the heavy drapes, flushed and spent. She sank onto the edge of an overturned sofa.

"I *had* you, you bastard!" she cried. "You were mine."

Louisa stared down at the shreds of the message littering the floor. So impersonal. So businesslike. The very thought made her ill. She hated to lose. The thought of the money she had stood to gain was bad enough. She had invested her time in the blackguard, and time was a precious commodity to any woman of her age. She had schemed. She had waited. She had done everything that was sure to win him over for good. And here she was—despite all of her efforts—discarded like a pair of soiled gloves.

Defeat hung in the chamber like a suffocating cloud, but Louisa stood up, forcing herself to think.

The mantel clock that had escaped her wrath had not ticked a dozen times before the thought came to her with brilliant clarity . . . there was another woman! There *had* to be! Someone had *stolen* what was hers. What else could it be?

This she knew how to deal with.

The room was a shambles, but Louisa strode through it with the air of some conquering war goddess. She paused before the mirror and admired her own reflection. Despite the disappointment, her eyes were sparkling, her skin smooth and fresh, her cheeks blooming with color.

"Let him have his tumble with the whore," she whispered haughtily to the reflection in the mirror. "But he will be mine once I rid myself of the bitch."

Louisa moved to the door and yanked it open, scattering glass and jewelry across the floor. In the corridor, her call rang with excitement. She actually smiled a moment later when the fearful face of the servant appeared on the stairway. Turning on her heel, she preceded the young woman into the dressing room and stopped by the window.

"Clean this mess, you little mouse! But before that, fetch Dore to pack my trunks. And send a footman to hire a carriage."

"You are going on a trip, m'lady?" the young woman asked fearfully, dropping a small curtsy.

"I am," Louisa answered, kicking aside a pillow as she made her way to the wardrobe. "I have decided to accept a long-standing invitation from an old friend to visit Melbury Hall."

As the servant started backing out the door, Louisa stopped her again. "And one more thing."

"Aye, m'lady?"

"I received no letter from the Earl of Stanmore today."

The woman's confusion showed on her face.

"Must I spell everything out, you dolt? Listen, then!" She glared across the room. "I left for Squire Wentworth's estate. Have you got that? And in the chaos of my departure, you stupidly forgot to deliver the letter to me."

The servant blinked and looked down at the shredded pieces of paper on the rug.

"Do you understand?" Louisa said menacingly.

"Aye, m'lady. You . . . you never received the letter."

The morning sun bathed the meadows rising above the lake on yet another day of spring's finest weather. Rebecca looked out her window at the morning sky, crystal clear and blue as a robin's egg. She sighed deeply and brushed away an errant tear.

As she had done the day before, Rebecca sent down word this morning that she was still a trifle unwell. It was a feeble enough excuse, but one that had succeeded in sending Jamey downstairs for the past two nights to dine alone with his father. The Earl of Stanmore was making an effort to spend time with his son, and the best thing she could do—she was quite certain—was just the opposite of what his lordship had requested. She had to keep her distance, stop her meddling, and allow a bond to form between father and son.

Even if it hurt her to do so.

"Bear up," she whispered, chiding herself for her selfishness. The earl obviously knew more about raising a boy than she had given him credit for. Jamey had been perfectly fine when he'd finally returned to Solgrave with his father two days ago, and Rebecca had been the one who had looked like a fool for being concerned about nothing.

Giving him up to this new world—a world in which she would play no role—was proving to be extremely difficult, for Jamey had been Rebecca's sole purpose in life for so many years. But she knew she must, and she firmly intended to unwind the reins of authority from her hands. He was Lord Stanmore's responsibility now . . . as he should be. The bright colors of the landscape outside her window blurred momentarily as they had done so often for the past few days.

There was nothing like a day spent in solitude, though, to force a person to seek answers. There were so many questions that pulled at her. More uncertainties than Jamey's relationship with his father distracted her, gnawed at her. Rebecca still didn't know the true cause of Elizabeth's flight with her baby. What was it in her marriage, in this man, that had driven her away so many years ago?

No one mentioned her name. There were no portraits of her in the gallery of family likenesses. In spite of being the only wife of the Earl of Stanmore and the mother of the future earl, she was more like a vapor that had drifted in on a breeze, only to disappear as quickly as she had come. It was as if she had never existed.

And if that were not distressing enough, Rebecca's own attraction to Stanmore was driving her insane. The memory of his kiss lingered, making sleep impossible and causing her to daydream like a fool in her waking hours.

But she could not go on like this.

Rebecca knew what she must do. First of all, she must assume a more appropriate position in the activities of the household. From the first moment of her arrival—despite the plain and worn clothing, despite the fact that she was a common working woman from the colonies—everyone at Solgrave had treated her like gentry, and she had allowed it. This, however, was a mistake that she would soon set to rights. Though she was not employed by his lordship, in rank and social status she was no higher than his servants. Guest or not, she would have Mrs. Trent move her to a less conspicuous room—nearer the servants' wing, perhaps. Then it would be easier for all of them to accept things as they really were. And she could begin to think of a way of repaying the earl for all of these new clothes.

Determined on her course of action, Rebecca left her room and set off down the corridor toward the narrow stairs that led to the kitchens and the servants' wing.

She had seen Jamey early, before he'd gone downstairs for breakfast this morning. He would be spending the rest of the morning and part of the afternoon with Mr. Clarke. Everything would work out better, she thought, if she could move from her room while the lad was occupied with his lessons.

She was halfway down the backstairs, though, when she saw a young serving woman carrying a silver tray upstairs. The servant's surprise showed on her face before she could avert her eyes.

"Mrs. Ford." The girl gave a small curtsy before looking up at her. "Mrs. Trent was told that you were still unwell, ma'am, so she sent me up with some tea and toast for you, if that suits you. If you don't mind me asking, are you feeling better, ma'am?"

"I am, thank you. I can take this now." Rebecca took the tray out of the woman's hands. "I was a little tired yesterday, but I feel much better this morning."

"Then perhaps you might like to have breakfast in the dining room. The earl is a very early riser—up and gone, he is—but Master James and Mr. Clarke are still—"

"Not this morning, Ellen. It is Ellen, isn't it?"

The girl gave another curtsy and smiled slightly. "Aye, ma'am."

"Has Mrs. Trent taken her own breakfast, yet?"

"She has, ma'am, hours ago. But I saw her talking to Daniel in the servants' hall not too long ago. Would you like me to fetch her for you?"

Rebecca glanced down the stairs. "I have a better idea. Why don't you lead the way, and maybe I can have my breakfast there while I'll speak with Mrs. Trent."

"With us serv . . . ?" A deep blush colored Ellen's freckled face. "If that's what you wish, ma'am."

There were at least a dozen people talking and having their morning meal at the long table in the servants' hall. But all conversation ceased the moment Rebecca entered the room. Everyone's gaze focused on the doorway, spoons and knives forgotten in their hands as she nodded tentatively at them. Instantly, everyone stood up.

Feeling the awkwardness of the moment, Rebecca clutched the silver tray in her hand and searched the room for familiar faces. There were many she knew, but they all simply stood in complete silence.

"Mrs. Ford thought she'd take her breakfast in the . . . here instead of in the dining room. She was . . . Mrs. Ford was looking for Mrs. Trent." Ellen's explanation only made the faces look more incredulous.

A sudden thought sprang up in Rebecca's mind that perhaps there was nowhere that she belonged at Solgrave. She was ready to back out the door when Daniel, followed by a taller and older-looking man, entered the servants' hall from another door.

"Why, Mrs. Ford! How wonderful to see you!" The steward approached, his greeting so enthusiastic that Rebecca felt the weight partially lift from her shoulders. "We're so pleased that you are feeling better. Please, ma'am, allow me."

He took the tray and handed it to the young serving woman.

"Ellen, take this . . . and tell the cook to send a fresh pot of tea to the library."

As soon as the girl ran off, Daniel lowered his voice and spoke in a confidential tone, "I hope there is no problem that required your presence in this wing? If there is anything that we have done that has failed to please you—"

"Not at all, Daniel. I needed to speak with Mrs. Trent on a matter of little importance. Other than that, however, I felt it is wise to allow Mr. Clarke and James to start their lessons this morning with no distraction from me."

"I understand, ma'am. If you so desire, I will tell her to meet you in the library. His lordship told me expressly to see that you are made to feel comfortable there. The view of the lake is absolutely stunning with the morning light, if I may say so. And between the books in his lordship's collection and newspapers that are sent down from London, perhaps—"

"I am truly feeling quite well," she assured the steward with a smile. "There is nothing that I need, Daniel."

"I am delighted to hear that, ma'am. I would be honored to escort you." He gestured with a bow toward the door through which he had entered.

Rebecca knew that Daniel was trying to tell her, in the gentlest of tones, that her status at Solgrave would be no less than that of a proper guest of Lord Stanmore, and her brow creased. This presented an unforeseen obstacle to her plan.

"I don't mean to be a burden. Perhaps I should wait in my room, and—"

"If I may speak bluntly, ma'am," the steward said encouragingly, ignoring the older man behind him who cleared his throat in obvious disapproval. "If I may be so bold as to say, ma'am, your company was sorely missed yesterday. Your presence would be very comforting for Master James . . . and for his lordship himself, I might add . . . if you are well enough to be about, today. May I?"

Rebecca didn't know what to say to the determined steward. So she nodded. Clearly, her only chance of making a change lay with Mrs. Trent. As she started to follow, though, she hesitated at the tall man standing behind Daniel.

"Ah! Mrs. Ford. Please forgive me. Allow me to introduce Philip, his lordship's steward in London."

At his deep bow, Rebecca nodded gently. Beneath his powdered wig, the man's face bore no expression whatsoever. Seeing the two men standing shoulder to shoulder, she recalled overhearing a conversation between a servant and a gardener outside her window yesterday. Something about "Daniel's granite-faced old tyrant of a brother."

"Why, I have heard something about Philip!" she said in pleasant tones, meeting the older man's unchanging gaze. "You must be Daniel's twin brother."

Chapter 15

M rs. Trent patted her on the hand and shook her head.

"I am afraid that is quite out of the question, my dear."

Frustration washed down Rebecca's back. The housekeeper had, at first, looked genuinely distressed when she expressed her wish to change rooms. The older woman's expression had quickly softened into looks of affection, though, as Rebecca had tried to explain. The refusal might be gentle, but it was definite.

"But Mrs. Trent, I have explained to you that the bedchamber I now occupy should be reserved for visitors of . . . of quality."

"Quality? Posh! A fine dress does not make someone 'quality,' dear. And I can tell you from years of experience that a title does not ensure quality either. Quality is a gift from the Lord above. And you have it. So let us not speak any more of this."

"But Mrs. Trent . . . I am no one of any account. I sincerely believe that if I were to move to quarters that were more appropriate—"

"Hush! Just hush that kind of talk, dear. I have lived in service here at Solgrave my entire life. I have seen all manner of highborn lords and ladies come and go through those front doors. I am speaking for everyone when I say you have more quality in one little finger than many of . . ." She stopped and took Rebecca's hand. "Nay, my dear. We'll just leave things be, I should think."

"Mrs. Trent . . ."

"Why, just look at how those of us in service are acting. My, dear, I never thought I'd live to see the day when Philip and Daniel would agree on a thing without a quarrel." The woman's round face broke into a broad grin. "'Tis true! On my way up here, I was stopped by Philip, only to have him remind me that I shouldn't be keeping you waiting. Now, mind you, this from Philip! Why, the man has never shown such . . . well, enthusiasm in all the time I've known him."

"That doesn't count," Rebecca argued, crossing the library to one of the large windows. "I happened to charm him by saying I thought he and Daniel were twins. Philip might be partial to me now, but Daniel will likely never speak to me again."

"Posh! Daniel lies awake thinking of ways we can better serve you." The heavyset woman started pouring tea into a cup. "It has been a long time since we've had a real lady here at Solgrave to care for. Now come and sit and forget about all this nonsense of moving anywhere."

"Mrs. Trent, I am in the way," Rebecca persisted. "I have the best of intentions, but as long as I am around them, I find myself trespassing into areas where I should no longer . . . where I have no right to be trespassing."

"I should think ten years of raising the lad on your own—and as well as you have in that land of Quakers and other barbarians— gives you every right, my dear! Could we sit here together for a moment or two?"

Rebecca stared at the cup of tea the housekeeper was holding to her. She had no choice but move away from her perch at the window and join Mrs. Trent.

"And don't start talking so soon of leaving, either, as it hasn't even been a week since you've arrived and that lad still needs you . . . as is only natural, to my way of thinking."

Rebecca felt her stomach lurch at the mere mention of the words. She was so far from ready to part with Jamey. Though things were progressing as she'd hoped, she still harbored unanswered questions about Lord Stanmore's past, and undiminished concerns about Jamey's future. Beyond that, she couldn't even bear to think about her own feelings or the empty life that awaited her back in America.

"But don't think you need to be looking over Master James's shoulder all the time. Between Mr. Clarke and the rest of us, he'll be closely tended. Still, you need to stay close enough for the young master to see that all is well."

Rebecca sipped the tea, but said nothing.

"I know this is the country, and not much seems to go on here. You might have enjoyed yourself more if the earl had arranged for you to spend some time in London, to my thinking, but—"

"I have no desire to go to London. I insisted that we come here."

Mrs. Trent gave her an approving smile. "Well, if you know where to look, there is plenty to do here at Solgrave. Why, the gallery has paintings that folks have come from nearly every capital on the Continent to view. And as you can see, his lordship has a fine library. And the countryside hereabouts has some very fine walks. Why, there is even a point where his lordship's mother had a seat erected at the base of an ancient oak. The view the spot commands is lovely, my dear, truly lovely. And if you ride, the paths through the park's woods are quite invigorating, they tell me, though I've never been a rider myself. And Knebworth Village, such as it is, lies not far from us. But of course, this Sunday after church, his lordship will surely be introducing you to some of the neighboring gentry. Aye, my dear, you'll see for yourself, we have much to recommend us here in the country."

"Oh, I don't doubt that in the slightest, Mrs. Trent. It's just that I . . . well, I am not accustomed to a life of such . . . well, leisurely activity." Rebecca knew this was another part of her problem. She knew that such enforced idleness would soon give way to fanciful thinking and dreaming, occupations she had no right to engage in. "Is there anything that I could *do* in the village?"

"*Do,* my dear? You mean work?" Mrs. Trent's eyes rounded in shock at the mere suggestion.

"Well, something constructive with which I might occupy my time," Rebecca replied hopefully. "Everything here at Solgrave is taken care of. Under Daniel's and your stewardship, the manor operates so efficiently. With James to spend most of his days with Mr. Clarke, I thought if there were a school for girls nearby, perhaps, that might have need for a tutor. Or a minister who knows of some charity work that needs doing."

The housekeeper's curious gaze softened, and she reached and placed her warm hand over Rebecca's. "You *are* precious. Wait until I tell this to Daniel and—"

"Oh, please don't!" she interrupted at once. "My intentions are to be of some use to someone else and to give myself some distance from Jamey's daily activities. The last thing I need now is people thinking of me as something more than I am."

The housekeeper tapped her on the knee. "Say what you will, my dear, but others around here know already what a good heart you have."

"Thank you," Rebecca murmured softly, taking a sip of tea to hide her blushing face. She was not very good with praise, especially when it was as lacking in foundation as this. "So is there anyone I could go and see, Mrs. Trent? Anyone at Knebworth Village?"

She placed the cup back on the saucer and waited patiently as the housekeeper gave her question some thought.

"As a matter of fact, there are two people in the village who I know for certain will jump at your offer of help. But before I go into that, there is something that you should know about our village." The housekeeper paused and poured more tea into Rebecca's cup. "The village stands on land that is part of Solgrave, and all the people living there are tenants of his lordship. But for the past eight years—since the father fell ill and the son took charge—there has been no collection of rents."

The Earl of Stanmore is a very generous man, Rebecca thought. A frown creased her brow at the realization that every day she was finding more things that she liked about the peer.

"His lordship has never held with the idea that a tradition needs to be preserved—if folks are suffering because of it. The village is self-supporting, between its farming and the tradesmen there, and the Stanmore wealth can easily do without what his lordship might be collecting from his tenants." Mrs. Trent cast a quick glance at the direction of the portrait hanging above the hearth. Rebecca followed her gaze, taking in the depiction of an older man. "I must be truthful with you, my dear, our Samuel Wakefield spent little enough time in the company of his father, and it was a good thing, too. Bless him, his lordship's father could not easily be called a generous soul. But I only tell you this so that you'll understand the esteem the village folk have for the master. And for the most part, if they think they are offering you something that might incur his lordship's displeasure, well . . ." She shook her head doubtfully.

Samuel Wakefield, the Earl of Stanmore. Rebecca recalled the first mention of the name as she'd faced Sir Oliver in the doorway to her rooms in Philadelphia. She looked about the spacious library. Her gaze was drawn once again to the formidable demeanor of the father looking down at them.

"Now where was I?"

Rebecca returned her attention to the woman sitting before her. "You were going to recommend some people in the village to me."

"Aye. The Reverend Mr. Trimble . . . and Mr. Cunningham. The first is the rector at the church, and the second is the schoolmaster for our little schoolhouse." Mrs. Trent held up a hand. "But before you ask why Mr. Cunningham wasn't asked to come and tutor Master James, I should tell you that the schoolmaster is quite busy enough with his duties about the area. He and Reverend Trimble have formed a partnership, of sorts, to poke their heads in wherever there's a need. And that is why I have to warn you . . . between the two of them, you might not find a moment's rest left to you. So you have to be specific in your asking. You are looking for something *little* to do. You don't want to spend your days at their beck and call. You—"

"I believe I'll take a walk down to the village this morning." Rebecca put the cup and saucer down. She was already feeling better about everything. This was exactly what she needed—a distraction and some distance from Solgrave . . . and its master.

"I'll have Daniel arrange for a carriage to be brought around."

Rebecca rose to her feet. "I prefer to walk, Mrs. Trent. I'd like to get a feel for the distances. May I use your name in way of introduction?"

"You will be needing no introduction, my dear. The village has been buzzing since you and the young master arrived. Everyone has been quite eager just to catch a glimpse of you." Mrs. Trent walked with her to the door. "I believe you will like Knebworth Village and its people. They are kindly, industrious folk, my dear—very much like yourself, if I may say so."

*   *   *

The path through wood and meadow that led to the village was peaceful and comforting, the quiet broken only by the twittering of the birds and the rustle of leaves as small, woodland creatures scattered at Rebecca's approach.

The stillness of the forest was one of the few things that she had missed while living in the midst of the hustle and bustle of a growing city like Philadelphia. Not really missed, she thought, for she had been too preoccupied with Jamey and with the demands of their everyday life to waste her time missing anything. But here at Solgrave, with each step that she took, there were reminiscences of her childhood walks in the fields and parks around Oxford that kept pushing their way into her head. Bittersweet memories of schoolmates who had traveled those paths with her. Friends now cut off from her by years and society . . . and the spilled blood of a villainous rake.

And with those memories, doubts she had carried since she was a girl burst to the surface. Doubts and fears she had pushed from her thoughts, questions to which she'd never sought answers. Walking toward Knebworth Village, Rebecca now found herself unable to dismiss them.

She tried to consider the discussion she'd had earlier with Mrs. Trent. The housekeeper had said such sweet things to her, even if they weren't true. It wasn't the first time she had been confused with something she was not. Even in Philadelphia, those whom she had known and worked with had always treated her as gentility. True, she had never been really accepted as one of them, but instead respected and treated as someone above.

Her friend Molly's words came back to her, comments about Rebecca's learning and wit. And even before that, when she'd first met Lady Hartington, her employer had been most impressed with the "certain something" that the new tutor possessed. That, added to the respected reputation of Mrs. Stockdale's Academy for Girls, Mary Hartington had considered Rebecca an excellent choice for her three children.

A sudden breeze pushed Rebecca's straw hat a-kilter, and she caught the end of the ribbons and removed it from her head. The feel of the spring air and the warm sun was heavenly on her face.

The person she was, and the incorrect assumptions people made about her background, was of course solely due to Mrs. Stockdale and the years Rebecca had spent at her school. There were so many things that she'd learned in that exclusive place. True, some of them were so frivolous for someone of her position in life that she'd never openly admit to them. Riding to hounds, the importance of grace and submissiveness in a lady's manner, the planning of parties—from afternoon tea to a proper ball—the proper steps to the "acceptable" forms of dancing, how to reply when addressed in terms of courtship by young men both superior and inferior in station. What use would Rebecca Neville ever have for such knowledge? What use would Rebecca Ford have for such foolishness?

How she had been able to afford the tuition of the fine school was in itself a mystery that she had long taken for granted. She had many times been told about the barrister whom she assumed was her benefactor. But Mrs. Stockdale's school was attended by the offspring of earls and barons, by the most eligible daughters of English society. She could still remember the fine carriages that rolled away each spring toward genteel homes in London and Bath and Bristol, homes she could only imagine. Etched in her mind, also, were the images of the carts of trunks filled with stylish new clothing that arrived each fall.

And she was Jenny Greene's daughter. At least, those were Sir Charles Hartington's words. They were burned into her brain. And with them, the memory of assault and murder and her own wild flight into the darkness. She tried not to think of that accursed night. Instead, she forced herself to focus on the only name she'd ever been given about her parentage . . . Jenny Greene.

She knew the name Jenny Greene. Everyone in England knew Jenny Greene. Once the darling of the London theater, she had held the hearts of both princes and paupers in her hand. Jenny Greene had led a life that was notorious for its freedom, a life that was seemingly above society's censure . . . for a while, at least. Rebecca flushed at the thought that this might be her mother.

But why, she wondered now, would the actress go to the tremendous expense of sending her daughter to such a place? Why would she never contact her in all the years that followed? This morning, while waiting for Mrs. Trent in Lord Stanmore's library, Rebecca had absently paged through a recent issue of the London newspaper, the *Daily Advertiser*. When she had found herself scanning the list of the plays being presented in the city's various theaters, she'd realized with a start that her true object had been to find a name. Jenny Greene's name. She did not even know if the woman—no, her mother—was still alive.

Rebecca paused at the crest of a hill and lifted her face to the caressing breeze. The view of the valley before her was breathtaking. Framed by the green edge of the forest, the meadows and pastureland rolled downward to a gently meandering river and Knebworth, a tidy little village snugly nestled within a patchwork quilt of farms. She turned and glanced behind her. Only the very top of Solgrave was visible from here. When winter had stripped these trees of their leaves, she mused, what a welcome sight those chimneys and sturdy walls would offer a cold and weary traveler.

"Not that you will ever see it, Rebecca Neville," she murmured.

Drawing a deep breath, she turned her back and started down the slope toward the village. Tucking loose strands of hair behind an ear, she was attempting to put the straw hat back on when the sound of an approaching rider made her step to the side of the path. An instant later, from around a bend of the trees, she saw the horse and rider come into view. Her treacherous heart beat faster at the sight of him.

"Mrs. Ford!" Lord Stanmore's surprise was evident in his voice, but Rebecca tried to focus on the broad chest of the prancing steed, rather than stare at the man who was controlling him. "Pray, don't tell me James has disappeared again."

"No, m'lord." She didn't have to look up to know he was mocking her. Tired of struggling with the hat and the wind, she pulled it off again and held the ribbons tightly in one hand.

"A very pretty hat, ma'am."

"Thank you. Since James is hard at his lessons, and the morning is so pleasant, I decided to take a walk to the village." She glanced at him as he dismounted from the gray hunter, frowning at the butterflies in her stomach.

"May I join you?"

She stretched a hand in the direction of Solgrave, then pointed in the opposite direction. "You surely . . . but you must be . . . really, I can find the way." She sounded worse than Mr. Clarke at his most halting moments.

He patted his steed on the nose and looked expectantly at her. "Would you mind very much if I joined you?"

His gentle tone drew her gaze. Looking into the silvery depths of his black eyes, she realized that she might just be incapable of denying him anything. Good Lord, she thought, panic washing through her,

"No, I don't mind," she heard herself say.

They started down the path toward the village in silence. Where the path wound through a grove of trees, the quiet of the woods was more pronounced than before. Rebecca glanced at the discreet space the earl kept between them as his horse clopped along behind. She wasn't afraid of him, Rebecca told herself. It was herself. Her panic admittedly stemmed from the sensations that he'd produced in her, memories he'd awakened in her. So vivid were those memories! Those were things that she'd tried so hard to forget. She stole a quick glance in his direction and found him staring straight ahead. He appeared to have accepted her words that the whole incident had been a mistake.

If she could only make herself believe it.

"It was distressing to hear that you had taken ill. I hope you are feeling better."

"I am sorry to have caused your lordship any concern." Rebecca twisted the ends of the hat's ribbons around her fingers and looked down at an abandoned stone quarry that suddenly opened up at the left of the path. She decided to speak the truth. "There was nothing the matter with me. But after giving some thought to your earlier observations, I found myself in agreement with you regarding the excessive and unnecessary protectiveness I feel for Ja . . . for your son."

"I see. You agree with me, and then you set out to punish us by staying away?"

"Punish?" Surprised, she cast a sideways glance at him and then focused on the path. "No, m'lord. I was applauding your judgment. I am trying to give James some distance so that he can adjust more readily to the new faces in his life."

"My dear Mrs. Ford, I know you don't consider me an expert in child rearing—and with good reason, of course—but from what you've just said, I think you know even *less* than I do."

She turned on him sharply. "Are you trying to be hurtful, m'lord?"

"Hardly! But I would suggest that you stop trying to force a bond to form between James and myself." His tone was gentle. "You were the one who advised me of the necessity of giving James time. I agree! He needs time. And I need time, as well."

"Aye, time to spend together. But this is what I am trying to give you."

He shook his head. "Deprived of your presence, we have had the most uncomfortable of dinners for two nights running." He stared straight ahead for a moment before turning to her. "James refuses to say a word or even look up from his food for the entire evening. His manners are fairly unexceptional, by the way. My compliments."

"Thank you."

"But his intractable silence hardly improves anything." He paused. "Not that Mr. Clarke noticed, of course. I made the grave error of asking him to stay to dinner last night. The man talked endlessly. I managed to maintain a polite facade. My years in the House of Lords have taught me to appear interested, even when my thoughts are drawn to . . . well, to more interesting people."

He fixed his gaze on her, and she fought to ignore the heat radiating in her belly.

"If you mean me, m'lord, I must protest strenuously that I am hardly 'interesting' and would have added nothing to the dinner conversation. In fact, I am quite certain that you would not have considered my presence any improvement."

"I disagree." His dark eyes smiled at her, and Rebecca found herself growing quite warm under his attentions. "Your presence might have silenced the tutor and would certainly have washed some of the gloom off James's face. Now, as far as my own response to your company . . . I think you know that I would have been honored to have you with us."

The path took them out of the woods and into the bright sunshine of the meadow. At the bottom of the hill, the village bustled with activity. Sanctuary, she thought.

"We are . . . almost there." She placed the hat on top of her head and again made an attempt to tie the ribbons in the face of the rising breeze.

"Allow me!"

The gentle touch of his hand on her elbow froze her. Holding the hat in place with one hand, she found herself helpless as he turned her around until she was facing him. She stared at the broad expanse of his chest, at the collar of white and the cravat showing beneath the black riding coat. She dared herself to look up at the firm, full lips to the dark eyes that were studying every flaw in her face.

Unhurriedly, he tied the ribbons at her throat. When he was finished, though, he did not release the ends of the ribbons. The horse's reins lay on the ground, and she felt the brush of his fingers scorching her skin as he pushed the hair out of her face.

"I envy the wind."

Startled, she swallowed the knot of fear in her throat as his head lowered. Torn between the desire to run and the even stronger desire to feel his mouth against hers once again, she stood rooted to the ground and closed her eyes.

The brush of his lips was gentle—but heat shot through her, firing her blood and reducing her bones to molten wax. Her hands were fisted for a moment, but then fluttered open against his chest. The desire sizzled in the narrow space between them and Rebecca's lips parted as the pressure of his mouth became more persistent. Their tongues danced, and suddenly, starved for more of this torturous heat, she rose onto her toes and wrapped her arms tightly around his neck.

A groan of pleasure sounded somewhere deep in his throat, and Stanmore's hands became eager as they pressed her to him so hard so there was not a breath of distance left between their bodies. She would have been perfectly willing to remain molded against his body, but he abruptly ended the kiss.

He drew back from her, and she forced open her eyes, even though she could not force herself to breathe. He touched her lips with his fingers.

"I shan't rush you again," he said, his voice husky and dark. "We have all the time in the world."

Chapter 16

As they approached Knebworth Village, Rebecca felt as if a thick fog had swept in around her. As if in a dream, she could almost see herself walking, one foot placed squarely in front of the other, the sun shining above, the breezes sending rippling waves through the sea of green around her. And yet, she could hardly feel her own body.

Only when they reached the first of the cottages nestled against the hill, did her senses begin to respond. The smell of the spring earth registered in her brain. The sound of a dog barking beyond the small market square. The constant *shush* of the river flowing through the triad of stone arches that supported an ancient bridge. The fog suddenly cleared, giving way to a nervous, sharp-edged clarity.

The same discreet distance as before separated them, and she threw a quick glance at him. His face showed nothing, and his eyes were fixed on the village ahead of them. One might think they were just two casual acquaintances whose paths had joined a moment earlier.

With only that momentary look, though, turbulent sensations in Rebecca's body and mind suddenly erupted into full-fledged gale. Fear and desire clashed in a tumultuous and primordial battle. She wanted to touch her own lips and feel where he had touched her last. And then she wondered how she would be able to recall the taste of his lips and recollect their soft texture during the eternity of longing that was to begin so soon.

So soon? she thought, looking at the roses spilling over a garden wall. The intensity of her feelings totally bewildered her. How did this happen? As they walked, she could feel the power of his presence beside her; she could feel herself being pulled toward him. It was as if a taut flaming cord had formed between them, tugging at the very center of her. And this thrilled her as much as it terrified her. After all, how could she—a woman who had always shunned such feelings—ever have fallen so hard and so quickly?

Rebecca knew what she was feeling. She was not a child. It had taken great effort to restrain her emotions after the kiss. It was taking even a greater effort to walk at his side and not look at him again, for she also knew that she must keep up some pretense of indifference. But how could she do that? she wondered desperately. When he turned his keen gaze upon her face, she knew he was reading her thoughts, peering into her very soul.

This was a dangerous game, and it was one that the Earl of Stanmore was clearly a master of. His look, his words, his touch . . . he was playing with her, body and soul. It was a mortal game where no surface was solid, no edge firm. Reach out to steady herself as she may, her grasp only found clouds and mists that dissipated, slipping through her fingers. It was a game so complicated that she knew she would surely drown in it.

But the irony of it all was that she knew her only salvation lay, along with her damnation, in the same forbidden touch. His touch. And she could not help herself. She did not want to help herself, it seemed.

His deep voice scattered her thoughts. "It is not Philadelphia, I'm sure, but welcome to our little village." He gestured ahead. "We boast a number of shops situated along the lane here. Knebworth is a fairly active country village, as far as country villages go . . . particularly on market days. And we have a church—that you can see just there—that dates back to Alfred the Great, as well."

"I was hoping to meet the rector . . . and perhaps the schoolmaster, as well." She looked past his coat, staring at the green hedge lining the lane.

"The schoolhouse is the second to last building at the far end of the village. The rectory lies up the hill from the church. You can see it there . . . it is the one with the slate roof and the new stable near it."

She glanced in the direction that he was indicating. "Thank you, m'lord. I had no intention of detaining you. Mrs. Trent gave me detailed directions. I can find the way."

Obviously ignoring the opportunity that she was offering him and leaving her, he glanced at a group of very young children playing a noisy game in the front yard of a cottage they were passing. "I know that Mr. Cunningham, our schoolmaster, is generally occupied during the day. I would be happy to introduce you another day. It will be my pleasure to escort you to the rectory, however."

Rebecca whispered her words of gratitude as he led the way down the village street. It was a lovely and busy village. The cobbler could be seen in his front window, hunched intently over his work. The Black Swan, a large half-timbered inn, boasted a garden with fruit trees and arbors of wisteria covered with the pale lavender flowers. In the yard of Stafford's livery stable, a number of well-appointed carts and curricles, and even a new four-wheeled phaeton, could be seen. Noting her interest, Lord Stanmore informed her that Mr. Stafford's brother built carriages.

As they walked along, a number of the inhabitants came out to exchange pleasantries and to be introduced. No one seemed to be at all concerned with formality here. In the market square, a carter greeted them loudly, and the earl made certain to stop by the man's wagon and introduce Rebecca and then ask about the man's family. A baker and his wife hurried out amid a cloud of flour dust, spiced mince pies in hand as gifts for the lord.

Beyond the square-steepled stone church, Lord Stanmore led her up a narrow lane. Stopping at the new stable, he handed his reins over to a cheerful young groom, and the two ascended a path past a tidy garden of vegetables and flowers to the door of the rectory.

"The good rector's curricle is not in evidence at his stable, and Reverend Trimble has been known to make a visit or two around the parish in the mornings. So you may not have the opportunity of speaking with him, either. Nonetheless, Mrs. Trimble, the rector's wife, is rather fond of company. I'm quite certain she will be eager to receive you."

As they waited for the door to be opened, Rebecca secretly

watched his handsome profile as he gazed thoughtfully into the garden.

"I pray you will forgive me, Mrs. Ford, but I will be leaving you in Mrs. Trimble's care for a while. I am afraid there are a few other matters that I need to see to this morning."

"There is hardly reason to apologize, m'lord. I can find my way back to Solgrave. I very much appreciate what you have done already."

"May I call back for you before noon?"

She found herself captured by his dark and inquiring eyes. "Well, I don't know . . . I have already troubled you far more than I should. Truly, I . . ."

"Since you don't mind, then, I shall return for you just before noon." As the door was opened, Stanmore smiled broadly into the face of a surprised servant, who hurriedly curtsied and pulled the door open wide. As the girl turned to lead them into the parlor, the earl's words were a whisper against her ear. "You do me great honor in allowing me the pleasure of your company twice in one day, Rebecca."

Taking her by the arm, Lord Stanmore led her to a sunny, pleasant room where a very tall and friendly looking woman rose to greet them.

As they were introduced, however, all Rebecca could do was to pray that her own flushed cheek would be attributed to the walk and not to the attentions of her escort.

Mrs. Trimble walked with a pronounced limp, but the older woman's lively wit and warm hospitality seemed to indicate that the rector's wife possessed a spirit undaunted by any personal affliction.

After introducing the two women, Lord Stanmore excused himself, and Rebecca and Mrs. Trimble sat together, their conversation punctuated by the pleasant sounds of birds singing in a cherry tree just outside the open windows.

Tea was brought into them in the parlor and, after some pleasantries about the weather and the village, Rebecca found herself completely at ease with the woman. There were no prying questions. Nothing asked about Rebecca's life in Philadelphia. No nosy queries about her past, or about Jamey's upbringing. As she sat sipping her tea, she realized that no one she'd met since her arrival at Solgrave had questioned her on these topics. And with very little prompting, Mrs. Trimble chatted easily about her life with the Oxford-educated Irishman, and about the eight years they had spent at the old village church. At one point, however, she paused with a slight frown clouding her face.

"Now, when my husband was offered this living at Knebworth Village so many years ago, he didn't hesitate to accept the position. He had met his lordship—that is, the present earl—while the previous Lord Stanmore was in his declining years. Reverend Trimble has always been genuinely impressed with his lordship's stand on the politics of our time." Mrs. Trimble leaned toward Rebecca and lowered her voice confidentially. "So you can imagine the distress my husband experienced when the neighboring manor came into the possession of Squire Wentworth during our third year in Knebworth. The changes at Melbury Hall were immediate and not for the better, let me tell you, in spite of the efforts of my husband and Mr. Cunningham, the schoolmaster."

Rebecca listened intently.

"Growing up in that troubled land of Ireland as he did, my husband has never been a man who could turn a blind eye to such conditions. And he has never been one, Lord bless him, to seek favor with other gentlemen at the expense of the downtrodden . . . at Melbury Hall or anywhere else!"

"Are the people openly mistreated there?"

Mrs. Trimble got up and placed her teacup on a sideboard. Rebecca could see from her movements that the woman's knee was quite stiff.

"Conditions were ghastly from the beginning. I've heard Reverend Trimble and Mr. Cunningham place blame for much of it on the succession of hard men that Squire Wentworth has employed to oversee the management of the manor and the farms. But the problem runs deeper. The squire keeps Africans as slaves, you know."

"I didn't know."

"Many of us know it to be a barbaric practice, but Squire Wentworth believes he has the model estate for the modern gentleman farmer."

"And Lord Stanmore stands with you on the issue?"

"Well, of course! He is a strong advocate in Parliament for abolition. And here in Hertfordshire, he has been very persuasive with his fellow landowners. Samuel Wakefield is a force to reckon with when it comes to such unfairness."

"Is he?"

"He and the squire have had a number of heated discussions, I'm told, about the keeping of slaves. Of course, the squire is not a man to defy Lord Stanmore openly . . . at least, not in so many words. I believe he envies his lordship's influence in society too much to make him an enemy. But no one thinks there is any love lost between the two men."

"Are conditions still so bad?"

"I believe Lady Wentworth has tried to do what she can. At least, I'd like to think so, but . . . well, those poor people are still kept like cattle!" Mrs. Trimble sat down again beside Rebecca. "Though she is good-hearted and far different from her husband, Lady Wentworth is a timid thing. Unfortunately, she also prefers to spend most of her time in London. Reverend Trimble and Mr. Cunningham have taken on the plight of those poor people as their personal mission, but there is only so much that they can do."

No matter how improved their lives might be and how kind the squire's wife was, Rebecca agreed that slavery was abominable and cruel by its very nature.

"May I ask if there is a way that I might assist Reverend Trimble in his efforts at Melbury Hall?"

Mrs. Trimble took Rebecca's free hand in hers. "Of course, Mrs. Ford! Both my husband and Mr. Cunningham could use your help in a dozen ways."

"Mr. Cunningham appears to be a great help to your husband."

"Indeed he is. As fine a young Scotsman as you'll ever meet." The woman gestured toward her own knee. "But more help is always welcome. Since my carriage accident, my assistance has been limited to what I can do around the rectory. Going as far as Melbury Hall is a little beyond me, I'm afraid."

"You clearly do so much. There is an aura of such beauty and happiness surrounding your home. Your house, the gardens . . . they all do you credit." Rebecca cast an admiring eye around the room. She turned her attention back to her hostess and was greeted with an appreciative smile. "But can you think of some specific way that I can be of some use? You see, I don't honestly know how long I shall be at Solgrave."

The woman nodded with understanding. "Thus far, the squire has not dared to try to disallow Reverend Trimble's visits to Melbury Hall. You could accompany him and check on the health of those living there. Mr. Cunningham has been trying to teach a little reading and writing, but the schoolmaster's presence there has been . . . well, only grudgingly allowed by the squire. If you have any aptitude for teaching, I know they would appreciate any help you could give them in—"

"I'd be *very* willing," Rebecca said, feeling her spirits rise. "Perhaps you could appoint a time that I should return to meet with your husband."

"Even better, Mrs. Ford, I'll make certain to have Reverend Trimble stop out and visit you at Solgrave tomorrow morning." Her hostess pursed her lips thoughtfully. "But perhaps we should arrange a meeting with Lady Wentworth first. Mr. Cunningham mentioned to us last evening that she has come down from London earlier than expected. Apparently, an acquaintance of hers—or her husband's—will be visiting at Melbury Hall. Expected to arrive last night, in fact."

"Whatever you think best, Mrs. Trimble," Rebecca murmured, glancing at the ornate clock above the hearth. There was still half an hour left to noon and her heart had already begun to drum along pleasantly at the prospect of Lord Stanmore's return.

"Now, the King's Birthday is less than a fortnight away," Mrs. Trimble continued, "and I would assume that Lady Wentworth will remain at Melbury Hall at least until then. I will see to it that my husband makes the arrangements for the two of you to meet."

Delighted with the thought of being useful again, Rebecca was starting to ask the rector's wife about the village school when the sound of voices drifting up the garden path and through the open windows drew her hostess to her feet.

"Well, how wonderful! They are already here."

Rebecca stood, as well, and joined Mrs. Trimble by the window.

"I'll introduce you when they come in, but here is Reverend Trimble accompanied by Lady Wentworth. The other lady must be the guest they were expecting from London."

Reverend Trimble was shorter in stature than his wife, but he had the same lean build. Rebecca's gaze traveled to the fashionably dressed woman standing at the rector's side and making some remarks about the gardens. Her deportment showed her to be a woman accustomed to command. The wide brim of her high, plumed hat hid the upper part of her face, but the golden curls framing the firm chin, the perfect nose, and the red full lips bespoke the finest of English gentility.

"Lady Wentworth is a great beauty," Rebecca said softly to her hostess.

"Lady Wentw . . . ? Oh no! That would be their guest." Mrs. Trimble nodded toward a woman crouching over a flower a little down the path, half hidden behind the full skirts of the guest. "There she is . . . behind the others."

Rebecca tried to look past the rector, but other than a tip of a parasol and the pale yellow of her skirts, there was not much more of Lady Wentworth that she could see. At that moment, however, the rector turned to usher the ladies up the path and noticed the presence of his wife at the window.

At the sound of his cheerful greeting, Lady Wentworth and her guest looked up, and Rebecca's blood ran cold in her veins.

Chapter 17

Feeling her knees ready to buckle under her, Rebecca reached for the sideboard and took a wobbly step backward. Horror washed through her as she watched the new arrivals climb the path to the house. She glanced desperately at the door, thinking there might still be time to escape.

It was too late. Even if she ran, they would surely hunt her down. She stood still and waited for her fate. Through the window, she could see Lady Wentworth, the former Miss Millicent Gregory—a friend and fellow schoolmate at Mrs. Stockdale's Academy for Girls in Oxford—climb the step to the front door.

Too late, Rebecca swore silently, as the deep voice of the rector sounded in the foyer, ushering his guests toward the parlor. She continued to back away until her legs came in contact with the cushioned chaise. She forced down the bile rising in her throat and stared at her hostess as she made her way toward the door.

"I am so delighted that you are here. Welcome, Lady Wentworth."

The two women entered the room first, and Rebecca half listened to Reverend Trimble's introduction of the visitor to his wife. Suddenly, he was standing in front of her, though, presenting himself to her.

His voice was kindly, and his handshake warm and friendly, but during the entire exchange, Rebecca hardly looked at him, hardly looked up from the floor. As the cleric moved away, though, she hazarded a quick look at Lady Wentworth, who was standing with Mrs. Trimble and the beautiful visitor.

Despite her own distress at being in the same room with an old friend, what she found strangely upsetting was the pale and dispirited vision that Millicent presented. Though never a beauty, in the years that Rebecca had known her, the young woman's cheerfulness and lively personality always managed to distinguish her from so many of the others. Now, however, she seemed to be nothing more than a pale, insipid shell of what she had been.

The visitor, on the other hand, was holding forth with Mrs. Trimble, completely comfortable in her position as the center of attention. After a moment, the hostess turned and gestured toward Rebecca.

"Lady Wentworth, may I present to you Mrs. Ford. Mrs. Ford is at Solgrave, the home of Lord Stanmore. Mrs. Ford, this is the Lady Wentworth of Melbury Hall of whom we were speaking earlier."

"Only kind things, I hope, my dear," Reverend Trimble joked, his deep laugh filling the room.

Rebecca froze as Millicent's indifferent gaze drifted upward to her face. She could feel the knot in her throat choking her as she accepted the gloved hand of the other woman.

"Mrs. Ford." Immediate recollection brought a spark into the pale depths of her gray eyes, and Rebecca desperately clutched the other woman's hand, applying slight pressure. A wan smile appeared on Lady Wentworth's face. "Rebecca! Well, I must say I am genuinely delighted to see you again . . . Mrs. Ford, did you say?"

"Again? How delightful! I had no idea you two were acquainted already!"

Mrs. Trimble's exclamation drew the curious gazes of the other occupants of the room, causing Rebecca to blush deeply as she continued to hold on to Millicent's hand.

"Surely, you must have me confused with someone else, Lady Wentworth," she said desperately, sending a pleading glance in the direction of her old friend. "True, my given name is Rebecca, but this is my first trip to England . . . so unless you were in the colonies . . . I don't know where the two of us could have met."

There was a moment of confusion in the other woman's face, but somehow Rebecca's consternation must have registered, for Millicent gave an understanding nod and withdrew her gloved hand.

"I must apologize for such an impetuous response. You do remind me of someone I once knew. But that was so many years ago, and my recollection is increasingly vague, I fear."

"How curious that *your* given name should be Rebecca, as well, Mrs. Ford."

Rebecca's gaze was drawn to the other woman in the room. She was dressed rather ostentatiously in a velvet walking dress of deep blue, a matching blue jacket, and blue hat with blue feathers. Her face and figure were truly beautiful, but her eyes were as cold as ice.

Mrs. Trimble saved Rebecca from answering by making the introduction first. "Lady Nisdale is a guest at Melbury Hall. She came down from London yesterday, I understand. Lady Nisdale, please allow me to present Mrs. Ford."

Rebecca accepted another gloved hand.

"But you are a Rebecca, as well?"

The chill in the voice, the superior manner, turned Rebecca's earlier fears into annoyance. She gave the other woman a cool smile before withdrawing her hand.

"A coincidence, I admit, but my name is fairly common,"

"Quite common," the haughty woman said with an ironic look. "And your stay at Solgrave? Have you taken a position there?"

Mrs. Trimble let out a gasp of surprise, and a flash of temper rose in Millicent's eyes as she stared reprovingly at Lady Nisdale. The rector was all too willing to offer an explanation and ease the tension in the room.

"Mrs. Ford is Lord Stanmore's guest, m'lady. She has had charge of Master James, the earl's son, for the past ten years."

"Ah, I see. A governess."

"No, m'lady," Rebecca answered quietly. "I am a guest."

Though she said nothing further, Lady Nisdale made little effort to hide the mocking look she now directed at Rebecca.

"Won't you sit down, ladies?" Mrs. Trimble offered brightly, calling for a tray of fresh tea to be brought in.

As Lady Nisdale ensconced herself in a chair by the doorway, Rebecca took a seat on the edge of the chaise and glanced discreetly in the direction of her old friend. She had to find a time, somehow, to meet privately with Millicent. They had been friends once, but she could not rely on that. She only hoped Lady Wentworth's compassion was the same as young Millicent Gregory's had been so long ago. Glancing at her now, though, Rebecca felt an uneasiness settle into the pit of her stomach, for the languid look she had observed through the window had once again taken possession of her old friend's demeanor.

"Mrs. Ford has come by today not just to pay us a visit, Reverend Trimble, but also to volunteer her time," Mrs. Trimble spoke cheerfully to her husband and directed a bright smile at Rebecca. "We were just trying to sort out some of the particulars when you arrived."

"Well, thank you, Mrs. Ford. Thank you, indeed." The rector bowed gratefully. "Between Lady Wentworth's plans to grace our neighborhood with her presence longer than we normally enjoy at this time of year, and your offer of assistance, there is so much that we can plan to accomplish this summer. Why, I can hardly wait to tell all of this to Mr. Cunningham. He will—"

"You *must* tell Lord Stanmore about our meeting here today, Mrs. Ford," Lady Nisdale commanded, cutting off the rector's animated speech. "For now that I have come down to this charming little corner of Hertfordshire, his lordship will surely wish to extend his own stay in the country . . . to show me around personally."

Hot jealousy flared unexpectedly in Rebecca's chest as she watched this stylish member of London's *ton* shake the blond curls so artfully arranged around her face.

"Are you acquainted with his lordship, then?"

An arched eyebrow above Lady Nisdale's haughty eye answered Mrs. Trimble's innocent question.

"Acquainted is an understatement, my dear lady. Stanmore and I have been close . . . very close friends for a long, long time. In fact"—she pouted in the direction of Lady Wentworth—"before you even think of any charity work, Millicent, you promised me a ball. One can see at a glance that life is far too quiet here. We shall need to create an occasion where I can wear at least one of the dresses I have brought along."

Without waiting for a response, she turned her attention to Rebecca.

"Being in charge of his lordship's son, it is too sad that you cannot attend a ball, Mrs. Ford. But then again, you are probably relieved of it. Dressing appropriately for such a fine occasion would be terrifying, don't you think?"

Without allowing anyone to put a word in edgewise, Lady Nisdale turned again to Lady Wentworth. "Now, Millicent, you know I would help you with the preparations if Stanmore would just spare me a moment, but knowing how demanding his lordship will be once he learns I am here . . ."

The words hung in the air as a servant entered the room.

"His lordship, the Earl of Stanmore."

Rebecca's eyes fixed on the tall dark figure filling the door. His demeanor was unreadable, and his gaze was fixed on Mrs. Trimble. She wondered, though, how much he had heard of Lady Nisdale's words.

Reverend Trimble immediately jumped to his feet in greeting as the peer crossed the floor to the rector and his wife. And as the two made a fuss over his arrival, Lady Nisdale sat in her chair, an impudent smile on her face. Disgusted, Rebecca stood and moved casually toward the window.

Lady Wentworth immediately joined Rebecca by the open window. They both stared at the flowerbeds stretching in the yard. "My husband and his guest practice city hours, Mrs. Ford. I, however, am quite fond of morning rides. Would you care to ride with me . . . say, tomorrow morning?"

Rebecca recalled that she had told Lord Stanmore that she would not be riding, but the situation demanded that she take up Millicent on her offer. She doubted very much that the earl's grooms would deny her a horse if she were to request one.

She met her old friend's gaze. "I would very much enjoy a ride with you, m'lady. If it is not too inconvenient for you, though, could we make it very early?"

"I am delighted. The earlier the better. I shall ride over to Solgrave stables shortly after dawn. My husband insists that I have my groom accompany me, but we shall have ample opportunity to talk and . . . get to know one another a little . . . as we ride."

"I shall be ready."

With a small nod, Lady Wentworth turned to the room and the company.

An odd sense of relief flowed through Rebecca with the thought that not everything she recalled of her younger years had been false. Millicent was at least giving her a chance. Rebecca looked across the room in time to see Lord Stanmore excuse himself abruptly from the company of the Trimbles. As he crossed the room, his gaze held hers.

"Mrs. Ford. I hope you forgive me for being late."

The intensely dark eyes searched and caressed every inch of her face, and Rebecca had difficulty keeping calm.

"You are not late at all, m'lord," she finally managed to whisper.

"Lady Wentworth." Stanmore bowed politely to Millicent.

Out of curiosity more than jealousy, Rebecca cast a fleeting look at Lady Nisdale and found the woman's pretty face showing signs of temper. The artificial smile she managed to maintain in light of still not being acknowledged by the earl appeared to be starting to slip, however.

She wanted to admonish herself for her vanity in being approached by Lord Stanmore first, but the emotion she was feeling at the moment was far too satisfying to allow it. Later, she thought. I will chastise myself later.

His eyes were fixed upon her face. "I have just explained to Mrs. Trimble that we cannot stay for the luncheon she has so graciously offered . . . as we have a previous engagement. I hope you haven't already made a liar out of me." He extended an arm to her. "So if you are ready, we shall be on our way."

She was more than ready, though still a little uncomfortable that a woman like Lady Nisdale could bring out such an immediate aversion in her. As Rebecca accepted the proffered arm, she noted the surprised look on her hostess's face. Mrs. Trimble, with a quick look at the aristocratic lady, clearly understood that the earl intended to leave without even acknowledging Lady Nisdale. Her husband, however, stepped forward.

"I suppose there is no need to make an introduction, m'lord. Lady Nisdale has informed us of your . . . er, close and abiding friendship."

Rebecca could have sworn she detected a note of amusement—perhaps even satisfaction—in the rector's tone. It appeared that she was not the only one to notice that, in spite of all her proud claims, Lady Nisdale was receiving nothing more than indifference from Lord Stanmore.

"London may seem to be the center of the world, Reverend," Stanmore announced coolly, "but it can also be a very small place. Lady Nisdale is, no doubt, acquainted with nearly *all* of the *ton*."

Without another word, the earl bowed to his hosts and calmly escorted Rebecca from the house.

The sun seemed brighter outside, the spring air fresher, and the flowers far more beautiful than she remembered them being as she had entered the rectory. As they reached the end of the garden path, Rebecca was surprised to see a handsome new phaeton awaiting them with a groom wearing the Stanmore livery at the head of a fine-looking pair of bays.

"But your horse, m'lord."

"Back at Solgrave." He held her hand to assist her in climbing up onto the high seat of the carriage. As she seated herself, Rebecca looked intently at the horses, trying not to think of just how easily he had handed her up. He climbed into the carriage and took the reins in his hands. I hope you don't mind the imposition, but I have with me a basket luncheon that I simply cannot finish on my own. I was hoping you wouldn't mind helping me with it."

Mind? By heaven, regardless of the fiery panic that ignited in her at the mere touch of his hand, she found herself more than desirous of his attention . . . his presence. But such an answer would never do, and Rebecca struggled to find a response.

"But . . . but what of the previous engagement you mentioned to Mrs. Trimble?"

"That was with you," he said simply, giving her a devilish half-smile and flicking the reins. "So will you do me the honor of having luncheon with me, Mrs. Ford?"

"The honor is mine, m'lord," she answered quietly as the groom swung up behind them.

As the carriage pulled away from the rectory, Rebecca looked up past the gardens and saw Lady Nisdale looking at the carriage through one of the large open windows of the parlor.

Beautiful she was . . . and elegant . . . and angry enough to spit fire.

The walls were lined with cream-colored silk spotted with age and mildew. The window seats were piled high with cushions of deeply faded velvet of a color that may once have been rose. The wool stuffing peeked out from more than a few edges. The carpet, worn and faded as well, sat askew on warped floorboards that had seen nothing other than neglect for many years.

The visitor stood stiffly in the parlor, sniffing at the smell of stale flowers and dust and damp soot. Dressed in a fine suit newly delivered from Oxford Street, he could not bring himself to sit on anything in the room. He glanced once at the heavy drapery that effectively excluded any ray of sunlight, and idly wondered who had been sitting on England's throne when they had been bought and hung. The miser's fire that struggled to stay lit in the old-fashioned fireplace flickered, but cast little light and no warmth. Why bother, he thought with a surly twitch of his lips.

He turned to the door as the sound of muttered words drifted into the room. A pregnant hush followed, like the moment before the curtain rises, and then in swept the rather unsteady figure of the once celebrated Jenny Greene.

It had been nearly ten years since they had last met face-to-face, but the passage of time had etched thrice the years on the woman's face, obvious in spite of the paint and the rouge. He frowned at the consequences of the excessive amounts of gin and revelry that were so much part of the life of the aging actress.

A cold look bordering on a snarl was all that the man received in return. But he'd expected no different a greeting.

"I was certain my servant had misread the calling card."

He offered no explanations and remained silent until Jenny turned and sank heavily into one of the parlor chairs. The eyes that had once bewitched every man now were puffy and lined. Even the blue seemed to have lost its luster. The distrust in them, however, was readily apparent.

"I assume this is not a social call," she spat out.

He consciously chose to ignore her abruptness and her vulgar refusal to address him with the respect that his title and position called for. He would not allow her to anger him at all, and even succeeded in coaxing his lips into a smile.

"Or perhaps . . . this *is* a social call," she said, misinterpreting his response. The fingers of her quavering hand traced a path over the curves of her ivory breasts above the neckline of her dress.

It was difficult not to be distracted by the gesture. Fading though she might be, Jenny Greene still possessed much of the sexual allure that had made her one of the most passionate actresses ever to grace the London stage. When she wished to use it, she still could wield that power. He knew she was a woman who could make her body seethe with sensuality . . . when she wanted to. The voluptuous body, the stormy eyes, the red hair—now powdered, piled high, and wrapped in a turban—had once attracted the attention of every man in London, and the admiration of every woman.

"Why, now that I think of it, this *does* have all the signs of a secret rendezvous! Arriving in a hired coach . . . no liveried footman or grooms . . . such an air of secrecy! It makes my heart flutter!"

"I am here because of Rebecca." He watched with satisfaction as his statement succeeded in draining the color out of the woman's face. "I wish to know if she has been in touch with you."

The pale hand moved from her breast to a glass sitting on a small table beside the chair. The glass, however, was empty. She held it for a moment and then set it down again. Her face was tightly controlled in an attempt to show nothing of her thoughts. She was truly an actress, he thought.

"The child has been dead for years. How could she possibly be in touch with me?"

"Unless you know something that you never shared with us, madam, we have never assumed her to be dead . . . simply missing."

From her chair, she reached around for the bell pull, but could not find it immediately. "I need a drink."

He saw Jenny try to push herself up and turn in her chair, but a hand slipped and she sank back weakly. A trembling hand covered her eyes. It was barely noon, and she was already drunk. Or still drunk, he thought with disgust.

"Mrs. Greene, does the name Ford mean anything to you?"

She glanced at him without answering, and again tried to reach the bell pull, succeeding this time. She sat back in the pose of a queen on her throne, frowning, her hands curled over the ends of the armrests.

"Why? What is the meaning of all these questions? What makes you think she is alive? And . . . and what is it to me if she is?"

The visitor stared at her for a moment. It had been useless to come here. Jenny Greene was as callously indifferent as ever, and as self-absorbed.

"I am having your house watched. If she comes to see you, madam, you will tell us."

A servant appeared at the door, and Jenny ordered the woman to bring a drink.

He turned to leave.

"She is nothing to me. Never has been." Her words caused him to stop and turn. "But tell me what you know. I've helped you before. I'll help you now."

"Very well. Someone has been making inquiries about a certain Rebecca Ford. My people have strong suspicions that the object of this search is no one but your long-lost daughter, Rebecca Neville. We will not let her disappear again." He paused and stared at the aging actress. "This time, I intend to find her."

Chapter 18

The phaeton rolled along paths lined on either side with gray-trunked beeches, knobby oaks, and chestnuts. They moved comfortably through sun and shadow, and Stanmore showed Rebecca the farms beyond the village. As he pointed them out, she asked him about the crops and the workers, and he explained with pride the progress they'd made over the years. He told her what Solgrave itself meant to his people.

He was to some extent surprised by her intelligence and interest, but he was genuinely impressed by her ability to keep their conversation on such neutral terms. There had been no personal questions. No mention of Louisa Nisdale's name. No overt display of interest in finding out the truth behind whatever it was Louisa had been saying about their liaison.

Unlike any other woman that Stanmore had spent time with in his life, Rebecca Ford appeared to have a nature that focused on affairs outside of her own desires. Indeed, she seemed to make every attempt to redirect attention—particularly his attention—away from herself.

But this honest and refreshing attitude only made him respect her more, he thought, casting a quick glance at her bright, lively profile.

He pulled off the lane and stopped his horses in a protected spot by a running stream where a patch of sunlight bathed the ground and the old beech leaves would lie warm and dry on the grass. Jumping down as his groom ran to the head of the team, Stanmore helped Rebecca out of the carriage before taking the basket down.

"By the way, when I went back to Solgrave, I looked in on Mr. Clarke. So you needn't worry about hurrying back."

"Lord Stanmore, you know I have promised not to worry about James."

"I thought your promise was not to *show* me that you worry about James."

"As you say, m'lord." Her smile was prettier than sunshine as she took a blanket from beneath the seat of the carriage and stretched it on the grass.

After instructing the groom to walk the carriage up the lane and into a field around the next bend in the river, he turned back to his companion.

"Mr. Clarke is planning to spend a little extra time with James this afternoon," he said. "And after the lad is done with his lessons, Daniel is going to have one of the grooms take him around to the stables, so he can choose a pony. He might even be given a first lesson today, if he so chooses."

The look she gave him was filled with tenderness, and Stanmore was once again touched by how much Rebecca's emotions depended upon James's well-being. Another unconscious display of the selflessness so often lacking in the people of his set. Of a nobility that stemmed from the purity of one's heart, rather than one's station.

"Jamey . . . James will be delighted with that, m'lord. He has always been fond of the horses, but living in Philadelphia, he's never had a chance to learn to ride."

As he placed the picnic basket on the blanket, she sat down beside it and lifted the cloth covering.

"Have you always lived in Philadelphia?" He sat down on the blanket as well.

"For the most part," she murmured as her eyes searched the contents of the basket.

"Where else have you lived?"

"I stayed for some time in New York."

Stanmore knew he wasn't offering Rebecca the same courtesy that she had shown to him in asking nothing of his past, but her evasiveness only served to stimulate his curiosity more.

"Was your husband from Philadelphia?"

"No." Her answer, almost too quick, surprised him. He eyed the blush rising into her cheeks. She bent her head over the basket until the brim of her hat robbed him of the pleasure of watching the rose bloom in the ivory of her skin. All he could see were the full lips, the perfectly shaped chin.

"Where was he from?"

She took the napery, silverware, and the plates out, setting them aside. "John Ford was from England."

With an impatient move, she undid the ribbons beneath her chin and laid the hat beside her on the blanket.

"From England, did you say?"

"You could never have known him, m'lord. He was a commoner. No position, no kin, nothing." Her eyes were that stormy shade of dark blue when they met his. "That is quite often the case with people of my station, you know. Many have been forced to flee their homeland and go far away to make something of themselves in the world, to find what is precious within them."

She turned her face a little, but the sadness in Rebecca's expression struck Stanmore deep in the chest. His hand reached out uncontrollably and cupped her chin.

"Some people are precious wherever they are." Stanmore leaned over the basket and brushed his lips over hers. At that moment, the power of the affection he felt toward her startled him.

He sat back and released her.

Rebecca averted her eyes, but sat for a long moment as if stunned, and then reached up with hesitant fingers and touched her lips. He wondered how long it had been since any other man had kissed those lips.

"We'd better think about eating this food, or I shan't be held responsible for my actions." Stanmore tried to lighten the moment.

Composing herself quickly, she smiled and reached inside the basket. Taking out pieces of roasted chicken and fruits and cakes and pies wrapped carefully in cloths, she laid them on the blanket.

"I can see your cook Harry's influence," she said. "There is enough food here to feed us for a week."

"And what a pleasant week that would be—just the two of us beside this brook."

She unwrapped a piece of chicken and took a bite. "Based on what I have heard Mrs. Trent and Daniel say of your lordship's schedule, I have difficulty imagining you would be satisfied for so long a period of time with so little to do."

"I have been known to steal a little time for myself, here and there—like this fortnight that I plan to spend here at Solgrave." He thought for a moment, adding as an afterthought, "True, there is less to do here than in London, but I am not speaking of social engagements, since I've never been fond of them."

"But your stay here could be considered work, as well. Valuable work!" She used a napkin to wipe the corner of her mouth. "You are here to spend time with your son."

She could believe what she wanted, he thought, watching the play of the breeze in her hair. He removed his jacket and put it aside. "I am not as casual about my responsibilities as many others in my position, but there are times when I long to get away, to leave everything totally, completely behind. Away from those who know me, away where there is no formality and none of the responsibilities that haunt me every hour of the day."

She pushed the food away and leaned on her hand, watching him. "And is there such a place of escape?"

"There is!" He smiled at her. "I go there for a month every fall. Have you ever been to Scotland, Rebecca?"

She shook her head, and he watched the tendrils of gold and fire dance around her face. She rubbed one cheek gently on the shoulder of her dress as she continued to lean on one hand. "I've heard it is a beautiful land."

He moved the basket aside and stretched out on the blanket, propping his head on his hand. "It is a wild land . . . a place of ancient untamed gods where, beneath a windswept sky of blue, mountain streams tear through black crags into tumbled glens of oak and pine. On rock-studded braes that seem never to have borne man's footstep, bracken and heather battle for a place. Above lochs that have no bottom, ice-covered peaks gleam in the sun one moment, only to disappear in storm clouds the next."

The enchantment was revealed in her warm smile. "You love Scotland."

"I don't believe in love." He trapped her hand beneath his on the warm blanket. She didn't try to withdraw. "But I very much believe in passion."

She remained silent, a thoughtful expression clouding her face.

"What do *you* believe in, Rebecca?"

She took her time to answer. "I believe in love. I have seen it in the eyes of a little boy resting in my arms. It has comforted me. It has given me peace." Blue eyes looked searchingly into his face. "But the other terrifies me."

"Why?"

"Because it is forbidden."

"By whom?"

"By me!" she said softly. "I cannot allow myself to feel something that cannot be controlled, something untamable and . . . and violent."

His fingers caressed the top of her hand, and he saw a shiver ripple across her skin and a blush color her cheeks, "Did you never feel passion for your husband, Rebecca?"

She turned her face away.

"Did you never experience the ecstasy of the marriage bed? The soaring sensations, the coming apart that passion brings?" He could feel the wild beat of the pulse in her wrist. She refused to answer, though. "There is intense pleasure that comes with losing control. There is indescribable peace that follows the violence of such unbridled passion."

Stanmore's fingers left the warm fingers and moved up her arm, touching the soft fabric of the dress, caressing,

"Did your husband not know where to touch you?" His fingers reached the exposed skin of her neck above the linen shawl around her shoulders, and he saw her close her eyes as he traced the beautiful column of her neck. "Did he never make you burn with that inner fire only the passionate lover can know?"

Her face turned to him. He held her gaze as his hand moved down and gently caressed one of her breasts through the dress. A surprised gasp escaped her lips, and his hand moved even lower, rubbed the fabric against her flat stomach.

"Did he never pleasure you? Cherish you? Touch you here?"

His hand moved lower. Her cheeks were flushed. Her blue eyes open and aware. She did not push his hand away.

"Did he never learn your secrets and master your fantasies?" His hand moved on top of hers again.

"Tell me what you feel now, Rebecca?"

She swallowed hard, and he pulled her gently down next to him.

"But this is all wrong!"

"Is it?" he whispered soothingly.

"But we shouldn't. You are—"

He cut off her complaint with a brush of his lips, and she answered the kiss. As he drew back slightly, her mouth followed, kissing him and firing his desire. He rolled a little, his leg pressing against her thigh. His hands slipped around her, pressing her softly against him, encouraging her. She continued to kiss him, and he didn't think she even realized it when he rolled them on the blanket until she was on top of him.

Slender fingers dug into his hair as Rebecca raised her face. Her lips brushed against his before continuing a journey of discovery across his cheek, his ear, his neck. Uncertain fingers moved down his chest, feeling the curves of muscle beneath the shirt. She shifted her weight, and suddenly Stanmore felt his control starting to slip. Rolling her over, he trapped her beneath his body, his arms around her.

He felt every muscle in her body go taut, and he shifted his weight to the side, leaning on an elbow. Her face was flushed, her eyes stormy, but there was fear there, too.

"Do you feel it?" he said huskily. "Do you feel the need of your body? The need of mine? This is passion!"

A tear welling in the blue eyes brought a great tightness into his own chest. He cupped her face with a large hand and stopped her from turning her face away.

"What is wrong? What are you afraid of?"

Sparkling beads of moisture escaped the corners of her eyes, disappearing into the golden hairline at her temples. He kissed away one tear and then another. Pulling back, he looked into her eyes again.

"Talk to me, Rebecca."

She closed her eyes, but the tears continued to flow. He rolled to his side and pulled her tightly into his embrace, caressing her back, gently kissing her forehead, her cheek soothing her as he'd never soothed another woman in his life. He found himself caring for her as he'd never cared for another person in his life. It was some time before she spoke again.

"I am not . . . I am not who you think I am!"

"Your insipid wife is being incredibly tight-lipped about this Ford woman!"

Squire Wentworth ignored her as his fingers hurried to undo the laces on the back of Louisa's fashionable French stays.

"Careful!" she chided as his strong pull pressed the stiff cane into her delicate flesh. "Just call one of the maids."

"Nay." His lips were already on the bare skin of her shoulders. "I couldn't bear to stay away another minute. Why didn't you let me in last night, hussy?"

"I was far too tired," Louisa said lazily, leaning her head back against him. "And don't you dare complain about this morning, either. Just because your wife chooses to leave your bed before the lark sings, I don't see why I must take you in."

"Leave *my* bed? I've told you the little fool doesn't share my bed." As Wentworth helped her shrug out of the corset, Louisa enjoyed the tingling in her breasts as his fingers lifted them and stroked the nipples through the thin chemise. The squire's own clothes lay in piles around the bedchamber, and he rubbed his exposed sex against her buttocks through the silk fabric. "You belong in my bedchamber . . . not here."

"You are a fool, Wentworth," she said with a laugh. "And what would your wife and your servants think of your guest taking up residence in the master's bedchamber? Oh, the scandal!"

He squeezed her breasts and bit on the side of her neck. "Scandal? You didn't care what anybody thought for all the time you came to me at my London town house."

"But that was different. When you lured me there . . ."

"Lured?"

". . . lured me from my poor late husband's bed, I might add, you were not married to this silly chit. And later . . . well, later your wife was never there."

"Such absurd shyness is not becoming, Louisa, in such a woman of the world."

One of his hands slid downward over her belly, and he cupped her mound roughly through the thin layer of white flowered silk, causing her to gasp.

"Discretion was certainly a secondary concern during the three years that you were married to that old goat Nisdale. If I recall, he would not give you what I was giving you." He squeezed hard, and she reached back one hand to grasp his powdered hair. "You openly enjoyed what I gave you—the money, the clothes . . . aye, even the rough and dirty tumble, now and again, eh?"

"I don't care to talk of that now, you disgusting ape."

He grinned as he lifted his head off her shoulder, pulling his hair out of her grip. "Aye, disgusting. And that's why you came down to Hertfordshire, did you not? You are here to be with me!"

Louisa decided that the question did not merit an answer, but smiled slyly over her shoulder. Kicking the corset away, she freed herself of the squire's grasp and moved toward the mirror standing by the window. Watching her own reflection, she slowly peeled off the thin silk chemise.

"I give you credit, Wentworth. Lately, it seems you have established a reputation among the ladies of the *ton* for your . . . well, unusual sexual preferences. Most of them are quite unsure whether they should be afraid of you or throw themselves at you. Quite the sensation, I should say." Her breasts were perfection, Louisa thought as she stared at the pink tips already extended because of Wentworth's handling. "Why, there is even talk of your absolute control over your wife."

"Is that so? Talk of me among the ladies?" She could hear the note of satisfaction in his voice.

"Indeed. They say the silly chit fears you . . . acts in complete obedience to your wishes." Louisa let her gaze travel down her own reflection in the mirror and linger to admire the triangle of soft hair at the juncture of her legs.

"It is a man's place to command."

"Pray, I wonder if all this manly command could be used to pry some answers out of that wife of yours."

"Answers about what?" he replied suspiciously.

She pushed gently at the blond hair piled high on her head. "About who this woman is, of course—this Mrs. Ford—and what she is to Stanmore."

She gasped aloud as a hand seized her by the hair, jerking her head roughly to the side. She hadn't seen him move—hadn't been aware of his approach. Her haughtiness disappeared instantly, as she felt herself thrown hard against the nearest wall. Stunned, she was still trying to regain her breath when she felt his hand encircle her throat.

She could hear the anger in his whisper. "Are you here to be with me or with Stanmore?"

More than anything else in the world, Louisa wanted to correct the brute on the ridiculousness of the question. Looking up into the murderous eyes and feeling the fingers pressing on her throat, though, she quickly recalled her intentions.

"Am I not here at Melbury Hall?" She gave him her most seductive smile and stroked his hip with the inside of her knee . "Of course, I am here to be with you. Do you wish me to kiss the rod, as well, you beast?"

Her pretense served its purpose as he lowered his hand from her throat to her leg. He was *still* clay in her hands, she thought, wrapping both legs about his waist. And a moment later, as the squire drove deeply into her, Louisa conjured her most convincing cry of ecstasy.

Like clay, she thought.

Chapter 19

"Perhaps, then, you should tell me who you are."

Rebecca stared at him, shame coursing through her. One moment she was acting like a harlot, the next she was as frosty as a glowering duenna. Trying to gather together whatever remained of her dignity, she pulled herself out of Stanmore's arms and seated herself about an arm's length away. He sat up as well, reaching out and wiping the tears from her face.

"I am not the woman you think I am!"

"And what woman is that?"

She could feel the weight of his gaze on her bowed head. Vanity had never played an important role in Rebecca's life, but right now she was incredibly conscious of how terrible she must look to him. She could just imagine the look of her red nose and swollen eyes, the wild hair that had come loose and no doubt conveyed an image of Medusa. She stared at the weave of the blanket while she tried to collect her thoughts.

"I am not . . . I do not . . . I've never engaged in this kind of activity before." She closed her eyes and let out a shaky breath. "This . . . this intimacy frightens me . . . terrifies me."

"Are you saying that, aside from your husband, you've never been with any other man?"

She shook her head first, before nodding furiously.

He moved closer, and Rebecca felt the warmth of his breath on her ear. "And how many years have you been a widow?"

"Eight . . . nine years," she managed to croak.

"To think, a woman of your beauty . . . your . . ." His warm hand moved caressingly over her back, and she shivered. "But what a fool I am to complain of the stupidity and the blindness of other men."

"This is just what I mean." She turned to him and was sorry the moment she did, for the look of tenderness in his eyes was something totally new, something she was not prepared for. "I . . . I have never sought the attention of men. I . . . I did not wish for this . . . this thing to be happening between us now."

"I had no wish for it, either." He looped a loose strand of her hair around his finger. "But it is undeniably here, as you say, between us. And we cannot ignore it."

"But we must!"

"Tell me why."

"I've said it before. It is wrong. It is . . ."

"Do you have someone who is waiting for you in America?"

"I do not! But this is not about another man's claim on me. It is all about how I was raised."

"How you are raised is very important, Rebecca, but are you still a child? Suppose I said that sometimes we try to hide behind traditions we have been taught because we think we can be safe there," he challenged. "Are you still an innocent child, Rebecca?"

"I am twenty-eight," she answered earnestly. "And you have no need to press this point, m'lord. I know I am far from innocent."

"Of course. For anyone who lives in this world, the age of innocence is past." A trace of amusement shone in his dark eyes. "But do you intend to join a convent after your return to the colonies?"

A flash of temper raised color in her face. "I hardly find it amusing that you should entertain yourself at my expense."

"I am doing no such thing. My interest, though, is purely pragmatic. No matter what my attraction to you might be, I *will* cease to pursue you if your intention is to engage in some religious life."

"You *are* making fun of me." Rebecca pushed herself to her feet and walked a few steps away before whirling on him. "I am to retain my reason, not only for my own sake, but for yours, as well."

"Is that so? And how is that?" he asked lazily.

He looked the part of some well-dressed highwayman stretched out on the blanket beside the water. He could be a Captain MacHeath or a Willmore come to life. Staring at him, she found it increasingly difficult to concentrate on her argument when he watched her with so much heat in his dark eyes.

"If we were . . ." She moved her hands desperately in the air.

"To become involved." He finished her sentence for her.

She nodded. "Then I know . . . well, that I will not be the same."

"And you think that would be so terrible!"

She nodded tentatively. "But consider how your life might change, as well. What happens then? I mean you appear quite happy with your life as it is now . . . and I think it would be very wrong to muddy up what is . . . perfect."

"You think I am perfect?"

"Hardly!" Her quick answer made him burst out in laughter. Rebecca couldn't hold back her own smile. "I meant no disrespect, m'lord."

"Of course you did."

"Very well, perhaps I did." She put her hands on her hips. "But, to speak honestly, how else am I going to deal with you? You are . . . well, reasonably handsome. You know you have both poise and charm that many women might find attractive. And you are incredibly arrogant to ignore my request that you direct your attentions elsewhere. You, m'lord . . . you should be dining with people . . . with women . . . of your own rank. I cannot understand why you should notice me at all!"

He sat up on the blanket. His voice was low. "Do you find my attentions so hateful, Rebecca?"

She closed her eyes and let out a frustrated breath. "Here you are, starting again."

"Answer me."

"Of course, they are not hateful." Rebecca was startled when she opened her eyes and found him standing before her.

"You like my attentions. Admit it, you enjoy them. You enjoy being with me."

She wanted to deny the truth that he was speaking, but she couldn't.

"I say that you like me, Rebecca. And I believe you desire me as much as I desire you. Now, if you would stop your endless quibbling for any length of time and gave this some honest thought, I

believe you'd see that there is no sound reason for stubbornly refusing to surrender to your wants." When she tried to turn her face
away, he reached for her chin and held her in place. "What are you
saving yourself for? Most importantly, why are you robbing yourself of something that offers a promise of real fulfillment?"

Rebecca felt the insides of her body vibrate with anticipation.

"Do not be afraid of what might happen after. I am not one who
shirks his responsibilities. I will take care of you." His face descended, but he didn't kiss her. "I will not, however, press you beyond your own desires. On the other hand, I will not go away,
either. I will just wait until *you* come to me."

Following a young black-skinned girl who carried a small bundle of bread in her apron, Jamey had easily found his way to the
half-circle of ramshackle dwellings where most of the slaves lived
on a stream by the edge of a grove beyond Melbury Hall.

Arriving by the perimeter of the cluster though, the boy hid himself behind the large trunk of a tree and stared for some time at the
pitiful sight before him. At the center of an opening on the muddy
bank of the stream, two black men sat side by side in stocks. At
least, one of them sat. The other, the larger and older of the two, lay
back on the wet ground, one arm draped across his face.

The younger man wore no shirt, and Jamey could see why he
was sitting. His back glistened with blood from a whipping he must
have received not very long ago. The boy felt his stomach turn over
at the sight of the open wounds. The other man had a shirt on, but
as Jamey stared, the man moved his arm. His face was misshapen,
no doubt from countless beatings, but what was worse, the boy
could see he had no ears. It looked to him as though they had been
cut off long ago, for the scars were long healed. The boy stared hard
at the face, so wretched and old and lost.

Watching them, he felt the anger seething within him.

Chickens pecked about in the yard, stirred up occasionally by
two little children who chased them with sticks, while pigs and
goats rooted about outside of small, fenced vegetable gardens.
Jamey could see a young man with a twisted foot in an open tan-
ner's hut, scraping the hide of a sheep. Lines of clothing were visi-

ble on a small knoll beyond the last cottage, and as the boy
watched, a woman came out of the cottage and carried a bucket
down to the stream.

On her return, she looked around and then quickly strode to the
stocks. Pulling a half-loaf of bread from her blouse, she dropped it
in the lap of the sitting man. Producing a wooden cup from the
same place, she dipped it into the bucket and handed it to him, hurrying on without a word.

The boy sent a prayer heavenward, and then continued to look
for his friend. Set off from the others, by the hut closest to a path
that Jamey figured must lead toward Melbury Hall, he could see
piles of stacked wood. Moving along a ditch, he slowly worked his
way toward the hut. When he was fairly close, he peeked up over
the embankment.

Israel was busy at work, chopping wood that had been sawed
into fireplace lengths. Sitting on a broad section of tree trunk, a
white man of advancing years sat smoking a pipe and talking continually at the boy. Jamey remained where he was until the man
stood up, stretched, and—with a final word of direction to Israel—
walked up the path toward the Hall.

As soon as he was gone, Jamey picked up a piece of bark off the
ground and threw it to where Israel was piling wood. The other
boy's head came up instantly. The flesh around Israel's hazel eyes
was still swollen from his beating two days earlier. He looked
around nervously as Jamey trotted toward the woodpile.

"What are you doing here?"

"I went to the cottage in the forest yesterday . . . and then again
today, but you never showed up." Jamey let himself be pulled back
behind a tree, away from the huts. "I was worried."

Israel looked up the path. "You shouldn't have come here. If I
am caught talking to you . . ."

"I'll take the blame," Jamey said. "They won't do anything to
me. And wait until I tell Mr. Clarke about the two men I saw in the
stocks. The people at Solgrave know nothing of what is happening
here. I'm sure of it."

"Stay," Israel pleaded, putting his hand on Jamey's arm. "You

mustn't say anything. The more you say, the rougher things will become for us."

Jamey opened his mouth to argue, but Israel's frown and quick
gesture toward the path silenced him. The two crouched behind a
pile of brushwood.

A moment later, a thin, well-dressed woman glided silently into
the opening, stopping by the pile of wood that Israel had been
working on earlier. She lay a gloved hand on a stack of wood and
glanced about searchingly.

"Who is that?" Jamey whispered.

"Lady Wentworth." Israel mouthed. "She is the squire's wife."

As the two of them watched, she suddenly sank onto the stump
the old man had been sitting on, and covered her face with her
hands.

Jamey could see she was crying. "What's wrong with her?"

Israel didn't answer and just shrugged, staring with a frown at
the weeping woman. At one point, Jamey thought his friend was
going to leave their hiding place and go to her. As Israel began to
stand up, though, Jamey touched his arm, stopping him.

Lady Wentworth didn't remain there for too long, though. Just
as Jamey was beginning to get that pins and needles feeling in his
legs, the woman wiped her face with a lace handkerchief. Standing
up, she turned and disappeared again into the woods.

Israel was on his feet as soon as the woman was gone.

"She doesn't look like a cruel mistress."

Israel shook his head. "She isn't!"

"What's wrong with her?" Jamey asked again, his curiosity eating him up.

"What's wrong with any of us?" Israel answered, unconsciously
raising his hand to his bruised cheek. "What's wrong with Jonah?
Why must he be whipped and placed in the stocks without reason?
And what of old Moses? He has already lost his wits from too many
beatings . . . why put him in the stocks over and over?"

This was the first time that Jamey had seen Israel's temper rise,
and he felt his friend's hurt and anger fuse with his own.

"Squire Wentworth is the cause of it all, isn't he?"

Without answering, Israel moved away from their hiding place and went back to his job of piling wood. Jamey followed him. "I'll tell Lord Stanmore about this—about these beatings. He'll do something about it."

"No white man will do a thing about us. No white woman either." He pointed in the direction that Lady Wentworth had disappeared. "She wants to help. But she cannot. So what does she do? She cries. She comes here and tends to our wounds and then goes away again to London as soon as she can."

"Stanmore will be different!" Jamey defended his earlier statement. "My tutor told me what he is trying to do in Parliament. He is trying to put a stop to the stealing away of people from their own homes. He is a good man, Israel. He will—"

"If he is such a good man, then why don't you want him for a father?" Israel's hazel eyes flashed with challenge as he faced Jamey. "If you think he is so noble, then why do you try to run away from him?"

Jamey suddenly found himself lost for words. There were things that he could say. Arguments he'd used before. But none of it seemed important in light of the differences in the lives that he and Israel led. His complaints seemed so petty compared to the suffering his new friend faced.

"I asked you before . . . I beg you now." Israel's voice was gentle again as he spoke. "Do not mention any of this to anyone. Not to your tutor. Not to your mama. And *not* to Lord Stanmore."

Squire Wentworth pushed away the correspondence on his desk and looked up at his bailiff.

"They're promising me thirty-five slaves before harvest. Have you given any thought as to where you shall put them?"

"Aye, sir. When we know we'll have them, sure, we can evict Shaw and his lot from the east vale. That'll house a dozen. The rest can put up shacks at the southern end of the Grove, or cozy into the existing huts. After the slave ships, they'll seem like palaces, I'd wager."

Wentworth frowned. "Doesn't the southern end flood in the spring?"

"Aye, so they tell me." Mickleby shifted his weight from one foot to the other. "But does it really matter, Squire?"

"Only in that I don't wish to spend the time or the money rebuilding the bloody houses every spring."

"I'll have the dirty buggers put 'em up on high enough ground, Squire."

"Very well, then." Wentworth closed the books before him and rose to his feet. "And you'll have enough work for them."

"Aye. They'll earn their keep." The bailiff smiled, stepping back and watching his employer come around the desk. " 'Tis fine seeing you in such good spirits, Squire, if you don't mind my saying, sir."

"Don't mind at all, Mickleby. It is good having a change of scenery in the house now and again." The squire's face darkened abruptly. "Now get out to the south barns. Those black bastards are surely robbing me blind this very minute."

The afternoon sun was still bright when Millicent Wentworth glided quietly into the parlor. The squire, playing whist with Lady Nisdale, didn't look up from the cards, but Louisa arched a thin eyebrow as she took in the wife's appearance. Millicent knew her shoes were wet, as was the hem of her dress. Even if her eyes were red-rimmed from crying, though, she cared not. What was the point of hiding such things from *this* guest?

"You *are* a forbidding sight, my dear." Louisa shook her head. "The lady of the manor looking less composed than a pantry maid . . . scandalous, I'm sure!"

Millicent clutched the back of the nearest chair and ignored the woman's insult. She kept her gaze fixed instead on her husband.

"Wentworth, I am surprised at you," Louisa taunted, reaching over and affectionately patting the man's free hand on the table. "In London, everyone praises your influence on your simple wife in matters of style, but here—"

"Sir, I need to speak with you." Millicent interrupted the other's condescending speech. "Alone!"

"Later," Wentworth said dismissively without looking up from his cards. A knowing smile broke across Louisa's lips. "It is your play, my pet."

"Ah!" Louisa withdrew her hand and pouted at the cards. "But this distraction has caused me to forget what's been played."

She might as well not exist, Millicent thought bitterly, feeling anger and fear coiling simultaneously around her heart. This very afternoon, she'd stood and watched her husband disappear into their guest's bedchamber, totally disregarding her presence in the corridor or the presence of two passing servants.

Not that she cared anything about his disgusting sexual liaisons, Millicent thought, as tears welled up uncontrollably in her eyes. True, treating her brutally and disdainfully and with a complete lack of discretion was foul and villainous. But to treat their workers in such a way! Even knowing what would follow, she forced herself to persist in her desire for an audience with him.

"Wentworth! I need to speak with you. This is important."

Perhaps it was the change in her tone—one that she'd never dared to use with her husband—that got his attention. She trembled uncontrollably as the man's hand visibly fisted and his glare flashed threateningly toward her.

His cool tone belied the fury she could see in his eyes. "I am not accustomed to having my commands ignored."

Louisa glanced from one to the other before laying her cards casually on the table and rising slowly to her feet, "I think I shall take a walk in the gardens before readying myself for this evening."

"Stay awhile, my pet," Wentworth ordered, clasping Louisa by the wrist and gently pulling her around the table until she stood beside his chair.

It was impossible not to see her husband's hand slip possessively around the woman's generous hips as he gazed haughtily at Millicent.

"You have one minute."

Millicent was almost relieved to realize that her anger did not increase at this insolence, but remained focused on the injustice that she'd witnessed in the Grove.

"During my walk this afternoon, I found Jonah and Moses in stocks. Jonah was—"

"Louisa," Wentworth interrupted, turning sideways in his chair and pulling their guest onto his lap. "Did I ever tell you about the arrangement between my wife and me?"

"Jonah had been whipped." Millicent raised her voice. "I want to know why!"

"Unlike you, my pet, my wife abhors my touch." He ran a finger on the edge of the low neckline of the dress and tugged down. One pink tip peeked out.

"Not now, Wentworth!" Louisa's face turned a shade of red with obvious embarrassment. She placed her hands on his shoulders to push out of his grasp. But his strong grip on her waist kept her where she was. He pressed his lips on the ivory flesh of her breast. She pushed his face away.

"No reason to fret, Louisa," he said with a short laugh. "She will go soon."

"Stop it, Wentworth," Louisa snapped, shoving harder this time and breaking free. She pulled her dress up in place as she took a step back.

"Actually, I am not astonished that you object to her watching us, considering"—he still kept his gaze on Louisa as she ran her hands up and down her arms as if warding off a chill—"considering my wife's sordid taste in men. But I would never dream of bringing her into our bed as we brought in that . . . what was her name?"

"There has *never* been any other man," Millicent cried out in disbelief. She stared for a moment. "Was this the reason for those poor men's beatings?"

"She favors the slaves, you know. Everyone knows. She goes into the park and allows the Africans to have their way with her. Last year, in fact, she tried to give birth to a bastard."

"That is a lie!" Tears again rushed down Millicent's face. "That child was yours . . . a child you forced on me. If you had believed me . . . if you hadn't beaten me . . . losing him . . ."

"But this year, Lady Wentworth has raised her standards." Malice was evident in every inch of the man's face. "She has been trying to lure that schoolteacher on, but I have been watching over what is mine. She thinks those slaves will not divulge the misdeeds of their own whore, but my wife is quite deluded on that count."

"It is not true." Millicent continued to shake her head as her husband rose slowly to his feet. "Mr. Cunningham's visits here have nothing to do with me. He comes here because he has compassion . . . for people who need him."

"Do you hear it in her voice, Louisa? Do you see it in her face? She dotes on him."

Louisa turned with distaste and stared out the window as Wentworth advanced on his retreating wife.

"And have you slept with him already, Millicent? Are you carrying *his* child, too?"

"Stop!" She gasped in pain as Wentworth grabbed her upper arm. "I am innocent! There is nothing between . . ."

"Innocent as a Covent Garden whore! And your dear Mr. Cunningham may enjoy the protection of our sanctimonious Lord Stanmore," the squire whispered, shaking her so hard that she fell against him. "But you are mine. To touch as I like. To punish as I see fit . . . and in just the same fashion that I will deal with those filthy brutes who think they can keep you as their whore."

"There is only one brute. . . ."

Millicent's words turned to cries of pain as the squire's blows rained down on her face and body.

And by the window, Louisa Nisdale stared with a face of stone at the hills above Solgrave.

Chapter 20

The dawning sun had barely broken free of night's grasp when Rebecca left her bedchamber. Making her way down the servants' stairs, she went out a side door and started down toward the stables.

This morning, she had put on, reluctantly at first, the new riding habit that had been delivered to her room the night before. It had come with the other dozen dresses and accessories Mrs. Trent had ordered earlier in the week. The cloth of plum velvet, edged with silky violet ribbon—with its matching hat—was one of the finest outfits she had ever worn. It was certainly a dress that she would never have chosen for herself, if for no other reason than its obvious extravagance. But in the face of Lady Nisdale's ridicule the day before, Rebecca found herself appreciating Mrs. Trent's choice.

The dark leather boots that had been delivered with the dress made a soft noise on the path as she neared the stables. She had practiced her request a few times in her head. She had met some of the grooms already. There was no reason why her request should be denied, Rebecca reminded herself, trying to ease the nervousness she was feeling—nervousness that actually had very little to do with borrowing a horse.

The source of her worries lay with how Millicent would react to what she was about to tell her. Yesterday, Rebecca had prayed that her old friend would be understanding of her past—of the crime she had been forced to commit and all she had been doing since. But walking toward the stables in the cool morning air, Rebecca reminded herself that people change. Cheerful, friendly Millicent Gregory of Mrs. Stockdale's Academy for Girls was now a very different Lady Wentworth of Melbury Hall. What made Rebecca think she could trust her?

The smoke from the smith's fire was drifting into the treetops, and half a dozen grooms were visible bustling about the stables. As Rebecca approached, she could see a number of horses being brushed or led out for exercise in the paddock areas, but her friend had not yet arrived. Rebecca drew a deep breath, almost relieved that she'd have a few more minutes to calm her jittery insides. But the sight of the Earl of Stanmore standing by a handsome black hunter and engaged in reflective discussion with a groom took Rebecca totally by surprise. His gaze flickered toward her and then returned with evident pleasure.

"Rebec . . . er, Mrs. Ford!" he greeted her, leaving the groom behind. "What a pleasant surprise!"

"Good morning, m'lord." Her insides ignited, and she forced out the words as he looked over her new attire with obvious approval. "I was . . . I met Lady Wentworth yesterday . . . and she invited me to go riding with her this morning. So I was hoping your lordship would not mind if I were to borrow a horse."

"Of course not!" He instantly turned to the groom and gave him a series of instructions. As the man hurried off to do as he was ordered, Stanmore's attention returned to Rebecca. "I was under the impression that you did not ride."

"I do not ride, generally. I mean, I have not for some years." She felt embarrassment flush her cheeks for the half-truth she had told him before. "I used to ride, though, so Lady Wentworth's invitation sparked my interest in trying it out again."

Rebecca noticed the frown that creased his brow. He picked up the reins of his own steed and led the horse through a gate into a meadow. Rebecca walked with him, closing the gate after Stanmore had passed through.

"Is . . . is Lady *Nisdale* also to join you for your ride this morning?"

"No, m'lord. I believe it will only be Lady Wentworth and myself."

He nodded once, and she felt his relief. He studied, for a moment, the shortening shadows along the edges of the meadow, and then looked back at her.

"I am happy that you accepted Lady Wentworth's invitation," he said gently. "In the years that she has been a neighbor here at Solgrave, I have yet to see or hear of her seeking out anyone's company . . . until now, that is."

Rebecca remembered her friend's reserve the day before. "She does appear quite unhappy . . . though I have a difficult time believing Lady Nisdale's visit will alleviate the problem. The two appear to be so . . . so different!"

An icy frown stole over the earl's features. "You are absolutely correct in your observations."

Rebecca glanced down the path and still saw no sign of her friend. She wanted Millicent to arrive, but at the same time she prized these private moments in his company. She considered bringing up another topic that had been gnawing away at her—her concern about the lack of rapport between the earl and Jamey.

Last night, after joining the father and son in the dining room, she had been genuinely disturbed by the show of indifference that still was so pronounced between them. Jamey had yet—so far as she knew—to speak a word in Lord Stanmore's presence. Even when asked a question by Rebecca, the boy simply nodded or shook his head. Rebecca knew she had taught him better behavior than what had been displayed at the dinner table and, following him to his room, she had spoken to him at length about the unacceptability of his conduct toward his father.

But Jamey was not even ten, and Lord Stanmore's cool silence had certainly been no better than the son's.

What else could she expect, though, since the two had spent so little time in each other's company since their arrival at Solgrave?

"I am returning to London today."

Her disappointment must have shown immediately, for a smile stole over his face. He reached over and took her hand. Though she found she could not bring herself to shake off the touch, Rebecca wished he would use some of that allure in winning over the affections of his son.

"An urgent message arrived late last night. My presence is required, it seems, in London. But I shall not be away more than two days at the most."

Rebecca swallowed her personal feelings regarding his absence and instead tried to focus on the more important matters. "When you return, m'lord, will you be able to spare a day perhaps?"

His dark gaze was deep, bottomless, drawing her in. She shivered with excitement as he slowly lifted her fingers and placed a kiss on the back of her hand. "I can spare much more than a day."

"Dare I ask . . . two hours a day . . . for the entire length of your stay at Solgrave, then?"

"Why do I have a feeling that you are planning something?"

She withdrew her hand and hid it in the folds of the skirt. "You do not sound very trusting, m'lord."

The sound of his laughter reverberating in the yard brought a smile to her lips. "What are you after, Rebecca?"

"Not much. Only two hours a day of your lordship's time."

"What for?"

"Instruction."

"What kind of instruction? Better yet"—his voice dropped low—"which of us is to do this 'instructing'?"

"You are teasing me, m'lord." She looked down at his high-topped boots, at the dark buckskin breeches that molded to his muscular legs. Her gaze hurried past his narrow waist to the short black jacket that hugged his impressive wide shoulders. She had thought to charm and fool him and have him agree without knowing the details—but as the warmth spread through her, she found it was she *herself* who was being charmed.

"You keep this up, and I'll cancel my trip to London." He leaned toward her until his voice was a husky whisper in her ear. "And I will see to it that you and I are locked up in my bedchambers for a fortnight . . . at least. And what do you think of *that* proposition, Rebecca?"

If the mail coach from London had been bearing down on her, Rebecca could not have moved an inch. Stunned, unable to breathe even, she felt the molten heat flow through her, scorching her from the inside.

"I . . . I . . ."

Stanmore's fingers caressed her cheek. It took great control not to lean into his touch.

"No pressure," he whispered. "You will tell me when *you* are ready."

The arrival of his groom from the stables caused him to withdraw his hand. She glanced at the beautiful brown mare, saddled and ready.

Stanmore pulled on his gloves. "Where do you plan to meet Lady Wentworth?"

"Here! We were to meet by the stables here. But m'lord, you haven't answered my earlier question. About your time? Those two hours a day?"

"One hour."

She watched him loop the reins over his horse's head. "A moment ago, you were threatening me with lengthy confinement. Now you are being exceedingly frugal with your time."

He climbed up onto his horse. "I am known to be a generous man . . . so long as the terms of the negotiations are set forth openly and honestly."

She frowned up into his handsome face. "I have been open about my request from the first day. But your lack of interest in the topic has forced me to pursue a different approach."

"I've provided everything for the lad that you've requested."

"Not everything, m'lord," Rebecca replied doggedly as a darkening temper clouded his brow. "James needs you. He needs *your* attention . . . *your* interest . . . far more than he needs any of the comforts Solgrave provides."

The steed impatiently pawed the hard ground, but Stanmore's firm hand kept him in check.

"Are these his words, Mrs. Ford, or yours?"

"It does not matter whose words they are. I know him better than anyone in the world. You forget, I have raised him as my own."

"I do not forget anything, and in this case you are mistaken. Regardless of the fine example of hard work and self-sacrifice that you have provided all these years, James was borne to Elizabeth. All the good intentions on your part will not hold sway over his breeding. It is her blood that runs in his veins. With it he has inherited her weakness and selfishness and arrogance."

"I disagree!" Rebecca was astonished by the raw emotion she saw in the earl's face, but forged on anyway. "Elizabeth . . . your wife . . . she was none of . . ."

She caught herself. How could she defend a woman whom she had supposedly never known?

"I mean . . . James has his own character."

"I have noticed."

"But you must give him a chance. What harm would come from spending an hour or two a day in his company?"

She feared what his answer might be. His cold gaze was already fixed on the road leading out of Solgrave. The groom, who had been holding her horse, was now standing a short distance away from them, discreetly checking the hooves of the mare.

A battle was raging inside Rebecca's head. She liked Lord Stanmore. She admired him. She desired him. In truth, she was caught in some invisible web and was quickly becoming too blind to care about the consequences. And yet she knew she could never surrender herself to a man who harbored such bitterness toward his own son.

"One hour!" he said curtly. "Tell the boy he will have to rise early. Our designated hour will be planned for the morning . . . prior to his lessons with Mr. Clarke."

"Thank you, m'lord."

Her soft whisper drew his gaze for a final farewell. What she saw in that look caused her heart to jump in her chest.

"Safe journey. We shall be waiting for you."

As he spurred his horse toward St. Albans and London, Rebecca prayed that this journey of hers might be only slightly less perilous.

The young maidservant carefully slid the sealed letter into the pocket of her apron before slipping out of Lady Wentworth's bedchamber.

Melbury Hall was still fairly quiet. The master, drinking late last night and playing cards with the guest, was still abed. Hurrying down the corridor until she reached the master's chambers, the girl held her breath and trod quietly past, keeping her eyes on the door leading to the servants' stairs at the far end of the carpeted hallway. Violet didn't want to think about what else had been going on, aside from the card playing. She would just keep her mind on her task.

Lord, how she hated the times when her mistress's presence was required in the country.

She hurried on. Jonah would be hauling ashes out of the kitchen ovens now, as he did at this time every morning. The young woman needed to pass her mistress's letter on to the slave before he left. She didn't know very much about the quiet man herself, but she knew Lady Wentworth trusted him completely. Jonah would deliver her mistress's letter to its recipient this very morning . . . without fail.

Violet didn't see the guest until the woman suddenly appeared out of the shadows, blocking her path. The maidservant gasped out loud and immediately shrank against the wall.

"Why the hurry? So out of breath!"

"Beg your pardon, ma'am. Caught me unawares, you did." The servant dropped a curtsy and kept her gaze riveted to the floor. "Hope you slept well, m'lady."

"You just came out of Lady Wentworth's room. How is your mistress faring this morning?"

The woman's concern struck Vi as a little odd, coming as it was from someone who had just left the squire's bed. The servant gave a quick glance at the woman. Her hair, bound up in a high scarf, tilted precariously to one side. She wore a robe of fine silk loosely tied at the waist. It did very little to hide the naked body beneath it.

"She is feeling a bit better, m'lady."

"Did you bring her any breakfast?"

"Nay, m'lady. Her ladyship had . . ." Violet backed away nervously as the guest took a step toward her. Her back bumped against the wall. "Her . . . her ladyship had no appetite."

"Then why did she call for you?"

The young woman thought of the letter tucked into her apron pocket and intentionally hid her hands behind her back. "She . . . she wanted me to . . . to tell Cook not to send a tray up."

"Of course." A sardonic smile blossomed on Lady Nisdale's full lips. The guest reached out and touched a loose blond curl that had escaped the servant's cap. "What is your name, girl?"

"Vi, ma'am."

"Very well, Violet. And how old are you?"

"Sixteen," she croaked nervously.

"You have lovely skin." Lady Nisdale let her finger trail down caressingly over the maidservant's cheek. Violet tried to turn her face away, but the woman's quick grip on her chin held her in place against the wall. "You are a very pretty girl, Vi. How long have you been in the service of Lady Wentworth?"

"I . . . I started . . . just a few months, m'lady."

"Not long enough to know the rules of this household, I see," Lady Nisdale cooed, keeping a grip on Violet's face. The guest moved closer, and the young servant cringed as she felt the pressure of the other woman's breasts against her own. "Many in this household think of me as a new guest, but I'll share a little secret with you."

Vi swallowed hard and pressed her back against the wall.

"I've known your master longer than you think. Longer than his wife. Longer than his present steward. Longer than almost everyone." Lady Nisdale's hand released Vi's chin. Again, she ran her fingertips over the skin of her cheek, her neck. "And it is because of my long . . . friendship with the squire that I can warn you of something. Everyone and everything falls into two groups in his sight."

The guest continued to gently caress the girl's neck, and Violet fought back the foul taste rising in her throat.

"The first group consists of those who are loyal to *him*—those who are trustworthy and keep him informed of everything that goes on. And the other group . . ."

She lowered her hand and took hold of one of the maidservant's firm breasts. The servant gasped in shock and tried to push her away, but Louisa pressed her weight against the girl's body, squeezing harder. Vi stopped struggling, feeling the world crushing down upon her.

"The other group," Lady Nisdale continued in a voice of satin, "consists of those who disobey him. And those are the ones that the good squire punishes. He is a good master, is he not, Vi?"

"Aye, m'lady," the girl whimpered, not looking up.

"Is he not correct in punishing the disobedient . . . the disloyal?"

"Aye, ma'am," she whispered, beginning to cry silently.

"You heard of the lashing of the two slaves yesterday, I am certain. And you surely saw your mistress's face this morning." The guest brushed away the tears running down the servant's face and leaned forward to whisper in her ear. "And what you saw is nothing compared to the bruises the wife has here." She squeezed the girl's breast hard. "And other places. Have you ever been touched . . . in those other places, Vi?"

The servant's tears turned to a soft sob as she shook her head. "Please, m'lady. I'm a good girl. Please let me go."

"That's all very well that you're a good girl, Vi. Your master will be delighted to know that you are a virgin. Perhaps I shall take you into him right now, in fact. He and I could start the day off quite pleasurably enjoying your plump little body."

"Please, m'lady!" Violet begged, continuing to shake her head. "Please!"

"Let me ask you again, Vi. What did your mistress want you for so early this fine morning?"

The girl's blue eyes rounded with fear. She looked down the hallway as a movement caught her eye.

"Vi . . . Squire Wentworth is known to be quite . . . hmm, quite manly in the mornings. Large and manly." Louisa pressed her hand against the juncture of the girl's legs. "He could very well tear you in half with his thick shaft. And all I need to do is drag you to his bed."

"A letter!" the girl sobbed. "It was a letter. You can have it."

Lady Nisdale pulled back slightly and let the girl reach into the apron and draw out a sealed letter.

"Not a word," Louisa threatened, taking the girl's chin in one hand and the letter in the other. "To anyone."

With tears coursing down her face, the maidservant slipped around Louisa and ran in terror down the hall. In a moment, she had disappeared down the servants' stairs.

Without waiting another instant, Louisa broke the seal and scanned the contents of the letter. A polite salutation to Mrs. Ford, followed by fictitious excuses why Millicent could not attend a previously planned meeting with the other woman. A vague promise of writing again and rescheduling their morning ride, possibly next week. Nothing of significance, Louisa thought angrily as she glanced over the end of the correspondence. Nothing more than she already knew or could have guessed.

But there had to be more, Louisa thought, her temper beginning to rise. Something had passed between the two women. They shared a secret, she was certain. Something significant enough that they would arrange this private ride this morning. Just as Louisa was ready to crumple the letter in frustration, her gaze fell on the last line before the signature.

Our dear Mrs. Stockdale would have reproved of this hasty postponement . . .

Louisa stared again. *Our dear Mrs. Stockdale. Mrs. Stockdale. Our Mrs. Stockdale!*

Scanning the letter again, a smile broke across Louisa's face.

He was standing in the open door of his bedchamber when she looked up, and she made no effort to hide the paper.

"What do you have?"

"A letter. How long have you been there?"

"Long enough to watch your rather enticing way of dealing with servants. I am disappointed, though, that you did not bring her to me. The thought of the three of us is indeed arousing, my pet."

"There is always tomorrow," she murmured, undoing the belt of her robe and gliding toward him. "But you shall need all of your vigor for me this morning, for I shall have to take leave of you for the day. You *do* want to enjoy these again before I go, do you not?"

Wentworth's gaze moved from the exposed breasts to the triangle of blond curls to the letter she was holding too casually in one hand.

"Give it to me."

"There is nothing in it." She handed him the letter without a protest. As he glanced over it, she slipped an arm around him and felt for him through his nightshirt. His manhood was already thick and hardening, rising quickly to her touch.

"This woman . . . this Mrs. Ford," he asked, "is she the one you two met yesterday at the rector's?"

"She is," Louisa cooed, pushing him inside the bedchamber and closing the door behind them.

"Did you know anything about this ride they were going on this morning?"

"Not a thing." She tried to guide him toward the bed, but he planted his feet in the middle of the room and stared again at the letter.

"She is a mouse . . . not much better than your wife," Louisa whispered against his neck. "Throw it away. We have better things to do."

Taking hold of the shirt, she tore it open, smiling at his surprise. With a coy look, she began to trail her lips down over his bare chest until she was on her knees.

Suddenly impatient, Wentworth grasped Louisa's hair—scarf and all—and dragged her mouth roughly to his waiting shaft. Feeling her wet mouth closing around him, he dropped the letter to the ground and let out a satisfied groan.

"Who is Mrs. Stockdale?" she asked, drawing back a bit and eyeing him as if she were about to devour him.

"Who?" He looked down at her wet lips, at the tongue already teasing the tip of his manhood. "Stockdale . . . some old hag in Oxford. Runs a school there. Academy for girls. Millicent went there. Teaches them how to be 'ladies.' But you, my pet, would have been expelled the first day."

She looked up at him with an expression of mock innocence. "But isn't this what a 'lady' does?"

"Aye," he said, tightening his hold on her hair and guiding her back to him.

Chapter 21

The day was pressing forward, and Rebecca was beginning to feel uncomfortable waiting at the stables. She had already returned to the house once, inquiring about a possible message from Lady Wentworth, but there had been none. Deciding finally that she may have misunderstood their meeting place, she asked for directions and mounted her horse. With a groom trailing behind, Rebecca headed off in the direction of Melbury Hall.

When the forest trails opened out onto rolling farmland, she found herself riding through fragrant fields of wheat, barley, oats, and hay. Eventually reaching the long, winding road that led in to Melbury Hall from the village, Rebecca was surprised to come upon a conservatively dressed man, about the same age as herself, riding a rather decrepit-looking horse and heading in the same direction. He greeted her in a friendly fashion, and she found him to be Mr. Cunningham, the schoolmaster at Knebworth. And he had already heard much about her from the rector and his wife.

Immediately at ease with the man, Rebecca dismissed the groom, and the two continued on together, chatting comfortably.

It had become his Friday routine over the past couple of years, she learned, to spend his mornings at Melbury Hall tutoring the servants' children for an hour and the young slave children for another hour. He also rode out during the week occasionally, but those visits were generally in the evening, with the intention of reading with a number of the adults in service. And he was delighted to hear of her offer to help in the work there.

"But what brings you out to Melbury Hall this morning?"

"Lady Wentworth and I had planned to meet by the stables at

Solgrave earlier and go riding," Rebecca replied. "But I believe one of us must have misunderstood where we were to meet. At least, she did not appear. So, I thought I would ride over and make sure she is not unwell."

Mr. Cunningham consulted his pocket watch with concern. " 'Tis quite unusual for Lady Wentworth to be careless in keeping an appointment. I do know that when she rides, though, by this hour she has generally returned to Melbury Hall."

Rebecca glanced discreetly at the teacher. He was medium in height and build, with regular features that were pleasing, but could never be considered handsome. The spark of intelligence in his dark eyes, though, and the absolute confidence that rang in every word he spoke, gave him a distinctive flair. Rebecca thought the schoolmaster's knowledge of Millicent's schedule interesting, however.

"It was probably just my error regarding the meeting place. At any rate, I was hoping she would receive me if I were to ride over. I would like to deliver my apologies in person, and perhaps impose upon her for another visit some time soon."

The man's intense face brightened as he turned to her. "That is quite delightful, Mrs. Ford. Quite the thing, indeed! Lady Wentworth could certainly use the company."

"This is the second time today that I've heard this sentiment."

"Have you?"

"Lord Stanmore's feelings were much the same."

The schoolmaster nodded with understanding. " 'Tis difficult to not be affected by that good woman's melancholy. She is not a very happy woman."

So different from the Millicent Gregory Rebecca had known so many years ago. She glanced at the rolling vista of farms to their right. She knew they had to be nearing Melbury Hall. In one field a number of black-skinned workers were toiling steadily.

Cunningham followed her gaze, frowning. "Do you know that there are thousands of African descent—both free men and runaway slaves—living in terrible poverty along the Thames, east of London?"

"I did not know that, though I fear conditions are not much better in some of the cities in the colonies." They rode in silence for a moment. "Mrs. Trimble informed me of the squire's practice of slaveholding. She also mentioned the past disagreements between him and Lord Stanmore on the subject."

"Those disagreements are hardly in the *past*. His lordship's efforts in Parliament toward abolishing this wicked practice are aimed directly at those in league with Squire Wentworth. Sad to say, the King himself condones the trade and the use of slaves. Like many others, the squire's involvement is not limited to keeping the Africans on his farms here; he is also deeply involved with using them on a number of plantations that he owns in Jamaica. There are also rumors that he has invested heavily in ships that carry on the slave trade, as well." Mr. Cunningham's strong voice reflected his conviction. "Wentworth thinks he is above the world of men... and the morality that guides us. But in truth, he is standing on the edge of a precipice, and the earl's hand may just be the one to push him over."

"With so much animosity between them, why then does he allow you and Reverend Trimble—two men who appear to be openly aligned with his lordship—to visit his farms?"

The schoolmaster smiled grimly. "You have been living in a different world, Mrs. Ford. Who Squire Wentworth is and what he says are two separate things entirely. Though I'm a Scot, I can say without prejudice that this is the Englishman's way. It is obvious to all who know him well that he hates Lord Stanmore, but he'd never show it publicly. He has too much to lose." Cunningham's hand gestured to the farms on their right. "I was already running the schoolhouse at Knebworth five years ago when Wentworth bought all this land and Melbury Hall. Those who knew the man's background and knew of the plantations that he ran in Jamaica had no doubt that he bought this property for the purpose of rising in society."

"Was Lady Wentworth... Millicent already his wife at the time of his acquisition of Melbury Hall?"

"Nay! But she was acquired within short months," the schoolmaster replied sullenly. "Melbury Hall gave him status. His new wife—because of her money and noble lineage—gave him an entrée into the upper classes."

The hostility that bristled in Mr. Cunningham's words was unmistakable, but Rebecca found she could not blame the man. The
little that she'd seen and heard only served to confirm the schoolmaster's words.

"Then has there been any improvement as a result of your efforts?"

"I must sound very ungrateful," Cunningham added after a long
pause. "Aye! Some arrangements *were* agreed upon by the squire
after Lord Stanmore insisted. Small improvements, such as allowing the African children to take an hour out of their workday on Fri-
days to sit with me. Or calling in for Reverend Trimble when
someone is on their deathbed. Or allowing a doctor to be brought in
when someone has broken a bone. But 'tis still so . . . so disheart-
ening in many a way. For every step we have taken forward on behalf of these people, there seems to be a vicious price that must be
paid."

Ahead of them, a young dark-skinned boy was trying to pull an
overloaded sledge piled high with wood across the road.

"What kind of price, Mr. Cunningham?"

"Beatings. Families broken up and scattered willy-nilly. Sometimes, I tell you, there has even been the loss of life!"

Feeling suddenly ill, Rebecca turned sharply to the schoolmaster. "Here? At Melbury Hall? What has been done about this?"

"The law protects the squire. And every death has been called an
accident. If no one cries out . . . if there are no complaints, there is
no need for a magistrate's involvement."

"But surely people will eventually cry out against such conditions. It is happening in the colonies. One can stand oppression for
only so long."

The man's intense gaze suddenly turned guarded, as he stared
straight at the boy ahead who continued to struggle with the weight
of the load.

"I do not think I should say any more, Mrs. Ford. You are a visitor at Solgrave. You are not here to stay. 'Twas wrong of me to
complain so recklessly."

"Mr. Cunningham . . ." She stopped, seeing the boy slip and fall
hard to the ground.

They both reined in their horses. Before she could dismount, though, the lad was back on his feet and attempting to haul the sledge out of their way.

"That is far too heavy a load, Israel lad! Look, you've sunk into the rut here."

Mr. Cunningham dismounted and walked to the young worker. Taking hold of the back of the sledge, he pushed it out of the rut as Israel pulled. Beyond the bumpy road, a path sloped gently downward toward a winding river.

"Today is Friday, lad. I thought you'd be waiting at the Grove for your lessons."

The young boy's gaze never lifted past the dusty boots of the schoolmaster. "I cannot come to the lessons today, master."

Rebecca studied the lad's long black hair tied at the back of his neck. The old breeches were frayed at the knees, his feet were bare. He didn't look much older than her Jamey. It sickened Rebecca to think that no matter how young, no matter how innocent, a human being had no ability to escape the evil of enslavement. She thought of the words of the Frenchman Rousseau that she had read in Dr. Franklin's paper—*Man is born free; and everywhere he is in chains.*

Just then the boy lifted his head slightly to answer a question Mr. Cunningham asked. Rebecca and the schoolmaster saw the bruises on his face at the same time.

"What happened to you, Israel?"

He didn't answer. Rebecca immediately dismounted and came near, as Mr. Cunningham lifted the lad's face for a better look. She winced at the dark bruises under the left eye and on the cheek—at the cuts and swelling that marred one side of his mouth. His fall appeared to have opened an earlier wound, and there was fresh blood on his mouth. The most beautiful hazel eyes, though, watched her with curiosity.

"Did someone beat you? Is this Mickleby's handiwork? I warned that bailiff. I told him the next time he raised a hand . . ." The teacher continued, but the young boy acted as if he were not hearing a thing. He continued to stare at Rebecca.

"Israel?" she said when the schoolmaster paused. "My name is

Mrs. Ford. I am staying at Solgrave for a while this summer. We are neighbors."

His gaze studied every aspect of her face. They took in the hat, the hair, the eyes.

"Aye, ma'am," he finally said softly.

"Your lip is bleeding. Can I clean it for you?"

His gaze lowered again. " 'Tis nothing, ma'am."

She took out her handkerchief and offered it to him. "I am sorry that I asked. Of course you are old enough to take care of this yourself."

He stared at the lace handkerchief in her hand.

"Take it. I want you to use it."

Still he continued to stare.

"You may keep it."

"Keep it, ma'am?"

"I want you to."

With hesitant hands he reached out and took the handkerchief. But instead of bringing it to his bleeding lip, he closed his eyes momentarily and inhaled the cloth's slight lavender fragrance. When his hazel-colored eyes opened again, Rebecca was further surprised by the tears welling up in them.

"Bless you, ma'am," he whispered softly before tucking the handkerchief safely inside his shirt and turning to the load of wood piled high in his sledge.

Mr. Cunningham and Rebecca watched him pull the sledge down the hill, but the memory of his response to the simple smell of a handkerchief lingered.

"Are there many like him here at Melbury Hall?"

"There are at least a dozen children of African descent who live in the Grove. Some of the wee ones were born here, others were brought over with their mothers from the squire's plantations in Jamaica." The schoolmaster led Rebecca back toward the horses. "But Israel is the only one of them who has no one. And that may be why he is treated worse than the others."

Rebecca could understand Millicent's melancholy the day before. She could see perfectly the reason for her low spirits. She herself had not even arrived at Melbury Hall, and already her mood was souring.

"Who is this Mickleby that you mentioned?" She accepted Mr. Cunningham's help onto the mare.

"He is the latest in a line of hard-handed bailiffs that the squire has employed. A brute of a man with a nasty temper and a quick fist."

"What do you mean the latest?"

The schoolmaster's face darkened with loathing. "'Tis an ongoing cycle, as sure as the winter ice follows the fall rains. Someone gets hurt at Melbury Hall. Then the word eventually reaches Reverend Trimble or myself. Then Wentworth blames his bailiff, fires him, and brings in another . . . worse than the last."

"And he continues to hire 'brutes' to oversee the slaves he keeps?"

"I think I have finally figured out how he goes about all of this." The chimneys of the house came into view in the distance. "Squire Wentworth says he fires them here, but I'm thinking he just moves them to his plantations in Jamaica. And then he simply brings in the new bailiffs from there."

As they rode on in silence, Rebecca considered the problems she had faced for the past nine years in Philadelphia. They all seemed so inconsequential, suddenly, to what was facing these workers. Prejudice against a single boy because of his deafness or his deformed hand might be fought against one person at a time, but how could one fight an established agricultural business practice? Perhaps the same way, she thought, one person at a time.

"This is where we must part ways," Mr. Cunningham said as they arrived by the circular driveway that led on to the main house. He motioned toward the courtyard entrance. "One of the grooms will see to your horse, and the footman will notify Lady Wentworth of your presence."

"And where do you conduct your lessons, Mr. Cunningham?"

"I shall be stopping at the kitchens first, ma'am. This hour is promised to their young ones first. From there, I shall go past the house and down that knoll there, just past that glen they call the Grove. That's where all of the slaves have their huts."

"Mrs. Trimble mentioned that you might be in need of some as-

sistance with teaching. I am available after my visit with Lady
Wentworth. May I join you at the Grove?"

"You are not obligated, Mrs. Ford, to—"

"I know I am not," Rebecca replied amicably. "But I want to."

"I have to warn you though, the conditions . . . that is, your expectations of a classroom might be a wee bit different. . . ." The
schoolmaster's words trailed off and he looked off toward the
Grove and gathered his thoughts. "How these people are housed
and treated and where I conduct the lessons may not be the most fitting place for someone of your . . . quality, if I may say so."

"Do not waste your energy with such concerns, Mr. Cunningham." She spurred her horse toward the Hall. "I shall meet you at
the Grove later."

"Her name is Rebecca Neville," Oliver Birch announced with
quiet confidence. Long, hard miles and too many hours combing
the roughest quarters of Bristol, Dartmouth, and the Thames waterfront had bought that confidence. "At least, this was the name she
went by ten years ago . . . when she left England."

"What else?" Stanmore asked shortly, remembering the lie she
had told him of always living in the colonies. He thought back over
her words carefully. No, she had not lied . . . only hinted. Eva-
sively . . . and uncomfortably.

"They boarded the ship together. Elizabeth was already obviously unwell. Later, it was apparent to those on the ship that an
arrangement regarding James had been made between the two
women before they'd started the journey. All the interviews that
I've conducted confirm that Rebecca Neville was an acquaintance
of your late wife."

Stanmore recalled their discussion this very morning. As always, her main concern had been for James, and as a result she had
nearly slipped and defended Elizabeth openly against his accusa-
tions.

"The unsettling matter is that in all of the inquiries I've directed
toward your deceased wife's family and friends, no one has even
hinted of such an acquaintance."

"And she definitely was not one of those my father's doctor hired to attend her during her confinement?"

"Definitely not. Each of those people has been accounted for." Birch looked down a list of names on a piece of paper in his hand. "But if your lordship could suggest more people that I might still question. . . ."

"Too bad that coachman was killed in that accident."

"I'm certain he would agree, m'lord."

Stanmore shot the lawyer a withering look. "What of her past, prior to going to the colonies. Have you discovered *anything*?"

"Very little, m'lord," Birch answered, hiding his embarrassment. "But I am far from nearing the end in this search. I had not expected your lordship in London so quickly, so my people have still not reported back. Still, though, we have learned some rather puzzling things."

"Such as?"

"Well, soon after Rebecca's departure with your wife, there were some rumors of a widespread inquiry concerning Miss Neville's whereabouts. So far, I have only been able to confirm that this is true. I have even been able to ascertain the names of the lawyers who were conducting the search for her. But as far as who was behind the query—or for what reason—that I still need to search out. There is no chance, m'lord, that your late father—"

"Definitely not. He engaged no lawyers or anyone else at the time." Stanmore rose to his feet in the lawyer's study. The good smell of ink and old leather from Oliver's law books pervaded the air. "Neville . . . Neville. It is an old name, but I do not believe I know anyone of that family."

"It is a very old English name. Since the time of the Conqueror, they have been the earls of Westmoreland, Salisbury, Northumberland. But the noble line of the family became extinct over a century ago. I intend to look further into that. There must be some descendants still around. Perhaps I can locate the parents or family of Mrs. Ford."

"Elizabeth's snobbery would not have allowed her to befriend anyone beneath her own rank," Stanmore turned impatiently to his lawyer. "But if Rebecca was from a good family and not . . . well, not in trouble herself, why should she agree to go to the colonies in such haste? In addition, what ever could have convinced her to shoulder the responsibility of raising James under the conditions that you have described?"

"As you say, m'lord . . . *if* she were not in trouble herself." Birch shook his head gravely. "There is a great deal that we still need to discover about her. I will keep you informed as we learn more. How long does your lordship plan to stay in London?"

"I am meeting with Lord North tomorrow at noon. Unless something unforeseen happens before then, I plan to return to Solgrave tomorrow afternoon."

"I do not expect any great advances in our inquiries over the next few days. But if there were any new developments . . ."

"Solgrave is less than half a day's ride away." Stanmore then ordered the lawyer, "Any news of significance about Mrs. Ford's past, and you will notify me immediately."

So much to clear up, he thought. Though Stanmore was certain that she had assisted Elizabeth, he could not bring himself to doubt her integrity. Rebecca's devotion to James during all those years . . . her devotion now . . . was so pure.

For too many years than he cared to count, he'd seen facades at work in society and in politics. As a result, he'd developed a keen ability to recognize lies and identify ulterior motives. But in Rebecca's case, from the first day, he'd been able to look onto her soul. She was good and pure, as beautiful inside as she was on the outside.

He'd demanded this investigation. He'd wanted the truth, but he realized now that with every layer of truth revealed by Birch, he'd been unconsciously preparing a defense himself. It was liberating to admit that after so many years, Rebecca had managed to pry open his own shuttered heart.

He had to get back to Rebecca. There was simply too much between them that needed to be said.

Chapter 22

"I am sorry, ma'am, but Lady Wentworth is not accepting visitors today."

Rebecca refused to wither under the steely gaze of the bewigged and liveried footman blocking the main entrance of Melbury Hall. The man's blunt refusal, however, only served to increase her growing concern that something was wrong.

Mr. Cunningham's words about the squire of Melbury Hall, combined with the noticeable signs she'd seen yesterday in her friend's demeanor, had made her think of a woman she'd known slightly in Strawberry Alley in Philadelphia. She'd seen her often, though, moving furtively along the alley, cringing from contact with anyone. The woman had been the wife of the candlemaker, and the magistrates had hung him after they'd found her buried in the cellar of their neat brick house.

Now, Rebecca was becoming worried about the true nature of Millicent's situation.

"Has she taken ill?"

"Good day to you, ma'am."

She put a hand out to stop the servant from closing the door in her face. Mrs. Stockdale had taught her girls well how to be haughty with those in service, and the man's abruptness brought out Rebecca's training instantly.

"I am here by an invitation. How dare you close the door on me! Inform the squire that I am here . . . immediately."

The man's ruddy face took on a brighter hue beneath his powdered wig. "My deepest apologies, ma'am," he said with a deep bow. "I was under the impression that you were calling for Lady

Wentworth, ma'am." He took a step back, opening the door wider. "If you would be kind enough to wait in the drawing room, I shall announce your arrival to the squire."

Rebecca stared at the open doorway. Somehow, her plan of explaining her own twisted past had fallen by the wayside. In its place, Rebecca now found the desire to help her friend in whatever was plaguing her life. Perhaps meeting the squire would provide some answer. Perhaps.

Nonetheless, she still needed to find a way to see Millicent.

"Very well."

"This is a most beautiful house," she announced loudly, slowing her pace as the servant tried to usher her past a wide stairwell. Her voice echoed beneath the vaulted ceiling. She only hoped her voice would travel up the stairs to where she assumed Millicent might be. "Tell me . . . have the squire and his wife occupied this house for very long?"

There was no answer, and Rebecca decided that the footman had exhausted his ration of civility for the day.

They passed a number of servants on their way to the drawing room, and Rebecca was instantly aware that the sullen mood of the lady of the manor was not limited to Millicent alone.

"Are you quite certain that the squire is expecting you, ma'am?" the footman challenged as he led her into the designated room.

"Are you questioning me?" she replied in her loudest and haughtiest tones.

At the sound of the door closing, Rebecca let out an anxious breath. Her palms were clammy, her heart beating unevenly in her chest. She decided against sitting on one of the plush, cushioned chairs, and—to calm her nerves—began pacing the room.

What was she doing? With every new Englishman she met, she thought suddenly, she was exposing herself to greater danger. Exposing Jamey to danger. And now, she realized, she was even exposing Lord Stanmore to public censure. And it was all her own doing.

It was true—since arriving in England, Rebecca had drifted with each passing day further from her original purpose. Settling

Jamey with his father had been the sole reason for returning. But now, not even a month had passed since setting foot on English soil, and she had already entangled herself in too many matters to count.

But then again, had life ever allowed her any other way?

Suddenly, a side door to an adjoining room opened a crack, drawing her attention. Rebecca stood still, waiting uncertainly as the door slowly swung back.

The face that peered through the opening made Rebecca gasp with dismay.

"Millicent!"

"Hush!" the other woman cried nervously, motioning for Rebecca to come closer. "Please do not say or do anything that would make my husband suspect that you have seen me. It would be dangerous . . . for both of us."

A bruise of purple and yellow and green spread in an ugly crescent beneath one of her eyes. Her upper lip, too, was swollen and discolored. She did not appear to be able to stand straight.

"What happened to you?"

"Please do not ask. If anyone should know, I . . . I could not bear the shame." The battered woman clutched at Rebecca's arms, her eyes darting constantly toward the door. "But for your own sake . . . for mine . . . do not tell him we know each other . . . that we are friends."

"But your face!" Rebecca raised a hand to touch the bruise above her mouth. Millicent caught her hand and pressed it frantically between her own.

"Make some excuses to him, but do not go. I need to talk to you." She glanced nervously toward the door. "But he cannot know."

"I am meeting Mr. Cunningham by the Grove in an hour. Could you come there?"

"I don't know!" Tears sprang to her desperate eyes. "I shall try! But I cannot let the schoolmaster see me like this. Please don't say anything to him, either. Please, Rebecca . . . I need your help! I cannot live like this anymore!"

Her anguished plea hung in the air as she backed out of the

room and pulled the door shut. Rebecca had had no time to gather her thoughts or compose herself, though, when the main door to the room opened. She whirled hastily and faced Squire Wentworth.

"Well! Mrs. Ford, I take it."

Rebecca dropped a small curtsy. Quite unlike the monstrous giant she'd assumed him to be, the squire was a man of medium height. He had not yet completely dressed for the day, but was comfortably though carelessly attired in breeches, slippers, and a satin brocade dressing gown. His hair, thinning and fashionably curled, was tied in the back. His features were regular, cocksure, perhaps even handsome, and—though a heavy odor of spirits wafted across the drawing room—the squire's face was certainly not the face of a brute.

But Rebecca was not fooled for a moment. Sir Charles Hartington had been considered handsome by many, as well. And as she thought this, the squire's gaze swept downward from her face, taking in her attire in a way that reminded her very clearly of her dead employer.

"I would like you to know that I have no intention of complaining. But unless my memory is failing me, I cannot recollect . . ." His lips curled into a smile. "And I would certainly remember extending an invitation to so lovely a visitor."

"Allow me to apologize, sir," Rebecca said quietly. "But I rode over to Melbury Hall this morning with the intention of assisting Mr. Cunningham with his lessons to those in your service."

"I see." The look of smooth sophistication slipped for an instant, but the squire quickly recovered himself.

"I thought it only proper to announce my presence to Lady Wentworth or yourself." She tried to not show her discomfort under the man's wandering gaze as he closely studied every inch of her face . . . followed by every curve of her body.

"I understand you are staying at Solgrave."

"That is correct, sir."

He walked toward her, and Rebecca fought the urge to take a step back. It was clear to her that he had already been drinking heavily, as early as it was.

"And you are a . . . friend of our illustrious neighbor, the Earl of Stanmore, Mrs. Ford?"

The tone of his question conveyed an impertinence, a nuance of disrespect. His attitude and his disordered condition put her off, increased her discomfort . . . made her feel vulnerable. Considering those feelings, she welcomed his invoking of Stanmore's name. There was protection in it.

"I am Lord Stanmore's guest, sir."

His careless look became a lecherous grin. "Damn Stanmore! His taste in women is damnably fine."

Rebecca opened her mouth to retort, but shut it again immediately. She refused to be baited, no matter what this man chose to think. He motioned toward a chair, but she declined the offer and glanced at the direction of the door.

"I believe I shall just take my leave, Squire Wentworth, now that we have been introduced. So if you do not mind, I shall go and join Mr. Cunningham. It was a pleasure meeting—"

"But I *do* mind!" the squire replied seriously. Crossing the room to a sideboard, he picked up a crystal decanter from a silver tray and poured himself out a generous portion of amber-colored liquid. "You must join me, Mrs. Ford."

She declined with a shake of her head. "I am not partial to drinking this early in the day."

"This early, did you say?" He raised his glass to her with an impudent wink. "Then I must drink alone . . . to intoxicating beauty."

Before she could move, the squire had drained the glass and banged it down onto the sideboard. As he sloshed more into the glass, she started for the door, but he moved quickly to cut her off, carrying his glass with him.

"Tell me, ma'am. What is Cunningham's attraction?"

She stopped. "Pardon me?"

"Cunningham . . . the blasted schoolmaster. The dog is a Scot. He is poor. Has no place in society. Even his damned looks are no asset. So answer me"—his face was growing flushed from the drink—"why do you women all throw yourselves at him?"

Temper heated the blood pulsing in her veins. "I hardly understand you. Your accusation, sir—and I believe I am not mistaken that you are accusing me—is entirely unfounded. I have known the schoolmaster only since this morning, and my offer of helping him in teaching some of your workers comes from charity and not from some . . . some infatuation, if that is what you mean!"

He laughed without a shred of mirth. "My deepest, humblest apologies. I am clearly mistaken," he said with a facetious bow. "Then I must assume you are still the dalliance *du jour* of Stanmore. Indeed, I must be correct. I can see my good neighbor still has you blinded with his charm. Well, the time will come, my sweet—and much sooner than you think—when he will be replacing you with the next pretty face that happens to cross his path."

She clamped her mouth shut, refusing to respond to such insolence.

"But there is a lot to be gained for a woman of your type in being my friend as well. A woman cannot have too many protectors these days, you know."

"I appreciate the offer, sir," she replied, infusing her tone with sarcasm. "But I am not presently searching for such 'friends.' And you are completely mistaken in Lord Sta—"

"But you should be, my dear woman. You should be." He threw himself carelessly into a chair by the door and pointed at her with his glass. "I am told you met Lady Nisdale yesterday . . . in that godforsaken village down the road."

Rebecca glanced at the door, wondering if the squire would physically stop her from leaving.

"Now she—very much like you yourself—was a woman with no title and even less means when we first met years ago." He took another long swig of his drink. "Of course, she'd show a little temper if she ever found out what I am telling you right now, but Louisa's conquests have gone right to her head. Now that I think of it, she may just be in need of a good setting down."

"If you'll forgive me, sir, Mr. Cunningham—"

"Let the bastard wait. I have important things to share with you . . . now that we're to be neighbors . . . for a time." He waved a hand in the air. "Did you know I was the one who broke in Louisa. Nay, of course, you couldn't know. Well, it was I who taught her everything that she knows about pleasing a man. It is an art, you know, to reduce a man to mere clay in your hands." His eyes focused on her breasts. "After that, of course, she had no trouble in finding a husband. Old and rich, that is what she went after. And title. And wealth. Aye, Nisdale gave her all of it during the three years the doting old fool survived in her clutches."

The fire in her veins quickly turned to ice. The man's gaze appeared to have become permanently fixed on her body.

"Of course, Louisa has made a fatal mistake in thinking that simply luring Stanmore to her bed would make him her next husband. Now, if she had talked to me first, I would have saved her the heartache she is going through as we speak. You see, it is only as a good neighbor that I share these things with you." His eyes were narrowed with mischief as he finally looked up into her face. "I know a secret about Stanmore's past that will explain why the earl will never . . . hear me, my sweet . . . *never* trust a woman enough to take as a wife."

It wasn't for the sake of her own personal interest that she should listen, Rebecca assured herself, but for the first time, she was curious in hearing what this man had to say. He must have sensed her change in attitude, though, for a smile broke across his lips.

"Are you aware that the boy—that cripple that you raised in the colonies—is not Stanmore's son?"

Rebecca stepped back, stunned by the man's words.

"Are you also aware that Stanmore knows who it was *exactly* his wife opened her legs to, while he was away playing the hero against the French at Quebec?" He leaned forward and stared with malicious delight into her face. "Did you know that my illustrious neighbor knows that his own father cuckolded him?"

The room whirled around her.

"Aye, the cripple is the old earl's bastard!"

Rebecca tasted the bile rising in her throat.

"So you see, Stanmore is not the marrying type, my pet. He has sworn on his father's grave never to trust a woman again." He sat back in the chair. "And who can blame him?"

The walls of the room were beginning to pulse, and Rebecca shook her head to clear it. Her feet seemed to be rooted to the floor.

"So, my sweet, that is why it is only in your best interest to sever your ties with the heartless cur of Solgrave . . . before he throws you over. I like what I see in you, and I am quite prepared to be your friend."

An age seemed to pass before she could find her voice.

"I shall remember your offer," Rebecca whispered, forcing her legs to move toward the door.

Nearly blinded by tears, she made her way from the room and pushed past a blur of stairs and arches and footmen. Suddenly, she found herself standing in the courtyard before the house, walls of brick and a high iron gate still surrounding her . . . and only fields with black workers were visible beyond.

Leaving the half dozen servant children with admonitions to read a little each day and say their prayers, William Cunningham went out through the kitchens, the only way that he was allowed in and out of the house.

As he went, he glanced past the neglected, old-style formal gardens—with their trellised roses and arbors—toward the more fashionable "natural" vista stretching out from the house. The view had been under construction for a number of years now, though Cunningham wondered whether Capability Brown—from whom the design had certainly been stolen—wouldn't think it somewhat hackneyed, vulgar, and overdone.

As he passed the entry to the formal garden, he was surprised to hear two voices coming over the enclosing wall. One voice he recognized, and he stopped with dismay, overhearing her words. Turning back to the gate, he looked in to see the two women inside huddled together on a stone bench. Neither noticed his approach until he was upon them.

"Please forgive me, m'lady!" the servant girl was saying. "I tried . . . I swear on my mother's grave . . . but she is the devil! I know she meant all those horrible—"

"Hush, Vi! No damage done! It was my fault to burden you . . ."

Lady Wentworth stopped abruptly as Cunningham drew up before them, trying to think of some apology for intruding upon them.

"Mr. Cunningham."

"Lady Wentworth." He bowed. The young servant quickly dropped a curtsy before running back toward the house. He watched her wiping her tearstained face as she ran. "I am sorry for . . . for disturbing you."

He stopped. The veil of a tall, brimmed hat covered the face to her delicate chin. Her dress was long-sleeved, the neckline high, in spite of the comfortably warm weather. She wore white gloves that hid every bit of skin. Cunningham, though, didn't have to see her eyes to know that there was something terribly wrong. The way she had turned her face from him told him a great deal. He stepped closer.

"Lady Wentworth, about my conduct the other evening . . ."

Holding up a gloved hand to him, she glanced toward the house. Without a word, she stood and walked quickly from the garden, turning her steps toward the path through the woods that eventually wound down to the Grove. Shocked by the suddenness of her action, Cunningham quickly followed. He saw her stumble once in her rush, but before he could reach her, she had recovered and disappeared into the trees. He hurried his steps.

"Lady Wentworth . . . Millicent!"

Not heeding his call, she continued rushing down the path. He caught her beneath the protective limbs of a great oak.

"Millicent!" Cunningham called out, taking hold of her arm. For the first time, he realized she was crying. "Stop and talk to me. Please, Millicent."

She struggled weakly as he turned her in his arms. When he drew her against him, though, her hands came up to push at his chest.

"I beg you!" he said softly. "I cannot concentrate on my work, knowing you are still angry with me."

Millicent turned her face away, but he saw the tremble in her chin and felt the soft sob that wracked her body. He cupped her hands between his own and bent his head over them. "I am sorry! I am terribly sorry for my transgression. It was wrong of me to try to kiss you. I . . . I have been so frustrated with everything at Mel-bury Hall, with the lack of progress here while you were away. And then . . . then you were here with me . . . and all that I felt for you . . . feel for you . . . spilled over!"

"Do not!" she whispered. "Please, William."

Cunningham lifted his head and found her veiled face before him.

"Please, refrain from such talk," she whispered again. She gently pulled her hands free of his grasp and stepped back. "You should not speak what is in your heart. I am committed to the vow I took . . . to my marriage."

"You are the only one who is," he said bitterly. "Your servants this morning were more eager to speak of your husband and Lady Nisdale than—"

"I am not interested in them." She shook her head and took another step back. "I respect you, Mr. Cunningham. I am . . . very fond of you. Please! Do not deprive me of your friendship. Allow me *one* thing that is good and true in my life."

He opened his mouth to protest. He knew Millicent felt much more for him than she was admitting right now. But her beseeching attitude—the pleading whisper of *needing his friendship*—gave him pause. More than anything else, he knew this was true. He bowed his head, surrendering to her wishes. For now.

"As you wish, m'lady. I am, as always, your devoted friend and servant."

"Thank you, William." Her gloved hand reached under the veil, and she wiped at her tears. "I was . . . I am to meet Mrs. Ford at the Grove."

"I am going there myself. May I accompany you?"

She looked back toward the house nervously. "I . . . I prefer not. Would you be so kind as to allow me to walk on ahead of you?"

He bowed again, suddenly feeling bruised by her lack of interest. As Millicent departed, the schoolmaster leaned a shoulder against the trunk of the great oak, biding his time impatiently and brooding over the ache in his chest.

What William Cunningham didn't see, though, standing nearby in the shadows of the wood, was a very interested bystander.

Mickleby, the bailiff, who had heard every word, smiled grimly at his good fortune.

The squire would, no doubt, reward him handsomely to hear even a portion of what he'd heard. Aye, the honest and proper Lady Wentworth might just prove to be a profitable little package for him, Mickleby thought.

Quite profitable, indeed.

Chapter 23

Though uncertainty filled her until she felt ready to burst, still Rebecca knew she could not leave Melbury Hall without seeing Millicent.

She was not daft enough to believe everything that Wentworth had told her, but something in the gleeful assuredness with which he had spoken filled her with dread. And Rebecca was hardly secure enough in everything that she had seen in the Earl of Stanmore and in his relationship with his son to discredit totally the squire's words. But the answers to her questions resided at Solgrave, and she was now painfully impatient to be returning there.

First, though, a woman . . . a friend . . . needed her.

Rebecca directed her horse down the path one of the grooms had told her would lead to the Grove. She saw the cluster of decrepit huts on the river at the same time as a large man of advancing years appeared out of nowhere and staggered into the path. It took all of Rebecca's presence of mind to yank the horse's head around. The black man stopped, gazing uncomprehendingly at the animal blocking his path. Rebecca slid off the horse's back and, holding the reins, peered at the distracted man over the back of the mare.

Taller than Stanmore and strongly built, the man stared without moving. Rebecca was shocked to see that beneath short-cropped hair of black and gray, both of his ears had been cut off and his face was marked with innumerable scars. Despite his size and the fierce look borne of his mutilated features, though, he appeared weak and faint.

Without thinking, Rebecca found herself going around the animal and standing next to him.

"I . . . I was in search of the Grove, but I believe I've found it."
She lifted a hand and patted the horse's neck. The man's gaze
drifted to the movements of her fingers as she combed the long
mane.

"She's a friendly one, so gentle that even a novice like me has
no trouble handling her."

"Beg pardon, ma'am." Rebecca turned with a start at the deep
voice of a man coming up from the river. She watched him drop a
large basket beside the path and walk toward her. "Moses meant no
harm. No harm, at all. I'll take him away, if you please."

"He did no harm," she said quietly to the newcomer.

This man—younger, shorter, and thinner than Moses—appeared
weak and ill, but still showed a protectiveness toward the older
slave that impressed Rebecca.

"I was hoping to meet Lady Wentworth . . . or Mr. Cunningham
here."

"I don't know if Lady Wentworth will be coming this way
today, ma'am." His somber expression told Rebecca that he must
know of Millicent's condition. Everybody at Melbury Hall seemed
to have the same look about the eyes. The same sadness. The same
downtrodden spirit. Even she herself was feeling the same oppres-
sive mood.

The newcomer touched Moses on the arm, and the big man
turned immediately to the other.

"Jonah . . ." The relief was instant—all traces of fear evaporat-
ing from the older man's expression. "Jonah . . ."

The younger man shook his head at his friend, and the other
went silent. "If you don't mind waiting here, ma'am, I'll find Mr.
Cunningham for you."

"Thank you," Rebecca whispered, watching the two of them
walk away. The backs of both men's frayed shirts were stained with
blood. Through a rip in Jonah's sleeve, she could see an oozing cut
that looked too much like the result of a fresh lashing. Rebecca's
stomach turned, and she grabbed at the bridle of the horse for support as the helplessness of these men's situation struck her with the
force of a club.

Millicent's appearance some time later did little to alleviate Rebecca's dismay. Though dressed and wearing a hat and veil that hid her bruises, she glided through the trees like some forest-dwelling ghost.

"Thank you for meeting me here."

Rebecca reached out and the two women embraced briefly before Millicent pulled back to wipe the tears away from under the veil.

"I am the one who must thank you . . . for keeping my secret yesterday."

"Walk with me a little?" Millicent asked, looking back the way she had come.

Rebecca nodded and tied the reins of the horse to the bough of a tree.

"Do not thank me yet. I may have done you a great wrong," Millicent said as soon as they stepped onto a path leading along the river. "I sent you a note this morning, apologizing and trying to reschedule our ride."

"But I never received it."

"I know. Lady Nisdale intercepted it before it ever left the house." Millicent's gloved hands clutched Rebecca's. "You have found a bitter enemy in that woman."

She didn't have to ask why. While Lord Stanmore's attention had elated Rebecca, she knew it had infuriated Lady Nisdale.

"She asked me many questions about you yesterday on our way back to Melbury Hall. None of which I answered, continuing the pretense of not knowing you. But I believe from the tone of my letter this morning—although I did not reveal your true name—she might guess at our deception . . . perhaps even our connection."

It was only a matter of time. She was to be exposed. Rebecca knew it. And it was no longer the fear of prosecution and death that horrified her, but the possibility of bringing dishonor to Jamey and to the Earl of Stanmore's name. Wentworth's words crowded her mind. What if he were speaking the truth about the illicit affair between Elizabeth and the late Lord Stanmore?

Stanmore's aversion to establishing any type of rapport with Jamey supported such a claim. She had been a fool to insist on something between the two that could never exist. And who, other than an honorable man, a man who was devoted to his family despite the lies of the past, would search out and bring this child back . . . and claim him as his own? It was time for her to let them be. Jamey already had much more than she could ever have given him in life. He was strong enough to stand on his own. It was time for her to go.

"Why *are* you denying your past, Rebecca. Your upbringing in England?"

Millicent's question drew her out of her reverie.

"Ten years ago, I killed a man."

A fallen tree lay on its side by the river, and the two women sat down beside each other. Having made up her mind to go, Rebecca found that she had no fear of telling the truth. All of it. From her first meeting with Mary Hartington, to the murder of Sir Charles, to the carriage ride and ocean journey with Elizabeth Wakefield . . . and Jamey. She even told her friend about her years in Philadelphia.

"My God, I admire you!" Millicent said when she'd finished. "All that you have done!"

They sat for a few moments without speaking, the gurgling sounds of the river filling the air.

Millicent stared at the rippling currents. "I wish I had the courage to kill *my* husband."

"There are better ways to deal with hardship than murder." Rebecca took her friend's hand. "I do not regret what I did that night so many years ago. The brutality of some men justifiably falls back on them. But if I had ever had an option—a family to escape to, to protect me, anything or anywhere outside of that doomed house that night that I could have gone—lives would have been saved. Mine *and* that evil man's."

"But Fate brought you life, too. If you had not acted when and as you did, you would never have found Jamey."

Rebecca didn't want to think of what her life would have been without him. True, she'd had an unexpected blessing. Still, though, as she watched Millicent slightly lift the veil on her face to wipe her tearing eyes, she could not wish her own path for her friend. Millicent had never done anything to prepare herself for such a life.

"You have family, wealth of your own. Why not leave the squire?"

Millicent shook her head and stared at the path leading back to the Grove. "I cannot. He will not let me go."

Rebecca watched her. The bruises, now visible with the veil pushed up onto the brim of the hat, were ugly marks of his viciousness.

"This is not the first time that he has treated you like this, is it?"

Millicent's silence was her answer.

"Does your family know of his cruelty?"

Fresh tears rolled down her bruised cheeks. "I am rarely allowed to see any of them now. And when I do, he is always there. But even if they knew, I do not believe they can do anything, anyway. My two older sisters are the only ones left. Each of them has her own husband and children to keep them busy. And my uncle . . . he was all too glad to get rid of me when he gave me away to Wentworth. He surely has no desire to have me back again. He would not brook such disgrace being brought to his doorstep."

Millicent was far more vulnerable than Rebecca had thought. "There must be other ways. What about your own income . . . from your family? With that in hand, perhaps you can move away . . . run away if you have to."

"He would kill me." Her voice was cold, passionless, defeated. "That is what he did to his first wife. I know it now. Wentworth told me himself after the first year of our marriage . . . after I threatened to leave him if he ever beat me again."

A breeze rustled the leaves in the treetops. Millicent shivered.

"To him, I am just property, like everything else here—the land, these poor workers, his horses and dogs and sheep and cattle. He sees it as his right to abuse us and cut us down when we are no longer useful to him. His first wife's family owned a number of plantations in Jamaica. That is where he made a small fortune, but just before he decided to move back to England, she mysteriously died." Millicent's gray eyes were empty of emotion, as if it were she who was dead. "Wentworth told me, in his drunken boasting, that she had worn out her value."

Rebecca placed her arm around her friend's shoulders. She was trembling.

"My uncle was more than eager to be rid of me. Twenty-three years old I was . . . and no eager suitors. So he gave me to him. Wentworth married me as many men of rising fortune marry—for name, for lineage, for connections in society. And now, after five years, he has gained everything that I could bring him. I too have worn out my usefulness, Rebecca. He is going to kill me. I know he is just looking for a way—one wrong step and I shall die. It is only a matter of time."

"Oh, Millicent!" Rebecca hugged the shivering woman tightly. "You cannot stay here. Come with me to Solgrave."

"I cannot!" She shook her head sadly before pulling out of the embrace and wiping her face. "If I cannot burden my own family, I certainly cannot drag strangers into it. You are the only one I have ever told any of this to. You are the only one I trust."

"Then . . . then come back with me to the colonies."

The idea unfolded in Rebecca's mind as quickly as it occurred to her. Everything was suddenly making sense. This was what was meant to be. She was losing Jamey, but gaining someone else to help and to nurture until Millicent was strong enough to stand on her own. She was a friend who desperately needed her help. This was her opportunity to give to someone what Elizabeth Wakefield had once given her—a second chance at life!

"I told you . . . no one found me there in ten years. It is a great new world! We can disappear in it together. He cannot find you there, Millicent."

"I shan't have any access to my income."

"Will you miss it?"

Millicent thought for a moment and then shook her head, her face brightening as a shred of fear dropped away. "I should be happy never to sleep in a real bed again. I would happily wear nothing finer than a rag, so long as no man could ever again raise a hand to strike me . . . or violate my body against my wishes."

"Then you will be happy there. Between the two of us, we shall work and make an honest living. I have done it before. We can do it again."

Millicent grasped Rebecca's hands fiercely in her own. "Do you really mean it? Will you take me back with you?"

"I shall! I promise you, we shall do it together!"

The message from the prime minister was urgent in its tone, and Stanmore went to the Downing Street residence certain that Lord North would be asking him about his possible involvement in recent attacks on the British slave trade. In the previous fortnight, there had been yet another commotion in a shipyard—this time in Liverpool—which had been contracted to build two new slave ships. And only two days ago, a slaver had burned in the Thames, sinking into the murky waters off Deptford.

In and out of Parliament, it was no secret that Stanmore indirectly supported factions dedicated to creating havoc for the slave traders. The prime minister had made a number of comments this spring, though, implying that the earl's support was perhaps more active than had been commonly believed. And there could be no doubt, Stanmore thought as he waited for Lord North, the target-shooting destruction of the five ships by the Royal Navy had caused the government some embarrassment.

Lord North's greeting, however, couldn't have been more cordial. Following the prime minister into his private study, Stanmore was greatly surprised to learn that the nature of their meeting was to be unofficial . . . of a personal nature, even.

"Just another case of my rather zealous secretary overreacting, I'm afraid. I simply wanted to see you the next time you were in London, Stanmore. During those last hectic days of Parliament, I never had the opportunity of congratulating you on your son's return."

Stanmore arched an eyebrow in surprise, but tried to relax his defenses as he sat down across from the prime minister in one of the large, comfortably upholstered chairs. "Thank you, m'lord."

The sound of children's voices and small feet running in the corridor drew Lord North's gaze to the doorway. With a look of contented amusement, the most powerful man in England waited until the footsteps had retreated toward other areas of the residence.

"Children are truly wondrous creatures. But they need room to run, fresh air to breathe. We are all ready for the country, I think."

Lord North was well known for his fondness for his children, and the affection showed as his prominent eyes continued to focus on the door.

"So we shall depart tomorrow for Banbury and Wroxton Abbey." A resigned sigh escaped his chest. "Unfortunately, I shall need to return to London shortly. I am expected to be at the White House at Kew, you know, to attend the King on his birthday."

His Majesty's personal friendship with the prime minister was no secret at Court. And Stanmore shared the feeling. Lord North's complete lack of haughty self-importance, along with his personal integrity and unblemished sense of honor, made him a refreshing change from many recent leaders in British government.

"And I hear that you have chosen the clean country air for your son, as well. Are you planning on having him remain at Solgrave for the summer?"

"He seems happiest there."

"His name is James. Is it not?"

"James Samuel. After my father."

"And I assume you have made arrangements for him to attend Eton?"

"Of course. He will be starting in the fall term, m'lord." He eyed the prime minister carefully. Perhaps it was simply his own suspicious nature, but Stanmore could not help but wonder at the purpose behind these questions. True, he thought, it could simply be an opportunity for the man to expand their acquaintance on a personal level. Although they'd both attended Eton and Oxford, they had not been classmates nor particularly close friends.

"My oldest boy is there, now, you know." Lord North propped his legs up on the table before him. "Ah, but you are a very fortunate man, Stanmore. I must tell you, even living as we do here in the center of culture and education—the 'capital of the world' as Horace Walpole put it—my wife has had a devil of a time finding governesses and tutors suited to seeing to our young ones' needs." He hooked his thumbs into his waistcoat pockets and considered for a moment. "Rumor has it, though, that your son, James, has had a very fine upbringing thus far, and under the care of a total stranger, no less . . . *despite* being raised in those infernal colonies."

"He has been provided with an excellent beginning," Stanmore answered truthfully. The rumors that had reached the prime minister had been intentionally started by the earl himself. It was much easier to control the shape of rumors' constructions if you laid the foundation yourself. Regarding the manner and condition of James's upbringing, though, there was not a single thing that he would fault Rebecca with. She had accomplished far more than anyone else with her limited financial resources could have possibly done.

"Indeed," Lord North said, breaking into his thoughts. "And this mystery woman from the colonies—the one who has done such an excellent job in raising your son—I understand she is staying with you for a time."

"She is, m'lord."

"And is she an angel of mercy or . . . something more mercenary, would you say?"

"Without a doubt, Mrs. Ford is an angel. Everything she has done has certainly been motivated by her compassion for James and my late wife. The woman brought him up with absolutely no expectation of any financial reward."

A curious smile broke out on the prime minister's face, and Stanmore realized it was the result of his quick defense of Rebecca. "She certainly sounds like a most enchanting woman. Tell me this, Stanmore, how long is she planning to stay in England?"

He didn't want to think about Rebecca's departure. "I assume she will be staying for a while yet. She believes that James should be completely settled before she takes her leave and returns to the colonies."

"A smart woman . . . and a benevolent one." Lord North pouted his thick lips as he considered for a moment. "To be the sole provider for a child as she has done for so many years—I must assume this Mrs. Ford is quite attached to your son. And yet, she is willing to sever the tender bonds that connect a mother and child—even an adoptive one, I should think—and leave him when her presence is no longer needed. She is certainly a remarkable woman."

Remarkable was too feeble a word to describe her. Stanmore looked away as the confusion surrounding Rebecca's true identity gnawed at him. She hadn't told him the truth about her past. But then again, neither had he shared anything of his own life.

"I would very much like to meet them."

Stanmore's attention snapped back to his host, who was studying him with great interest. "I beg your pardon, m'lord?"

"I said I would very much like to meet both your son and your fascinating Mrs. Ford." The prime minister put his feet on the floor. "You cannot blame me for being impressed with her. Perhaps she would consider accepting a position in my household instead of returning to that haven of troublemakers in Philadelphia."

"She is not seeking a position, at all." His objection to the offer was immediate and his tone sounded curt, even to his own ears. But something had clicked inside of his head. The world suddenly looked different to him. He didn't *want* Rebecca engaged by someone else. He didn't want her dependent on anyone else. By the devil, he was able to support her and provide for her, and that was the way it would stand.

This possessiveness he was feeling about her future unsettled him, though. For the first time, a sense of permanence had edged into his perspective. In his mind's eye, even now he could see her beautiful face, her eyes, her hair, her smile. The devil take him . . . he missed her!

"Well, I should still like to meet her before she leaves," North persisted. "In fact, would you object to me paying you a visit down in the country?"

"I thought you mentioned that your lordship was planning to travel to Wroxton Abbey . . . and then with the King to Kew."

"Indeed, I am. But I shall return to London by the way of Hertfordshire before the King's Birthday. Come, Stanmore, you will surely extend your hospitality to a weary traveler?"

"You are always welcome at Solgrave, m'lord," Stanmore said, though he doubted Lord North noted much enthusiasm in his face.

Chapter 24

Rebecca's decision had been made, but she knew she could not go until she had some answers.

As delicate a matter as it was, thus far she had avoided raising the suspicions of those whom she had questioned. Unfortunately, neither Mrs. Trent nor Daniel had been able to shed any light yesterday on the late Lady Stanmore. To both of these people, Elizabeth Wakefield had been a spoiled young woman who had left the pampering of her own family and had expected the same treatment from her husband's family. The fact that she had chosen to stay away from Solgrave for the short duration of her marriage only added to their suspicion and hostility. Rebecca had quickly turned her discussions with them to more mundane topics.

Discarding any hope of gaining any information from Daniel and Mrs. Trent, she had decided to focus her efforts in bringing up the topic with Philip. Despite the London house steward's reputation for a dour humor and for brevity, Rebecca had found the older man to be nothing short of charming from the first day they had met.

Saturday morning dawned gray and wet and unusually cold for a day so near the end of May. Jamey, free of Mr. Clarke and schoolwork, was at Rebecca's door shortly after dawn, restless and seeking her company. It was time together they both needed. They had shared many moments like this in Philadelphia, and she cherished them. At the same time, she knew this was perhaps one of the last mornings like this they would ever have.

Snuggled together, she told herself she was able to leave him. She wasn't as worried about him as she'd been when they first arrived. He had once again managed to get his feet under him, as he had done in the streets and on the wharves before. But with this renewed sense of independence, she noticed the loss of naïveté that was part of being a boy. Somehow, he seemed to be maturing so quickly. His questions no longer centered on his own needs, now focusing—curiously enough—on more worldly subjects. Jamey seemed genuinely interested in the running of an estate like Solgrave. He actually asked about his father—his involvement in politics, his influence—questions that had totally surprised Rebecca.

Without a hint of pride, Jamey appeared to be accepting who he was and where he was destined to be. And this eased Rebecca's own guilt regarding her decision to wait to reveal the truth of her departure until the very last moment possible. To shift the attention from her own misery regarding their future separation, she told Jamey about Stanmore's promise of taking him out for a ride around the estate every morning. Although he tried to hide it, she thought he actually looked pleased.

Shortly after breakfast, as Jamey ran off through the misty weather toward the stables to spend some time grooming the pony that he'd chosen last week, Rebecca sought Philip out. She found him overseeing the work of Lord Stanmore's valet.

"Philip, would you be kind enough to give me a tour of the galleries?" She hid a smile at the valet's look of gratitude, and noted that even Philip brightened. Unlike Daniel, who was busy with his normal routine of running Solgrave, the older man was apparently bored beyond measure with the earl gone.

They had begun their tour in the lower gallery, passing before centuries' old portraits of some of the earl's ancestors. With Philip providing a litany of names and titles, and the mark each subject had made on history, they had paused before each portrait. It wasn't until they'd stopped before a more recent painting of a beautiful, dark-haired young woman standing with Solgrave in the background, though, that Rebecca had found herself entranced. The woman was holding a child.

"Lady Margaret. The daughter of the late James Graham, fourth

Marquis and first Duke of Montrose. The mother to the present Earl of Stanmore."

"The resemblance is remarkable," Rebecca murmured. The same high cheekbones, the full lips, even the eyes—with the exception of their expressions—were the same. Lady Margaret was an incredibly striking woman, and so was her son. "What happened to her?"

"Happened? Why, nothing!" Philip said, surprised. "Lady Margaret Buchanan—as she prefers to be addressed now—is doing quite well, living at her family holding in Scotland."

Rebecca had already learned that the way to motivate Philip to reveal more was not through asking questions. Instead, patience and simple interest encouraged him the most. She was not disappointed as he lowered his voice somewhat, speaking to her in a tone that she understood to be confidential.

"Lady Margaret and the late Earl of Stanmore had what is vulgarly called an arranged marriage. I am sorry to say that there never existed any affection between the husband and wife—no camaraderie ever grew between them. The good lady abided by her family's wishes, however, and stayed with his lordship until their son was raised to the age of five. Then she took her leave and retired to Buchanan House in Scotland . . . near a place called Loch Lomond."

No wonder Stanmore had such a negative view of love, Rebecca thought. Though she herself had not grown up in a family, she had seen it for herself . . . been a part of it . . . in the Strawberry Alley home of Molly and John Butler.

"If I may be allowed to speak candidly, ma'am, no one ever blamed her for leaving. For all of his good qualities, James Wakefield was, at best, a very difficult man. And—just between us—as the years passed, his lordship became . . . well, nigh to impossible." The steward stared thoughtfully at the portrait. "You should know that, regardless of the miles between them, our present Lord Stanmore has a far better rapport with his mother than he ever had with his father."

"His lordship mentioned to me that he spends a month in Scotland each fall."

"That he does," Philip confirmed. "It began as a tradition when he was a lad . . . to appease Lady Margaret's family. But if the truth be told, he always enjoyed the holiday. Still does."

Rebecca moved reluctantly away from the portrait, looking at the others. As she and Philip continued to move on along the gallery, she realized that, even here, there were no reminders of Elizabeth.

"I believe James will enjoy viewing this gallery."

"He already has." Philip nodded approvingly. "I found him here yesterday afternoon engrossed in the pictures, so I offered to be his guide and he accepted it, fine lad that he is. I hope you will accept my congratulations, Mrs. Ford, in the way that you have raised the young master."

"All the credit is due to him," she said softly. "He is a most intelligent and good-hearted boy. Was there anything James was looking for in here particularly?"

"Indeed, ma'am. A picture of his mother," he replied, hesitantly glancing in her direction.

"All as it should be," she replied. "For James to accept his lineage, he needs to see that someone far better than I brought him into this world."

"Not *better*, if I may say so, Mrs. Ford. Master James was only brought into the world by someone *other* than you."

She looked down at her hands, resisting the urge to speak in Elizabeth's defense. Her battle was not with this man, she reminded herself.

"Thank you," she said a moment later. "All the same, is there a portrait of James's mother anywhere for him to see?"

Philip shook his head. "Not at Solgrave, ma'am. No time for a portrait to be done. You see, they were married in July of 1759. Less than a month after their marriage, his lordship took his place as a major in His Majesty's 45th Regiment of Foot and sailed to the colonies to join in the taking of Quebec. He was away for two years. With Samuel Wakefield gone, Lady Stanmore stayed mostly in London." Philip stared at a Dutch painting of a city at the edge of a storm-tossed sea. "Quite soon, we could see she was not herself. She had a most difficult time carrying Master James, and she spent much of her time secluded and bedridden. There was never any time to have a portrait of her done after the marriage. But I am certain that her own family . . ." Philip's voice trailed off.

Rebecca's heart sank like a stone. Stanmore had left in August. James had not been born until the following July . . . the day Rebecca and Elizabeth had first met.

"You say she was ill during the confinement?"

"Indeed, ma'am. When the child was born in May, the doctor required that she remain in seclusion indefinitely. The house was closed to all distractions and company, since both mother and child were too frail after the ordeal."

"An announcement *was* made in May?"

"A rather bleak one, if I might say so. As far as any of us knew in the household, there was not much hope for the young master surviving."

"But Lord Stanmore's father *did* announce that a boy had been born . . . and announced his name, as well."

"Indeed, ma'am. James Samuel Wakefield." Philip was looking at her curiously.

Rebecca looked hard at the Dutch painting. Above church spires, the sky was filled with battling clouds of white and gray and pink.

"Did you attend the mother and child yourself, Philip?"

The steward stiffened at the memory. "No one, with the exception of the old earl and a number of attendants the doctor brought in, was allowed to see to their needs."

He was born only this morning, Elizabeth's words, as if spoken this very day, came back to her clearly.

"Her ladyship remained in their care, cut off from the world for two months, ma'am. And then one morning, the house fairly exploded with activity. She'd just up and taken the child during the night. They were gone, ma'am!"

Rebecca's head echoed with the lies that had surrounded Jamey's birth. She had no doubt that he was only a day old when she had first set eyes on him. If a year had passed, and Stanmore had returned from Quebec, it would have been impossible for the father to know the true age of the child.

But Rebecca was certain of what had happened. Stanmore's father had announced the birth before it actually took place, hiding the mother away until the child was really born. It was almost too horrible to consider, but she wondered what would have happened if a girl had been born to Elizabeth.

But with the husband in Quebec, she puzzled, what was it exactly that drove the young woman to take her son and run away? Rebecca smoothed the furrows lining her forehead and glanced up at the portrait that they were standing before now.

"This one is the portrait of the last Earl of Stanmore. The great Sir Joshua Reynolds painted this the summer before all of this."

The brooding man standing before a statue of Zeus was striking enough to capture anyone's attention. Graying hair was the only hint of his age. Strong of build, with a carriage that exuded confidence and power. Rebecca pondered momentarily whether his was a presence that Elizabeth had perhaps found comforting.

She closed her eyes for an instant. How could she blame Elizabeth? Who was she to say that the young woman was the one at fault? It very well could have been that the late earl had been the pursuer. Perhaps she had been nothing more than a victim. This was, of course, assuming that no other man had been involved. All the secrecy surrounding the birth of James had been for the sake of preserving the respectability of the Stanmore name.

She looked hard at the picture again. Yes, she saw the resemblance—the painter had captured the peculiarly piercing quality in the eyes that Jamey shared with both Stanmore men. And there were other small resemblances that the boy shared only with the man in the painting—the line of the chin, the shape of the ears.

"Two years after this portrait was completed, Lord Stanmore suffered a fall from his horse and lost the use of his legs."

Rebecca turned to the steward. "And . . . and the present earl was away for all of this."

Philip nodded gravely. "It was difficult for him when he came home—his wife and son gone, his father crippled. And I'm sorry to say that losing the power to walk was not the only thing that plagued the old earl. He became increasingly ill and, with each passing year, more and more angry, belligerent . . . almost mad at times."

"When was it that his lordship passed away?"

"It has been slightly over a year."

A year. The father's death had brought about the search for the younger son. Rebecca followed the steward as he moved away from the portrait. Wentworth had somehow tapped into the truth about this family's past, but knowing it herself did nothing to lessen her respect for Lord Stanmore. He was the one, she now knew, who had taken it on himself to set so many wrongs to right.

Rebecca turned and looked out the diamond-paned windows at the lake and the road leading out of Solgrave. In the end, it only made things more difficult. She had lost her heart to Samuel Wakefield, but she was also about to leave him behind.

Fastidiously dressed young women. Serenity. Order. Etiquette. Punctuality. Femininity. Propriety. As Louisa Nisdale watched a young woman glide out of the receiving room, she felt her skin crawl. Mrs. Stockdale's exclusive girl's school in Oxford was the epitome of everything that Louisa Nisdale abhorred in society. As a young girl, her parents had never had the means of sending her to such a place, but even if she had been blessed with a fortune, a school such as this would have killed her the very first day.

Hiding her contempt behind a honeyed smile, Louisa listened and tried not to gag at Mrs. Stockdale's speech about the seemingly endless virtues of the academy. She had wanted to meet with the pedantic old fool the day before, but the schoolmistress's schedule had not permitted it. Apparently, a dinner engagement with Reverend Somebody or Other simply *couldn't* be broken!

Annoying as it was to have to stay over in the dusty old university town, the wait actually had done Louisa a great deal of good, though, as she'd been able to question the innkeeper's wife where she was forced to take rooms for the night. Apparently, she learned, Mrs. Stockdale was not particularly susceptible to bullying, but neither would a direct approach get Louisa any of the information she wanted from the old battle-ax. Pretense was the name of the game—a game in which Louisa Nisdale just happened to be a master.

"So how old did you say that your daughter is now, Lady Nisdale?"

Louisa smiled with just the right blend of haughtiness and sociability. "The little dear is only five! Too young to be sent to you, of course, but hearing so much of your excellence in teaching from my dear friends, I—"

"Five is *not* too young!" the gray-haired woman asserted. "Although we do not, as a rule, take children so young, we have had a number of girls sent to us over the years. Of course, they have come with private governesses and the like. Nonetheless, because life presents us with so many hardships, we try to remain open to the needs of our families. You know . . . cases of mothers passing away at birth, widowed fathers who are in the service of the king and cannot see after—"

"Indeed. I assure you my situation does not call for any exceptions. As I was saying, I was simply intrigued by your school, having heard such generous praise from a number of your past students."

"My girls are my best reference, Lady Nisdale."

"Well said." Louisa pushed a crimped curl into place. "Why, just a couple of days ago, I was visiting Melbury Hall and Lady Wentworth . . ." Perceiving a blank expression from the schoolmistress, Louisa added, "She was Miss Millicent Gregory as a pupil here."

"Of course! Of course! Naturally, I remember Miss Gregory quite well."

"Well, Lady Wentworth told me a great deal about her days here at your dear academy. Why, she went on and on about the excellent education that she received here, and about the friends that she'd made. In fact, one young woman's name specifically was mentioned again and again. What was it? Rebecca . . . a good friend of Miss Gregory's . . . I mean, Lady Wentworth's. Rebecca . . . hmmm . . ." Louisa rested a hand against her brow and glanced up distressingly at the high ceiling. "I am losing my mind. The name was Rebecca . . ."

"Neville?"

"That is it!" Louisa smiled brightly. "Rebecca Neville! Lady Wentworth spoke a great deal about her dear old friend Miss Neville and how sad it was that after leaving your good school she lost touch with her dear friend."

A reflective expression clouded the woman's wrinkled face, and she stared toward the open window of the room.

"But that is life, is it not, Mrs. Stockdale? Our most carefree days are the ones when we are young. Marriage, social responsibilities, children . . . all designed, it seems, to tear us from those we once held so dear." Louisa thought herself quite clever to come up with such balderdash. "My dear friend Lady Wentworth—after hearing that I was coming here—was insistent that I should inquire after Miss Neville. She was quite curious to know where her old classmate might be."

Louisa placed her hands demurely in her lap and waited, but Mrs. Stockdale continued to frown out the window.

"Lady Wentworth is so eager to arrange for a reunion," she prompted. "If you could shed some light on where Miss Neville has come to reside since leaving your fine care. Or anything . . ."

"I am very sorry, Lady Nisdale." The woman's sharp eyes turned on Louisa's face. "But I realize I should not have divulged even the name of Miss Neville. You see, I am most sensitive to my former pupils' privacy. But having said as much, perhaps we could direct our interview away from Lady Wentworth's curiosity, and instead discuss any questions you might have about the arrangements for your own daughter. This *is* the reason for your visit, Lady Nisdale . . . is it not?"

When the two men rode out of the darkness, reining in their steeds before the walls of Solgrave, shouts and servants with torches and grooms running from every direction marked their arrival.

"Do you believe horrible moods are hereditary?" Sir Nicholas Spencer climbed down from his horse and tossed the reins to the waiting stableman. He glanced at his friend's brooding expression and followed him toward the door. "I can see you choose not to answer. Very well! Do you believe ghastly moods are contagious?"

The long strides of the baronet matched the earl's. "By 'sblood, Stanmore, you must answer this one. After spending so many hours in your insufferable company today, I must know if my highly enviable charm is seriously threatened."

"As usual, Nicholas, your timing is appalling."

Nicholas glanced ahead at the open door. Two stewards and the housekeeper were standing on marble steps, ready to receive their master. "You might have told me this was a bad time for a social visit."

"I *did* tell you this was a bad time for a visit . . . several times!"

"Well, I suppose you did, now that you mention it. But as your most devoted friend, Stanmore, I know it to be my responsibility to ignore even your threats . . . and I do recall a threat or two. Nonetheless, it is my sworn duty to badger you until such time as you have left behind your deplorably unfashionable gloom."

"Spare me your charity."

Nicholas ignored the retort, instead exchanging pleasantries with the housekeeper as the earl spoke with his stewards. The London *ton* was absolutely abuzz with talk of the swarm of visitors in Hertfordshire. Lady Nisdale, Squire Wentworth, Lady Wentworth, Lord Stanmore, his newly recovered son . . . even Lord North was said to be heading into the country. But then, of course, there was the mysterious Mrs. Ford, about whom everyone talked so much. And yet, no one in society had actually met her. The whole thing seemed a delightful mess—one that Nicholas would have normally have kept at arm's length. And he would have . . . if he had not met Stanmore yesterday and realized that something had seriously changed in him since the last time they'd spoken.

So Nicholas Spencer had insisted on riding down to the country with his friend. His sense of duty required it. Well, duty and curiosity.

"Master James and Mrs. Ford have already dined, m'lord," Mrs. Trent offered in answer to Stanmore's question about the two. "The lad is already asleep in his room, but the last I checked, Mrs. Ford was reading in the library."

Daniel spoke just as Philip was ready to whisper something in the earl's ear. "Would you care for some dinner, m'lord? I can have Harry—"

"No need. Sir Nicholas and I stopped at that new inn on the other side of St. Albans."

"A dreadful place," Nicholas put in. "I believe one of Harry's brothers is the cook there."

The older steward leaned again toward the earl. "I believe Mrs. Ford has been waiting up for your return, m'lord."

Nicholas heard the hushed words and raised an eyebrow at the look of open anticipation that Stanmore sent in the direction of the library.

"Daniel, if you would be kind enough to escort Sir Nicholas to his room . . ."

"Not quite yet." Nicholas gave his cloak and hat to the steward and started toward the library. "Coming, Stanmore? It was a long ride, and I am in desperate need of a glass of your best port before I retire for the night."

"The devil you do! Then I shall have a bottle sent to your room." Stanmore glowered as he caught up to him.

"Not a chance!" Nicholas glanced back and found the housekeeper and the two stewards had not moved. He lowered his voice. "You cannot hide her forever, my friend. Face it, man. A simple introduction and I'll be on my way."

"Busy as a mother hen, you are, Nicholas. Well, tomorrow will be soon enough for introductions."

Nicholas paused by the door of the library with a hand on the latch. He was genuinely surprised at the expression he saw. So unlike the forever controlled friend he had always known.

"By the devil! She has you in tatters."

"Nonsense!"

"By 'sblood, now I have seen it all. The implacable Lord Stanmore *discomposed* by a woman."

"Nicholas!"

Ignoring the threatening drawl, he pushed the door open. The room was as spacious and comfortable as he remembered it. Though he was not a particularly bookish man, Nicholas loved the feel of a well-appointed library. The heavy curtains had been closed to keep out the dampness, and the light of dozens of candles infused the room with a soft glow. Nicholas's gaze swept over the place, and as Stanmore pushed by him, a woman's slender frame rose from a divan like morning mist off a tranquil lake.

"M'lord!" Her delighted greeting was directed at Stanmore. Nicholas could see that her magical blue eyes perceived nothing but the man standing beside him.

Nonetheless, Nicholas Spencer drank in her beauty. Soft waves of hair the color of fire and gold draped over slender shoulders, framing a face that glowed with warmth. Full lips, high cheeks, exquisitely shaped breasts that hinted at perfection hidden beneath the low neckline of her dress.

He looked back up into her face. There was something about her. Something familiar. Something in the sensuality, in the hint of passion that hung caressingly about the eyes, on every curve of her cheek. . . .

That was it! he thought. He *had* seen her before . . . well, someone very much like her. In the portrait of the most beautiful woman he had ever seen . . . in the villa of the great actor David Garrick at Hampton.

Nicholas Spencer stared into the face that had illuminated the London stage for decades . . . up until a few years ago. The woman was the very image of the actress who had once been the toast of kings—the magnificent and beautiful Jenny Greene.

Chapter 25

It was some time before Stanmore's dark gaze released her and she became aware of the other man in the library. Still though, Rebecca's jittery insides would not allow her a full breath as she watched the earl walk into the room a little. Something warmed deep within her. His glowing eyes had conveyed more than his happiness to see her. Far more.

"Mrs. Ford, please allow me to present to you the most villainous of friends, Sir Nicholas Spencer."

Rebecca dropped a small curtsy as the man raised her hand to his lips.

She politely withdrew her hand a moment later, but the newcomer continued to study her in the most unsettling manner. His look was not a lascivious one; it was more the look of someone trying to make a decision about something. Nonetheless, he was already beginning to make Rebecca uncomfortable.

Sir Nicholas was approximately the same height as the earl, but one would never be confused for the other. His broken nose and long, wavy, blond hair tied back with a black ribbon gave the blue-eyed giant a rakish look that was a far cry from his friend's appearance. He was handsome enough, she supposed, but a hint of the untamed seemed to be lurking just beneath his refined manners.

"Nicholas only stopped in for an introduction," Stanmore said, drawing her attention. "He assures me that he is *quite* tired from the long ride and is *on his way*—"

"Your incredible loveliness"—his friend interrupted with a small bow—"your flawless beauty overwhelms me, Mrs. Ford. You are truly refreshing for the eyes of the road-weary traveler. But what is truly astounding is that this blackguard has been hiding such a treasure away here, depriving his few friends—of which he has a rapidly diminishing number—the pleasure of such company these past weeks."

Rebecca felt the heat rush into her face, and she clutched the book she had been reading tightly in one hand. She glanced quickly at Stanmore, who was glaring at Sir Nicholas. She fixed her eyes on the pattern of the rug.

Oh God, she thought. What had she been thinking? Clearly, she had been in the wrong to dress as she had tonight. She certainly had never expected this response from anyone. But far worse, it had been wicked of her to want to flaunt herself before Stanmore after deciding that she was going away. What right did she have to plan and hope for something when going away made it so wrong? Well, this was clearly her punishment—getting noticed by the wrong man!

"And blushing modesty, as well. An enchantress. There is no end to this lady's charms."

"Enough, Nicholas!" Stanmore warned. "Your roguish tongue has moved you from simply being a nuisance to that of the rake that you truly are."

Rebecca had not needed a protector for many years and needed no one now to speak in her defense.

"I cannot speak to your charge of Sir Nicholas's character, m'lord, but your guest is not being a nuisance." She met the earl's gaze before turning to his grinning friend. "If I am blushing, sir, it is just that I am not accustomed to flowery compliments. And as a result I am not readily armed with any retort worthy of this good gentleman's highly imaginative praise—even if they are no doubt the result of his admitted weariness. The problem lies not with Sir Nicholas, but with me and my inexperience."

Nicholas placed a hand over his heart. "I swear to you, madam, that there is nothing imagined in my praise of you. Every word I uttered came from the deep well of my esteem."

"You must be tired, my good sir, to lower your guard to the point that even an amateur like me can inflict a wound."

"A wound, Mrs. Ford?"

"Well, to conjure such accolades from the *deep well* of your esteem . . ." She shook her head. "Well, it seems to me, sir that only
a shallow and empty well could produce such noisy praise for a
total stranger."

The rogue laughed. "You have wounded me, Mrs. Ford."

Stanmore moved beside her and placed an arm protectively
around her waist. "Better her than me, Nicholas. And you have already overstayed your welcome."

Sir Nicholas bowed again and addressed Rebecca. "Only because I can be assured of renewing our acquaintance in the morning, I will allow this black-hearted tyrant to dispose of me tonight.
But what about tomorrow, Mrs. Ford? May I beg the pleasure of
your company . . . perhaps for a ride or a casual walk in his lordship's deer park?" He held up a hand as she started to speak. "But
before you decline my invitation, I give you my word of honor that
I shall leave behind my *roguish tongue* and speak only the absolute
truth."

"Excellent," Stanmore growled. "Since you'll be leaving your
tongue behind, shall I nail it to the stable door where you can find
it?"

Rebecca realized that she actually liked Sir Nicholas. He was
certainly a womanizer, but he was also a charmer who did not of-
fend.

"I shall have to answer your invitation in the morning, sir, after
I have had an opportunity to assess your references with our host."

It was a slight move, but she felt the pressure of his large and
comforting hand at her waist. She didn't dare look up at Stanmore
for fear she might see him smirking at his friend.

Sir Nicholas was glowering with mock fierceness at the earl.
"Just watch *your* tongue, my friend, for there is no end to the damage *I* can cause."

"Be on your way, Empty Well."

With a wink, Sir Nicholas bowed to Rebecca before turning to
leave. At the door though, he paused—suddenly serious.

"She would be older than you by twenty years . . . perhaps
thirty."

"Who is that, Sir Nicholas?"

"The actress. Jenny Greene. Do you know her, Mrs. Ford?"

A knot formed instantly in her stomach, and Rebecca felt her entire body tense at the question.

"Only the name, sir."

Stanmore felt Rebecca shiver as Nicholas went out, and he looked down at her face. A sudden paleness had flushed all color from her cheeks. Seeing the change in her, he pulled her into his arms.

"You are cold." She came willingly, her arms wrapping around him, her head tucked beneath his chin.

Her trusting movement knotted his throat. She wasn't seeking passion, only comfort. She just wanted to be held. Everything about her bespoke her innocence, and this only caused his heart to open a little wider, drawing her deeper into long-protected regions. It was so strange. They had not spoken any words of commitment. They had yet to fulfill the longing of their bodies. But she was already a part of him . . . more than he'd ever before thought possible.

"Did I stay away too long?"

Her head moved up and down on his chest, and he smiled.

"Might I be bold enough to assume that you were waiting up for me here tonight?"

She pulled back slightly and looked into his face. "You do not have to assume, m'lord. I willingly admit it. But dressed as shamelessly as I am, I believe everyone who has seen me this evening must have guessed at my intentions."

Stanmore was charmed by the intensity that brought color again to her cheeks. He glanced down at the neckline of the dress and with difficulty tore his gaze away from the graceful curves of her ivory breasts. His hand caressed the delicate line of her back.

"You are dressed in the height of fashion. I believe anyone would feel blessed just to follow you here and feast on your beauty."

She smiled and her hands moved from his back to rest against his chest. "And I believe you have spent too much time today in Sir Nicholas's company. You are starting to sound like him."

"There is a distinct difference. Nicholas praises all women who are exceptionally beautiful. I praise only the one whom I have desired for an eternity of days. The one woman who stirs my insides and sets my blood afire with need. The only woman who has ever managed to insert herself beneath my skin and reach into my heart. The one whom I have failed to be able to push from my mind from the moment I first saw her." His hand moved lower on her back and he pressed her closer until his arousal was pressed tightly against her belly. A flash of awareness darkened her blue eyes. "Do not confuse me with him, Rebecca."

She stared up at him with eyes so large that in them he could see her giving heart, her besieged soul. In them, he could also see his own reflection . . . the image of a man in love for the first time.

"I could never confuse you with anyone," she whispered finally, before raising herself on her toes and pressing her lips softly against his.

He did not know it before tonight, but Stanmore realized that he had been so ill for so long . . . and Rebecca was the cure.

Stanmore's blood pulsed. Desperate as he was to peel away her fears and see her rejoice in the passion that was ready to burst forth between them, he held back, controlling his desires, determined not to frighten her again.

Rebecca's hands slipped around his neck, her fingers threading into his hair. Her mouth slanted beneath his, her lips pressing harder. In her innocent way he felt her coaxing him to take charge. Careful to slip only a single thread of his control, he let his affection and his passion flow into the kiss. In the giving and taking of their mouths, in the delicate imitation of the sexual act, he felt himself soar.

Her moan of pleasure was the sweetest sound he'd ever heard. Her body molded to his, softened, formed itself to him in ways he'd only dared to dream. He let slip another thread of his restraint, allowing his hand to roam over her back, pressing her closer, cupping her bottom, savoring the perfect fit of their bodies.

Stanmore tore his lips away from her mouth and trailed kisses on her face, along the column of her neck. He lifted her in his arms and his lips came in contact with the round flesh of her breasts. He found himself becoming ravenous with need as her slender fingers guided his movements, pressing him to go on.

"Is this it, Rebecca?" Stanmore managed to ask as he carried her to the divan and lowered her onto it. "Are you ready?"

Her answer came as a whisper. "I am. For the first time in my life, I am ready."

And he was ready, as well. He knew what he wanted for today, for tomorrow, for eternity.

"I do not want our first time to be here." The layers of skirts draped across his arms as he lifted her again and started for the door. "But there is no stopping, now. No changing our minds."

She shook her head and kissed him on the lips. "No stopping. No regrets. Just the opposite." She smiled shyly at him. "But I am not accustomed to being carried off to anyone's bedchamber while an entire household looks on."

He hesitated by the door and then put her gently on her feet. Discretion had rarely been an issue with any of the women he'd known.

"Of course. We will do this in the way that will please *you*." Her warm smile and the affection that shone in her blue eyes rewarded him for his words. "However, if I allow you to retire to your room ahead of me now, do you give your word to let me in later?"

She nodded and brushed a kiss over his lips.

"And do you promise to remain impatiently by your door, dressed as you are?"

She nodded again and smiled shyly.

"One more thing, Rebecca," he asked as she turned to go. "What was your name . . . before your marriage?"

Stanmore watched the color rise from her neck into her face. Her gaze, though, did not waver.

"Neville," she said softly. "My name was Rebecca Neville."

The old woman snatched the coin out of the lady's palm and peered at it in the darkness of the closed carriage. She glanced quickly at the drawn shade. She had met the carriage at the appointed place—an alley by Christ's Church—but she could no longer hear the sounds of High Street.

"What is it you want to know?" she asked nervously.

"Rebecca Neville. Tell me everything you know."

"Been a long time since I've heard that name, yer ladyship."

Louisa Nisdale impatiently reached inside her purse. "Talk to me and there is another shilling in it for you."

The woman eyed the purse. "Miss Neville was well off, I should think, but kept to herself, she did. Polite to us servants, unlike the rest of them snooty ones . . . begging yer pardon, mum. The girls lived upstairs. We was in the attic rooms, but I worked in the kitchens, and I don't know much more about her, to tell the truth."

"What happened to her?" Louisa took out two coins this time and held them close to the woman's face. "Where did she go? What were her *secrets*?"

"Can't say I knows any of this, mum." Her eyes narrowed. "But even if I knew some, that's a lot of questions for the little ye be offering."

Louisa angrily reached inside her purse again and took out a gold coin. "Tell me anything worth knowing, and you shall earn this."

"That's more friendly-like, mum." The servant snatched the coin, holding it tightly in her fist. "We're talking years ago, of course."

"Of course!" Louisa hissed impatiently. "Go on!"

"Well, shortly after Miss Rebecca left, there was confusion in the house, mum. You see, Mrs. Stockdale had found the miss a paying job in London town, but whoever her kinfolk were, they didn't take to it much. Fit to be tied, as far as we could see . . . especially after nobody could find her."

"What do you mean, no one could find her?"

"Well, that's just it, mum. She just kind of disappeared, she did. Went to that paying job and disappeared quicker than a dog with a bone."

"Who were these people that she went to work for? Give me a name."

The servant shook her head. "That I can't, mum. I mean I don't know. Where them girls come from or go don't reach us much in the kitchens."

Louisa leaned forward and took hold of the woman's wrist. "Then you find out. Do you hear me? You ask around and find out to whom she was sent in London."

"'Twill cost you another gold one"—the woman wrenched her wrist free—"for that kind of work."

"Tomorrow!" Louisa said fiercely. "You bring me that name tomorrow."

Rebecca paced the room with a nervousness that had everything to do with lies . . . and nothing to do with passion.

She could not go through with it. She couldn't hurt Stanmore again. She would not treat him the way those other women that he'd cared for—his mother and his wife—had treated him. She couldn't leave him without a word.

What made it all so shockingly unfair was the thought of making love to him and then simply disappearing. All along, he had given her a choice, an option to go forward with their affair or to back away. Now, it was only right that she should offer *him* the same. This decision had to be his.

The soft knock set Rebecca's heart pounding even faster than before. She moved quickly to the door and took a deep breath before opening it. He had discarded his jacket and waistcoat. Almost involuntarily, she studied every inch of him as if trying to stamp on her memory this moment, this man. It was a memory that would need to last for more years than she cared to count.

"May I come in?"

She was scorched by the heat of his gaze. Extending her hand in invitation, their fingers entwined, and he entered. As soon as the door closed behind them, he caught her up in his embrace, holding her, pressing every curve of her body against his until she could almost feel his heart beating in her own chest, feel his need spreading through every inch of her body, feel his desire become her own.

"I cannot remember ever wanting anything in life as I have wanted you."

An aching knot formed in Rebecca's throat, and she swallowed hard. "Before we do . . . this . . . there are things that I need to tell you. Things about myself . . . about my life . . ."

His powerful arms held her close, and she paused to muster her courage. She had to speak the truth now, while she had the nerve.

"Before I even start, though, you should know that . . . that everything that I have held back from you . . . the truth that I did not reveal . . . that I could not reveal . . . the *reason* I held back . . . had nothing to do with deceiving you . . . nothing to do with wanting to bring harm in any way to James . . . or to your family's name. I had to deceive you because . . . because of the person I once was . . . because of the life I once had . . . and needed to escape."

She was babbling. She was crying. She was a mess. And still his arms did not release her. This realization only made the tears come faster—made the knot in her throat grow larger. She shook her head.

"I am sorry. I . . . I just . . ."

"Hush!" One strong hand caressed her back. The brush of his lips against her brow was filled with tenderness. If she could only hide in his arms and forget her past! If she could only continue to live her life in a lie, then she would have the memory of this night to take her through the rest of her life!

But she couldn't. She would not hurt him for all the happiness in the world.

It was some time before Rebecca was able to find her voice. "I have failed you miserably in the promise I gave you downstairs."

"You have yet to fail me, Rebecca."

His words were charged with meaning, and she drew a breath. "I . . ."

She stopped, pushed out of his embrace, and walked a few steps away. She couldn't think clearly so near him.

"The first thing that you should know is . . . is that there never was a John Ford. That I was never married. As I told you downstairs, my true name is Rebecca Neville. But I have not used that surname for nearly ten years." She turned to face him. The expression on his face was hidden by the shadows of the room. "When I arrived in Philadelphia so many years ago, I was an unmarried woman with a child whom I was claiming as my own. I was in search of a position by which I could live. I decided then that it would be much easier . . . safer . . . if others saw me as a married woman.

There were other husbands away at war." She shot a glance at him. "As far as anyone knew, he could return any day. With such an invention, I could keep off men's attentions, and I could start our lives anew."

Stanmore moved to the nearest chair and sat down, but Rebecca could not look at him. She didn't want to gauge his mood before she was finished saying everything that she had to say.

"My design worked. I was able to find a place to live and employment that supported us. After that, I simply let the lie stand. Some months later—after I was secure in our haven—I made it known to those around me that I had received word of my husband's death . . . at Quebec."

She moved away from him and toward the window.

"When your attorney, Sir Oliver, found us in Philadelphia this spring, I had to lie to him about how I originally came to have James. Who I was . . . the life I had made . . . it was all based on the invention of this imaginary husband, on the fictitious life I had created for him and for myself. No one around me knew that I had not been born and raised in the colonies."

Rebecca felt a damp, aching cold seeping into her. With each word that she spoke, she knew she was moving farther away from him.

"The first time I met your wife, Elizabeth, was on the night that she was leaving England."

"The same day that James was born." His words from across the room brought tears again to her eyes. So he did know the truth of that, she thought.

"She was alone and very ill from the childbirth . . . and I was . . . I was in need of help, myself." She stared into the emptiness that separated them. "She helped me . . . paid my ship's fare. And I promised to stay with her . . . to take care of James afterward if . . . if something were to happen to her."

Rebecca leaned against the windowsill and brushed away her tears. "She died less than a week into the journey. I, on the other hand, won a treasure from the bargain. I had James. I left England with only the clothes on my back, though, so upon arriving in New York . . . I sold the jewels your wife gave me. With what I received from them, I took James to Philadelphia, and we started our new life."

Rebecca leaned her head against the window, vainly hoping that the coolness of the pane would penetrate her feverish skin. "Sir Oliver asked me in Philadelphia why it was that in all these years I never thought to seek James's father . . . to return him to his rightful family. The answer I gave him then was different than the truth I have held in my heart.

"If things were different . . . if I had the financial means and the courage to return to England on my own, I . . . I still would not have returned him to you. Elizabeth may have given me the initial means to go on, but James was the one who gave me the courage. Raising him taught me about life. Taught me independence. Made me forget my fears and seize all that life might offer. Selfish of me, it was . . . but I would not have come back if you had not sent for him. The two of us might have been out of place in some ways, but we had each other."

She reached up to wipe a tear from her face, but his fingers were the ones that brushed the bead from her cheek. He had moved close to her, and she had not been aware of his advance.

"Why were you running?"

She was trapped by the touch of his fingers, by the dark gaze that caressed her face.

"You must not ask me that!"

"Rebecca!"

She shook her head, and his fingers released their hold on her face. "I have told you everything that concerns James . . . and you and your family. But as far as my past . . . you must allow me to remain silent. In return, I promise I shall not jeopardize your good name, m'lord."

Rebecca let out an unsteady breath and stared at the open collar of his shirt. "In fact, in order to keep that promise, I have come to a decision. I am returning to the colonies. I shall leave for Bristol this coming Friday."

"How can you . . . ?"

"When we first arrived, I spoke to the masters of half a dozen ships on Broad Quay. I shall have no problem securing passage."

"Everything so neatly arranged." His tone had become cold, restrained.

"Not everything," she replied, trying to keep up her courage. "I have told James nothing about my leaving . . . or his staying. I know he is ready, though. I know he will be able to deal with my absence much better now than at the beginning. Still, though, I thought . . . it would be best if . . . if I waited on telling him . . . until the last moment."

His face was a mask, but his eyes were daggers, piercing her very soul.

"And what would have happened if I had taken you—as you were offering yourself—downstairs in the library earlier? Would you have waited then and told me at the last moment, as well? Or would you have been happy simply to go . . . and let me hear the news from someone else?"

She winced at the harshness of his tone, but her pride forced her to lift her chin and meet his gaze. "My past might be a perverse lie . . . my future not much of an improvement . . . but the person before you now, m'lord, would gladly step into a lion's den rather than knowingly hurt you. I would have found a way to tell you . . . even if we were to . . . to stay in your library."

"Damn you, Rebecca!" His fingers were rough as he grabbed her shoulders. "Why must you do this to me?"

"Because you . . . matter too much!" She pushed herself against his hard body and pressed her lips to his. He stood rigid, not responding. But she was not deterred. She had seen the hurt in his eyes.

"Please," she coaxed, brushing her lips against his again, wrapping her arms around him and molding her body to his. "You want this. . . ."

His strong fingers pulled her back again, and he glowered menacingly. "And is this another bit of charity? Another selfless act? Helping Elizabeth. Helping James. Of course, why not spread the good works to Stanmore? Give them all what they need!"

"No!" She shook her head. "No! *This* is for me."

"I do not believe you."

"You *must* believe me!" Her fingers clutched at his shirt. "You have awakened in me a need . . . a passion . . . that I never knew existed. You have made fires light up inside me with your looks . . . with your kisses . . . with the sound of your voice. I have few regrets about my past, but I know my greatest disappointment would be if I failed at this moment to take this . . . memory . . . of us into the future."

"Damn you!" He kissed her, attacking her mouth. His hands moved unabashedly over her back, her arms, turning her slightly to feel her breasts through the dress.

His eagerness made Rebecca come alive in his arms. She no longer feared, but sought. Her mouth became as ravenous as his, her fingers as probing, as rough. She pulled his shirt from his breeches, hungry for the feel of his skin.

She felt her dress drawn down in front. Her nipples tightened at the feel of the air and then one rough hand cupping and shaping her flesh. The sweetness of the ache was excruciating.

Rebecca knew if they were to slow down, he would have time to think. She knew he would stop, and this knowledge added to her frenzy to please him—to keep him mindless in this reckless moment of passion. She was inexperienced, but her instincts guided her as she suckled his probing tongue, her hands kneading the hard muscle of his buttocks.

In a flurry of motion, she suddenly found herself on the bed, and a thrill raced through her as they sank into the bedclothes.

Stanmore's lips left her mouth and trailed roughly down her neck and to her breasts. He was down on one knee, and his hands were impatient as they pushed beneath her skirts. Rebecca gasped at the feel of his warm mouth suckling her breast. Her fingers dug into his hair as she felt the brush of his hand moving up the inside of her thighs.

The shock of his fingers inside her wet folds made her cry out aloud. His palm pressed at the moist surface, his fingers retreating and entering again. Rebecca found herself short of breath. Her body was suddenly humming with sensations so new. His mouth moved up to her face and captured her lips again, his fingers were still relentless in their sweet torment.

She was possessed by him. He had enthralled her body in a timeless, frenzied world of sensation and passion. The climax exploded within her with the awesome power of a summer storm. Somewhere in a more conscious world, she could hear a woman's voice—no, it was her own voice—crying out exultantly. Her hands were pushing him away at the same time that she fought fiercely to hold him closer. She could not breathe. And then, she was simply floating, weightless in a crystalline sky, colors she had never before seen flashing around her.

Stanmore held her as she descended, kissing her softly until she found she was still in his arms. A moment later, he turned her slightly and began pulling roughly on the laces of the dress.

The sensations in her body continued to recede in waves, but as he worked at the clothing, she felt her excitement and desire growing once again. She heard a tear in the gown, felt the hardness of him through the layers of clothes and shivered in anticipation of what was yet to come. Suddenly, he pulled her to her feet and peeled the dress and petticoats without ceremony from her body. Sweeping her into his arms, he kicked the pool of clothing clear. Bare to the skin and vulnerable to the onslaught of his gaze and his lips, she arched her back, offering herself willingly to him as he placed her once again on the bed.

Even in the haze of frenzied delight that followed, even as his mouth moved over her belly, her thighs, loving her in ways that made her cry out for release . . . even then, he astonished her. Wave after wave assailed her, lifted her, shattered her, and still he continued.

Even then—her bones dissolved into liquid, her flesh tingling and spent—he refused to shed his own clothes and take from her even a little of the joy he was so generously giving.

Later, Rebecca cried softly as she lay tenderly enfolded in his arms. She cried because he was granting a wish—giving her that memory—but that was all he was willing to give.

Chapter 26

Dawn lightened the sky beyond the hills far to the east, but still Stanmore had no desire to leave Rebecca's bed. For the first time in his life, he wanted to stay, cherishing the spell she'd cast over his heart.

He'd had many hours to think during the night. Many hours to recollect everything that had been said and done between them. Many hours to contemplate his life.

Stanmore had always recognized the emptiness that had defined him. He'd learned long ago to accept it as a way of life. But everything had changed the moment she stepped into his life.

Rebecca made a small sound in her sleep, and he felt his throat tighten. Stirring a little, she reached for him just as she'd done numerous times during the night. He placed a kiss against her brow and tightened his own arms around her, pressing her head against his chest.

Last night had been a first for her . . . and a first for him.

For her, it had offered the first experience of her birthright as a woman. For him, it had offered the first realization that an ache of a longing heart ran far deeper than the throb of a body's desires. Somewhere between the time her eyes had closed and the first gray hint of day, he'd come to the realization that no matter what the obstacles were between them, he could not let her go. Somewhere, somehow, the union of two hearts had emerged from a woman who had feared passion and a man who had feared love. Last night, he had found that the two of them had formed a bond. For love . . . for life . . . forever.

He needed her. Although he'd not said the words, he now understood the meaning of love. He wanted to marry her, have children with her, grow old with her. But having heard the determination in her voice last night—understanding her devotion and her willingness to sacrifice herself—he knew she would not agree to stay unless he could solve the mystery of her past and release her from its stranglehold.

From all that she'd told him and all he'd learned from Oliver Birch, Stanmore did not have to stretch his brain to guess that a crime must have been committed the night she had fled. Whatever the crime, he knew that scandal was attached to it.

Before last night, he'd known that she harbored a deep fear of men. He remembered their kiss by the old mill, her panic whenever she came near him, their picnic by the stream. Rebecca's words came back to him—*it would be much easier . . . safer . . . if others saw me as a married woman. . . . I could keep off the men's attentions. . . .* He wondered if the crime involved a man . . . perhaps an attack on her.

She had the beauty of an angel and the integrity and industry of a saint, and yet she was twenty-eight years old and still a virgin. He brushed his lips against her sleeping brow and tried to not think of the smooth, naked body beneath the linen sheets. *His* virgin, he repeated silently, ignoring the ache in his tightening loins. After last night, he was a candidate for sainthood himself.

Six days! She had threatened to leave in six days. Oliver was on the right trail. What he'd discovered corresponded perfectly with everything that Rebecca had revealed last night. But six days were too short a time to solve the rest.

Stanmore knew he had to convince her, charm her, make her as mad about him as he was about her. Perhaps then she would listen to his plea for more time.

The soft knock on the door woke Rebecca with a start. She clutched at the sheets before looking frantically up into his face. Her voice was a panicked whisper. "Jamey!"

"I latched the door," he whispered back before being pushed out of bed ahead of her.

He watched with great interest her attempt at modesty in her haste to pull on a robe. The sheet, dragged from the bed, successfully covered her breasts, but Stanmore had an unobstructed view of her flawless back and perfect bottom. He wondered how it was that he'd lasted through the night, and what he could possibly have been thinking of, for now he couldn't wait to make love to her.

There was another soft knock, and Rebecca turned to him pleadingly as she wrapped the robe around her. "He cannot find you here! What am I to do?"

Stanmore rose from the edge of the bed and, before she could object, planted a kiss on her full lips. "Send him to the stables. Tell him I want to meet him there in half an hour." He ran his finger down her neck and into the open neckline of the robe. She colored beautifully and caught his hand. "I seem to recall some pixy tricking me into giving an hour of each day to a certain lad. Well, tell him this is the designated hour, and he'd better not keep the Earl of Stanmore waiting."

Brightening, she gave him a quick and affectionate hug and ran to the door.

Standing in the shadows of the room, Stanmore watched them. He was a fool. What he witnessed pass between them—the touch, the soft word, the embrace—made him understand for the first time the nature of the bond between Rebecca and James. This wasn't *attachment,* as he previously had called it. This was *love.*

The smell of hay and horses drifted out of the open doors of the stables and mixed with the dampness of dawn. Jamey took a deep breath and savored the already familiar scent. Since being allowed to choose a pony of his own four days ago, he'd come back to the stables every day—insisting on learning how to take care of Strawberry himself. Porson, the groom who had been teaching Jamey things about the horses, had laughed and had asked the reason for the name. Jamey explained that the reddish mane of the large pony reminded him of strawberries and, besides that, he lived in Strawberry Alley in Philadelphia. The pony made him feel like he was at home.

Porson stopped laughing.

Jamey walked inside the stables and went to the stall where his pony was waiting. He didn't know how he felt about going riding with the earl every morning. His mama had insisted on it, so he knew he *had* to do it. But he couldn't wonder if this was the earl's doing, or if he was being forced, like Jamey himself, to go along.

The problem was that he just didn't know how he felt about the

Earl of Stanmore anymore. He still didn't *want* to like him. He could never be a replacement for the parent whom he already had. But at the same time, he'd heard so many workers praise him at Solgrave that Jamey was having a hard time believing that he could be too bad a person.

The Earl of Stanmore is the only one who can make a difference, Mr. Clarke had said when Jamey asked the teacher about the use of slaves at Melbury Hall.

Jamey remembered his own conversation with Israel and his friend's challenge. *If he is such a good man, then why don't you want him for a father?*

Confusion battering his brain, he began saddling the pony. He didn't know where to start—how to take the first step so the man would like him. He didn't know how a son could make his own father accept him.

"Well, I am glad to see you are an early riser."

Jamey whirled and stared at the open door of the stall and at Lord Stanmore standing in it. Habit kept the boy from speaking, but he nodded in greeting. He shot a second look at the man, though. Stanmore looked different today. It was the curious expression on his face, as if he were really looking at Jamey. The earl gazed at the pony—and then back at him.

"That's a rather spirited pony. It takes a fearless lad to handle one that lively so soon after learning to ride."

Jamey looked away, but felt a strange feeling of pride wash through him.

"I assume you have had no breakfast yet?"

He shook his head.

"Nor I. And I am hungry, too. But I suppose a good morning's ride will help run off some of this Parliamentary fat, eh?"

Jamey stared at the man. He was as fit as anyone he'd ever known, tall and muscular. A groom appeared, leading the earl's black hunter past the stall.

"Nonetheless, go easy on me this morning, will you?"

He turned to go, and Jamey turned to hide the unexpected grin tugging at his lips.

When they were outside in the stable yard, Porson the groom appeared and talked to the earl for a moment about what he had and had not taught Jamey so far.

"I thought we'd head toward that gamekeeper's cottage this morning," Lord Stanmore said as the two of them trotted their mounts along the drive leading past the lake. "It is not often I ride in that direction, but the past couple of times that I've come looking for you, that seems to be a favorite haunt. You're doing well with that sprightly fellow."

Jamey thought of bringing up Melbury Hall and Israel, but he felt awkward saying anything. The longer he refrained from speaking to the earl, the more difficult it was becoming to start.

"Train yourself to manage your pony with a light hand," Stanmore said a little later. "Firm when you want him to respond . . . brook no nonsense . . . but handle him with a light hand otherwise. That's it. You have a natural touch, James."

Jamey smiled shyly, feeling his face grow hot. Luckily, the earl was not looking at him, though, and in a moment the trail wound into the trees.

"It is fascinating to me that you found that cottage so soon after arriving at Solgrave. That ruined hut was *my* hiding place when I was your age, as well."

He needed to hide, too? The boy shot him a sidelong glance, Lord Stanmore *did* look different today. His feelings were showing so plainly on his face. And Jamey had never heard him so talkative.

"We used to play 'storm the keep' out at the cottage. There were generally six of us from Solgrave—the two sons of the woodcutter and Mrs. Trent's three boys and I—against a half dozen farm lads, and sometimes more, from Melbury Hall."

"Were the lads from Melbury Hall slaves back then, too?" Jamey didn't realize that he'd asked the question aloud until Stanmore's surprised gaze snapped around. The earl turned his attention back to the trail, but Jamey shifted his weight uncomfortably on the back of the pony. These were the first words he'd ever spoken to his lordship.

"No slaves back then," he answered. "Melbury Hall was owned by someone else when I was a lad, and they did not keep Africans as slaves."

Jamey studied the hardness that had crept into the earl's face as he stared ahead into the woods.

"I noticed that someone has been doing some work on the cottage."

The boy decided not to make a comment. He didn't want someone else getting angry at Israel for touching something that wasn't his.

"I am glad of it," Stanmore continued, as if reading his thoughts. "If you know who the person is that is doing the work—or if you happen to meet with him or them—pass on my thanks, will you?"

"Aye," James replied, relieved.

As they rode on in silence for a while, Jamey tried to think of the best way to bring up the subject of slaves again. He'd promised Israel not to say anything about the beatings, but there were other questions that he had. Questions about how it was that Squire Wentworth got away with being so cruel. And was there any place these workers could escape to, so they could become free?

As they broke out of the woods into the edge of the meadow, Jamey could see the top of the cottage in the distance. Perhaps, he decided, he could ask his questions once they arrived there. He could show the earl all the work that Israel had done on the place and then try to get some answers.

"Seeing how well you are handling this pony on your own, I believe Mrs. Ford will have no problem with you riding over here whenever—"

A sharp cry sliced through the morning air, cutting into Jamey's heart.

"Israel!" he whispered in panic, digging his heels into the sides of the animal and racing toward the cottage as another cry rang out.

"Israel!" Jamey shouted. Stanmore's horse thundered past him toward the old building.

By the time Jamey had arrived at the cottage, Stanmore had dismounted from his horse and checked the cottage.

"There is no one inside," he said, striding back to Jamey. His fierce gaze studied the dense trees. They both heard the third cry, and Stanmore was immediately running toward the trees.

Jamey slid off the back of the pony and looped the reins around a low branch. Racing down a path after the earl, he stopped short at the sight of Stanmore driving a powerful fist into the face of a giant of a man.

The boy immediately picked up a large stick lying on the ground as he saw the giant push the earl back roughly and throw himself at him. Stanmore moved quickly to the side, shoving the man hard into a large tree. On him instantly, the earl pounded the giant's face into the ground.

Jamey had seen many fights along Philadelphia's waterfront, and had been in a few himself. Once, he had even seen a knife fight broken up outside The Admiral's Head by the wharf. In his experience, though, fights were usually just some pushing, perhaps a few punches were thrown, ending with tough talk.

For the first time in his life, though, he hoped he would see Stanmore beat this brute to a bloody pulp.

He raised the heavy stick, ready to join in if Stanmore needed him. Then he caught sight of Israel.

His friend lay curled up in the dirt, his shirt and back turned into raw streaks of flesh and blood. Jamey cried out loud, running to him and crouching down. He bit back tears as he looked into the freshly battered face. Israel's eyes were closed, and he did not seem to be breathing.

"No!" His own shout was piercing, his fury spewing out, his spirit demanding revenge. He picked up the stick that he'd just dropped to the ground and turned to see Stanmore fling the giant to his knees.

"You killed him! *You killed him!"*

The tears were blurring his vision, but he felt the stick connect solidly with the man's shoulder. As he lifted the stick to strike again, he felt the earl's strong arms grab him around the waist and lift him off the ground. Seizing the moment, the giant staggered to his feet and ran unsteadily off into the woods.

"Let me go!" Jamey struggled against the steely grip for a moment, and then felt the stick pulled out of his hand. "He killed him. He killed Israel."

The tears were running down his face, but he didn't care. The anger and sadness were churning so tightly in his chest that he had to gasp for breaths.

"He won't get away with this." Stanmore's voice was determined and yet calm. "You and I will see to it."

His strong arms held Jamey against his chest, soothing him. It seemed ages before Jamey thought that he could take a breath.

"Stay here and let me look at the lad!" Stanmore ordered grimly as he stood Jamey on his feet. The earl frowned over in the direction of the small body.

Jamey shook his head, and angrily wiped at the tears on his face. "Nay, Israel is my friend!"

Stanmore was looking at him, his eyes grave. He had a cut on the side of his chin that was still bleeding a little. As the earl placed a hand on his shoulder, Jamey saw his knuckles were scraped and beginning to swell. Together, they both walked toward the body, and Jamey crouched beside him as the earl gently pressed a finger against the side of Israel's neck.

"He is still alive," he murmured, looking carefully at Israel's face and back. "I think this blow to his head rendered him unconscious. We need to get a doctor for him. I cannot tell for certain, but he might have a few broken bones, as well."

"Please . . . !" Jamey pleaded, "We cannot take him back to Melbury Hall! They shan't take care of him there. Please, m'lord, this is not the first time Israel has been beaten. Last week, he was bruised, too. . . ."

"Why didn't you tell me?"

The earl's hard glare immediately brought more tears to the boy's eyes. "I . . . I should have. I am so sorry I didn't. But Israel made me promise to say nothing. He thought telling would make it worse for everyone else. I saw two other men who had been whipped and put in the stocks at the Grove, but I said nothing about that, either."

"You have been to Melbury Hall?"

"Aye, m'lord," Jamey confessed. "Then I . . . I just didn't know what to do . . . or how I could help them . . . and I could not talk to you . . . didn't know how . . . and . . ."

"Enough of that, lad." The earl's large hand closed tenderly on Jamey's arm. "This is not your fault. The man who just ran off: his name is Mickleby. He is the bailiff at Melbury Hall. Reverend Trimble tells me that all who work there are terrified of him. Now I can

see why . . . but we shall see to that soon enough. For now, let us get
Israel to Solgrave."

Jamey wiped at his face. "Does this mean you will not take Israel
back to them?"

"Not a chance, lad. Your friend is going back with us . . . where he
can get the care he needs."

"Get out. I shall call you when we are finished with our business."

Louisa's maid looked once at the old woman standing in the sitting room Lady Nisdale had taken at the inn, and went out, closing
the door behind her.

Louisa stared at Mrs. Stockdale's serving woman standing uncomfortably in the middle of the floor.

"Did you get a name for me?" she demanded, not getting up from
her chair.

The woman looked back at the door before flashing ruined teeth
at her. "Aye, mum. Took some doing, but I got the name, I did. Mistress Rebecca went to a household in London, sure"—she lowered
her voice to a whisper—"never to be heard of again."

"What's the name?" Louisa snapped irritably, getting up and
crossing the floor to the servant.

" 'Twill cost ye two gold sovereigns."

Louisa's hand lashed out so fast that the old woman didn't even
see it. But a second later, the woman was gasping in pain at the feel
of the sharp nails digging into the wrinkled skin of her throat.

"What is the *name*?"

"H . . . H . . . Hartington!" the woman croaked, wide-eyed. "Sir
Charles Hartington, Baronet! 'Twas his household that Miss Neville
was sent!"

Chapter 27

Jamey galloped ahead of Lord Stanmore, arriving at Solgrave far enough in advance to alert the household. Minutes later, the earl was handing Israel into the waiting arms of Daniel and Philip, and immediately dispatched a groom to St. Albans for the doctor.

It seemed to Stanmore that Israel had only just been settled in a room—with Mrs. Trent and Rebecca tending his injuries—when Daniel reappeared, red in the face.

"Squire Wentworth has arrived, m'lord," the steward announced, crossing the room to where Stanmore sat watching the proceedings.

"We shan't let him take Israel!" James announced from his perch beside the earl. "Tell him he can just go to the devil."

The steward nodded approvingly to the lad as Rebecca whirled to look at the three.

"Ahem . . . indeed. However . . ." Daniel continued. "The squire has situated himself in your library and demands an audience with you. If you agree with Master James, however, I would be more than happy to fetch several of the grooms and throw the man out."

"I do not think so, Daniel." Stanmore pressed a hand on the boy's shoulder, encouraging him to stay put, and headed for the door himself. "I want that pleasure for myself."

"Wait!" Rebecca caught up to him as he started down the stairs. "Would you allow me to come with you?"

Stanmore stopped and touched her cheek tenderly. "This is between the squire and myself."

"He is a horrible man," she said quietly, casting a killing look in the direction of the library. "I met him this Friday past when I went in search of Millicent. His bailiff is not the only one who is a brute. The squire, I believe, is even worse."

"I know him quite well, my love." Stanmore's words drew Rebecca's worried gaze away from the stairs and to his face. The turbulent sea of emotion he could see in her stormy blue eyes was a gift from heaven. "Fear not. I have known the man for quite a while. I am very well prepared to handle him."

She appeared to acquiesce, but only for a moment. As Stanmore started down the stairs again, she clutched at his arm.

"Wait! If the squire mentions anything about stealing . . . about Israel stealing a handkerchief . . . or perhaps a scarf that might have belonged to me . . . you should know that I gave the handkerchief to Israel myself on Friday. Mr. Cunningham was with me when I gave it to him. And Jamey just told me that he gave his friend my scarf at the cottage the day he went swimming by the old mill."

He laid his hand over hers. "You heard what James said. We shan't let him take Israel."

She nodded gratefully, and Stanmore seized her hand, placing a kiss on her palm. "But if you would be so kind as to restrain that angry cub of yours. I do not want him coming to my rescue."

"I have never seen him so proud of anything or anyone as he is about you, at this moment."

"I am the one who is feeling quite proud, to tell the truth. That swine of a bailiff is surely ten times the size of the lad, but James showed no fear whatever in attacking the knave in retaliation for what he had done to Israel." Stanmore reluctantly released her hand. "You have raised a fine lad, Rebecca. I think you should stay at Solgrave . . . and in London . . . just to make certain that I do not ruin him in the coming years."

The mixture of confusion and longing in her eyes was exactly what he'd hoped for.

"I do not ask for an answer now, but I should like it very much if you would consider staying with us . . . staying with me."

Standing on the landing above them, Sir Nicholas Spencer was more than a little disturbed by the tender exchange he'd just witnessed between Stanmore and Mrs. Ford.

Naturally, he wanted his friend to be happy. Over the past decade, he would have done anything to see Stanmore's attitude toward women ease somewhat. He himself had tried to interest him in the right sort of woman, but with no success at all.

Nicholas had been through a great deal with Stanmore. He'd seen his friend bow to his father's wishes in marrying a woman he didn't love. He'd been with him in Quebec when the news finally reached them that Elizabeth had run off with their two-month-old child. And he'd witnessed his friend's fierce struggle to overcome frustration and unhappiness when they returned to England.

But all that seemed to be behind him. Stanmore's philanthropic causes, his work in Parliament, his efforts here at Solgrave had seemed to succeed in pushing the pain of the past into some small and manageable place within him.

And if he wanted a wife, he could have any woman in England. Heiresses, beauties, women of learning or position—any woman he wanted was his for the choosing. But to pick someone like Rebecca Ford—with her unknown background, her lack of family and fortune! Nicholas feared his friend was about to make another mistake. True, she was extremely pleasing to look at, and tremendously charming in conversation. But why not simply engage her in an affair and leave it at that? Why the devil should he ask for her hand in marriage? Nicholas frowned on the landing, considering carefully what he had overheard. If that wasn't a proposal of marriage, then the devil take him!

He turned his thoughts to the woman. There was something about her—some hesitancy, some furtiveness—that Nicholas was not certain sat right with him. Perhaps if he were to do a little searching into her background . . . just for safety's sake. Certainly her resemblance to Jenny Greene was as good a place to begin as any. And though Mrs. Ford had recovered quickly, she'd nearly jumped out of her skin when he'd mentioned the name.

He turned from the stairs and ran into Philip coming down the hall. "Well, the earl seems to be exceptionally busy this morning."

"Indeed, sir."

"Would you be kind enough to tell Lord Stanmore that I had totally forgotten about a dinner engagement this evening, and I was forced to ride up to London this morning."

"I shall tell him, sir."

"Also, Philip, kindly tell him that I plan to return to Solgrave in a few days, so he shall not be so easily rid of me."

"I shall relay the bad news, sir."

With a discreet bow, the older steward headed down the hall again, but Nicholas remained where he was, staring at the man's back and wondering when Philip had developed a sense of humor.

The man's face might as well have been chiseled out of ice, for there had been no change in his expression at all during the squire's harangue.

Ready to grab the earl by his well-tailored jacket front, drag him out of his chair, and hammer a fist or two into his frosty face, Wentworth planted his large fists on top of the peer's desk. "Have you been listening to anything I have been saying? Do you have nothing to say in your own defense? Do you even deny hiding my slave—my *property*—here at Solgrave? Do you seriously think the beating of my bailiff—for no reason—is not to be considered a serious breach of civility?"

"I deny nothing, Wentworth. Further, I shall *not* tolerate cruelty to innocent people. Your barbaric practices will stop." Stanmore's warning was spoken so coolly that the squire's anger flared even hotter. "But be advised . . . my watchmen have been instructed to shoot Mickleby on sight. It is your own choice if you want to keep the brute employed or not. And with regard to Israel . . . he will remain indefinitely at Solgrave as my *guest*."

"You high and mighty ones . . . you think you are above the law!"

"You are free to charge me with criminal conduct, as you see fit, Wentworth." Stanmore leaned forward. "But if you do, I shall break you."

Fury boiled within the squire. He wanted a drink. He knew that as a member of the peerage, Stanmore was answerable only to the House of Lords—and none of them would side with Wentworth against one of their own.

"You must look at the evidence," the squire bellowed. "That filthy little bugger is a thief! I have brought the proof of what he stole from you yourself."

Stanmore glanced at the shawl and the handkerchief Rebecca had warned him about, lying on the chair.

"I have already told you. Those articles were given to Israel by my son and by Mrs. Ford."

"Your son and Mrs. Ford! Ha!" Wentworth spat out. "A crippled bastard and a whore!"

Stanmore's fist connected with his jaw with a crack that echoed in the squire's brain. Before he could shake his stunned head to clear the flashing lights in front of his eyes, though, a second blow to his ear sent him crumpling to one knee.

"If I ever hear you refer to my family or guest in such a manner again, Wentworth, I'll hunt you down and kill you myself."

Through the continuing haze, Wentworth saw Stanmore open the door of his library and motion for his steward and two footmen to enter.

"Escort our visitor to his horse. And Daniel, return to me immediately, for I will be sending a letter to Sir Oliver in London." The earl turned to the squire, who was struggling to his feet. "My lawyer will be instructed to settle on a price with you for the purchase of Israel. But just so we are clear . . . the lad is here to stay."

"You will pay dearly. . . ."

"I expect to. He is worth it. Now, Daniel, throw this creature out."

Stanmore waited until the congregation had dispersed after the Sunday service before pulling Reverend Trimble and William Cunningham aside and explaining the events of the morning.

"Israel was conscious when we left for the village a couple of hours ago. The doctor thinks the lad has sustained a concussion as well as some broken ribs."

"I saw him on Friday," the schoolmaster put in solemnly. "He was already bruised then. He must be a mess now."

"His face looks like a side of mutton," Stanmore said grimly.

"Poor fellow." Reverend Trimble shook his head.

"We cannot risk angering the squire any more than I already have. William, I want you to stay away from Melbury Hall for a few days." He turned to the minister. "And you, too. I want to make certain the tempers are cool—especially Wentworth's—before anyone who has *any* association with me crosses the squire's path."

"But the people there have come to expect our visits," Cunningham protested.

"I understand that! But I also understand that these same people would prefer to have you alive rather than dead."

Reverend Trimble looked gravely into the earl's face. "Do you believe it is that bad, m'lord?"

"It is, today." Seeing the frown on the schoolmaster's face, though, he shook his head. "You shall start again soon enough. But when you do, you shall go with one of my grooms as an escort."

"But, m'lord . . . !"

"Accept my wishes in this, William. I do not need your blood on my hands."

The young man nodded solemnly. "As you wish, m'lord."

After few more general inquiries about the village and the school, Stanmore walked toward the phaeton, where Rebecca was speaking quietly with Mrs. Trimble.

With all that was going on, he could have lingered here all day, just to admire the way she looked and spoke in the company of the villagers. But this afternoon Stanmore wanted Rebecca Neville all for himself. Having heard the doctor's report about Israel and knowing that the lad was in good hands with James looking on, she'd reluctantly agreed to come with him to the Sunday service, and this gave Stanmore great encouragement.

Moments later, they were following a road that wound alongside the river.

"True, this is not the most direct route back to Solgrave, but I want to hear no objections from you," he growled teasingly. "Daniel and Philip are prepared to defend the manor house. The doctor and Mrs. Trent have everything under control with Israel. James is at the lad's bedside, as well." He looked over at her. "You can take an hour for yourself."

Her blue eyes warmed with affection. "Do you truly believe you can keep Israel at Solgrave?"

"I can and I will!" he said confidently, taking the phaeton expertly across a ford where the river widened. "Wentworth knows he cannot force me to give back the lad, so he'll come up with an outrageous price for him."

"And you will pay it?"

"Of course! Happily."

A tear rolled down her flawless cheek, and she pressed her head affectionately against his shoulder. "You are the most . . . most honorable man to have walked on English soil, m'lord.." Her voice was a broken whisper.

"You would not think me honorable at all," he whispered in her ear, "if you knew exactly what is going through my head right now."

Her face lifted and a pretty blush crept into her cheeks. "What is it . . . exactly?"

He leaned down and captured her mouth in a kiss. Her lips instantly parted, and Stanmore's tongue rubbed against hers in a seductive dance. Hearing her soft moan, he moved the reins to one hand and let the other brush against her breast and move down to tease the inside of her thigh through the layers of her dress. When he pulled back, a deep blush had her cheeks burning and her blue eyes were clouded with passion.

"Have I fallen in your assessment, yet?"

She shook her head. "Not a whit!"

"Then you leave me no choice but to convince you otherwise."

Ten minutes later, the phaeton topped a hill and the old mill came into view, with the shining waters of the lake visible beyond. Reining in the sprightly pair, Stanmore helped Rebecca down and removed a blanket from the seat. After directing his groom to return the carriage to the stables, the earl turned to her.

"You wouldn't mind if we walked back from here."

"Of course not," she said with a smile.

As the phaeton disappeared toward Solgrave, Stanmore watched Rebecca lifting her face to the sun and closing her eyes, savoring the feel of it.

Today she had dressed in a blue gown and hat that were roughly the same color of her eyes. The white lace detailing the conservative neckline, the long sleeves, the fall of the skirts—all drew his gaze in turn. But it was just the ornamentation of perfection. He wanted her, body and soul. He hungered for what he knew lay beneath the layers of clothing. He saw in his mind the long and slender limbs, the full breasts and pink tips that so easily came to life at the touch of his lips. He longed for her—naked and unadorned—radiant in her natural state, exposed to his gaze, and wanting him, too.

Stanmore clenched his jaw, forcing down such thoughts. The passion she induced in him was staggering. And last night, as much as he'd wanted to have her, the thought of her walking out of his life had held him back. But now . . .

Miss Rebecca Neville would have thought him a *most* dishonorable man if she had any inkling of his thoughts and plans.

Stanmore spread the blanket on the grassy meadow near the stone wall of the mill before walking slowly toward her. Her eyes widened at his approach.

She put her hands behind her back. "Do you believe I might have offended your friend, Sir Nicholas, last night?"

He came to a stop so near her that he could smell her scent of lavender.

"Nicholas is never offended by women." His hands lifted to her chin, and he undid the ribbons of the hat, dropping it on the grass. He pulled the pins out of her hair and watched the ringlets of gold and fire make a mockery of the sun's brilliance.

"Then . . . why did he leave so soon and so unexpectedly?"

His fingers played with her hair, threading into the silky locks and pulling it over one shoulder until her ivory neck was exposed to his heated gaze.

"That is Nicholas," he said vaguely. "He plans nothing. He comes and goes as he pleases."

Her fingers moved up to his jacket, slowly working their way beneath the cloth. "Does that mean . . . that he can drop in on us . . . here . . . now?"

"I am afraid I would have to kill anyone who would interfere with what I have conspired to do to you this afternoon." His lips pressed against her throat, and he felt the shivers run through her body.

"Would you be kind enough to tell me . . . what it is exactly that you have planned?"

"Why, to make love to you."

She seemed to stop breathing as he backed her slowly toward the stone wall of the mill.

His fingers were already working on loosening the laces of her dress. "Do you remember our first kiss . . . here at the mill?"

She nodded, rising on her toes and capturing his lips in a kiss. His body pressed against hers, his hips rubbing intimately against hers. She broke off the kiss and, laying her head back against the wall, looked up to him in wonder. Stanmore could no longer see any fear in those eyes—only awareness and anticipation.

"I have dreamed of making love to you against this wall—on this grass, in that lake—since that day." His hand cupped her breast through the dress, and her eyes closed. Hearing the moan deep in her throat, he brushed his lips against hers. "What say you, Rebecca? Is this a day dreams are made of?"

"I am yours to take!" she whispered fiercely. "Heart, soul, and body! Yours to have for—"

Stanmore captured her mouth before she could finish. *For now!* He had no desire to hear such things. All that mattered was now . . . but the future began now, as well!

And right now he wanted her to become frenzied with need. Continuing to kiss her mouth, he captured one of her hands and guided it downward from his chest to the front of his breeches. The hard fullness of him must have startled her at first, for she immediately withdrew her hand. But an instant later, she sought him out—timidly, slowly, feeling him, exploring him. A low groan of pleasure emitted from deep within him, and this appeared to give her the courage that she needed.

"You must tell me if I am doing anything wrong."

"There is nothing you can do to me that would be wrong." His fingers finished undoing the laces, and he pulled down the dress and lace chemise from her shoulders. He stroked her full breasts with his palm. "But you are only allowed to stop when I drop at your feet unconscious."

The sound of her soft laughter warmed him, and he thought of all the years they could have together, enjoying each other and sharing such a life.

He bent his head to her breasts and took her sweet flesh into his mouth, but she was clearly determined not to allow him to again lift her alone into a state of bliss. Not this time. Coaxing his mouth back to her lips, she seduced his mouth with her lips and tongue and with soft murmured cries in her throat. Before he could recover from that, she was undoing the buttons of his breeches with timid fingers.

Stanmore was lost the moment she reached inside and actually touched him. Of all the control he'd employed last night, he could not summon any of it this afternoon. His hands were shaking when he drew her down onto the blanket with him and pushed up her skirts. "This is too quick," he groaned when she lay back, pulling him on top of her.

"No! Give me all of you!" With an air of absolute certainty, she guided the tip of his manhood to her wet folds, and he was a lost man. He drove into her with a single motion and stopped, forcing himself to retain some semblance of control. She gave no cry, but the tears gathering in the blue orbs bespoke her pain. He waited—fighting the urge to pull back and imbed himself deeply again—and instead made love to her mouth and teased her breasts until she was writhing beneath him and pulling him into her. He rolled them on the blanket until she was on top of him, and her eyes opened in surprise.

"Can we make love this way?"

"You'd be surprised at all the ways."

She looked down at him in awe, but he was the one dazzled by the sight above him. Her dress lay open, her exposed breasts caressed by the breeze and kissed by the sun. Her skirts billowed around them, hiding the most intimate contact of their flesh. Her face took on a questioning look, and he smiled. Stanmore reached beneath the skirts and, cupping her buttocks, lifted her and lowered her again, sending her on the journey to fulfillment. And as her straining body writhed in the rhythmic dance of love, he reveled in her cries of ecstasy.

Rolling her again beneath him, he heard Rebecca's whispered declaration, and an instant later Stanmore burst into a place he never thought existed this side of heaven.

She felt the dampness of the shirt on his back and gathered him tightly in her arms. Last night, and for the first time, she had experienced a sexual release. But not until moments ago had she realized what it was like to have the earth stop turning and time stand still, to have the very breath catch in a lover's chest as they flew toward their mutual fulfillment. In the span of these few precious moments, Stanmore had been able to open a most wondrous door. He had forced her to glimpse the beauty of a life that lay beyond it, a life that emanated from two people committed eternally to each other, a life that she could never have dared herself to dream.

Rebecca fought the painful knot that was forming in her chest. She brushed her lips against his hair as he rested so serenely on top of her. She could feel the pounding of his heartbeat beginning to slow. She cherished the feel of his weight. The strength that flowed from him. She turned her attention to the present and tried not to mourn what was to come.

Chapter 28

"I do not understand this. Have I died and gone to heaven?"

"Only if I am there, too." Jamey jumped onto the bed and pulled his feet up, sitting cross-legged. "You are at Solgrave."

"But they shall come after me . . . to take me back!" Israel glanced anxiously toward the door, where a young serving woman had just gone out with an empty bowl of broth that she'd been cheerfully spooning into him.

For as long as he'd been awake, there had been people around him. White people. Taking care of him. The doctor. Mrs. Ford. The kind old housekeeper, sending servants in and out as she herself had seen to his face and back. This morning, Israel had even been stunned to see the Earl of Stanmore come in to ask after him, before taking Mrs. Ford away. In fact, this was the first time that he and Jamey had been left to themselves.

"No one is taking you, Israel. Squire Wentworth was already here, but my father sent him on his way."

Israel's turned his battered face questioningly to Jamey. Through his swollen eyelids, he met the other boy's gaze. "The bailiff must have followed me to our cottage. He caught me there with your mama's wrap and . . . and he was set to kill me." His ribs and body ached so badly that he wanted to cry, but he blinked back the tears. "Outside . . . when he was beating me with that old stick of his— and kicking me, too, for good measure—I saw the earl coming. I heard him shout once at Mickleby before the bailiff clubbed me in the head again. After that, I don't remember a thing . . . until waking up here with all your folk around me."

His fingers touched the soft linen of the sheets hesitantly.

"Never in my life have I slept in a real bed." His body was too beaten up to feel anything but throbbing pain, but he knew this bed was softer than any cloud in the sky. And the people seeing to him had been nicer than any angels he'd ever dreamed of running into in heaven. "His lordship saved my life, Jamey. You were right. Lord Stanmore is different."

"You should have seen him. He beat that dog of a bailiff real good. I think my father would have killed him if the cowardly cur hadn't run away."

Jamey had said it twice already. *Father.* Israel wanted to smile at his friend and tell him. But he decided Jamey already knew that he was looking on the earl in a different way. Besides, it hurt too much to smile, and he was getting very tired.

"From now on, you'll be living at Solgrave like me. I heard Daniel tell Mrs. Trent that my father is settling accounts with the squire, so no one at Melbury Hall will have any hold on you."

Israel's gaze drifted up to the ceiling that seemed to be as high as the sky. If he looked really hard, he thought he could even imagine stars smiling down on him. "I know his lordship will be a good master. For years, I've heard Mr. Cunningham and Reverend Trimble sing his praises. I'll do my best to be a hardworking slave."

"Not a slave, Israel." The man's deep voice in the doorway drew both of the boys' faces. Lord Stanmore was leaning against the jamb. "You are to be free now, lad." He walked to the bed. "As free as James here." He ruffled the other boy's hair and sat down on a chair. "And you shall grow up as a free man."

The earl was far bigger than Squire Wentworth. He looked even stronger than Mickleby. But Israel was not afraid. Though his face was stern and he had a gaze like some black-eyed cat, there wasn't a shred of meanness in his looks. In fact, his lordship made him feel safe—inside and outside.

"I don't know where I was born—or who my parents were, m'lord. I don't know what being free means." Israel's words were a quiet whisper.

The earl looked down at his hands, and Israel saw his face harden in a frown. "I know that is true, Israel, and I am sorry about it. But you were born in the same way that James and I were born.

God meant for all of us to be free." He touched the blanket. "Being
free means no one will claim it as a right to mistreat you. It means
you shall control your own life. When you are grown, you shall
choose where you wish to live and how hard you want to work and
how you spend the fruits of your labor."

"But, m'lord, I have no place to live!"

"You shall live at Solgrave," the earl answered. "And when
James goes away to Eton for the fall term . . ." he paused, and Israel watched as the father's and son's gazes met. There was no
longer fight in Jamey's expression—only respect and acceptance.
The earl's gaze turned to Israel again. "You shall go to school in the
village. You have done too much work with your hands for someone so young. I believe you might just enjoy working your mind a
little now."

"I shall need to earn my keep, m'lord," Israel promised.

"I am certain you will, lad! Daniel makes sure everyone at Solgrave earns their keep. But you shan't be beaten for it, and you shall
earn a wage for the work you do." The earl looked from one to the
other and then rose to his feet. "I think you two will want some time
to yourselves. Knowing Mrs. Trent, she shall be up here any moment, scolding James and me for not giving you enough rest."

As the Earl of Stanmore left them, Jamey turned to Israel. "I do
not like being sent away to school, but I shall go because the earl
thinks I should."

"And I shall be here waiting for you when you come home."

The boy smiled and placed his hand on top of Israel's. "This is
very good, don't you think so?"

Israel blinked back the tears and tried to not think of the other
slaves still at the Grove. He tried to not think of the whippings and
worse that the others would still be living with every day. He tried
not to see Moses in his mind's eye—a giant of a man who cried
every night in his sleep and wet himself at the very sight of a whip.

"Very nearly," Israel whispered solemnly. "This is *very nearly*
heaven."

The stage floor had been rolling beneath her feet tonight, the
faces of the audience indistinct. But Jenny had heard them well

enough. By the devil, rowdy and lewd they were in the pit! True, she may have imbibed a little too much spirits this afternoon and hadn't remembered a few . . . well, more than a few of her lines, but it hadn't mattered much to this rabble. With the uproarious laughter and the vulgar hilarity going on in the pit, no one would have heard a thing anyway.

Jenny Greene groped toward the small changing room they all shared backstage. Rustics! Addle-brained fools! Just because she'd tripped and fallen twice coming on for her first lines, that was hardly reason enough to carry on so throughout the play! This Covent Garden crowd was becoming lewder and lower every year. Not like the old days, when she had played Ophelia and Rosamond and Lady Macbeth at Drury Lane.

"Send him my way when you are finished with him, will you, Jenny?"

"What?"

"Never seen *this* one. Have you?"

"He is a *dream*, Jenny!"

Jenny leaned a hand against the wall to steady herself and looked confusedly at the three actresses who were pushing their way out of the dressing room.

"There, love. You have the place all to yourself!" The fourth girl winked at her before slipping out the door.

Lord, she thought. And still they come.

After dealing with those rolling floorboards all night, though, Jenny was feeling a little queasy about lifting her skirts for yet another admirer. But her vanity soon quelled the thought. Now that she thought of it, it had been a long time since anyone of *significance* had been waiting backstage for her. Perhaps she'd just take a look at him. She reached inside the neckline of her dress to adjust the weight of her breasts and noticed the long tear in the side of the bodice. That first fall onstage must have torn it. Nice of her fellow actors to tell her, Jenny thought. No wonder they'd laughed in the pit.

She saw the bottle of gin and the cups long before noticing the flowers and the gentleman.

"Mrs. Greene, you are a marvel, ma'am."

It was difficult to tear her gaze from the bottle, but she forced herself to look at the handsome man towering over the dressing table. He was younger than the ones she'd been seeing lately and far better dressed. A lovely sword, as well. Quite lovely.

"Performing dries an actor's throat like little else." She sauntered as casually as she could toward the bottle. "What is your name?"

"Sir Nicholas Spencer . . . at your service, ma'am."

She picked up the bottle and tried to pour a drink, but the cup moved. It seemed to be moving more and more of late.

"Please allow me, Mrs. Greene."

She watched the man's sure movements as he took the bottle from her hand and filled two glasses. He looked good—smelled good—she was certain he would even taste good. It had been a very long time since anyone had succeeded in whetting her appetite. Jenny let her gaze travel appreciatively down to the front of his breeches. Very long, indeed.

"It is far too public in here for two people to get properly acquainted," she cooed, accepting the cup from his hand. "Allow me to finish this, and we shall go back to my place. It isn't far."

"Perhaps you will allow me to finish my drink, as well."

He put aside a pile of costumes that had been heaped on two chairs and set one of them by the dressing table for her. Jenny concentrated hard and successfully negotiated the seat on the first try. She took another long drink and eyed his muscular thighs as he sat down near her.

"Are you fond of the theater, Nicholas?"

"Indeed, ma'am. Though I've not much interest in the highbrow stuff."

"And do you attend often?"

"As often as my schedule permits." He leaned over, and when Jenny looked down, she found the cup in her hand already filled. "But the truth be told, I mostly attend the plays in which my favorite actresses command the stage."

The cup felt heavy in her hand, but she wasn't willing to part with it. She took another drink . . . to lighten it. "And do you have many favorites?"

"If I may be so bold, ma'am, there is none I esteem more highly than the inimitable Jenny Greene."

Jenny felt the excitement ripple through her—a thrill so long forgotten—a feeling far stronger and more pleasurable than anything gin could produce. Staring into the young man's adoring blue gaze, she could see the legions of men who used to wait for her after the curtain fell. The gifts, the balls, the attention, the jealous looks of other women who knew they could never compete with Jenny Greene.

"When was it you first saw me on stage? Was it at Drury Lane? At the Haymarket?" The young man paused an inordinately long time, she thought, and a pang of insecurity sent the cup again to her lips. As the liquid slid down her throat, it no longer tasted quite so pleasant, however. She downed the rest of it, nonetheless, and reached for the bottle herself, getting it on the first try.

"To be honest, ma'am, it was your portrait that I saw first . . . before I ever saw you on stage."

She saw him watching her hand on the bottle. Or was the rogue looking at her breasts? she thought with satisfaction.

"I had never seen anything so beautiful in my life up to that moment. I recall standing there, for an eternity it seemed, staring at a woman who was surely a recreation of Venus herself."

She felt the snarl pulling at her lips, but she hardly cared a whit. He was enchanted with the woman she *was*. The beauty she had once possessed. She didn't bother with the cup and the mouth of the bottle banged against her lips, spilling some of it down the front of her costume. She brushed at it without much concern. The damned thing was torn anyway. She peered at him and held the bottle tightly.

"And where . . ." she said with an air of majesty, "where was this portrait?"

He reached over to take the bottle from her, but she hugged the spirits against her breast.

"Where was it?" She must have shouted her question, for there was a ringing in her ears afterward. Sir Nicholas, however, showed no sign of anything amiss, only a slight frown of concern crossed his face when she tried to take another drink from the bottle. Well, the devil take him!

He shrugged his broad shoulders and laid his gloves over his knee. "I first saw the portrait when I was a lad. It was in the gallery of a villa in Hampton. My father had taken me to visit his friend, the great actor David Garrick."

"David!" She sank back against the chair, a piercing melancholy stabbing at her heart. "My beautiful, sweet, unfaithful David."

"You were on stage together for years, I believe."

"We were, indeed," she whispered, her mind warming with reminiscences of the past. "He discovered me, you know. He was in love with me."

"How could he avoid it?"

"True," she murmured. "They all were."

"When was that portrait painted, Mrs. Greene?"

Her grip on the bottle must have loosened, for she saw him take it from her lap and put it on the table. He placed her cup beside it.

"You looked very young and innocent in that portrait," he persisted.

"Young. That is true enough, but innocent . . . ?" She smiled and shook her head, starting the room spinning nicely. "David had me sit for that portrait right after I gave away my child. It was a reward, you know . . . for doing the right thing . . . for making the correct decision."

"You gave away Garrick's child?"

"No! No! No!" She shook her hand in the air impatiently. "I was already carrying someone else's child when I first saw David. He was playing Richard III at Drury Lane. I fell in love with him . . . and he with me."

"And he asked you to rid yourself of the child?"

"It was not like that!" She reached for the cup but it was out of her range. "Give me a drink, sir . . . sir . . . what is your name?"

"Nicholas," he replied, holding out the cup to her. "What do you mean, it was not like that?"

"I mean . . . David was trying to do the right thing . . . but it was for that fool Guilford . . . and for me." She took the filled cup from him. "Aye, Guilford was the father . . . and he was in love with me . . . but he was married. Still, he was stubborn and high-minded and . . . well, he meant to do right by me . . . you know, in providing for the child. And then, when David and I fell in love, I wanted no part of him . . . or his family . . . or his help." Jenny stared down into the cup. "And, to be truthful, I was not sure that I even wanted his child anymore. So that is when David talked me into . . . into giving the baby to the father and washing my hands of the whole thing."

"And you did? You gave up your child?"

"Gladly! And everyone was perfectly happy." She raised her cup and took a sip, immediately spraying the liquid across the room. "What the devil is this?"

"Water," he said calmly before sitting down. "Do you know what became of your child?"

Jenny frowned and threw the cup to the floor. "I do not want to talk about her. Ask about me and David—about the stage and the theater. About all the fun we had together until . . . until he cheated on me and married that bitch . . . that Viennese harlot . . . that . . . dancer."

"Everyone knows about that part of your life, Jenny." His voice was gentle, soothing to the ear, and she suddenly felt very tired. "But I do not believe many people know anything about this mysterious daughter."

"Of course not!" she said heavily, finding the chair suddenly very uncomfortable. "People know nothing of her . . . and no reason they should. Except that other gent . . . Heartfelt . . . Hartingford . . . Hartington . . . that's it. Except for Hartington, you are the only other gentleman who's ever been interested in this." She peered at him suspiciously. "Do you know him?"

"Hartington?"

"Aye. When was that? He'd hired her . . . it was a long time ago. He came to see me . . . fancied me, he said. A bit of a romance, we had . . . I think. And then I come to find out my Rebecca was working for him." Jenny reached over for the bottle on the table, but it was gone. "I need a drink. . . . No, wait! We shall go over to my place and . . . and get acquainted properly."

He rose to his feet and she had a sinking feeling from the look on his face that it wasn't eagerness to go home with her.

"Another time, Mrs. Greene," he said cheerfully. "I shall have my carriage take you home, though. I don't know if there will be a chair available at this hour."

"Your carriage?" she huffed. "Damn your impudence! I need no sympathy from a water-mongering whelp!"

"Do not mistake my offer as sympathy. I should be truly honored if you would accept the use of my carriage." He took her hand and helped her to her feet. "Mrs. Greene, I believe you were the most beautiful actress that has ever lived."

Her throat was dry. She was tired. She needed his strength even to take a step. And he supported her until they were outside and she was tucked safely in the carriage.

"Any regrets, Jenny?" he asked before closing the door of the carriage. "Do you ever wish that you had kept your daughter?"

She glanced at the well-appointed but empty interior of the carriage. She thought of the cold bed that was awaiting her at the house. And then, in her mind's eye, she saw the crowd on their feet before a stage. The repeated shouts of her name. The lines of admirers.

"No!" she said haughtily. "Only a *fool* would trade what I have had for a mere child."

The sky beyond the window seat was a shade lighter, and Rebecca knew the dawn was about to break. Carefully, she lifted Stanmore's arm from around her waist and slipped from his embrace. He stirred slightly, and she felt the temptation to curl back into his warmth.

The polished wood was cool and smooth on the soles of her feet as Rebecca padded across the floor to the window. Pulling a quilt around her, she looked through the glass panes. The moon had dropped low in the night sky, making the drive leading out of the estate and back to the St. Albans road eerily white. She sharply turned her gaze to the silvery and magical reflection of the moon on the lake.

Rebecca wanted this scene branded in her memory . . . the moon, the lake, the bridge, the meadow climbing upward from the water's edge. She wanted something that she would be able to recall of Solgrave during the empty years ahead—something other than the man and the boy whom she loved more than life itself, but had to leave behind.

"Why are you out of bed?"

His voice was a warm whisper in her ear. Rebecca's breath hitched in her chest as she felt his warmth close around her. She couldn't bring herself to tell him the truth—of already mourning the time when she had to leave. "I . . . I couldn't sleep."

His hands gently pulled the quilt off her shoulders, and Rebecca felt the cloth pool at their feet as his naked body pressed against her own from behind. "Then you should have awakened me."

Rebecca felt his teeth scrape over the sensitive skin beneath her ear, and she shivered with excitement. "I . . . I wanted to . . . but I felt so bold . . . after everything we shared . . . during the night."

One hand cupped her breast, the other slid down her stomach . . . and lower to cup her already damp folds. She leaned her head back against him as his teeth nibbled her earlobe.

His voice was a husky growl. "Don't you already know that I cannot get enough of you?" The play of his fingers in and out of her flesh had her body humming to the most tantalizing song. "Call me selfish if you will, but knowing that you are afflicted with the same suffering makes me a very happy man, my love."

She leaned to one side and threaded her fingers in his hair, kissing him deeply.

Although they'd already made love several times during the night, the force of his passion at this moment was unmatched. He turned her toward the mirror hanging above the dresser beside the window, allowing Rebecca to look at their reflection as he entered her. She watched through a thick haze of passion how one expert hand cupped and caressed her breast while the other continued to coax the pleasures of womanhood within her. He slid into her again and again, and Rebecca stared with utter disbelief at the image of these two people rising together on undulating waves of passion before finally coming apart in an explosion of ecstasy.

Breathless before the power of what she'd witnessed, Rebecca closed her eyes and etched in her mind this memory, too.

Chapter 29

The church was deserted but for the two women speaking quietly by the ancient crypt.

"Everyone is afraid. Since yesterday morning, even his own people scatter when he comes around. And I do not think . . . it is anger. There is something more—a madness has taken hold of him. He is in his cups *all* the time. He never sleeps, as far as I can tell. This morning, he beat one of the scullery maids for not knowing when Lady Nisdale was coming back. And then he ordered one of my maids—Vi, a young and innocent thing—to be brought to him in his study." Millicent shivered. "We had to hide the terrified creature in one of the slave huts in the Grove and lie and say the girl had gone to St. Albans to look after her sick mother. I am hoping he forgets about her."

Rebecca's hand rested on her friend's arm. "How about you? Will you be safe there until the end of the week?" With the netting pushed up, she had a clear picture of Millicent's hideous bruises.

"I am already defeated as far as he cares." Her voice was flat and empty. "He is now on a rampage to crush those who have any life left in them. I am more docile than I have ever been."

"How about the bailiff? Is he still there?"

"Mickleby is still there, but his bluster is only a veneer. The rumors that Lord Stanmore has ordered him to be shot on sight have clearly frightened the bully. I heard one of the maids say the coward would swim to Jamaica if the squire released him and paid him the wages he's owed. For now, though, he is still there." Millicent's gaze met Rebecca's. "But how is Israel?"

Rebecca told her friend about the lad's broken ribs. But she also mentioned how much better the boy was, even after only a day, and how Jamey was keeping a vigil at the bedside.

"Are you still . . . still planning to go?"

Rebecca quickly pushed aside all of her own hurt and longing and painted a smile on her face. "We are . . . the two of us will go this Friday. I have already asked one of the grooms at Solgrave to hire us a carriage. You must meet me at the end of the orchards, by the road to Melbury Hall, early Friday morning."

"I shall be there!" Millicent said excitedly, clutching Rebecca's hand. "I have only a little money, and some jewels. I shall be leaving with not much more than the clothes on my back. But it does not matter . . . nothing matters. I shall be free . . . and happy for the first time in my life!"

Rebecca's hands patted her friend's back as Millicent hugged her tightly. Blinking back her own tears, she tried to not think of what she herself would be leaving behind—Jamey, Stanmore, and all that they meant to her. Rebecca fought back her rising anguish and tried to not think of the happiness that her past was robbing her of. Millicent was right . . . *it does not matter . . . nothing matters.*

"I'll wait for you by the orchards."

The lawyer stared incredulously at the visitor. "And does his lordship know *anything* about what you are up to?"

"Do not discourage me, Birch," Nicholas warned. "This is the noblest thing I have yet done in my life. In fact, now that I think of it, this is quite like something Stanmore himself would do." He shook his head. "This is not good. I have been ruined by him after all. You mustn't tell anyone. Think of my reputation!"

Birch started pacing the room. "I hardly think his lordship would be pleased to know of your involvement in his affairs."

"You mean, if you were to *tell* him that I was the one who discovered this most damaging information about Mrs. Ford."

"Miss Neville," Birch corrected. "I received a letter from his lordship yesterday. She has confirmed what I discovered earlier . . . and through my *own* efforts." He paused, glowering at Nicholas. "Her name is Miss Rebecca Neville. There never was a husband, after all, and she was not an acquaintance of Elizabeth before they sailed."

"So the mystery lies in . . ."

"What caused her to run and change her name ten years ago."

"Which brings us back to her early years in England and . . . perhaps to a possible employer?"

Birch stopped pacing. "I am not denying the significance of what you have learned, Sir Nicholas. It is just . . . well, because of the sensitive nature of this matter . . ."

"How sensitive an issue is it?"

"He plans to marry her"—the lawyer glanced at the letter from Stanmore lying on his desk—"soon . . . perhaps this week."

"That is exactly what I was afraid of." Nicholas sank into a chair.

"I can assure you, there is *nothing* to fear. Mrs. Ford . . . I mean Miss Neville is an absolute exemplar of propriety, a paragon—regardless of her mother's reputation. Of course, we must search out this Mr. Guilford, whoever he is."

Nicholas let out a low whistle. "So you are attracted to her, too. You and Stanmore both. And that is not all of it. Daniel, Mrs. Trent, even that old grump Philip. Everyone she meets falls prey to her charm, it appears."

"I hardly think the term 'falls prey' applies here. In fact, I might argue that perhaps the fault lies with you, Sir Nicholas, as you appear to be so wholly unaffected by such a rare and wonderful woman. Far superior to any you might find among the *ton*, I should add."

"No doubt. But who says I am unaffected by the woman?" Nicholas responded in self-defense. "I am only concerned with Stanmore's rather precipitous intentions. I do not believe that either you or I would like to see him hurt again."

Birch ran a hand over his face. "I certainly do not."

Nicholas jumped to his feet. "Then it is settled. We shall proceed with my plan."

"I still believe it would be best if you allowed me to visit this . . . Hartington residence on my own."

"No chance of that, Birch," Nicholas warned, picking up his hat and gloves. "Like it or not, I am involved and will remain involved until the woman is raised to sainthood or damned forever."

Disgruntled, Birch moved behind his desk. "I shall send my card to this Sir Charles Hartington and appeal for a meeting with him tomorrow."

"Do not bother with Sir Charles. Send your card directly to Lady Hartington."

"And why is that?"

"Because the present baronet is not yet twenty years of age."

"Twenty?"

"His father, the previous Sir Charles, was killed years ago. If there is anyone who can give us any worthwhile information about our mysterious Miss Neville, it will be the mother."

They tried to be discreet. Stanmore would come to her bedroom late in the night, only after the household had retired. And in the mornings, he'd reluctantly leave her before dawn, going back to his own chambers to wash and change and meet James by the stables for their morning ride. But despite their discretion, as Rebecca made her way to Israel's room to check on him before going down to breakfast, she felt as if everyone could see right through her.

True, she was a little dreamy eyed from all she and Stanmore had shared last Sunday by the lake and in the course of two nights of blissful ecstasy. She was deliciously tender from his repeated lovemaking, yet always ravenous to see him again. He knew exactly how to bring her body to life and make her wild with desire. He knew how to strip away the encumbrances of her heart and her mind until she was freely whispering words of love to him. Not that any of it was a surprise, for Samuel Wakefield, the Earl of Stanmore, was the only man she had ever loved. The only man she would ever love.

As she approached the dining room, Rebecca tried to fight back the grief that was welling in her eyes and knotting her throat. She had a lifetime in the colonies to ponder the emptiness of her existence, a lifetime to cry for her two men.

Philip was in the dining room when Rebecca entered. Pleasant as always to her, the steward was positively animated by news of the distinguished visitor that they were to expect at Solgrave before the end of the week.

"Lord North, the prime minister, will be stopping *here* . . . on Thursday!"

Though Rebecca tried to exhibit some enthusiasm, she honestly hoped no one would visit until she and Millicent had gone. It wasn't the entertaining that she minded, of course, but rather the further loss of precious time she had to spend with the ones she loved. She accepted a cup of tea and admonished herself for her selfishness.

"Indeed, I remember reading about the King's new First Minister when I was in the colonies. He took office early this year, I believe?"

"He did, ma'am." Philip motioned to one of the servants to serve Rebecca her breakfast. "His lordship is a great favorite of the King. I believe they have known each other since boyhood. In fact, if I may be so forward . . ."

He paused, waiting until the servant had completed his task and backed away. He lowered his voice, speaking confidentially.

"In fact, ma'am, there is such a close resemblance between the King and Lord North that it is rumored they may even be related. Lucy Montagu, the mother to the present Lord North, was known to be an attractive young woman and widely rumored to be quite *intimate* with the King's father."

Rebecca paused with the cup halfway to her mouth and raised an eyebrow at Philip. She would never have taken the steward as a gossip.

"Of course, this is just disgusting rumor based upon—did I say close?—*slight* physical resemblance between the two men . . . and upon court talk, which I would be loath to credit with any truth whatever!"

Rebecca hid a smile, deciding that Philip would be disappointed if she were not to pursue the topic. "Is Lord North's father still alive?"

"Of course!" The steward added, "The old earl, who served as the King's Governor in His Majesty's minority, you know, is quite advanced in years now. Spends most of his retirement at Wroxton Abbey near Banbury, I believe. In fact, that is where the prime minister shall be traveling from this Thursday. Despite all that scandalous chin wagging, it is well known that Lord North is quite fond of the old man."

The appearance of Jamey and Stanmore saved Rebecca from having to ask any more questions. She was elated by the lad's crushing embrace, and watched with a sublime sense of happiness as the boy attacked his food. Fighting an urge to send Stanmore the look of longing that was in her soul, she simply smiled at him. His dark answering gaze, though, heated her entire body.

"Shall I tell her, or are you going to?"

Rebecca looked from Jamey to Stanmore and back.

"I believe you should," the earl replied casually.

Jamey turned his bright face to her. "We are going to Scotland for an entire month this August. That is earlier than his lordship goes every year, but he is changing his plans this year, so we can all make the trip before I go off to Eton."

Rebecca sent a smile of gratitude at Stanmore. Jamey would need just that kind of attention once she was gone.

"Is this not the most exciting news?" the lad asked. "And we can take Israel, too."

"You shall all have the best of times," she replied encouragingly.

"But you will, too!" Jamey asserted. "His lordship thinks you shouldn't be frightened of Lady Meg . . . that is my grandmother. He says she is all bark and no . . . no teeth?" He glanced questioningly across the table.

"All bark and no bite."

"That's the phrase! She shall love you. The same way that we *all* love you." Jamey's pleading eyes lifted up to hers. "You *will* come with us? Say you will!"

Rebecca felt as if someone had wrapped a fist around her heart and was squeezing hard. An uncomfortable silence fell over the room. She felt the weight of everyone's gaze on her.

"Mama?"

She no longer deserved it, but he continued to call her by the name. Rebecca saw Jamey's eyes fill with tears, and she struggled for an answer.

"I shall . . . I shall need to talk with his lordship about it." She turned to Stanmore. "We shall speak more about it."

The look on the earl's face was no less disappointed than the look on Jamey's.

Not one to enter into any situation unprepared, Birch had succeeded in learning a few things about the Hartington family before he and Sir Nicholas climbed the steps to the handsome town house.

Although eight years had passed since the murder of Sir Charles Hartington in Vauxhall Gardens by an unknown assailant, Lady Hartington was still known to bristle at any mention of the incident. The lawyer was given to understand that the woman's aversion to discussing her husband's demise was largely due to Sir Charles's roguish style of living. Sir Charles was a known womanizer whose sexual exploits were directed at any woman who passed his way, regardless of age, class, or marital status. And to add to the family's misfortunes, it was rumored that it had been a disgruntled husband—waterman or some such thing—who had put the knife blade between Sir Charles's ribs.

Not entirely uncommon, Sir Oliver thought, but certainly reason enough for a respectable woman like Lady Hartington to shun such discussions.

Upon arriving at the house, he and Sir Nicholas were seen into the lady's receiving room, where she received them civilly, albeit coolly. Sir Oliver was surprised to find she was indeed a very pleasing-looking woman, and younger looking than he'd expected.

"How curious it is that I should receive visitors twice in one week, asking the same question about the very same person."

Birch glanced at Sir Nicholas, only to find him looking as baffled as he himself was feeling. He turned his attention back to their hostess. "Did you say someone *else* was here inquiring after Miss Rebecca Neville this week?"

"Indeed!" Lady Hartington pressed her hands together on her lap—a movement that the lawyer found extremely charming. "Lady Louisa Nisdale. She was here on Monday, claiming that she was a long-lost friend to Miss Neville. She was hoping, she said, to find any news she could of her missing friend."

"Ah, indeed. Lady Nisdale." Birch frowned at the thought of Stanmore murdering Louisa. But a glance at the fury in Nicholas's eyes, and he wondered which one might kill her first. "Did Lady Nisdale mention . . . how she had discovered any connection you might have with Miss Neville?"

"She claimed to be an old school friend of Rebecca's . . . and she claimed that their old schoolmistress had offered the connection." Unexpected temper colored the woman's cheeks. "Of course, as soon as she said it, I knew the woman was *not* telling the truth. I have known the director of that school for a long time. In fact, I continue to correspond with her, for my own daughter Sara—she is sixteen now—is a pupil in that fine school. I *know* the woman would *never* divulge information of that sort to anyone. She has built a reputation on her integrity and her discretion. Needless to say, I sent Lady Nisdale on her way without being able to offer any answers."

Birch buried his sigh of relief. He had enough to be concerned about this week, and he didn't need Louisa's jealous involvement added to it.

"If I may be so blunt as to pose the question, how did *you* learn of my connections with Miss Neville?" Lady Hartington waited patiently for an answer.

Birch's practiced answers had not addressed this specific question. Sir Nicholas's quick response was a blessing.

"Your name was given to us by Miss Neville's mother. She is . . . was a well-known actress on the London stage. Your husband . . . your late husband had visited the lady at some point in time and told her that Rebecca was being employed by him."

The mention of her husband indeed succeeded in bringing a frown to the woman's face.

"We apologize for the discomfort that our reference to your deceased husband is causing you, m'lady," Birch spoke gently. "But it is crucial for us to know the length and nature of Miss Neville's employment while she was here, and also the circumstances surrounding her departure."

The lawyer noted the whitening of the Lady Hartington's knuckles in her lap, and the blush that once again crept into her cheeks.

He knew if their questioning had not been conducted on behalf of the Earl of Stanmore—a distinguished leader of the House of Lords—she might have dismissed them at this very moment. She looked up and fixed him with a steady gaze.

"Miss Neville came to us from Mrs. Stockdale's Academy for Girls ten summers ago. I hired her as a tutor for my three children, who at the time were of the ages six, eight, and ten. My eldest was going off to Eton in the fall. Rebecca came here highly recommended by the schoolmistress."

"From what I have heard of that fine academy," Nicholas put in, "the young women who attend it are not generally those who have a need to go into service."

"You are correct, sir," Lady Hartington answered softly. "I felt very fortunate to have her, but I guessed, even from the beginning, that she would not be staying with us long."

The woman hesitated, causing Birch to shift uncomfortably in his chair. He couldn't pressure her, but at the same time the need to learn everything that there was to learn was driving him mad. He wanted confirmation that Rebecca was as pure as he had judged her to be. He *wanted* to prove that Stanmore was doing the right thing in making her his wife. She deserved it more than any other woman he had ever known.

"And?" Sir Nicholas was not inclined to be so patient.

"Rebecca was here for a month," Lady Hartington continued. "And I have to say that she was everything that Mrs. Stockdale had promised and more. She was absolutely the best tutor my children *ever* had."

"But she left after a month," Nicholas probed.

"She did."

"Why?"

"I . . . I do not know."

"Did she ask for any references before her departure?"

The woman touched her brow in a nervous gesture. "She did not."

"Did she give you any notice of any kind?" Nicholas asked again.

"She did not."

"Did she collect what you owed her . . . her salary before her departure?"

Birch, quite impressed, stared at Sir Nicholas. He certainly had missed his calling in not studying at the bar.

"I hardly think . . ." Lady Hartington finally whispered.

"Did she take her belongings?"

"Rebecca did not have much here with her."

"Did she take them?"

"She did not." Her answer was weak. The color was now gone from her face.

"Are you telling us that Rebecca Neville did not leave . . . but simply *disappeared* one day?" At the woman's silence, Nicholas stood up, drawing her frightened gaze.

"See here, Sir Nicholas . . ." Oliver protested as Stanmore's friend barreled on.

"Were you not at all concerned, ma'am, that something might have happened to her? Was she not your responsibility while staying at your household?"

She turned her face away, so neither of the men could see it.

Birch's tone was much softer—more compassionate. "Were you at home, m'lady, the day . . . or the night . . . that Miss Neville left?"

She shook her head and rose to her feet.

"Was your husband at home?" Birch continued.

Without another glance at either of the men, Lady Hartington glided toward the door. As she reached for the latch, she spoke her parting words. "I have told you everything I can, gentlemen. Now, if you will forgive me, I am unwell. My butler shall see you out."

The two men's gazes met as the door closed behind the woman. "We did not get everything that we came for," Birch said solemnly.

"But at least we know it was the husband!" Nicholas angrily stared at the door. "It is obvious that the filthy rake had his way with her!"

"Or tried, Sir Nicholas. We must not jump to conclusions."

"True enough. She may have simply run to escape his lecherous claws."

"There is more that Lady Hartington knows," the lawyer said

confidently. "Another meeting with her, and I will learn a great deal more."

Nicholas was smirking knowingly at him.

"What is that look supposed to convey, if I might ask?"

"For an old bachelor, Sir Oliver, when you are attracted to a woman, you are about as subtle as the Temple Gate." They started toward the door. "But I don't believe Stanmore has ten years to waste while you pursue your own amorous interests."

"My own amor . . ." Sputtering a little, Birch bit back his own retort as a butler entered the room.

They were not even out of the receiving room when Nicholas laid a hand on the brawny butler's arm. "Say, are you not the same fellow I saw fighting at Wetherby's last week?"

"Aye, sir. That would be me."

"I won a bundle on you, my man. That was a fair bit of brawling, I should say. You've a devastating right hand."

Before they reached the ground floor, the lawyer was listening with great amusement as the two men discussed the fights last week and the wagering that was likely to take place at the area boxing clubs this week. It was amazing to Oliver that someone of Sir Nicholas Spencer's education and family—a man bred to travel in the highest circles of society—could carry on with equal comfort in the very lowliest.

Shaking off such thoughts, he focused on *his* next move, and the question of whether it would be worthwhile sending a letter revealing their findings to the earl yet.

"And this last butler . . . the one before you . . ."

"Robert, sir."

The lawyer focused again on the discussion. The three of them were standing in the open door, looking out onto the residential street.

"That's it . . . Robert. You will pass on my message to him, won't you, George?"

The man looked around him first before giving a discreet nod. "Absolutely, sir."

"My money will be on you next week, George. Watch for me."

"Aye, sir. That I will."

Birch had to wait until they climbed into the carriage before voicing his curiosity.

Nicholas immediately broke into a grin as he seated himself across the way from the lawyer. "You would do far better if you could keep your attention off the skirts, Birch."

"Sir Nicholas! Please!"

The man laughed, but immediately grew serious. "My new friend George tells me he has been butler for the Hartingtons for only two years. But the man before him—a fellow named Robert—had been working for them since before the fall of Troy."

"And presumably was there at the time of Rebecca's short-lived tenure in the household."

"Precisely. From what George tells me, Robert was dismissed for doing a little gambling with the housekeeping money. But apparently, the man also harbors a great resentment toward his old master, the late Sir Charles Hartington."

Oliver rubbed his hands together. "So when can we go and meet with him?"

"Robert will be instructed to come to your rooms in the Middle Temple tomorrow evening. George here believes there is *no* secret in the Hartington household that Robert would be unwilling to reveal . . . for the right price, of course."

Chapter 30

The dinner served by Mrs. Trimble had been delicious, but William Cunningham had hardly been able to swallow a bite. The topic of conversation had filled him with dread. Though he and Reverend Trimble had continued to stay away from Melbury Hall, the rector had been getting reports from a number of sources. All of them were the same, stories of unprecedented violence and abuse.

As he made his way home, the darkness that enveloped the village was complete. The sky was black, not even a single star was visible overhead.

Nonetheless, the familiar whistle that came from the east wall of the school drew his attention, and he moved cautiously toward the sound. Jonah was waiting.

"How are things there, my friend? How is Lady Wentworth?" He led the man to the back of the building where they could speak without fear of discovery.

"Lady Wentworth asks that you come the back way to the Grove right at dawn tomorrow morning. She asks that you bring a carriage."

"Is someone hurt? We can go immediately."

The man shook his head. "The squire's watchman will kill you if you come now. In the morning, she thinks you'll be safe enough."

"Am I bringing someone back with me? One of the workers?"

"Aye," Jonah said. "Lady Wentworth's maid Vi. The squire has taken a fancy to the girl, and she is frightened enough to kill herself. We've been hiding her in the Grove for two days now. I must be going, sir."

"Very well, Jonah. Thank you for coming."

"You'll be there at dawn?"

"Indeed I will," Cunningham answered, and then watched the man slip away in the darkness.

"Where are you taking me?" Rebecca asked, following Stanmore into a wing of Solgrave that she had not visited before.

"No questions, just come with me," Stanmore encouraged, holding a burning candelabra in one hand and leading her with the other.

She glanced about at the closed doors. She could smell the musty scent of rooms that had not been aired in quite some time. She looked up at the images of the paintings on the walls as the light from the candles brought each one momentarily to life. They came to a halt before a closed set of double doors. She glanced up at Stanmore's grim face and felt his hesitation.

"What is this?" she asked softly.

"My father's rooms," he answered, pushing the doors open and walking inside.

Rebecca paused at the threshold, unable to tear her gaze away from the man she loved. He placed the candelabra on a table by the foot of a heavily curtained bed. His face reflected the despair that was his legacy from the past. His eyes studied every aspect of the large chamber, and the open doors leading to adjoining rooms.

"This was his prison for nearly eight years." His voice echoed off the walls. "That bed served as his place of crime and punishment, all in one."

Rebecca wanted to go to him. To embrace him. To make his pain go away the only way she knew how—by loving him. But she could hardly offer a remedy that held no promise of eternity.

"For eight years my father lay in this bed. Refused to leave this room. Snubbed everyone who wanted to help him. He simply lay there, basking in his own self-inflicted misery and guilt." He pulled back the curtains roughly and stared into the emptiness. "For eight years, he lay here . . . and one day revealed his sins to me."

Rebecca wanted to tell him that she already knew, but his need to speak kept her silent.

"James is not my son. But I believe while you have been here—

witnessing my cold, hard behavior toward the lad—you must have guessed at the truth."

All she could do was give a small nod.

"He was born to Elizabeth after an affair that my wife and my father had shortly after I went away. He told me about it—about the endless hours they spent together. About her unhappiness with our alliance—about her enchantment with him and of his with her. He told me how her untimely pregnancy was a shock to them both." He turned again to the empty bed. "But my father was a schemer. He knew how to avoid scandal. He planned to pass off the child as mine. The two month's difference between my departure and the start of her pregnancy was no great obstacle . . . to a man like him."

She quietly walked into the room and closed the doors behind her, leaning against them.

"He arranged for Elizabeth to be secluded, pretending she was having difficulty with the pregnancy. Of course, this just created more of an opportunity for the two of them to indulge their passion." He turned to a portrait of his father on the wall. "At the designated time, when Elizabeth should have had the child—that is, if the child were to be seen as mine—he even made an announcement."

He ran a hand impatiently over his face. "He was so secure in his lies that he even announced the child to be a boy. He told me he already planned to give the infant away if a girl was born instead. He would simply claim illness had taken the life of the babe.

"And Elizabeth went along with everything. She was a willing accomplice . . . until the day that James was born. When she found out that, because of his deformed hand, my father was going to give him away, anyway, she could no longer go along with his plans. You see, he was a perfectionist. Any aberration was a reflection against his name—his status in the eyes of the world." He paced away from the bed before turning around again. "I believe this was the first time in her entire life that Elizabeth showed any courage. Some maternal instinct must have awakened in her the courage to act."

Stanmore faced her. "She ran away. She took James in a display of independence that was so uncharacteristic of the person that she was. She fled so she could keep the child . . . and keep him safe."

His eyes shone with unshed tears when they met hers. "I have never talked about the past with anyone. I have refused to allow anyone to question me about Elizabeth . . . or about my father. I have fought against allowing anyone to enter *here*"—he touched his chest with a fist—"where I know they would see my weakness, my failure."

Eternity be damned, Rebecca thought, walking to him and wrapping her arms around him. His hands were fierce as they pressed her close to him.

"There is nothing that I want hidden from you, Rebecca. I want you to know the truth about me. I am flawed—in many ways I am quite as bad as my father. I would never have searched for James or Elizabeth if my father, on his deathbed, had not begged me to forgive him and made me promise to bring James back. It was that promise that sent Birch in search of you. It was only an unexpected blessing that the same promise brought you here, as well."

A tear fell from his eye and mingled with hers as she raised her lips and kissed him.

"I love you, Rebecca, and whatever haunts your past matters naught. I cannot let you go." He cupped her face with his hands and she tried to calm her sobs.

"I need you. James needs you. You have given both of us a second chance at life." His lips tasted the tears on her face. "I want you to marry me. I want you to stay."

Rebecca buried her face in his neck. Though her very life depended upon it, she could think of no way to end the sorrow that would tear their hearts apart.

Her words were muffled against his chest, but she forced them out. "I killed a man. Though I struck out at him in self-defense and to protect my virtue, I killed him. And then I fled. And I must run again . . . for it is only a matter of time before I will be discovered."

She held him tightly, not wanting to look up and see his reaction to the shocking truth. "I know I am a coward for running. But I cannot afford to be caught while I am . . . somehow associated with you or James. I can never allow any of my shame to taint your good name."

"The devil take my name," he said roughly, pulling her back and staring into her face. "I know you, Rebecca. You would not hurt a creature if you could avoid it. I shall use every connection I have to secure some pardon for you. I shall go to the King himself—"

"No!" She shook her head. "I cannot chance it . . . I cannot chance your lives . . . your names . . . I have to go."

"Then I shall go with you."

She didn't deserve such a gesture. Tears coursed down her face, and her body was wracked with sobs.

He gently took hold of her chin. "I never even glimpsed true happiness before I met you. James is the next earl. The family name shall survive as my father so desperately wished it. But I need none of it. We shall go to the colonies together. We shall start—"

"Stop!" She placed her hand against his lips and shook her head. "You cannot leave him here. He needs you. Your people need you. The work you are doing . . . the good things that you are bringing about . . ."

"Rebecca!" He forced her to look into his face. "You and I are destined to be together. I will not stand here and argue this. Instead, I am telling you that somehow—in whatever way we need to make it work—we shall be together . . . and for the rest of our lives."

She gazed deeply into his eyes. There was no point to be gained in arguing now. Their fates, their futures, were as far apart as the earth and the sky. For now, though, she wanted no rancor between them. With so few days left, she wouldn't allow anything to cast a shadow over the moments of happiness that were left to them.

His lips took hers in a frenzy of need, and Rebecca responded.

"I shan't let you out of my sight for a moment." He took the candelabra from the table. One arm remained around her. "And propriety be damned! I shall drink in the sight of you for as long as you allow me. Tomorrow morning, you will join James and me in our morning ride. In the afternoon, you can come with me to the village to meet with Reverend Trimble and Mr. Cunningham. . . ."

Stanmore continued to talk, and she simply listened, basking in the warmth of his affection.

And as they left the musty chambers of a sordid past, Rebecca tried to think only of the present and of his loving arms around her. The decisions that would tear them apart had already been made, but the future held time enough for tears.

Night still lay like a blanket over Melbury Hall when Millicent slipped out of the house and ran through the darkness to the Grove. As soon as they saw her, Jonah and Violet appeared in the clearing.

"Mr. Cunningham should be here shortly!" Millicent said, looking down the dark pathway. "Perhaps we should start out and meet him."

Violet shivered in the chilly predawn air. "Do I have time to run to the house for a minute, m'lady?"

"You cannot be serious! What if you are discovered?"

"I shall be in and out in a lightning flash," the girl whispered convincingly. "I have my mama's locket still under my bedding in the attic. I also want to get the shawl my grandmum made for me when I was a wee thing. That's all, ma'am. Those are the only two things I want to take with me."

Millicent heard the thump of the horses' hooves. A moment later, she saw a dark figure holding a lantern and leading the carriage into the clearing. She rushed toward him with Vi at her elbow.

"Mr. Cunningham—" She whispered her greeting. "I cannot thank you enough for all you are doing."

"Lady Wentworth!"

The schoolmaster made no attempt to hide his frown as he held the lamp up to her face. Millicent took an involuntary step back as she remembered that she was wearing no hat or veil to cover the ugly bruises on her face.

"Millicent," he said more gently. "What has happened? Who did this to you . . . as if I need to ask?"

"May I go, m'lady? May I run to the house?"

"Go, Vi," she whispered, turning her face to the girl. "But hurry!"

Without pausing, the young servant lifted her skirts and ran as fast as she could toward the main house. The servants' door through the kitchen was open, and she slipped in without a sound. Climbing carefully, she made her way toward the rooms in the attic. The soles of her shoes were quiet. Vi knew that the other girls would be waking very soon, and she needed to get in and out before the others made a stir.

The sound of heavier footsteps behind her as she neared the top made her freeze in terror. Whoever it was, he carried a candle. She cringed and hugged the shadows of the wall. If he came up to the attic, he would find her for sure.

No one knew that Lady Wentworth was having her taken away this morning. No one but the lady herself and Jonah and the four black women who had hidden her in their hut.

The footsteps were as hurried as her own, but the man turned off at the landing below her and went down the hall toward the master's and mistress's bedchambers. Vi breathed a sigh of relief and looked at the stairs leading upward, and then made no move to climb any farther. There was something terribly wrong, she thought. With furtive steps, she quietly retreated to the landing below and followed the person down the dark corridor.

She heard the impatient tap on a door and still crept ahead—keeping to the shadows. There was another knock, and she saw a door fling open. The dawn was breaking, for the squire's bedchamber was brighter than the corridor.

"What is it?" Wentworth's angry bark echoed through the house.

"Cunningham is here!" The bailiff's pleased voice chilled her. She pressed her back against the wall and waited. "He is here with a carriage. She must be running away with him."

They knew she was running away, Vi thought, turning to retreat again.

"I had no desire to tell you, master. But her ladyship's been lifting her skirts for him. I saw them at the Grove not a week past. And then, Monday, she went down to the village to meet him. And now she is going to run off with the snake."

"I think not. I'll kill them both, by the devil. Get my gun."

Wentworth's shout sent Vi running back to the stairs. Crazy with fear, she broke from the house and ran past the gardens.

She needed to warn them. Running down the path, she could see Jonah at the edge of the trees. Even if they started now, they wouldn't get far. And Lady Wentworth wouldn't run, anyway. Vi knew she needed to get help.

"Jonah," Vi panted, taking hold of his arm. "Go and warn her ladyship. The squire thinks she's running off with the schoolmaster. He's coming, and he's got his gun. Run and warn her. Hurry! I'm going to Solgrave for help!"

Chapter 31

They moved to the edge of the stream. Standing with him, Millicent glanced back at the black workers who had gathered in the clearing. If Vi did not leave soon, and the slaves did not move out into the fields, Mickleby would surely be coming down here to find out what was the matter.

"You must come with me, too." Cunningham's gentle hand cupped Millicent's jaw. "I cannot stand by any longer and see what he is doing to you. He is dismembering you, limb from limb, body from soul."

"No, William. My soul is my own." She let the tears roll down her face. "I cannot go with you. If I do, he shall find you . . . find us . . . and then where should we be?"

"We can go to Scotland. I know of places where he can never find us. Come away with me, Millicent!"

She wrapped her own hand around his wrist and placed a kiss on his palm. "You have been the most precious of friends. Take Vi today. Arrange for the girl to be sent back to her family. If I knew of a place where the rest of these people could be safe, I'd ask you to take them, too. Nobody deserves to be left here, subjected to this cruelty."

"Nobody but you?" he asked angrily. "Staying here does not make it any easier for these people. He does not torture them any less because he has just used his fist on your face—or just abused your precious body."

"Please, William," she begged, placing a hand against his lips and lowering her own voice. "I *am* going away. Someplace where he cannot ever find me or touch me."

"Going? Going where?"

"Do not ask me! But please trust me when I say that I shall be taken care of. It is just these people . . . that I have to do something about."

He held her shoulders, bringing her closer to him. "But what about me? About us? Please Millicent . . . will you never understand? I love you."

She brushed her cheek against his. For the first time, she went willingly into his arms and allowed his strength to flow into her. "You mean so much to me."

Jonah's cry of alarm as he ran down the hill from the house jerked Millicent out of Cunningham's arms. They quickly returned to the carriage and watched the man run toward them.

"He is coming!" he spoke hoarsely. "The squire is coming, m'lady, and he is bringing his gun. He thinks you're running away with the schoolmaster."

Millicent frantically looked toward the house. "Where is Vi?"

"She's run to Solgrave for help. She says he is ready to kill someone, m'lady. You'd best go."

She turned to Cunningham. "Go! Please, just go. He shall kill you if he finds you here."

"You must come with me."

She shook her head. "I cannot! I have to prove to him that he was wrong, or . . ." She looked around at the throng of workers. "Or there is no telling what he'll do! Please go . . . go now!"

"I shan't," he said stubbornly, refusing to move even when she tried to push him toward the carriage. "The monster will take it out on you. I shall stay and explain. I was here . . . I came here . . . because someone was sick. This is not the first time I have been here."

"You do not understand! Please . . . !" She began to sob, glancing constantly toward the pathway and the house. "Wentworth will hear no explanation. He has been looking for a reason to kill you . . . to kill me. Do not let him find us here together. *Go!*"

Cunningham had his hands on her shoulders, trying to argue with her when Squire Wentworth strode into the clearing with Mickleby following behind. All Millicent could do was gasp in ter-

ror and turn in William's arm, shielding his body with her own as
the barrel of the gun was lifted toward them.

The dawn was breaking in the east when the three riders left the
stables of Solgrave and started out on their morning ride.

"I cannot believe that you told me once that you do not ride,"
Stanmore said as he watched her graceful handling of the horse.

Rebecca smiled at the compliment and met Stanmore's warm
gaze. "It was not a lie. I had not ridden a horse since I was a student
at Mrs. Stockdale's school in Oxford."

"So she is the one who is responsible for *all* your flaws. I have
heard of the school."

"Flaws?" she whispered in mock anger. She glanced up at James
riding his pony a safe distance ahead of them. "As I recall, you were
describing me in terms of absolute perfection only an hour ago."

He lowered his voice even further and leaned toward her—a
suggestive gleam in his dark eyes. "And were you not perfectly
naked with me buried deep inside of you at the time?"

She blushed deeply and tried to turn her face away, but his gentle touch on her knee drew her gaze back. "You *are* absolute perfection, my love—clothed or not. And my reference to your flaws?
You have none . . . so I must give Mrs. Stockdale some credit for
helping form the woman that I love."

Rebecca placed her hand in his, warmed inside and out by the
way he placed a kiss on her fingers and then her palm.

As Jamey slowed his pony and turned toward them, they both let
go of the other's hand and shifted guiltily in their saddles. The boy
looked from one to the other before speaking. "May we ride toward
the old woodcutter's cottage? I promised Israel to check on the
place this morning while we were out riding."

"We shall go where you lead us."

Stanmore's encouraging tone brought a smile to the lad's face,
and Jamey spurred his pony on ahead of them again.

"Is that the place where you found Israel?" Rebecca asked
softly, glancing at the sword that the earl had taken to wearing on
their rides.

Stanmore nodded. "But I believe this is also the place where the two boys first met. It is near enough to Melbury Hall . . .

The earl's eyes narrowed and Rebecca looked up in time to see Jamey reining in his pony. Across the meadow a young woman was running toward them. Drawing up next to the lad, they stopped as she neared them. She was crying out incoherently, and the earl immediately dismounted and took her by the arm.

"He has a gun, m'lord. He is going to kill Mr. Cunningham and m'lady. Hurry, m'lord. Please hurry!"

"Who has a gun?"

"Squire Wentworth, m'lord. He thinks my mistress is running away with Mr. Cunningham. But she isn't . . . 'tis all a lie Mickleby's done given him . . . and . . . the schoolmaster came in to take me back to my family. . . . The squire was going to hurt me. . . ."

"James, ride back to Solgrave as fast as you can go, and tell Porson to bring some men to Melbury Hall." He leaped onto his own horse as James yanked his pony around and galloped back the way they'd come. "Rebecca, take this girl—"

"I am coming with you," she responded, cutting him off. "Millicent is my friend. I have to come."

Stanmore frowned fiercely, but nodded.

"Very well, but stay behind me and keep your distance," he warned. "Wentworth is fool enough to hurt anyone who stands in his way."

"I promise to stay clear of him," she whispered. "Be on your way."

As Stanmore charged ahead, Rebecca looked down at the weeping girl. "Make your way back to Solgrave and wait there. Ask for Mrs. Trent when you get there. She will see to you until we get back."

"I am worried to death about my mistress, ma'am. She is—"

"His lordship will see to it. You did very well in coming after him. Now be on your way."

Rebecca spurred her horse after Stanmore, suddenly frantic with worry herself. And if Wentworth were even to touch Stanmore, she found herself thinking she would kill again.

*   *   *

Millicent pressed her back against William and refused to be pushed aside. "Let him go, Wentworth. This is not what you think."

"The whore and her court." He laughed crudely, glancing at the black workers gathered around her. "So this is what I have been doing wrong for the past five years. This is why you push me away. Her ladyship likes an audience. Or is it that she likes more than one in her at a time?"

"You are abominable. Do not dare to speak to her that way." Cunningham pushed Millicent aside, and took a step forward. "You are a vile pig, Wentworth. You disgrace yourself . . . you disgrace everything that—"

The shot echoed off the trees and the huts, stunning everyone with its suddenness. The horse that was harnessed to the carriage leaped ahead a few steps at the sound, but stopped by the water.

The schoolmaster, thrown backward by the shot, was sitting and staring in disbelief at the hole in his chest. Pressing his hands to the wound as blood began to pour out, he looked up at Millicent and then stretched flat on the ground.

"No!" she screamed, dropping to her knees beside him. The blood formed a thin black river beneath him and spread out on the dirt. She pressed her hand against his chest, but to no avail.

"No! Please do not die, William. Please . . . !"

She touched his face, her fingers marking his brow, his cheek, his still lips with blood. His eyes were open, but stared sightlessly into the dawn sky.

Wentworth handed the gun to Mickleby and drew his sword. "And who is to die next, Millicent?" He walked to the line of workers standing silently around her. At his approach, no one cowered. No one withdrew.

"Kill me!" Millicent sobbed, bending over the dead body of the schoolmaster. "Kill me and be done with it."

"All in good time, my pet." His eyes took in the hostile faces of the gathering—at the gazes that no longer turned away from him. "You *will* die this morning. But before I grant you your wish, it is only fitting that you witness what your actions will cost some of these creatures."

Millicent stared through a sheen of tears as Wentworth laid the edge of the sword against the chest of the person nearest him. She gasped aloud as he slashed the skin deep enough to draw blood. The man barely flinched. Wentworth lifted the point of the weapon, pointing at the man's face before moving down the line, studying each face as he went.

"We must do this in the correct order, my pet. We shall kill your friends in the correct order."

Millicent held her breath and stared in horror at the bloodlust playing over her husband's features. When he came to a stop before Jonah and raised his sword to the man's throat, she scrambled to her feet and ran toward them.

"Please do not kill him," she sobbed. *"Please, Wentworth, I beg you. Have mercy!"*

Millicent couldn't get to him fast enough. Wentworth sneered at her, raising his elbow to thrust the weapon.

The sneer turned to a look of surprise, however, and the sword dropped to the ground at his feet. Reaching behind him, the squire opened his mouth to speak, and then sank to his knees in the dirt. As he fell, Millicent watched Moses release the handle of his knife, leaving the squire to twitch in his final agony.

The old slave turned slowly and stared at his friend. "Jonah," he whispered, tears on his weathered face.

The roar coming from behind her shook her from her trance.

"You filthy scum! I shall kill every one of you."

Millicent turned and watched Mickleby advancing on them, sword in hand.

"No . . . ! Run, Moses! Stop, I say, Mickleby!" She tried to throw herself at the bailiff, but hands took hold of her. She twisted in terror. "Jonah . . . run!"

Neither of the men moved, and Millicent felt the hands pull her out of the bailiff's path. She could hear herself screaming, saw Mickleby advancing as in a dream. Then, around them, the line of workers suddenly began scrambling backward, dragging her with them. The sound of thunder filled the air. The bailiff stopped, sword raised, when he was almost upon the two men. He turned his head, and Millicent saw a flicker of fear in his eyes.

That was all the time Lord Stanmore needed. As the black

hunter tore past, the earl's sword arced through the air, cutting the bailiff down with a single deadly stroke.

Millicent stood stock-still as the hands holding her loosened and then released her. She watched Stanmore dismount and, with a quick glance at her, go directly to the body of Cunningham. Frowning fiercely, he closed the young man's eyes a moment later with unsteady hands. His examination of Wentworth and Mickleby, however, was cold and brief.

Rebecca rode into the clearing and dismounted from her horse, coming immediately to her. Millicent accepted her friend's embrace, but her gaze remained on Moses, who was still standing over the body of the squire.

"I killed him!" Moses said evenly to the earl, pointing at Wentworth's body. "He killed the teacher. . . . He was going to kill Jonah. . . . I killed him. . . . I killed him with this." He crouched down and gestured to the hilt still protruding from the squire's body.

"Oh, Moses . . . !" Millicent cried.

Stanmore looked at her briefly before putting his hand on Moses's shoulder. Millicent held her breath.

"Those who saw this will tell you that you are mistaken, Moses. You did not kill Squire Wentworth . . . I killed him." He bent down and pulled out the knife, wiping it clean and handing it back to Moses, saying gently, "Can you remember that? You killed no one."

Moses looked in confusion at Jonah who, in turn, nodded to him.

"He can remember that, m'lord," Jonah said quietly.

Stanmore nodded and his gaze swept the group. He pointed to Mr. Cunningham. "This great man, our friend, is dead, but these other two deserved what came to them. It would be better for all of us to forget what happened today."

There were nods among the workers.

"Very well, then. Jonah, perhaps you had better have someone go up to the Hall and get help. And we shall need to bring Reverend Trimble here from Knebworth . . . to settle the formalities."

*   *   *

The willingness of the old butler to answer each one of their questions spoke clearly of the man's lingering bitterness toward his late master and his family.

"He had the morals of a cat and the self-control of a goat. He cared not a rush who it was . . . or when . . . or how many." Robert sat in a chair facing the lawyer. Sir Nicholas stood comfortably by the window. "Sir Charles would pick up a girl in the Strand, take her to the Haymarket Theater and leave with her on one arm and some handsome actress on the other. Off to the Rose Tavern or Ranelagh Gardens they'd go, and about dawn he would pick up some whore in St. James's Park on his way home." The man shook his head in disgust. "Everyone in the house knew when Sir Charles had got himself the clap. The girls would be praying for it to last . . . as it meant he'd be staying off of them while the burning lasted."

"And Lady Hartington put up with all of this?"

Robert shrugged at the lawyer. "What was she to do? She had three young children by him, and after that we all thought she was happy to have his lecherousness aimed at other women and not at her." He shook his head. "Nay, sirs. I think she minded none of it, so long as he was halfway discreet about it . . . and stayed away from her bed."

"I assume Sir Charles took a fancy to Rebecca Neville."

Robert looked over the younger man. George had spoken very highly of Sir Nicholas and the old butler could see why. Highborn the fellow might be, but he was down to earth in his manner.

"That he did," Robert answered. "But from the beginning she'd have no part of him. You see . . . she ain't like the others. She was no servant in the house . . . at least, that was our understanding. And Lady Hartington treated her like she was quality or something."

The former butler glanced at the two gentlemen waiting attentively, waiting for him to continue. For all the years he'd worked for Hartington, Sir Charles had never treated him with half the civility of these two. "As I was saying, he pressed her first the same as he did with all the help. But she would not budge. And then one night, and when the wife was out, he became impatient, I suppose you could say, and ordered me to bring her to him."

"Did you?" the lawyer asked, horrified.

"I might have been paid by the filthy codger, but I ain't a pimp. And I never forced any woman into that man's bed." The man shook his head in self-defense. "All I did was tell Miss Neville about the master's order. The rest was up to her."

"Did she go?"

"She told me to tell him that she was leaving. In the middle of the night . . . with no place to go . . . she was willing to go on the street rather than wait around and be used so by the master." Robert shook his head at the memory. "Sir Charles about had a stroke when I told him."

"What did he do?"

"He cornered her on the stairs and accused her of stealing his wife's jewelry and silver. Then he dragged her back into his study—latching the door behind them."

Neither men spoke. Both were staring at him gravely. He knew they thought the worst.

"He didn't get what he wanted. Miss Rebecca wouldn't give it up. Instead, the plucky lass dinged him one on the head with a poker and ran off."

"What happened next?" the lawyer asked impatiently.

"I believe she thought she'd killed him. I mean, we all thought that, seeing all the blood spilling out on the rug. She ran out of the house and down the street. Someone told us they saw her get into a passing carriage. But we never saw her again."

The two men looked at each other.

"Elizabeth," Sir Nicholas said.

The lawyer turned back to the butler. "And Sir Charles?"

Robert laughed mirthlessly. "Embarrassment and trouble followed for him. He was out cold until well after his wife got home and sent us to fetch a doctor. She was not particularly happy at the sight of him . . . you know, lying there with a gash in his head and his breeches open and . . . well, sirs, his intentions were very clear."

"And that was the end of it?"

"Not at all, sir!" Robert chuckled again. "Sir Charles ended up with a scar on his head that even a wig couldn't cover. And despite his wife's objection, he wanted to have Miss Neville chased down and hanged for what she'd done. Of course, he'd already changed his version of what happened. She was a thief and a murdering slut, in his telling. But as soon as he started making noise like that, the sky fell on him."

"What do you mean?" Sir Nicholas asked.

"Miss Neville's family showed up."

"Her family?"

Robert nodded at Sir Oliver. "First, a handful of lawyers showed up accusing him of everything but starting the Great Fire. Then the two lords showed up in a carriage finer than any Sir Charles ever dreamed of having. None of us knew anything about it before. But we knew certain enough then that the girl was *real* quality, but somehow distanced from her kin. But the long and short of it, sirs, was that the Hartingtons were in deep water for not taking care of her, for nobody could find her after that." The man smiled with grim satisfaction. "It was quite ugly."

"What was the family's name?" the lawyer asked. "Do you remember?"

"Of course, sirs." The man nodded. "It was North. All of us were sworn to secrecy, but I don't mind telling you. She was the daughter to the earl of Guilford. You know, Lord Guilford of Wroxton Abbey. Can you imagine . . . *our* Miss Neville, sister to Lord North, the King's own prime minister!"

Chapter 32

"I cannot leave, Rebecca. I cannot leave Melbury Hall tonight . . . and I cannot leave it on Friday."

From the time Rebecca had arrived at the Grove this morning—from the moment she had seen her friend standing with the workers over the body of the squire she had guessed at this decision.

"William should not have died." Millicent looked down into her lap and dashed a tear from her face. "But the inevitable truth is that he *is* gone. Wentworth left no heir, so I am to inherit everything. . . ." She waved a hand vaguely. "It is all mine now—Melbury Hall, the plantations in Jamaica, his slave holdings. There is so much to undo, and it is up to me to do it. But for the first time in my life, I am not afraid."

Rebecca gently touched her friend's knee and drew her gaze. "You will do well in all you have to do. I cannot tell you how proud I am of you."

"Then you are not angry with me?"

"For not running away?" Rebecca smiled and shook her head. "I wish I had half of your courage. No, I am not angry, Millicent . . . only proud to be your friend."

"But do you *have* to go?" she asked softly. "What are the chances of anyone discovering you . . . of learning your secret? You can stay with me . . . we can—"

Millicent stopped speaking as Stanmore returned to the room.

"Have you made the arrangements, m'lord?" Rebecca asked.

The two listened intently as the earl explained what had already been done. Millicent accepted the earl's offer to send Philip over for a few days to Melbury Hall to see to the hiring of a new steward and bailiff and servants. It was a welcome offer, for Lady Wentworth had decided that any of the household staff who had allied themselves with the squire must go.

When Stanmore and Rebecca were ready to leave, Millicent held her friend in a long embrace. "Will I ever see you again?" she whispered in her ear.

"Of course," Rebecca murmured in a husky voice, knowing that if she spoke the truth now, she would quite probably lose both her composure and her courage.

The suite of saloons at Lady Mornington's palatial home overlooking Grosvenor Square was filled with the usual crowd of men and women plying their skill at the various gaming tables.

"I never thought I should ever see you so easily defeated, Louisa." Lady Mornington cast a sly glance at her friend as they sat together on a chaise. "But this sulking is not becoming in the least."

"One must wage a war before accepting defeat!" Louisa's gaze fanned over the well-dressed crowd. "In Stanmore's case, a war was not worth the prize."

"So this . . . this Mrs. Ford was a more worthy opponent than you first assumed!"

"Who?" Louisa asked breezily.

Lady Mornington inclined her head toward her young friend. "You were a smart woman to leave the battlefield while you still have your head attached to your shoulders. Stanmore has not been known to take too kindly to women who, upon being dismissed, arrive uninvited at his doorstep."

Nothing is sacred, Louisa thought. That little slut of a maidservant must have told everyone about Stanmore's letter.

"I did not go down to Hertfordshire to visit Solgrave," she lied. "I was visiting an old friend."

"I have heard about that, too." The older woman smiled. "And how *is* Squire Wentworth these days? Does he still amuse himself by mistreating that unfortunate wife of his?"

"I could hardly say anything about that." Louisa tucked a strand of her powdered hair in place before turning her pouting face away.

"You should mix with better company than Wentworth, my dear.

Considering the man's reputation, even someone as clever as you would not fare very well with him for long." The older woman's gaze swept the crowd before returning to Louisa. "I did have someone in mind tonight that you should meet, however. A certain distinguished gentleman who should easily cure you of your loss of Stanmore. He could restore you to complete health, my dear, both in your pocket and in your bed."

Louisa couldn't help but be interested.

"Ah, there he is." Lady Mornington waved to a well-dressed man across the room. The gentleman started their way. "Augustus Fitzroy—the third Duke of Grafton. He is filthy rich *and* recently divorced."

"Of course!" Louisa lifted a brow in admiration as the handsome man approached. "Lady Mornington, you are doctor of the first order. I believe you just found the cure for melancholy."

Rebecca awoke to the sound of carriages pulling into the drive. She looked beside her and found Stanmore was already gone. Daylight poured in from the windows, and a glance at the clock on the mantel told her that she had slept far later than usual.

Stanmore had wanted her to come riding with James and him this morning, as well. But with everything that had happened at Melbury Hall yesterday, she wondered if the two had decided against it.

She pushed the covers aside and pulled on a brocade robe. Sweeping the long mane of hair over her shoulder, she quickly walked to the window in time to see the last of the visitors disappearing inside. A dozen equerries, footmen, and grooms milled about the drive for a moment before leading the carriage and horses toward the stables.

"Oh, no," she groaned. "The prime minister . . . already!"

Philip had warned her about the visit today. Well, she thought, she would simply stay in her room this morning. The fewer people she met, the fewer questions would be asked, and easier time Stanmore would have explaining her disappearance when she was gone.

She did, however, need to meet with Jamey this afternoon.

Alone. Her time with him was drawing rapidly to an end, and she had to say good-bye.

As she washed her face, a sharp tapping at the door drew her attention. She closed the robe tighter around her and went to answer it. Mrs. Trent and four maidservants were waiting outside.

"I am so happy that you are up already, my dear," the housekeeper said breathlessly. "We have to get you ready."

Not giving Rebecca a chance to utter a word, the woman motioned for the servants to follow her inside the room. Her best dress was laid out on the bed while Mrs. Trent and two of the girls sat her before a mirror, her hair brushes and combs in hand.

"What is this all about?" she managed to ask, between Mrs. Trent's hurried instructions to the hairdressers.

"Why, the prime minister is waiting for an introduction, of course. Lord Stanmore is already with him. The house is in a complete uproar . . . I mean, with Sir Nicholas and Sir Oliver arriving before dawn this morning, and his lordship spending an hour behind closed doors with them before having his coffee, even! And no sooner is he finished with his discussions there, but who is driving down the lane . . . the prime minister's party!" The housekeeper selected the underclothes herself. "Now, I know his lordship has not even breakfasted yet . . . and you know how he is before he eats. . . ."

Ravenous, Rebecca thought, hiding a smile.

"Well, I saw him . . . just for a moment as he moved from one room to the next . . . and he certainly did not have the look of a hungry man. In fact, he looked . . . well, I don't know how to describe it!"

Without taking a breath, the housekeeper went on, chiding the girls for their slowness in getting Rebecca ready. "Now, if you had not given me such a hard time about your new wardrobe, I would have chosen an ivory dress with gold ribbons for you to wear today—but then perhaps I shall just have one ordered anyway. There is still the entire summer to enjoy."

Rebecca's mind drifted to Stanmore and his houseful of guests. She prayed he was not exposing himself to scandal in trying to arrange a pardon for her. And how strange, that Sir Oliver and Sir Nicholas should ride down in the middle of the night!

"More beautiful than a summer flower." Mrs. Trent nodded approvingly, making the final adjustments on the dress.

Thoughts of rebellion flashed in Rebecca's mind. If she decided not to go downstairs, then Stanmore might not feel compelled to reveal her past to a stranger. Then he wouldn't be opening himself up to . . .

"She is ready!" Mrs. Trent took Rebecca by the arm and led her toward the door before she could even formulate a workable plan.

She should have gone yesterday. She should not have told him the exact date. She should have known that he'd do something to stop her. He'd said as much himself.

Curiously enough, she was not angry. But she *was* frightened. Perhaps this was what walking to the gallows felt like.

Rebecca's feet were leaden as she descended the stairs. Somehow . . . somewhere . . . after leaving her room, Mrs. Trent and the maidservants had stayed behind. At the bottom of the stairs, she saw Sir Nicholas and Sir Oliver standing on the landing. Both men looked up and watched her. She could not understand why they were smiling. Everyone seemed to have lost their mind this morning.

The lawyer walked toward her and took her hand as Rebecca reached the last step. "Just know this, m'lady. It has been a pleasure to serve you!"

Rebecca wanted to ask what he was speaking of, but the door to the earl's study opened at that moment, and she saw Stanmore step out. Her heart pounded at the change in his expression when he saw her. His look was filled with such love and hope, but even as the thought registered in her brain, his features grew serious again.

His steps were purposeful when he walked toward her. Rebecca reached out her hand, needing his strength to proceed another inch.

"Good morning, Rebecca! Have I told you today that I love you?" He kissed her hand and then, with no regard to their audience, kissed her lips with such longing that she had to clutch his jacket to save herself from melting against him.

When he pulled back, she was still unsteady on her feet. He brushed a kiss against her ear.

"You did not kill Hartington, my love," he whispered in her ear. She clutched his lapel tighter, hardly understanding the words she had just heard. "The cad survived that night and lived long enough to inflict himself on more innocent women . . . before being murdered by an angry husband eight years ago."

Rebecca's stomach was a painful knot. She stared into his face with disbelief. "Please do not jest with me."

"I would never jest about something so serious." He shook his head and motioned to Birch, who was standing nearby.

"What his lordship has said is the truth, m'lady. Sir Nicholas and I interviewed Lady Hartington and Robert, the butler who served the family ten years ago. There is no doubting the facts."

"My God!" She covered her mouth with a hand as tears sprang to her eyes.

"You mustn't cry!" Stanmore took her in his embrace again, placing kisses on her forehead.

"Am I the only one not invited to greet the enchanting Miss Neville?"

Rebecca quickly brushed away the tears and tried to compose herself at the sound of the visitor's voice. Stanmore released her, but continued to hold her hand as they turned to their guest.

"Lord North, may I present—"

"No introductions are necessary." The man spoke gently as he approached. "I would have known this lady anywhere and at any time. It is so unfortunate that fate has kept us apart for so long."

Rebecca curtsied to a man whom she was certain she had never met before.

The prime minister took her hand from the earl's and started back toward the library. Rebecca cast a questioning look over her shoulder at Stanmore, who continued to stand by the foot of the steps.

"Are you coming, Stanmore?" the prime minister called. "As future husband of my sister, I think you are entitled to be told of the madness that runs on our side of the family. But then again, she looks to be made of much better and healthier stock."

Rebecca was certain that everyone had gone mad this morning.

Epilogue

A month. A month would have changed everything!

A month's difference and the Earl of Guilford would have returned from the Continent in time to collect his daughter Rebecca Neville—named after the earl's own mother—to introduce her properly into London society. A month's difference and Rebecca would not have gone to the Hartington household as a tutor. A month's difference and she would not have run away thinking she'd committed a murder. A month's difference and she would never have encountered Elizabeth Wakefield and begun a new life in the colonies.

A month's difference and she would never have found Jamey . . . or Stanmore.

Indeed, for all the hardship it had brought, that month had made all the difference in the world in securing for her happiness that transcended her wildest dreams.

The list of wedding guests had been extensive, to say the least. And on it, Rebecca noticed, Stanmore had personally added the name of Mrs. Jenny Greene. The gesture warmed her heart, even though the aging actress had sent a note declining the invitation. A "previous engagement . . ." she had written in shaky, uneven script. But no refusal could spoil Rebecca's happiness, for she had made her own peace with the past. Today and all the days to come were what mattered.

The news of the Earl of Stanmore's upcoming wedding to Miss Neville—a long-lost "relation" of the prime minister—was well covered by the various newspapers and gossiped about incessantly

among London's *ton*. The wedding promised to be the event of the
Season.

The actual nuptial day started off misty and gray. But as carriages rolled into Knebworth Village from near and far, the clouds
had gradually parted, and the dew had glittered like diamonds on
the landscape. Even now, the late summer sun was smiling down
upon the sizeable gathering and the couple who had just finished
exchanging their vows on the steps of the old church.

Rebecca looked up and met Stanmore's loving gaze as the
throng looked on in anticipation. With a final flourish, Reverend
Trimble blessed their union, and the world around her exploded in
a cacophony of cheers. All Rebecca could hear, though, was her
husband's declaration of undying love. All she could see was the
mist in his eyes as he drew her into his embrace.

"I don't believe there ever was a man happier than I am at this
moment." Her lips met his, and they were both lost in a moment of
tenderness that was solely their own.

The crowds around them, though, would not allow the couple to
remain undisturbed for very long. The Earl of Guilford was at their
elbow the next moment. Rebecca's new brother, Lord North, and
his wife and children, pushed forward impatiently to reach the couple. Lady Meg, Stamore's mother, smiled from her place just beyond them. She had made the journey from Scotland to meet
Rebecca, and the two women had bonded the moment they'd met.
And now she stood ready to welcome her new daughter into the
family.

Regardless of the jubilant adults crowding the newlyweds,
though, Jamey was the first to receive the attention of the two. As
the boy left the side of Lady Meg, Rebecca reached for him, and
Stanmore lifted the lad in his arms. Together, the three of them
turned to bask for a moment in the warm wishes of the assembled
guests.

"Are you ready, m'lady?" Stanmore asked some time later, after
congratulations had been made, and Jamey had skipped back to
Lady Meg's side. The crowd had parted to allow them a path to
their waiting carriage. "Ready to go and receive our guests at Solgrave, my love?"

All Rebecca could do was nod and accept his arm, for she did not think she could speak right now and still keep her emotions under control. Together, they moved down the steps of the church and through the crowd.

With well-wishers lining the street, they rolled toward the feast awaiting them all at Solgrave.

"Are you happy?"

Tears rolled down her face as Rebecca turned and nodded to her husband. "Thank you, my dearest. Thank you for the gift of your love . . . your honor . . . your promise of a future. . . ."

"I had no future without you." He pulled her into his arms and kissed her. "I was incomplete without you, Rebecca. You are the one who has made me whole."

She smiled up at him. "You keep talking like this, and I might be forced to persuade you to take an indirect route back to Solgrave."

"We can arrange for a lengthy stop by the old mill." His eyes shone with mischief. "Or perhaps we should just leave the entertaining of the guests to my mother and start for Scotland this instant."

As he glanced toward the coachman, she took hold of his chin and drew his face to her. "We couldn't really do that. I mean it sounds perfectly wicked . . . and wonderful . . . but there is just so much . . ."

Rebecca's words trailed off as her eyes focused on an older, fashionably dressed woman sitting in an open carriage by the side of the road. As their own carriage passed by, Rebecca stared at the oddly familiar face. A knot formed in her throat, and she raised a hand hesitantly in greeting. The woman's gloved hand rose as well, but she did not wave. Rebecca watched her instead wipe tears from her face and look away.

Rebecca looked back at the proud figure of Jenny Greene for a long moment.

"Shall I stop the carriage? This is the perfect time for all of us to meet."

Rebecca shook her head. "I don't believe my mother is ready for anything more just yet."

And even as the words were spoken, the two saw Jenny's carriage start off in the opposite direction.

"I'm sorry!" Stanmore whispered in her ear as he drew Rebecca into his arms. "I'm sorry that this day couldn't be perfect."

"But it is," Rebecca replied, brightening and pressing a hand against her husband's heart as she met his affectionate gaze. "I have everything that I ever wished for. Everything that I ever dreamed of in my life. This is simply as perfect as life can be!"

Author's Note

For those readers who have been following our stories, we hope the jump from a Scottish medieval setting to the England of George III was as much fun for you as it was for us!

For our new readers, we wanted to thank you for sharing in a story that we have been dying to tell for some time now. As always, we have tried to depict a place and a time in a way that mingles the real and the imagined in an entertaining way. Lord North, Lady Mornington, even the Philadelphia "coachee" driver John Butler (the husband of Rebecca's friend Molly), were actual historical figures. Strawberry Alley and the Friend's School in Philadelphia, Berkeley Square, the Covent Garden Theater in London, and Broad Quay of Bristol were actual places.

The issue of slavery in America is one that is well known to most of us. Very few of us here might be aware, though, of the struggle abolitionists carried on to eradicate the evil in England. It was through the efforts of a few progressive thinkers, beginning in the middle part of the eighteenth century, that Parliament eventually did away with the slave trade in 1807. In 1833, they would successfully pass a bill to abolish slavery in all British dominions.

On a personal note, we would like to extend our sincere thanks to Dr. Marjie Bloy of Rotherham, England, for her gracious help with so many questions about eighteenth-century politics, the House of Lords, and Lord North and his family. Your kindness, your expertise, and your warmth know no bounds. Thank you. Stitch and bitch, forever, Marjie!

As always, we love to hear from our readers.

May McGoldrick
P.O. Box 511
Sellersville, PA 18960
mcgoldmay@aol.com
www.Maymcgoldrick.com

Please read on for
an excerpt from

The Rebel
by May McGoldrick

coming from Signet
in Summer 2002.

London
December 1770

The snow lay like blue icing over the stately plane trees and the walkways of Berkeley Square. Dinner guests, bundled in fine woolen cloaks and mantles of fur, scarcely spared the picturesque scene a look, though, as they hurried from the warmth of Lord and Lady Stanmore's doorway to their waiting carriages. Across the square, a wind swept up from the river, raising crystalline wisps from the barren tree branches, and flakes of snow curled and glistened in the light that poured from the windows of the magnificent town house. Soon, all but one of the carriages had rolled away into the darkness of the city, the sounds of horses and drivers and wheels on paving stones muffled by the fallen snow.

Inside the brightly lit foyer of the house, Sir Nicholas Spencer accepted his gloves and overcoat from a footman and turned to bid a final farewell to his host and hostess.

"Spending Christmas *alone*!" Rebecca chided gently. "Please, Nicholas, you *must* come with us to Solgrave for the holiday."

"And intrude on your first Christmas together?" Nicholas shook his head with a smile. "This first holiday is for you. For your family. I wouldn't impose on that for the world."

Rebecca left her husband's side and reached for Nicholas's hand. "You are not intruding. My heavens, that's what friends are for. When I think of all the years that James and I were alone in Philadelphia. If it weren't for the hospitality of our friends—especially at the holidays—how lonely we would have been!"

Nicholas brought the young woman's hand to his lips. "Your kindness is touching, Rebecca, and you know how hopeless I am about denying you anything. But I've spent more than my fair share of holidays with that beast you call your husband. Besides, I understand you have some rather joyous news that you'll be wanting to share with young James. . . ."

The prettiest of blushes colored Lady Stanmore's cheeks, and she glanced back at her husband.

"I am slightly better at keeping state secrets, my love." Stanmore reached out and took her tightly into his embrace.

Nicholas stood and watched as his friends slipped into a world that included only the two of them. The bond that linked their hearts and their souls was so pronounced, so obvious . . . and Nicholas frowned at the unwanted ambivalence pulling at his own heart. As happy as he was for them, he could feel something else squirming about inside of him.

He looked away, forcing the frown from his face. Only a fool, he told himself, would be envious of a life that he had avoided like the plague.

He already had his overcoat on and was pulling on his gloves when the two became aware of him again. Nicholas couldn't help but notice the protective touch of Stanmore's hand on Rebecca's waist, the intimate entwining of her fingers with his.

"Come anyway." Stanmore spoke this time. "Come after Christmas, if you must wait. You know my family likes to have you with us . . . though God only knows why. Seriously, though, I know James will be anxious to tell you about his term at Eton, and Mrs. Trent will love to fuss over you."

Nicholas nodded. "I'll do that. That is, if my mother and sister don't go through with their threat of coming across from Brussels for a visit. From the tone of my mother's most recent letter, that brat Frances has become too much for her to handle alone. The latest threat is to leave her in England so that she can finish her schooling here."

"Well, that is very exciting news," Rebecca chimed in.

"Not for me." Nicholas shook his head and took his wide-brimmed hat of soft felt from the footman. "I know nothing about how to deal with sixteen-year-old children who talk incessantly, without the least semblance of reason . . . and still think themselves mature beyond measure."

"There is a season for everything," Stanmore countered as he and his wife followed Nicholas toward the door. "It is all part of the great scheme of life. Marriage. Children. Moving the focus of our attention from ourselves to those we love. As Garrick said so eloquently at Drury Lane the other night, 'Now is the winter of our discontent made glorious summer.' "

Any other time and Nicholas might have made some light-hearted retort about humpbacked, wife-murdering kings; but as he looked at Rebecca and Stanmore, the words knotted in his throat. Somehow, even the words "happy and carefree bachelor" seemed difficult to conjure at the moment.

Nicholas leaned down and placed a kiss on Rebecca's cheek. "Merry Christmas."

Outside, the snow was coming down harder, the wind picking up in earnest. Nicholas pressed his hat onto his head and gave a final wave to his friends from the street. As the door closed against the weather, though, he found himself still standing and staring—considering for a moment the events that had brought such happiness to that house. He finally roused himself and turned to his groom.

"Go on home, Jack, and get warm. I believe I'll walk from here."

A gust of wind whipped at the capes of Nicholas's overcoat, and the groom moved on as he was ordered.

The baronet turned up the collar of his overcoat and walked past the fashionable houses lining the square. The handsome windows were still lit in many, in spite of the lateness of the evening. It was the season for entertaining. A solitary leaf danced along the snow-covered street, pressed forward by a gust before being caught in a carriage track. The chill wind burned the skin of his exposed face, reminding him of the warm fire in the Stanmore's library. The image of his friends in the foyer kept pressing into Nicholas's thoughts.

The improvement in Stanmore was so marked. For all the years since his first wife had left him without a word—taking James with her and disappearing—he had been a tormented man. And now, since he'd found the lad and had married Rebecca, Stanmore was so obviously happy. "Fulfilled" was perhaps the best word. The change was stunning . . . miraculous, perhaps.

It was not long before Nicholas's house on Leicester Square came into view, but he was far too restless to settle in for the night. The snow was beginning to let up, so he turned his steps toward St. James's Park.

Since coming back from the colonies over ten years ago, Nicholas Spencer had worked diligently to keep his life as uncomplicated as possible. He had wanted no ties. He had endeavored to inflict no pain. During his years as a soldier, he'd seen enough suffering in those wounded and killed, and enough anguish in those families that were left to endure the loss, to cure him of ever desiring any kind of attachment. Life was too fleeting, too fragile.

Somewhere over the years, he'd also found that women were more than willing to put themselves in his path for their mutual amusement and enjoyment. Live while we can. *Carpe diem.* No harm in it for anyone.

Wealth only meant having enough for good clothes, good horses, a little meaningless gambling, and a bit of concealed philanthropy. It mattered little to him that the most polite reaches of society scoffed at his roguish style of living. He knew that they perceived him as a gambler and a womanizer, as a sportsman who had chosen to shrug off the responsibilities of his position in society.

And Nicholas Spencer did not dispute this reputation. He was proud of it. He'd earned it. He'd worked hard to establish it. He had never wanted to be answerable to anyone.

So when, he thought, had he become so discontented?

He strolled through an open gate onto the tree-lined walks of St. James's Park. The usual prostitutes and gallants who frequented the park—even this late—appeared to have searched out warmer haunts, out of the wind and the weather. He left the paved walk of the mall, moving out into the open field, his boots crunching on the dry snow.

Indeed, he was as independent as an eagle, but something unexplainable was happening to him. Why, for example, had he felt driven to spend so much time over the past six months with Rebecca and Stanmore? Of course he cared for them deeply, but spending time in their company often did nothing to lift his spirits. On the contrary, it only served to point up how empty and insignificant his own life was, in comparison with theirs.

Fight it as he may, it seemed a desire for belonging, for permanency, had been edging into Nicholas's heart. It was an odd sensation, new to him, though he knew it was a condition as old as time. Nonetheless, he didn't want to believe it. He was happy with who he was.

Or so he thought. . . .

"Spare a ha'penny, sir? Jist a ha'penny fer my sister an' me?"

Out of the dark shadows of a grove of trees, he saw the boy's scrawny bare arms extended in his direction. Nicholas paused to look at him.

"A ha'penny, sir?" Walking on feet wrapped in dirty rags, the waifish figure came cautiously nearer. The top of his head barely reached Nicholas's waist. Even in the darkness, the boy was pale as death, and the baronet could hear his teeth chattering from the cold.

Nicholas glanced past the thin shoulders of the child toward the bundle of bare legs and arms curled into a ball and lying motionless beneath the tree. Hanks of long dark hair covered the other one's face.

"Is that your sister?"

The boy tugged at Nicholas's sleeve. "A ha'penny, sir . . ."

He teetered slightly, and the baronet put out a hand to him. As Nicholas took hold of the boy's arm to support him, he was immediately dismayed by the thin ragged shirt that covered the bony frame. He took his gloves and his hat off and handed them to him.

"A ha'penny, sir?"

It wasn't until Nicholas had taken off his overcoat and was draping it around the boy that he smelt the spirits emanating from the child.

"If you and your sister follow me to a safe house I know, I'll see to it that there are hot food and warm clothes . . . and half a *shilling* in it for you."

Dwarfed by the size of the clothes, the boy stared at him blankly and said nothing.

"No harm will come to you or your sister, lad. You have my word on it."

Nicholas turned his attention to the girl on the ground. She was much smaller than the boy, and as he pushed back the dark mangle of hair, the baronet was stunned by the angelic look of innocence in the sleeping face. Like the brother, she was dressed in nothing more than thin rags that barely covered her. He touched her face. It was deathly cold.

Nicholas immediately gathered the child in his arms, stood up, and turned to the brother. The boy was gone.

The frail bundle of bones and skin in his arm concerned him more, however; so he started across the park in the direction of the house on Angel Court, off King Street. There, he knew, a couple of good souls would look after this child while he searched out the brother.

The loss of his coat and hat was not what concerned him. The boy was welcome to them. What bothered Nicholas was the money he would be finding in the pockets. There was enough there to keep a man drunk for a fortnight. For a child who would use it for pouring spirits and beer down his throat, there was enough money to kill him.

The girl weighed no more than a kitten, and Nicholas frowned fiercely at the smell of alcohol that her body reeked of, as well. The excessive drinking of both rich and poor was still one of the curses of England. While the rich could afford to take care of themselves and their families, though, the misery of the poor passed early on to their children.

A face appeared at the window when Nicholas knocked at the house on Angel Court. At the sound of his voice, the door quickly opened. The old woman's face, bright with recognition, immediately darkened when she saw the bundle in Nicholas's arms.

"I found her in the park." He brushed past her. "I think she is unconscious with drink . . . though the cold surely hasn't helped her any."

The old woman hurriedly opened up a door to the right, leading him into a large room, where a small fire spread a warm glow over a dozen beds lining the walls. A few children peeked from beneath their blankets, wide-eyed with curiosity.

"Which one, Sadie?"

The old woman pushed a basket of mending off an empty bed, and Nicholas laid the child gently on the clean blanket.

"Go fetch Martha for me, dear," Sadie said to a boy on the nearest cot.

As the child hurried out of the room, Nicholas stood back, watching the older woman's wrinkled hands as they moved over the girl's face and neck.

He was no expert on children's ages, but he guessed this young one couldn't have been more than five. Small curled hands lay on the blanket. Dirty feet stuck out from beneath her rag of a dress. Nicholas's gaze was drawn to the dark hair framing the innocent features of the face. Long eyelashes sat peacefully against cheeks pale beneath the dirt.

Looking at her, Nicholas found his mind racing, planning. The city was a difficult place for a child on her own. Perhaps he could bring this helpless waif to Solgrave when she was a little better. He was certain Stanmore wouldn't mind it, and Rebecca would embrace the idea. After all, they had given shelter to Israel, and he was a new lad entirely after only six months. She would thrive in the country. She could go to the village school in Knebworth. She could become a child again.

Sadie's sharp glance in his direction stopped him. He went nearer, and the woman stood up.

"The poor thing has already gone to her Maker, sir."

He stared at the woman's mouth as she quietly spoke. A sudden need to deny her words welled up in him, but he restrained the utterance.

He took a step back. With a slight nod, he turned and in a moment was on the street.

Oblivious to the harshness of the winter night or the time,

Nicholas Spencer walked the streets. The injustice of such a death was so wrong. And more innocents—helpless and dying—surrounded him. And what he had been doing about it was clearly not enough.

A shelter here and there. A house to offer meals and a safe bed off the street. All well and good, but where did these children go from here? How had his insignificant acts of charity in any way changed their lives? What had he done to keep them from ending up drunk or abused or dead on the streets?

There had to be something more that he could do. A house in the country where they could grow up healthy. A school where they could learn to fend for themselves. They needed something like a permanent home.

Suddenly, he found himself back at Berkeley Square, staring up at the darkened windows of his friends. Even the night and winter could not hamper the glow of warmth radiating from inside.

Nicholas was getting old and he was terrified of it. The admission hurt less than he'd imagined. But for so long, he'd been battling the emptiness and coldness of his life, that now coming to terms with his ailment was an incredible relief.

An image of the innocent face of the dead child came before his eyes. His life had become a waste and there *was* so much more that he could do. He would need to make a few changes, though. A new life for himself. A real home where he could truly influence the fate of these lost souls.

But such a thing required a wife, and where on earth would he find her?

PENGUIN PUTNAM INC.
Online

Your Internet gateway to a virtual environment with
hundreds of entertaining and enlightening books
from Penguin Putnam Inc.

*While you're there, get the latest buzz on
the best authors and books around—*

Tom Clancy, Patricia Cornwell, W.E.B. Griffin,
Nora Roberts, William Gibson, Robin Cook,
Brian Jacques, Catherine Coulter, Stephen King,
Ken Follett, Terry McMillan, and many more!

**Penguin Putnam Online is located at
http://www.penguinputnam.com**

PENGUIN PUTNAM NEWS

Every month you'll get an inside look at our upcoming books and new features on our site. This is an
ongoing effort to provide you with the most
up-to-date information about
our books and authors.

Subscribe to Penguin Putnam News at
http://www.penguinputnam.com/newsletters